George Gilfillan, Thomas Campbell

The Complete Poetical Works of Thomas Campbell

George Gilfillan, Thomas Campbell

The Complete Poetical Works of Thomas Campbell

ISBN/EAN: 9783337401917

Printed in Europe, USA, Canada, Australia, Japan

Cover: Foto ©Raphael Reischuk / pixelio.de

More available books at **www.hansebooks.com**

THE

COMPLETE

POETICAL WORKS

OF

THOMAS CAMPBELL.

WITH

A MEMOIR OF HIS LIFE, AND AN ESSAY ON
HIS GENIUS AND WRITINGS.

Illustrated with Fine Steel Engravings.

NEW-YORK:
D. APPLETON & COMPANY,
443 & 445 BROADWAY.
1868.

SKETCH

OF THE

LIFE OF CAMPBELL

THE following spirited and evidently truthful account of the Life of Thomas Campbell, appeared in Fraser's Magazine for November 1844.

I WISH to write about Thomas Campbell in the spirit of impartial friendship : I cannot say that I knew him long, or that I knew him intimately. I have stood, when a boy, between his knees ; he has advised me in my literary efforts, and lent me books. I have met him in mixed societies—have supped with him in many of his very many lodgings—have drunk punch of his own brewing from his silver bowl—have mingled much with those who knew and understood him, and have been at all times a diligent inquirer, and, I trust, recorder of much that came within my immediate knowledge about him. But let me not raise expectation too highly. Mr. Campbell was not a communicative man ; he knew much, but was seldom in the mood to tell what he knew. He preferred a smart saying, or a seasoned or seasonable story ; he trifled in his table-talk, and you might sound

him about his contemporaries to very little purpose
Lead the conversation as you liked, Campbell was
sure to direct it in a different way. He had no
arrow-flights of thought. You could seldom
awaken a recollection of the dead within him ; the
mention of no eminent contemporary's name called
forth a sigh, or an anecdote, or a kind expression.
He did not love the past—he lived for to-day and
for to-morrow, and fed on the pleasures of hope,
not the pleasures of memory. Spence, Boswell,
Hazlitt, or Henry Nelson Coleridge, had made
very little of his conversation ; old Aubrey, or the
author of Polly Peacham's jests, had made much
more, but the portrait in their hands had only been
true to the baser moments of his mind ; we had
lost the poet of Hope and Hohenlinden in the
coarse sketches of anecdote and narrative which
they told and drew so truly.

Thomas Campbell was born in Glasgow, on the
27th of July, 1777, the tenth and youngest child
of his parents. His father was a merchant in that
city, and in his sixty-seventh year when the poet
(the son of his second marriage) was born. He
died, as I have heard Campbell say, at the great
age of ninety-two. His mother's maiden name
was Mary Campbell

Mr. Campbell was entered a student of the High
School at Glasgow, on the 10th of October, 1785.
How long he remained there no one has told us.
In his thirteenth year he carried off a bursary
from a competitor twice his age, and took a prize
for a translation of " The Clouds" of Aristophanes,
pronounced unique among college exercises. Two
other poems of this period were " The Choice of
Paris," and " The Dirge of Wallace."

When Galt, in 1833, drew up his autobiography,

he inserted a short account of Campbell. " Campbell," says Galt, " began his poetical career by an Ossianic poem, which his ' schoolfellows published by subscription, at two-pence a-piece ;' my old schoolfellow, Dr. Colin Campbell, was a subscriber. The first edition of ' The Pleasures of Hope' was also by subscription, to which I was a subscriber." When this was shown to Campbell, by Mr. Macrone, just before the publication of the book, the poet's bitterness knew no bounds. " He's a dirty blackguard, sir," said Campbell ; " and, sir, if Mr. Galt were in good health, I would challenge him ; I feel disposed to do so now, the blackguard." " What's to be done ?" said Macrone ; " the book is printed off, but I will cancel it, if you like." Here the heading of the chapter " A Two-penny Effusion," attracted Campbell's attention, and his thin, restless lips quivered with rage. " Look here, sir," said Campbell, " look what the dirty blackguard's done here !" and he pointed to the words, " A Two-penny Effusion." Two cancels were then promised, and the soothed and irritated poet wrote with his own hand the following short account of his early efforts :—" Campbell began his poetical career by an Ossianic poem, which was published by his schoolfellows when he was only thirteen. At fifteen he wrote a poem on the Queen of France, which was published in the Glasgow Courier. At eighteen, he printed his Elegy called ' Love and Madness ;' and at twenty-one, before the finishing of his twenty second year, ' The Pleasures of Hope.' "

Before Campbell had recovered his usual serenity of mind, and before the ink in his pen was well dry, who should enter the shop of Messrs. Cochrane and Macrone, but the poor offending author,

Mr. Galt. The autobiographer was on his way home from the Athenæum, and the poet of "Hope," on his way to the Literary Union. They all but met. Campbell avoided an interview, and made his exit from the shop by a side door. When the story was told to Galt, he enjoyed it heartily. 'Campbell," said Galt, " may write what he likes, for I have no wish to offend a poet I admire ; but I still adhere to the *two-penny effusion* as a true story."

On quitting the Glasgow University, Mr. Campbell accepted the situation of a tutor in a family settled in Argyleshire. Here he composed a copy of verses, printed among his poems on the roofless abode of that sept of the Clan Campbell, from which he sprung. The Lines in question are barren of promise—they flow freely, and abound in pretty similitudes; but there is more of the trim garden breeze in their composition, than the fine bracing air of Argyleshire.

He did not remain long in the humble situation of a tutor, but made his way to Edinburgh in the winter of 1798. What his expectations were in Edinburgh, no one has told us. He came with part of a poem in his pocket, and acquiring the friendship of Dr. Robert Anderson, and the esteem of Dugald Stewart, he made bold to lay his poem and his expectations before them. The poem in question was the first rough draft of " Pleasures of Hope." Stewart nodded approbation, and Anderson was all rapture and suggestion. The poet listened, altered, and enlarged—lopped, pruned, and amended, till the poem grew much as we now see it. The first fourteen lines were the last that were written. We have this curious piece of literary information from a lady who knew Campbell

well, esteemed him truly, and was herself esteemed
by him in return. Anderson always urged the
want of a good beginning, and when the poem was
on its way to the printer, again pressed the neces-
sity of starting with a picture complete in itself.
Campbell all along admitted the justice of the
criticism, but never could please · himself with
what he did. The last remark of Dr. Anderson's
roused the full swing of his genius within him, and
he returned the next day to the delighted doctor,
with that fine comparison between the beauty of
remote objects in a landscape, and those ideal
scenes of happiness which imaginative minds
promise to themselves with all the certainty of
hope fulfilled. Anderson was mote than pleased,
and the new comparison was made the opening of
the new poem.

> " At summer eve, when Heaven's ethereal bow
> Spans with bright arch the glittering hills below,
> Why to yon mountain turns the musing eye,
> Whose sunbright summit mingles with the sky ?
> Why do those cliffs of shadowy tint appear·
> More sweet than all the landscape smiling near ?
> 'Tis distance lends enchantment to the view,
> And robes the mountain in its azure hue.
> Thus, with delight we linger to survey
> The promised joys of life's unmeasured way ;
> Thus from afar, each dim-discover'd scene
> More pleasing seems than all the past hath been ;
> And every form that Fancy can repair
> From dark oblivion, glows divinely there."

There is a kind of inexpressible pleasure in the
very task of copying the Claude-like scenery and
repose of lines so lovely.

With Anderson's last *imprimatur* upon it, the
poem was sent to press. The doctor was looked
upon at this time as a whole Wills' Coffee-house

It was said of Campbell, that by the time

> " His hundred of gray hairs
> Told six-and-forty years,"

he was unwilling to remember the early attentions of Dr. Anderson. He certainly cancelled or withdrew the dedication of his poem to Dr. Anderson, and this is the only act of seeming unkindness to Dr. Anderson's memory which we have heard adduced against him. But no great stress is to be laid on this little act of seeming forgetfulness. He withdrew, in after-life, the dedication of " Lochiel' to Alison, whose " Essay on Taste," and early friendship for Campbell, justified the honor ; and omitted or withdrew the printed dedication of " Gertrude of Wyoming," to the late Lord Holland.

As soon as his poems had put money in his pocket, an early predilection for the German language, and a thirst for seeing some of the continental universities, induced him to visit Germany. He set sail for Hamburgh, where, struck with the sight of the many Irish exiles in that city, he strung his harp anew, and sung that touching song. " The Exile of Erin," which will endear his name to the heart of every honest Irishman. On his road from Munich to Linz, he witnessed from the walls of a convent the bloody field of Hohenlinden, (Dec. 3, 1800,) and saw the triumphant French cavalry, under Moreau, enter the nearest town, wiping their bloody swords on their horses' manes. But he saw, while abroad, something more than " the red artillery" of war ; he passed a day with Klopstock, and acquired the friendship of the Schlegels.

He was away altogether about thirteen months, when he returned to Edinburgh, to make arrangements with Mundell about the publication, in London, of a quarto edition of his poems. Mundell granted at once a permission which he could not well refuse, and Campbell started for London by way of Glasgow and Liverpool. At Liverpool he stayed a week with the able and generous Dr. Currie, to whom he was introduced by Dugald Stewart. Currie gave him letters of introduction to Mackintosh and Scarlett.

"The bearer of this," Dr. Currie writes to Scarlett, " is a young poet of some celebrity, Mr. Campbell, the author of ' The Pleasures of Hope.' He was introduced to me by Mr. Stewart, of Ed inburgh, and has been some days in my house. I have found him, as might be expected, a young man of uncommon acquirements and learning, of unusual quickness of apprehension, and great sensibility.

" He is going to London with the view of superintending an edition of his poems, for his own benefit, by the permission of the booksellers to whom the copyright was sold before the work was printed ; and who, having profited in an extraordinary degree by the transaction, have now given him the permission above-mentioned, on condition that the edition shall be of a kind that shall not interfere with their editions. He is to give a quarto edition, with some embellishments, price a guinea ; the printing by Bensley. You must lay out a fee with him ; and if you can do him any little service you will oblige me and serve a man of genius."

Currie's letter is dated 26th February, 1802, so that we may date Campbell's arrival in London (there was no railway then) on or about the 1st of March.

" When Campbell came first to London," said

Tom Hill to the collector of these imperfect 'Ana, "he carried a letter of introduction to Mr. Perry, of the *Morning Chronicle*. He was then a poor literary adventurer, unfitted with an aim. Perry was so much pleased with him that he offered him a situation on his paper, which Campbell thankfully accepted. But what could Campbell do ? he could not report, and he was not up to the *art* of writing *leaders*. At last it was agreed that he should receive two guineas a-week, and now and then contribute a piece of poetry to the corner of the paper. He did write, certainly," said Hill, "but in his worst vein. We know what newspaper poetry is, but some of Campbell's contributions were below newspaper poetry—many pieces were not inserted, and such as were inserted, he was too wise to print among his collected poems." Tom Hill's means of information were first-rate ; he was, moreover, the intimate friend of Perry, and Campbell's neighbor for many years at Sydenham.

The quarto edition of his poems, which Campbell was allowed to print for his own profit, was the seventh. This was in 1803. The fourth edition, corrected and enlarged, was printed in Glasgow in 1800. His own edition is a fine specimen of Bensley's printing ; but the engravings are of the poorest description of art.

In 1803, and before the publication of his subscription quarto, he printed, anonymously, at Edinburgh, and at the press of the Ballantynes, his "Lochiel" and "Hohenlinden." The title is simply "Poems," and the dedication is addressed to Alison. "John Leyden," says Sir Walter Scott, "introduced to me Tom Campbell. They afterwards quarrelled. When I repeated "Hohenlinden' to Leyden, he said, 'Dash it, man, tell the fellow I hate him, but, dash him, he has written the finest verses that have been published these fifty years.' I did mine errand as faithfully as one of Homer's messengers, and had for answer, 'Tell Leyden that I detest him; but I know the value of his critical approbation.'" Scott knew "Hohenlinden" by heart; and when Sir Walter dined at Murray's in 1800, he repeated at the table, as Wilkie tells us, Campbell's poem of "Lochiel."

What Campbell's profits or expectations were at this time I have never heard. When a poet is in difficulties, he is sure, said William Gifford, to get married. This was Campbell's case, for I find in the Scotch papers, and among the marriages of the year 1803, the following entry:—"11th Oct., at St. Margaret's Church, Westminster, Thomas Campbell, Esq., author of 'The Pleasures of Hope,' to Miss Matilda Sinclair, daughter of R. Sinclair, Esq., of Park Street."

The fruit of this marriage, the most prudent step the poet could have taken at that time, was a son, born at Edinburgh on the first of July, 1804, Thomas Telford Campbell, a helpless imbecile, still alive. If there was any one point in Campbell's character more amiable than another, it was his affection for his son. They were much together; and, before his imbecility became confirmed, it was a touching sight to see the poet's fine eyes wander with affection to where his son was seated, and, at any stray remark he might make that intimated a returning intellect, to see how his eyes would brighten with delight, and foretell the pleasures of a father's hope.

In the volume of *Johnson's Scots Musical Museum* for 1803, there is a song of Campbell's, addressed to his wife, when Matilda Sinclair. It is in no edition of his poems that I have seen, and can make no great claim for preservation, beyond any little biographical importance which it may bear.

> "O cherub Content, at thy moss-cover'd shrine
> I would all the gay hopes of my bosom resign ;
> I would part with ambition thy votary to be,
> And breathe not a vow but to friendship and thee.
>
> "But thy presence appears from my pursuit to fly,
> Like the gold-color'd cloud on the verge of the sky :
> No lustre that hangs on the green willow tree
> Is so short as the smile of thy favor to me.
>
> "In the pulse of my heart I have nourish'd a care
> That forbids me thy sweet inspiration to share ;
> The noon of my youth slow departing I see ;
> But its years as they pass bring no tidings of thee.
>
> 'O cherub Content, at thy moss-cover'd shrine
> I would offer my vows, if Matilda were mine ;
> Could I call her my own, whom enraptured I see,
> I would breathe not a vow but to friendship and thee."

This is poor poetry, after the passionate love-songs of Burns, in the earlier volumes of the same publication.

On the 28th of October, 1806, Campbell had a pension granted to him from the Crown, payable out of the Scotch Excise, of one hundred and eighty-four pounds a year. It was Fox's intention to have bestowed this pension upon Campbell, but that great statesman died on the 13th of the preceding month. His successors, however, saw his wishes carried into execution, and the poet enjoyed his pension to the day of his death, a period of nearly eight and thirty years.

He now took up his residence in the small hamlet of Sydenham. Here he compiled his " Annals of Great Britain, from the Accession of George

III. to the Peace of Amiens." Forty years of eventful history, compiled without much accuracy of information, or any great elegance of style. This was a mere piece of journeyman's work, done to turn a penny. Few have heard of it, fewer seen it, and still fewer read it. The most intelligent bookseller in London was, a week ago, unaware of its existence.

Some small accession of fortune about this time, and the glorious certainty of a pension, enabled him to think seriously of a new poem, to outstrip his former efforts, and add another stature to his poetic height. As soon as it was known that the celebrated author of "The Pleasures of Hope" was employed upon a new poem, and a poem of length, expectation was on tiptoe for its appearance. The information first got wind in the drawing-room of Holland House. Then the subject was named—then a bit of the story told by Lord Holland, and a verse or two quoted by Lady Holland; so that the poem had every advertisement which rank, fashion, reputation, and the poet's own standing, could lend it. The story was liked— then the metre was named and approved—then a portion shown; so that the poet had his coterie of fashion and wit before the public knew even the title of the poem they were trained up to receive with the acclamation it deserved.

Nor was public expectation disappointed, when it became generally known that the poet had gone to the banks of the Susquehanna for his poem— had chosen the desolation of Wyoming for his story, and the Spenserian stanza for his form of verse. The poet, however, was still timidly fearful, though he had the *imprimatur* of Holland House in favor of his poem. I was told by Tom

Hill that Campbell sent the first printed copy of his poem to Mr. Jeffrey, (now Lord Jeffrey.) The critic's reply was favorable. "Mrs. Campbell told me," added Hill, "that, till he had received Jeffrey's approbation, her husband was suffering, to use his own expression, 'the horrors of the damned.'"

A Whig poet was safe in those days, when in the hands of a Whig critic. He had more to fear from the critical acumen of a Tory writer; but only one number of the Quarterly Review had then appeared. If Gifford had dissected "little Miss Gertrude," he might have stopped the sale, for a time, of a new edition: but no critical ferocity could have kept down "Gertrude of Wyoming" for more than one season. But Gifford was prepossessed in favor of Campbell; he liked his versification and his classical correctness; so the poem was intrusted to a friendly hand—one prepossessed, like Gifford, in his favor—the greatest writer and the most generous critic of his age —Sir Walter Scott.

No poet ever dreaded criticism more than Campbell. "Coleridge has attacked 'The Pleasures of Hope,' and all other pleasures whatsoever,' writes Lord Byron; "Mr. Rogers was present, and heard himself indirectly *rowed* by the lecturer. Campbell will be desperately annoyed. I never saw a man (and of him I have seen very little) so sensitive;—what à happy temperament! I am sorry for it; what can he fear from criticism?"

His next great work was the "Specimens of the British Poets," in seven octavo volumes, published in 1819. This was one of Mr. Murray's publications, and one of his own suggesting. His agreement with Campbell was for 500*l.*, but when the

work was completed he added 500*l*. more, and
books to the value of 200*l*., borrowed for the publication. Such fits of munificence were not uncommon with John Murray; he had many deal-
ings, and dealt fairly, straightforwardly, beyond
the bounds of common liberality. We wish we
could say the same of Campbell in this transaction.
No second edition of the "Specimens" was called
for before 1841; and when Mr. Murray, in that
year, determined on printing the whole seven volumes in one handsome volume, he applied to
Campbell to revise his own work, and made him
at the same time a handsome offer for the labor of
revision. Campbell declined the offer, and set his
face at first against the publication. What was to
be done? There was a demand for a new edition,
and it had been a piece of literary madness on Mr.
Murray's part if he had sent the book to press with
all its imperfections on its head—not the imperfections, be it understood, of taste and criticism, but
of biographical and bibliographical information.
Good taste can never change—it is true at all
times; but facts, received as such, for want of better information, may be set aside by any dull fact-
monger who will take the pains to examine a par-
ish register, a bookseller's catalogue, or a will in
Doctor's Commons.

Mr. Peter Cunningham, at the eleventh hour,
was called in by Mr. Murray to superintend the
reprint, and correct the common errors of fact
throughout the seven volumes. Various inaccuracies were removed; some silently, for it had been
burdening the book with useless matter to have
retained them in the text and pointed them out in
a note; while others, that entangled a thought or
gave weight, were allowed to stand, but not with-

out notes to stop the perpetuity of the error. A·
quiver of rage played upon the lips of the poet
when he was informed that any one had dared to
revise his labors : but when he saw what was done,
and knew the friendly hand that had gone with so
much patient care through the whole work, he
expressed his unfeigned pleasure, and, as we have
heard, thanked Mr. Cunningham for ·his useful
services.

The Essay is a charming piec▸ of prose, fresh
at the fiftieth reading, and the little prefatory no-
tices abound in delightful criticism, not subtle and
far-fetched, but characteristically true to the genius
of the poet. He is more alive to beauties than de-
fects, and has distinguished his criticism by a
w.der sympathy with poetry in all its branches,
than you will find in any other book of English
criticism. Johnson takes delight in stripping more
than one leaf from every laurel—he laughs at
Gray—Collins he commends coldly, and he even
dares to abuse Milton. Dryden and Pope, the
idols of Dr. Johnson's criticism, are the false gods
of Southey's :

"Holy at Rome—here Antichrist."

Campbell has none of this school of criticism ; he
loves poetry for its own sweet sake, and is no ex-
clusionist.

The great fault of Campbell is, that he does not
give the best specimens of his authors ; but such
pieces as Ellis and Headley had not given. Of
Sir Philip Sydney, he says, " Mr. Ellis has exhausted the best specimens of his poetry. I have
only offered a few short ones." No one will go
to a book of specimens for specimens of a poet in
his second-best manner, or his third-rate mood.

We want the cream of a poet, not the skimmed milk of his genius. A long extract from Theodric would not represent Mr. Campbell's manner in the fiery Hope, or the more gentle Gertrude. Specimens are intended for two classes of people —one who cannot afford to buy, and the second who do not care to possess, the British Poets in one hundred and fifty odd volumes. The poor want the best, and the other class of purchasers want surely not the worst.

In the year 1820 Mr. Campbell entered upon the editorship of the *New Monthly Magazine,* which he conducted, we are told, " with a spirit and a resource worthy of his reputation, and of the then palmy estate of periodical literature." We doubt this. He drew his salary regularly, it is true, but contributed little of his own of any merit. The whole labor, and too much of the responsibility, rested on the shoulders of the assistant. The poet's name carried its full value ; the Magazine took root and flourished, and the pay per sheet was handsome. He soon drew a good brigade of writers around him, and placing implicit confidence. in what they did, and what they could do, he made his editorship a snug sinecure situation. " Tom Campbell," said Sir Walter Scott, " had much in his power. A man at the head of a Magazine may do much for young men ; but Campbell did nothing, more from indolence, I fancy, than disinclination or a bad heart."

A series of articles appeared in the *New Monthly Magazine* when Campbell was its editor, entitled " Boswell Redivivus," a catchpenny name, given by Hazlitt to a collection of Northcote's conversations and sayings, uttered, as was urged, by Northcote. in all the confidence of friendship. An ill-natured saying or two brought the painter into trouble and Northcote wrote to Campbell, complaining of their appearance, in a letter in which he calls Hazlitt a wretch who had betrayed him Campbell's answer is a striking illustration of the system he pursued in editing the *New Monthly*.

" I am afflicted beyond measure," says the poet, " at finding my own inattention to have been the means of wounding the feelings of a venerable man of genius. Dictate the form and manner of my attempting to atone for having unconsciously injured you, if I can make any atonement. The *infernal* Hazlitt shall never more be permitted to write for the *New Monthly*. I mean not to palliate my own want of watchfulness over the magazine which has occasioned such a paper being admitted. I only tell you the honest truth, that a crisis in my affairs, which is never likely to occur again, fatally tempted me this last month to trust the revision of some part of the number to the care and delicacy of another person ; that person, like myself, has slept over his charge."

This want of watchfulness was, we fear, a monthly failing, not, as is here set forth, a rare occurrence.

The success of " Gertrude" induced him in 1824 to put forth another poem, a dramatic tale, entitled " Theodric." A silence of fifteen years put expectation upon tiptoe, but when " Theodric" appeared it was much in the condition of Jonson's " Silent Woman," *there was no one to say plaudite to it.* The wits at Holland House disowned the bantling ; the *Quarterly* called it " an unworthy publication," and friend joined foe in the language of condemnation. Yet Campbell had much to encounter : he had to outstrip his former efforts, and fight a battle with the public against expectation and the applause awarded to his former poetry. There is a conscious feeling throughout the poem that the poet is fighting an unequal battle; he stands up, but his play is feeble, he distrusts himself, and is only tolerated from a recollection of his bygone powers.

"I often wonder," says Sir Walter Scott, "how Tom Campbell, with so much real genius, has not maintained a greater figure in the public eye than he has done of late." Scott is writing in 1826. "The magazine seems to have paralyzed him. The author not only of 'The Pleasures of Hope,' but of 'Hohenlinden,' 'Lochiel,' etc., should have been at the very top of the tree. Somehow he wants audacity, fears the public, and, what is worse, fears the shadow of his own reputation." * * * "What a pity it is," said Sir Walter to Washington Irving, "that Campbell does not write more and oftener, and give full sweep to his genius! He has wings that would bear him to the skies, and he does, now and then, spread them grandly, but folds them up again, and resumes his perch, as if he was afraid to launch away. The fact is, Campbell is in a manner a bugbear to himself; the brightness of his early success is a detriment to all his further efforts. *He is afraid of the shadow that his own fame casts before him.*"

In 1827 he was elected lord-rector of his own mother university at Glasgow. He was elected by the free and unanimous choice of the students, and was justly proud of his election.

"It was a deep snow," writes Allan Cunningham, "when he reached the college-green; the students were drawn up in parties, pelting one another, the poet ran into the ranks, threw several snowballs with unerring aim, then summoning the scholars around him in the hall, delivered a speech replete with philosophy and eloquence. It is needless to say how this was welcomed."

When his year of servitude had expired, he was unanimously re-elected, the students presenting him at the same time with a handsome silver punch-bowl, described by the poet in his will as one of the great jewels of his property.

On the 9th of May, 1828, he lost his wife. This was a severe blow to him. She was a clever woman, and had that influence over him which a wife should always have who is a proper helpmate to her husband. I have heard him say, and with much emotion, " No one can imagine how much I was indebted to that woman for the comforts of life."

In 1829 and 1830, he quarrelled with Colburn, threw up the editorship of the *New Monthly Magazine*, and lending his name to another publisher, started a magazine called *The Metropolitan*. A Life of Sir Thomas Lawrence, in two octavo volumes, was advertised, with Campbell's name to it, about the same time. The Life was soon abandoned, and the new magazine, after a time, transferred to Saunders and Otley, with two editors instead of one, Tom Campbell and his friend Tom Moore. The after history of the magazine is well known—the two poets retired, and Marryat, with his " Peter Simple," gave it a swing of reputation which it had not before.

The sorrows of Poland, and the ebullitions of bad verse, occupied much of Campbell's time when editor of *The Metropolitan*. He lived in the Polish Chambers, and all his talk was Poland. Czartoryski and Niemciewitz were names everlastingly on his lips. A tale of a distressed Pole

,was his greeting when you met, and an alms or subscription the chorus of his song. Boswell was not more *daft* about 'Corsica than Campbell about Poland. Poor Tom Campbell, he exhausted all his sympathy on the Poles, and spent all his invectives upon Russia. Yet he did good—he was the means of assisting many brave but unfortunate men, whilst his ravings against Russia passed unheeded by, like the clamorous outcries for liberty of Akenside and Thomson.

In 1834, he published, in two octavo volumes, the " Life of Mrs. Siddons." Our great actress had constituted Campbell her biographer, and Campbell has told me, more than once, that he considered the work a kind of *sacred duty*. No man ever went to his task more grudgingly than Campbell ; and no man of even average abilities ever produced a worse biography than Campbell's so-called " Life of Mrs. Siddons." The *Quarterly* called it " an abuse of biography," and its writer " the worst theatrical historian we have ever read." Some of his expressions are turgid and nonsensical almost beyond belief. Of Mrs. Pritchard he says, that she " electrified the house with disappointment." Upon which the *Quarterly* remarks, " This, we suppose, is what the philosophers call negative electricity."

Since Mr. Campbell's death, Mr. Dyce has addressed a letter to the editor of the *Literary Gazette*, disclaiming any partnership in the composition of what he calls " that unfortunate book." There was a rumor very rife, when the book appeared, that Mr. Dyce had had a main-finger in the pie ; but the gross inaccuracies of the work gave the best answer to the rumor. Mr. Dyce's accuracy deserves to be proverbial, and no one could suspect that he could have had a hand in any thing like " a very large portion" of the unfortunate performance.   However, in disclaiming the share assigned he lets us a little behind the scenes on this occasion.   We see Mrs. Siddons in Tom Campbell's *tiring-room.*

" Soon after Campbell had received the materials which Mrs. Siddons had bequeathed to him for her biography, he wrote to me on the subject ; informing me, that, as he had'a very slight acquaintance with stage-history, he dreaded the undertaking, and offering me, if I would become his coadjutor, one-half of the sum which E. Wilson was to pay him for the work.   I refused the money, but promised him all the assistance in my power.   He next forwarded to me his papers, consisting chiefly of Mrs. Siddons' memoranda for her life, and a great mass of letters which she had written, at various intervals, to her intimate friend Mrs. Fitz-Hughes. Having carefully gone over the whole, I returned them with sundry illustrations ; and subsequently, from time to time, I sent him other notes which I thought might suit his purpose.   As, on one occasion, he had spoken slightingly of the letters to Mrs Fitz-Hughes, (calling them ' very dull,' and saying that ' the mind of Mrs. Siddons moved in them like an elephant,') and was evidently inclined not to print them, I strongly urged him by no means to omit them, since they appeared to me, though a little pompous in style, extremely characteristic of the writer.

" While he was engaged on the biography, a report reached him that Mrs. Jameson was about to publish Memoirs of Mrs. Siddons, and that Miss Siddons (now Mrs. Combe) had furnished her with many anecdotes. At this he was excessively angry; and showed me a letter which he had written to Miss Siddons, indignantly complaining that she should patronise Mrs. Jameson's work, when she must be aware that he had been specially appointed her mother's biographer. As the letter in question was perhaps the most extraordinary ever addressed by a gentleman to a lady, I entreated him to throw it into the fire; but he positively refused. Whether it was eventually sent or not, I never learned : if it was, Mrs. Combe cannot have forgotten it. He had afterwards some communication with Mrs. Jameson, in consequence of which she abandoned her design."*

I have heard Campbell say that a little girl of eleven would write better letters of their kind than any half dozen addressed by Mrs. Siddons to Mrs. Fitz-Hughes. The poet was introduced to the actress by Charles Moore, the brother of Sir John Moore.

With the money which the publication of a bad book brought him, Mr. Campbell set off for Algiers. He told on his return more stories than Tom Coryatt, and began a series of papers upon his travels for his old magazine, the *New Monthly*. These papers have since been collected into two volumes, entitled, " Letters from the South."

His subsequent publications were a ' Life of Shakspeare," a poem called " The Pilgrim of Glencoe," the very dregs and sediment of his dotage ; " The Life and Times of Petrarch," concocted from Archdeacon Coxe's papers, (a sorry perform-

---

* *Literary Gazette*, 22d June, 1844. Mr. Dyce's letter is dated the 18th, three days after Campbell's death. After ten years of possessing his soul in peace—he might have waited a little longer.

ance ;) and "Frederick the Great and his Court and Times," a publication far below any thing which Smollett's necessities compelled him to put his name to, and only to be equalled by the last exigencies of Elkanah Settle.

In 1837, he published his poems, in one handsome octavo volume, with numerous vignettes, engraved on steel, from designs by Turner; but Campbell had no innate love for art, and his illustrated volume, when compared with the companion volume of Mr. Rogers, is but a distant imitation. Mr. Rogers, it is true, had a bank at his back, and Campbell had little more than Telford's legacy of 500*l.* to draw upon; but this will not account for the difference which we are to attribute altogether to an imperfect understanding of the beauties and resources of art.

When Mr. Campbell accepted the editorship of the *New Monthly Magazine*, he forsook his favorite Sydenham, and leased the house No. 10, Upper Seymour-street West. It was in this house that Mrs. Campbell died. His next remove was to Middle Scotland Yard. Here he gave a large evening party, and then grew tired of his house. Milton's biographers pursue their favorite poet through all his garden-houses and tenements in London : I am afraid it would be no easy task to follow Campbell through the long catalogue of his London lodgings, for the last fifteen years of his life. I recollect him lodging at No. 42 Eaton-street ; in Stockbridge-terrace, Pimlico ; in Sussex Chambers, Duke-street, St. James; at 18 Old Cavendish-street ; in York Chambers, St. James-street ; and at 61 Lincoln's-Inn-Fields. In November, 1840, he again set up house, for the sake of a young niece, to whom he has bequeathed the whole of his little property. The house he chose was No. 8 Victoria-square, and here he made his will.

The last time I saw Mr. Campbell was in Regent-street, on the 26th of September, 1843. He was dressed in a light blue tail coat, with gilt buttons, an umbrella tucked under his arm, his boots and trousers all dust and dirt, a perfect picture of mental and bodily imbecility. I never saw a look in the street more estranged and vacant; not the vacancy of the man described by Dr. Young, " whose thoughts were not of this world," but the listless gaze of one who had ceased to think at all. I could not help contrasting to myself the poet's present with his past appearance, as described by Byron in his Journal. " Campbell looks well, seems pleased, and dressed to *sprucery*. A blue coat becomes him, so does his new wig. He really looks as if Apollo had sent him a birthday suit, or a wedding garment, and was witty and lively." This was in 1813, in Holland House. He has drawn a picture of himself in the streets of Edinburgh, when the " Pleasures of Hope" was a new poem ; " I have repeated these lines so often," he says, " on the North Bridge, that the whole fraternity of coachmen know me by tongue as I pass. To be sure, to a mind in sober, serious, street-walking humor, it must bear an appearance of lunacy, when one stamps with the hurried pace and fervent shake of the head, which strong, pithy poetry excites."*

Mr. Campbell died at Boulogne on the 15th of June, 1844, and on the 3d of July was buried at Poets' Corner, about one foot above the ground.

* Lockhart's Life of Scott, i. 342.

and over against the monument to Shakspeare. I
have heard that he had a wish to be buried in the
Abbey—a wish which he expressed about a year
before he died, at a time when a deputation of the
Glasgow Cemetery Company waited on the poor
enfeebled poet to beg the favor of his body for
their new cemetery. Who will say that Campbell
lived unhonored in his native city?

Mr. Campbell was in stature small but well made.
His eyes were very fine, and just such eyes as
Lawrence took delight in painting, when he drew
that fine picture of the poet which will preserve
his looks to the latest posterity. His lips were
thin, and on a constant twitter—thin lips are bad
in marble, and Chantrey refused to do his bust because his lips would never look well. He was
bald, I have heard him say, when only twenty-four,
and since that age had almost always worn a
wig.

There was a *sprucery* about almost every thing
he did. He would rule pencil lines to write on, and
complete a MS. more in the manner of Davies of
Hereford than Tom Campbell. His wigs, in his
palmy days, were true to the last curl of studious
perfection.

He told a story with a great deal of humor, and
had much wit and art in setting off an anecdote
that in other telling had gone for nothing. The
story of the mercantile traveller from Glasgow,
was one of his very best, and his proposing Napoleon's health at a meeting of authors because he
had murdered a bookseller, (Palm,) was rich in the
extreme.

Campbell was very fond of forming clubs—he
started a poets' club at his own table at Sydenham,
when Crabbe Moore, and Rogers were of the

party. "We talked of forming a poets' club," writes Campbell, "and even set about electing the members, not by ballot, but *viva voce.* The scheme failed, I scarcely know how; but this I know, that, a week or so afterwards, I met with Perry, of the Morning Chronicle, who asked me how our poets' club was going on. I said, 'I don't know—we have some difficulty in giving it a name; we thought of calling ourselves *The Bees.*' 'Ah,' said Perry, 'that's a little different from the common report, for they say you are to be called *The Wasps.*' I was so stung with this waspish report, that I thought no more of the Poets' Club." Whatever merit is due to the foundation of the London University, I believe belongs by right to Campbell: he was the founder, moreover, of the Literary Union, an ill-regulated club which ex pired in the spring of the present season,

<blockquote>" Unwilling to outlive the good that did it,</blockquote>

like the Ipswich of Wolsey, as described by Shakspeare.

It is well known that Campbell's own favorite poem of all his composition was his "Gertrude." "I never like to see my name before 'The Pleasures of Hope;' why, I cannot tell you, unless it was that when young I was always greeted among my friends as ' Mr. Campbell, author of The Pleasures of Hope. 'Good morning to you, Mr. Campbell, author of The Pleasures of Hope.' When I got married, I was married as the author of 'The Pleasures of Hope;' and when I became a father, my son was the son of the author of 'The Pleasures of Hope.'" A kind of grim smile, ill-subdued, we are afraid, stole over our features, when

standing beside the poet's grave, we read the in
scription on his coffin :—

"THOMAS CAMPBELL, LL. D.,
AUTHOR OF THE 'PLEASURES OF HOPE,'
DIED JUNE 15. 1844.
AGED 67."

The poet's dislike occurred to our memory—there
was no getting the better of the thought.

There is a vigor and swing of versification in
"The Pleasures of Hope" unlike any other of
Campbell's compositions, the "Lochiel" excepted :
yet it carries with it, as Sir Walter Scott justly
observes, many marks of juvenile composition.
The "Lochiel" has all the faults and all the de-
fects of his former effort, and, as if aware of a
want, he sat down, when busy with "Gertrude of
Wyoming," to amend the poem. The last four
lines originally ran :—

> "Shall victor exult or in death be laid low,
> With his back to the field and his feet to the foe !
> And leaving in battle no blot on his name,
> Look proudly to Heav'n from the death-bed of fame."

A noble passage nobly conceived ; but hear how it
runs as appended to the first edition of " Gertrude
of Wyoming :"

> "Shall victor exult in the battle's acclaim,
> Or look to yon Heav'n from the death-bed of fame."

The poet restored the original reading on the re
commendation of Sir Walter Scott : he had succeeded in squeezing the whole spirit from out the
passage.

I remember remarking to Campbell, that there
was a couplet in his " Pleasures of Hope," which I
felt an indescribable pleasure in repeating aloud

and filling my ears with the music which it made ;—

> " And waft across the wave's tumultuous roar,
>   The wolf's long howl from Oonalaskal's shore."

' Yes," he said, " I tell you where I got it—I found it in a poem called ' The Sentimental Sailor,' published about the time of Sterne's ' Sentimental Journey.' " I have never been able to meet with this poem.

Campbell deserves a good biography and a good monument. His own works want no recommendations, but his friends may do much to perpetuate the memory of the man. Surely his letters deserve collection, and his correspondence should not be suffered to perish from neglect. There is a subscription on foot to erect a monument to his memory in Poets' Corner. This is as it should be—but let it be something good. We have more than enough of bad and indifferent in the Abbey already.

ESSAY

ON THE

GENIUS AND CHARACTER OF CAMPBELL

BY GEORGE GILFILLAN.

IT is a fortunate thing for a poet to make a hit at starting. Once write a popular poem, or even song, and your
name cleaves its native night, and obtains that floating
notoriety which is rarely, if ever, lost, and which secures
attention, if not fame, to whatever else you write. Not
only are the booksellers forever after your obedient humble servants, but the public, when once familiarized with
a name, after once relaxing its sage face into a smile of
complacency, is loath to write itself down an ass, by recalling, however it may modify, its verdict. Otherwise
with one whose struggles after renown, however vigorous, have altogether failed of introducing him into any
circle of admirers, much wider than that which any tal-
ented man can command by the private exercise of his
abilities. His name, if alluded to by any of his devoted
friends, comes like a staggering blow to the ignorance
of the portion of the pensive public which never heard
of him or of his works before. Its mention, accordingly, is resented as an impertinence, and inch by inch
must he continue to climb the sides, and probably die
ere he reach the summit of the difficult hill. Fortunate,
in truth, for a poet is the early culmination of his name ;
but only in a secular point of view, or when he happens

to be a disinterested and enthusiastic devotee of his art.
If he have no high religious purposes in its prosecution
—if he be greedy of its immediate gains—if he love the
hasty garlands of reputation better than that slow, deep,
rich flower of fame which God, " who hardens the ruby
in a million years, and works in duration in which Alps
and Andes come and go like rainbows," rears by a long,
late process—his rapid and instant popularity is a curse,
and not a blessing to his genius.   Not every one can,
like a Schiller or a Goethe, dally awhile with the mer-
etricious mistress, reputation—drink from her hand the
daintiest cup of her enchantments, and then, rejecting
the wanton, bind itself up, by severe and solemn training,
to gain the chary and chaste, but divine hand of fame
—of that fame which is indeed " the spur that the clear
spirit doth raise ;"—

" The last infirmity of noble minds."

Too many besides Thomas Campbell tarry in the Ca
lypso island till the sun be down, and Ithaca is still afar.
   And yet we readily admit that this true poet began
his career with a strong and pure love, if not the pro-
foundest insight into the meaning and mystery of his
art.   Nowhere shall we find the poetical feeling more
beautifully linked to the joyous rapture of youth than
in the " Pleasures of Hope."   It is the outburst of genuine enthusiasm ; and even its glitter we love, as re-
minding us of the " shining morning face" of a school-
boy.   But why we quarrel with Campbell is, that this
precipitate shine of fame upon his young head has dazzled his eyes, has satisfied his ambition, chilled his love
of his art, and excited the suspicion, that his real object
all along has been the dowery of the muse, and not her
sacred and inestimable self.   The " Pleasures of Hope"
bears no more proportion to the powers of its author than
does the " Robbers" to those of Schiller, or " Werter" to
those of Goethe.   But where is Campbell's " Wallen-
stein," or his " Faust ?"   We have instead only such

glimpses—the more tantalizing that they are beautiful
—of a rare and real vein of original genius as are fur
nished in the " Last Man," " Hohenlinden," and
" O'Connor's Child."

Campbell's great power is enthusiasm—subdued.   His
tempest moves on gracefully, and as to the sound of
music.   His muse keeps step at the same time that she
shakes the wilderness.   You see him arranging the dis-
hevelled and streaming hair, smoothing the furrowed forehead, compressing the full and thrilling lips of inspiration.
He can arrest the fury of his turbulent vein by stretching
forth the calm hand of taste, as an escaped lunatic is
abated in a moment by the whisper of his keeper, or by
his more terrible tap of quiet, imperious command.
There is a perpetual alternation going on in his mind
He is this moment possessed by his imagination ; the
next, he masters and tames it, to walk meekly in the har-
ness of his purpose ; or, to use his own fine image,
while his genius is flaming above, his taste below, " like
the dial's silent power,"

> Measures inspiration's hour,
> And tells its height in heaven.

He is inferior thus to the very first class of poets, whose
taste and art are unconscious.   His are at once conscious to himself and visible to others.   Their works,
like Nature's, arrange themselves into elegance and or
der, amidst their impetuous and ecstatic motion ; their
apparent extravagancies obey a law of their own, and
create a taste for their appreciation ; their hair, shed on
the whirlwind, falls abroad, through its own divine instinct, in lines of waving beauty ; their flashing eye en-
riches the day ; their wild, uncontrollable step, " brings
from the dust the sound of liberty."   But if Campbell
be too measured, and timid, and self-watchful, to apper-
tain to those demi-urgi of poetry, he is far less to be
classed with the imitative and the cold—the schools of
Boileau and Pope.   He not only belongs to no school ;

but in short, deep gushes of genuine genius—in single thoughts, where you do not know whether more to admire the felicity of the conception, or the delicate and tremulous finish of the expression—in drops of spirit-stirring or melting song—and in a general manliness and chastity of manner, Campbell is perhaps the finest ARTIST living. His mind has the refinement of the female intellect, added to the energy of the classic man. His taste is not of the Gothic order, neither is it of the Roman; it is that of a Greek, neither grotesque nor finically fastidious. His imagery is select, not abundant; out of a multitude of figures which throng on his mind, he has the resolution to choose only the one which, by pre-established harmony, seems destined to enshrine the idea. His sentiment is sweet, without being mawkish, and *recherché* without being affected. Here, indeed, is Campbell's fine distinction. He never becomes metaphysical in discriminating the various shades, nor morbid in painting the darker moods of sentiment. He preserves continually the line of demarcation between sentiment and passion. With the latter, in its turbulence—its selfish engrossment—the unvaried, but gorgeous coloring which it flings across all objects—the flames of speech which break out from its white lips, he rarely meddles. But of that quieter and nobler feeling, which may be called, from its stillness, its subdued tone, its whispered accents, its shade of pensiveness, the moonshine of the mind, he is pre-eminently the poet. His lines on " Revisiting a Scene in Argyleshire," and those on " Leaving a Scene in Bavaria," are the perfection of this species of poetry. They are meditations, imbued at once with all the tenderness of moonshine, and all the strength of sunshine. Manly is his melancholy, and even his sigh proclaims the breadth and depth of the chest from which it is upheaved.

" To bear is to conquer our fate," is the motto of this brave philosophy, which contrasts well with the wayward recalcitration of Byron against the still strong order of things—with the whimper of poor Keats—with the unearthly shriek by which you track Shelley through his wildest wanderings in the mist—and with the sad propensity of the Lakers to analyze their tears ere they permit them to fall to the ground; to refine away their robust emotions into shadow; and to cover from their eyes the real calamities of existence by a veil of dream.

Campbell is *par excellence* the poet of the fair sex. There are no works which are more relished by cultivated females. His flight rises precisely to that pitch where they are able fully and gracefully to follow. The manly elegance, moreover, of his mental costume; the unaffected and becoming purity of his speech, so distinct from finical purism; the homage done to the private affections and gentle domestic ties,—these being the qualities which please them in a man, are sure to fascinate them in a poet. "Gertrude of Wyoming" has brought this enviable kind of popularity to a point. It strives to embody all the quiet, without the insipidity of domestic life; and by the picturesque accompaniments of American woods, flageolets echoing from romantic towns, war-drums heard in the distance, tomahawks flashing in the sunset, Indians bursting across the stage, it does, to some extent, relieve that tedium and common-place, through which too often "glides the calm current of domestic joy." It is not, however, on the whole, an artistically finished work. It has no story; at least the tale it tells has little interest or novelty, and is somewhat wiredrawn. The characters are rather insipid. Gertrude's father is a volcano burnt out. Gertrude herself is a pretty, romantic Miss of Pall Mall, dropped down by the side of the Susquehanna, where, undismayed by the sight of the dim aboriginal woods, she pulls out her illustrated copy of Shakspeare, and, with rapt look, and hand elegantly lost in the tangles of her hair, proceeds to study the character of Imogen, or Lady Macbeth, or Mrs Ann Page. Her lover is a " curled darling," who

4

has gone the grand tour—has seen the world, and returned like a good-mannered youth, from the saloons of
London, and the carnivals of Venice, in search of this
beauty of the woods. Of Brandt something might
have been made, but nothing is. The poet thinks him
hardly company for Master Henry the picturesque, and
Miss Gertrude the romantic : Fvon Outalissi, ere qualified for intercourse with these paragons, must have his
whiskers clipped, his nails pared, and become a sent'-
mental savage, who shall go off with a fine nasal twang,
(talking in his pathetic death-song, by the way, of a
clock that had found out the perpetual motion ; for surely more than eight days had elapsed from the departure
of the happy pair to the last song of the Indian, and
yet he says, " Unheard their clock repeats its hours.")
Nevertheless, the poem contains some of Campbell's
finest things—brief and sudden escapes of his richest vein.
What can be finer than such lines as the following :—

Led by his dusky guide, like morning brought by night.

Till now in Gertrude's eyes their ninth blue summer shone.

Nor far some Andalusian saraband
Would sound to many a native roundelay ;
But who is he that yet a dearer land
Remembers, over hills and far away.
Green Albyn, &c.

Oh, earthly pleasure, what art thou in sooth ?
The torrent's smoothness, ere it dash below.

That fled composure's intellectual ray,
As Etna's fires grow dim before the rising day.

And the exquisite words of Outalissi to his Henry :—

But thee, my flower, whose breath was given
By milder genii o'er the deep,
The spirits of the white man's heaven
Forbid not thee to weep.

The dying speech of Gertrude is beautifully tender ;
but a few sobbed out words, in the circumstances,

would have been more natural, and far more affecting
Shakspeare or Schiller would have made a monosyllable
unlock the human heart as effectually as Campbell does
by all the eloquence and linked sweetness of this artifi-
cial harangue. Let poets remember that the most affecting, and, on the whole, the most powerful words
ever written by man, are probably those in Lear,
" Prithee undo this button; thank you, sir." . The
opening description of Wyoming reminds us, at a distance, of that which commences the Castle of Indolence ; but is less distinct in its grouping, less rich in its
coloring, and unluckily, no more than it, resembles any
actual scenery. So, at least, declare all Americans.
It were ridiculous, therefore, to speak of Gertrude as a
great poem. It is only a second-rate poem containing
many first-rate things ; a tame and tremulous string,
supporting many inestimable pearls. Its tone is feeble ;
its spirit apologetic ; the author is evidently afraid of
his reputation. With gleams of truer genius than any
thing in the " Pleasures of Hope," it wants its frank,
fearless, and manly enthusiasm, and neither has been,
nor has deserved to be, one tithe so popular ; except,
indeed, with those who prefer it because in preferring
it they stand alone.

In " Theodric," again, and the " Pilgrim of Glencoe,"
you find the same sensitiveness as to renown, and sense
of inferiority to his former self, attempting to conceal
themselves under, we know not what, of a jaunty air
of nonchalance and affected defiance. Intensely aware
of the ludicrous aspect an old man would present mounted on a boy's stilts, he goes to the opposite extreme, and
assumes a garrulous, free and easy, and somewhat pert
and snappish tone, which we cordially dislike. " Theodric," indeed, is quite unworthy of its author's reputation,
has scarcely a fine thing in it, and is little else than
middling prose twisted into unmusical and shambling
metre. In the other you see now and then robust
vigor ; but, on the whole, the wicked exclamation

" *Eheu quantum mutatus ab illo,*" forces itself up into your lips at every turning of the bald and spiritless page It is with a mixture of feelings, half pleasurable, half melancholy, that you revert from this faint reflection of the tartan to " Lochiel's Warning," the most sublime and spirit-stirring of all Campbell's minor poems. Nowhere, save in some of Scott's battle scenes, or in Macaulay's " Lays of Ancient Rome," do we find the old Homeric spirit in finer preservation. The poet has shot into it all his nighland blood, like the *insanis vim leonis* by which the daring son of Iapetus inspired his primitive man. No one but a descendant of the Cullummore—who had slept in his plaid nights together mid the mists—who had crossed the foaming friths of the Hebrides while the spirit of the storm was shrieking above the white waves —who had been lost for weeks among the mountains— who had sallied forth with Christopher North, in dead of winter, from Glasgow College to Campsie Glen, and spent three days in making a snow man, " a great fellow, with a noble phrenological development, and face after the most improved Lavater shape," and then spent other three in taking him down—who had shuddered at broad-day at finding himself alone with the ravens and the streams on the solitary hill-side, and trembled lest his every footfall, as it startled the deep silence, might awaken something more fearful than a ghost—who had thrilled to the scalp at hearing in the far distance the long yell of the pibroch piercing the mist, or heard fitfully through the lulls in the autumn hurricane—who had once or twice, in wild frolic, drunk destruction to the house of Brunswick, and the memory of Prince Charlie, in draughts of usquebae, unchristened by revenue and unmitigated by water, and rising up from the fierce potation a " prophet in drink," while the mountains reeled around him, and the streams sang double, and two terrible suns flared in the afternoon heaven—no one who had not done all this, and, though born in Glasgow, much of this he actually did—could

have risen to the height, or sustained the swell of
" Lochiel's Warning." How finely contrasted are the
language and the attitudes of the parties in this almost
Shakspearean interlocution!—the chieftain serene, yet
stern, collected in his conscious courage and integrity ;
his arms folded ; his look bespeaking a calm indignation ; the one erect, fixed, yet tremulous feather in his
bonnet, but a type of the unity of his resolve and tho
chivalric determination of his soul. The wizard, bowing
under the burden he proclaims, pale in the prospect of
the measureless ruin which is at hand ; his eye shot
from the socket by the pressure of the bursting vision ;
erect before his chieftain, but bent low before his God ;
—the language of the one firm, direct, and contemptu-
ous, tinged too with poetry, for he has a vision of his
own, and his eye and his language kindle as he sees,

> " Like reapers descend to the harvest of death
>   Clanronald the dauntless, and Moray the proud,
>   All plaided and plumed in their tartan array ;"—

that of the other abrupt, involved, vehement—all on
end with the strange images of death which crowd in
upon his soul, from the burning eyrie, beaconing tho
blackness of heaven, to the bridle of the riderless steed,
" red with the sign of despair,"—from the sighs of the
iron-bound prisoner to the embers of tho far-flaming
summit, " like stars to the firmament cast." And fine
at length it is to see how the terrors of the future pale
before the courage of the present, as though a ghost
were to tremble, and turn before the ghost-seer ; how
the blue clear steel cuts the shadowy circle, and dis-
solves the dreadful spell, and the warrior leaves tho
stage, towering above his mystic adviser, and defying
destiny itself. Baffled and gloomy, you see the wizard
melting into his clouds, rolled together like the wounded
spirit of Loda, while the hero steps onward with a step
which seems to tread on necks, and a port which carries in it the assurance, if not of victory, at least of r
glorious death.

In a softer style Campbell has written " O'Connor's Child," the sweetest and most plaintive, and most romantic of all his strains. It is a poem, indeed, which can receive no adequate criticism but tears. Who durst make remarks on a production, while his eyes were making marks more eloquent and impressive far upon the blurred and blotted page? A tear is the truest and noblest Longinus. " To Barry we give loud applause, to Garrick only tears." We pass this poem by in silence. Never did the noblest harp that rung in " Tara's halls" send forth a strain so sweet and subtle, and mournfully desolate, as this. Soft as the voice of gentlest woman is the flow of the verse—heart-rending the pathos of the description, yet wild and high as the " Cameron's Gathering" rises the swell of the grandeur ; and you say, as you might of that subterranean music which Humboldt describes rising from a cavern in South America, or as Ferdinand says of Ariel's music, " This is no mortal business, nor no sound that the earth owns."

" The Last Man" is in a more ambitious style. It was a ticklish and terrible topic, out of Campbell's usual track, and verging on a field where the " giant angels" of genius have alone a right to disport themselves. It was such a subject as would have suited Dante, (and what a " Last Man" would he himself have made ! what an abrupt and haggard terminus had he been to the species, turning up that scathed face in gloomy triumph to the darkening sun and the reeling constellations !) or Michael Angelo, or him who drew Medusa " gazing on the midnight sky upon the cloudy mountain peak supine." And yet with what easy mastery has Campbell treated it ! With what a firm and tender hand does he bear the " pall of a past world !" In what terse, yet bold language, does he describe the " twins in death !"—yonder the sun darkening at his meridian height, as the black hand, of which eclipse is one premonitory finger, passes over him ; and here the solitary son of Adam receiving on his eye his last light,

and addressing him as they enter together into the eternal shadow. We have seen the taste of the idea
questioned; but surely, if there be poetry in the thought
of a first man—alone between the virgin earth and the
abyss of stars—there must be more in the figure of a
last man, forming a momentary link between an earth
that is dissolving and a sky that is rolling together as a
scroll. If there be poetry in the thought of the last man
of the deluge, standing on the last peak of a drowned
world, there must be more in the idea of one, dauntless
as, from the sepulchre of a perished earth, he is about
to leap into the arms of death, and feels gaining on him
the slow shadow of everlasting darkness. The execution of the poem is admirable—no exaggeration—no
appearance of effort; and herein we deem it superior to
Byron's " Darkness," which, in all but its dire literality
and distinctness, is a dream of nightmare, where, murky
as the gloom is, it is not dark enough to conceal the
sneer of the central object—the poet himself—making
mouths, which he imagines unseen, at the great funeral.
Campbell's " Last Man" is very properly nameless—
his previous history unknown—the interest is given him
by the circumstances in which he stands, and he rises
to the grandeur of his position while feeling himself sole
mourner at the obsequies of a world. Perhaps, to make
him a Christian was an error, because, first, the whole
idea of the poem is inconsistent with Christian truth;
and, secondly, as a mere artistic matter, the dreary
magnificence of the scene had been enhanced, had he
been represented as the last projection of the entire
human family, about to be sucked down into the sea
of annihilation. The poem altogether discovers in our
poet a new and extensive district in his mind, which
he has never cultivated, but left shadowy, silent, and
unbroken in the recesses of his spirit.

Had we been asked to give our vote for one best
qualified to be the laureate of the rainbow, we should,
even previous to experience, have preferred Campbell

His genius, pillared indeed on earth, yet rising by ethereal stages toward heaven, mildly reflective, rather than dazzlingly original, was just the genius to chant the praises of that fine old show of heaven, at which the "countryman stops to gaze," at the sight of which the little child claps his hands,—that arrowless bow which "encompasseth the sky with a glorious circle, and the hands of the Most High have bended it." On the green, glad, and glittering earth, and between the father Sun, and the fairest of his daughters, spanning the dark and dripping east, stands up the poet and sings a strain which ascends like "a steam of rich distilled perfumes," which arrests and eternizes the brief beauty of the apparition, and which seems now the song of the earth's gratitude, and now the voice of the sun's tenderness for his evanishing child. Campbell's "Rainbow" is not one of those "tearless rainbows, such as span the unclouded skies of Peristan," nor does it bear aloft his thoughts to that region where round the throne there appears a "rainbow like unto an emerald,"—his is of this "dear green earth,"—its beauty is the beauty of tears—it is the very rainbow which appeared in the departing clouds of the deluge, and—

> "As fresh in yon horizon dark,
> As young its beauties seem,
> As when the eagle from the ark
> First sported in its beam."

It is not the rainbow as he has seen it shining above the Thames, and with hardly an eye among those of thousands marking its slighted loveliness : but the rainbow as he has seen it, binding Beneaw to Benvenue, Benmackdui to Cairngorm—the delight of the solitary shepherd or huntsman on the hill. And as we said, that never shall a shell be seen without recalling to the enthusiast the lines of Landor, so we can at least answer for ourselves, that never do we behold a rainbow, whether bridging the Highland valley, or seen by our eye alone over the silent and smokeless morning city, without re-

calling the lines of Campbell ; and never shall we think
of his genius but (if we may use the words) as " clothed
with a rainbow."

Our author's " Lines to Emigrants" are in the style of
his earliest poem, but chastened down into severer beauty. In them he waves a white poetic hand to his departing brothers, and boldly furrows up, by the wing of
his imagination, those primeval forests " where now the
panther laps a lonely stream," and becomes a pioneer
and prophet of the glorious future ages which he is priv-
ileged to read in their germ—

> " As in a cradled Hercules we trace
> The lines of empire in his infant face."

It is characteristic of Campbell, and how much does
it say for his powers, that whatever he does is in its own
line the best. Thus, next to " Scots wha hae," " Hohenlinden" is the best war-song ever written. It catches
as in a cup the spirit of the " revelry" of war—that
wild steam of intoxication which hovers over the battle
field, till the genuine soldier awakens from a fight as
from a giddy and gorgeous dream, and like Caliban,
" cries to sleep again." And in his two celebrated sea-
songs how proudly does he pace the deck ! With what
rough, tar-like confidence, does he face the terrors of
the tempest of the sea-fight ; and the " meteor flag of
England," blazing over the smoke of battle, is a gran-
der spectacle to him than a comet's hair, or than one of
the serene and steadfast stars.

As a poet, he is already, what Byron is not—a classic secure of immortality—his works already exalted to
the same shelf with those of Goldsmith, Collins, and
Thompson.

His prose is liable to the charge of over-ambition, if
not of affectation, but is clear, energetic, and felicitous.
His critical dicta, as given forth in his " Specimens of
the British Poets." in his " Life of Mrs. Siddons," " Sir
Thomas Laurence," &c., have often a decisive vigor

about them which reminds us of the oracularities of Dr Johnson. He paints his author; and though you may dispute an opinion, who can deny a likeness?

Campbell, at college, was eminent for three things, his poverty, his wit, and his scholarship. A poor, little black-eyed boy, with his toes protruding through his shoes, he was wont to haunt the stove in the logic class; and when driven from it by tall dunderheads from Belfast, used to pelt them with extempore epigrams till, to his infinite delight, he got them to chase him through the class-room; and then the little vagabond, wheeling around, regained his warm corner. It was a high moment for him when he was raised to the post of Lord Rector in his native university. Unbounded was the enthusiasm which prevailed. Such crowding! such cramming! such questioning! " Have you seen him? and you? and you?" and after he was seen, and his fine, frank inaugural address was delivered, " Does he come up to your expectations? isn't he a better speaker than we thought he had been? what fine dark eyes he has got!" And better still when he mingled so familiarly with his constituents, walking arm in arm with them, and giving them (trembling to the very toes) the other and the other grasp of his warm right hand. What proud men we all were, when each of us received a copy of his first inaugural oration, with the magic words, " To so and so, from Thomas Campbell." We remember being in a debating society one evening, when the news arrived that the Lord Rector had unexpectedly come down from London on some matter affecting the interests of the students. It was an eccentric and chivalrous move on his part, and out rushed we in a body to meet and welcome him with respondent enthusiasm. We found him in his brother-in-law's, sipping his coffee, were most cordially received; and after some delightful chit-chat, and a warm-hearted speech or two, left him in a transport of admiration. He, too, felt his fame; and never—not when composing the " Pleasures of

Hope,"—did his blood boil higher; and never was his tongue half so eloquent, as in his meetings with, and his buoyant and cordial speeches to, the students of Glasgow. In memory of the halcyon days of the "Good Lord Rector," some of the cleverer of his admirers established a Campbell Club. He was the first poet we ever saw; and for us to meet, hear, feel the tingling touch of the author of "O'Connor's Child," was "a thing to dream of, not to see." Great as was the enthusiasm of all the red-gowned electors, there was none in whose heart it beat more warmly than in his, who now indites this feeble but sincere tribute to his fame

Alas! since the above was written, the poet of Hope (who, doubly alas! had ere his death become the walking image of despondency) has departed from among us. And with him has passed away that era of literature which stretched between the fall of Pope and the rise of Wordsworth. In Westminster Abbey now lie entombed, not only the remains of a fine though frail spirit, but of one beautiful age of English poetry. Peace, but not oblivion, to their united manes!

CONTENTS

CONTENTS. liii

CONTENTS

THE

PLEASURES OF HOPE.

ANALYSIS—PART I

Tʜᴇ poem opens with a comparison between the beauty of
remote objects in a landscape, and those ideal scenes of
felicity which the imagination delights to contemplate—the
influence of anticipation upon the other passions is next de·
lineated—an allusion is made to the well-known fiction in
Pagan tradition, that, when all the guardian deities of mankind abandoned the world, Hope alone was left behind—the
consolations of this passion in situations of danger and dis
tress—the seaman on his watch—the soldier marching into
battle—allusion to the interesting adventures of Byron.

The inspiration of Hope, as it actuates the efforts of genius,
whether in the department of science or of taste—domestic
felicity, how intimately connected with views of future happiness—picture of a mother watching her infant when asleep
—pictures of the prisoner, the maniac, and the wanderer.

From the consolations of individual misery a transition is
made to prospects of political improvement in the future state
of society—the wide field that is yet open for the progress of
humanizing arts among uncivilized nations—from these views
of amelioration of society, and the extension of liberty and
truth over despotic and barbarous countries, by a melancholy
contrast of ideas, we are led to reflect upon the hard fate of a
brave people recently conspicuous in their struggles for independence—description of the capture of Warsaw, of the
last contest of the oppressors and the oppressed, and the
massacre of the Polish patriots at the bridge of Prague—
apostrophe to the self-interested enemies of human improvement—the wrongs of Africa—the barbarous policy of Europeans in India—prophecy in the Hindoo mythology of the ex·
pected descent of the Deity to redress the miseries of their
race, and to take vengeance on the violators of justice and
mercy

PLEASURES OF HOPE.

At summer eve, when Heaven's ethereal bow
Spans with bright arch the glittering hills below,
Why to yon mountain turns the musing eye,
Whose sunbright summit mingles with the sky?
Why do those cliffs of shadowy tint appear
More sweet than all the landscape smiling near?—
'Tis distance lends enchantment to the view,
And robes the mountain in its azure hue.
Thus, with delight, we linger to survey
The promised joys of life's unmeasured way;
Thus, from afar, each dim-discover'd scene
More pleasing seems than all the past hath been,
And every form, that Fancy can repair
From dark oblivion, glows divinely there.
    What potent spirit guides the raptured eye
To pierce the shades of dim futurity?
Can Wisdom lend, with all her heavenly power,
The pledge of Joy's anticipated hour?
Ah, no. she darkly sees the fate of man—
Her dim horizon bounded to a span;
Or, if she hold an image to the view,
'Tis Nature pictured too severely true.
With thee, sweet Hope! resides the heavenly light,
That pours remotest rapture on the sight:
Thine is the charm of life's bewilder'd way,
That calls each slumbering passion into play.

Waked by thy touch, I see the sister band,
On tiptoe watching, start at thy command,
And fly where'er thy mandate bids them steer,
To Pleasure's path, or Glory's bright career.
　Primeval Hope, the Aönian Muses say,
When Man and Nature mourn'd their first decay,
When every form of death, and every wo,
Shot from malignant stars to earth below ;
When Murder bared her arm, and rampant War
Yoked the red dragons of her iron car ;
When Peace and Mercy, banish'd from the plain,
Sprung on the viewless winds to Heaven again ;
All, all forsook the friendless, guilty mind,
But Hope, the charmer, linger'd still behind.
　Thus, while Elijah's burning wheels prepare
From Carmel's heights to sweep the fields of air,
The prophet's mantle, ere his flight began,
Dropp'd on the world—a sacred gift to man.
　Auspicious Hope ! in thy sweet garden grow
Wreaths for each toil, a charm for every wo ;
Won by their sweets, in Nature's languid hour,
The way-worn pilgrim seeks thy summer bower ;
There, as the wild bee murmurs on the wing,
What peaceful dreams thy handmaid spirits bring !
What viewless forms th' Æolian organ play,
And sweep the furrow'd lines of anxious thought away
　Angel of life ! thy glittering wings explore
Earth's loneliest bounds, and Ocean's wildest shore.
Lo ! to the wintry winds the pilot yields
His bark careering o'er unfathom'd fields ;
Now on Atlantic waves he rides afar,
Where Andes, giant of the western star,
With meteor-standard to the winds unfurl'd,
Looks from his throne of clouds o'er half the world !
　Now far he sweeps, where scarce a summer smiles,
On Behring's rocks, or Greenland's naked isles :
Cold on his midnight watch the breezes blow,
From wastes that slumber in eternal snow ;

And waft, across the waves' tumultuous roar,
The wolf's long howl from Oonalaska's shore.
  Poor child of danger, nursling of the storm,
Sad are the woes that wreck thy manly form !
Rocks, waves, and winds, the shatter'd bark delay ;
Thy heart is sad, thy home is far away.
  But Hope can here her moonlight vigils keep,
And sing to charm the spirit of the deep :
Swift as yon streamer lights the starry pole,
Her visions warm the watchman's pensive soul ·
His native hills that rise in happier climes,
The grot that heard his song of other times,
His cottage home, his bark of slender sail,
His glassy lake, and broomwood-blossom'd vale,
Rush on his thought ; he sweeps before the wind,
Treads the loved shore he sigh'd to leave behind ;
Meets at each step a friend's familiar face,
And flies at last to Helen's long embrace ;
Wipes from her cheek the rapture-speaking tear !
And clasps, with many a sigh, his children dear !
While, long neglected, but at length caress'd,
His faithful dog salutes the smiling guest,
Points to the master's eyes (where'er they roam)
His wistful face, and whines a welcome home.
  Friend of the brave ! in peril's darkest hour,
Intrepid Virtue looks to thee for power ;
To thee the heart its trembling homage yields,
On stormy floods, and carnage-cover'd fields,
When front to front the banner'd hosts combine,
Halt ere they close, and form the dreadful line
When all is still on Death's devoted soil,
The march-worn soldier mingles for the toil !
As rings his glittering tube, he lifts on high
The dauntless brow, and spirit-speaking eye, ·
Hails in his heart the triumph yet to come,
And hears thy stormy music in the drum !
  And such thy strength-inspiring aid that **bore**
The hardy Byron to his native shore—

In horrid climes, where Chiloe's tempests sweep
Tumultuous murmurs o'er the troubled deep.
'Twas his to mourn Misfortune's rudest shock,
Scourged by the winds, and cradled on the rock,
To wake each joyless morn and search again
The famish'd haunts of solitary men ;
Whose race, unyielding as their native storm,
Know not a trace of Nature but the form ;
Yet, at thy call, the hardy tar pursued,
Pale, but intrepid, sad, but unsubdued,
Pierced the deep woods, and hailing from afar
The moon's pale planet and the northern star,
Paused at each dreary cry, unheard before,
Hyænas in the wild, and mermaids on the shore ;
Till, led by thee o'er many a cliff sublime,
He found a warmer world, a milder clime,
A home to rest, a shelter to defend,
Peace and repose, a Briton and a friend !
  Congenial Hope ! thy passion-kindling power,
How bright, how strong, in youth's untroubled hour ;
On yon proud height, with Genius hand in hand,
I see thee light, and wave thy golden wand.
  " Go, child of Heaven ! (thy winged words proclaim)
'Tis thine to search the boundless fields of fame !
Lo ! Newton, priest of nature, shines afar,
Scans the wide world, and numbers every star !
Wilt thou, with him, mysterious rites apply,
And watch the shrine with wonder-beaming eye !
Yes, thou shalt mark, with magic art profound,
The speed of light, the circling march of sound ;
With Franklin grasp the lightning's fiery wing,
Or yield the lyre of Heaven another string.
  " The Swedish sage admires, in yonder bowers,
His winged insects, and his rosy flowers ;
Calls from their woodland haunts the savage train,
With sounding horn, and counts them on the plain—
So once, at Heaven's command, the wanderers came
To Eden's shade, and heard their various name.

" Far from the world, in yon sequester'd clime,
Slow pass the sons of Wisdom, more sublime ;
Calm as the fields of Heaven, his sapient eye
The loved Athenian lifts to realms on high,
Admiring Plato, on his spotless page,
Stamps the bright dictates of the Father sage :
' Shall Nature bound to Earth's diurral span
The fire of God, th' immortal soul of man ?'

" Turn, child of Heaven, thy rapture-lighten'd eye
To Wisdom's walks, the sacred Nine are nigh :
Hark ! from bright spires that gild the Delphian height,
From streams that wander in eternal light,
Ranged on their hill, Harmonia's daughters swell
The mingling tones of horn, and harp, and shell ;
Deep from his vaults the Loxian murmurs flow,
And Pythia's awful organ peals below.

" Beloved of Heaven ! the smiling Muse shall shed
Her moonlight halo on thy beauteous head ;
Shall swell thy heart to rapture unconfined,
And breathe a holy madness o'er thy mind
I see thee roam her guardian power beneath,
And talk with spirits on the midnight heath ;
Inquire of guilty wanderers whence they came,
And ask each blood-stain'd form his earthly name ;
Then weave in rapid verse the deeds they tell,
And read the trembling world the tales of hell.

" When Venus, throned in clouds of rosy hue,
Flings from her golden urn the vesper dew,
And bids fond man her glimmering noon employ,
Sacred to love, and walks of tender joy ;
A milder mood the goddess shall recall,
And soft as dew thy tones of music fall ;
While Beauty's deeply-pictured smiles impart
A pang more dear than pleasure to the heart—
Warm as thy sighs shall flow the Lesbian strain,
And plead in Beauty's ear, nor plead in vain.

" Or wilt thou Orphean hymns more sacred deem,
And steep thy song in Mercy's mellow stream ;

To pensive drops the radiant eye beguile—
For Beauty's tears are lovelier than her smile ;~~
On Nature's throbbing anguish pour relief,
And teach impassion'd souls the joy of grief?
  " Yes ; to thy tongue shall seraph words be given
And power on earth to plead the cause of Heaven ;
The proud, the cold untroubled heart of stone,
That never mused on sorrow but its own,
Unlocks a generous store at thy command,
Like Horeb's rocks beneath the prophet's hand.
The living lumber of his kindred earth,
Charm'd into soul, receives a second birth,
Feels thy dread power another heart afford,
Whose passion-touch'd harmonious strings accord
True as the circling spheres to Nature's plan ;
And man, the brother, lives the friend of man.
  " Bright as the pillar rose at Heaven's command,
When Israel march'd along the desert land,
Blazed through the night on lonely wilds afar,
And told the path,—a never-setting star:
So, heavenly Genius, in thy course divine,
·Hope is thy star, her light is ever thine."
  Propitious Power ! when rankling cares annoy
The sacred home of Hymenean joy ;
When doom'd to Poverty's sequester'd dell,
The wedded pair of love and virtue dwell,
Unpitied by the world, unknown to fame,
Their woes, their wishes, and their hearts the same—
Oh, there, prophetic Hope ! thy smile bestow,
And chase the pangs that worth should never know—
There, as the parent deals his scanty store
To friendless babes, and weeps to give no more,
Tell, that his manly race shall yet assuage
Their father's wrongs, and shield his latter age.
What though for him no Hybla sweets distil,
Nor bloomy vines wave purple on the hill ;
Tell, that when silent years have pass'd away,
That when his eye grows dim, his tresses gray,

These busy hands a lovelier cot shall build,
And deck with fairer flowers his little field,
And call from Heaven propitious dews to breathe
Arcadian beauty on the barren heath;
Tell, that while Love's spontaneous smile endears
The days of peace, the sabbath of his years,
Health shall prolong to many a festive hour
The social pleasures of his humble bower.
    Lo! at the couch where infant beauty sleeps,
Her silent watch the mournful mother keeps;
She, while the lovely babe unconscious lies,
Smiles on her slumbering child with pensive eyes,
And weaves a song of melancholy joy—
"Sleep, image of thy father, sleep, my boy;
No lingering hour of sorrow shall be thine;
No sigh that rends thy father's heart and mine;
Bright as his manly sire the son shall be
In form and soul; but, ah! more blest than he!
Thy fame, thy worth, thy filial love at last,
Shall sooth his aching heart for all the past—
With many a smile my solitude repay,
And chase the world's ungenerous scorn away.
    "And say, when summon'd from the world and thee,
I lay my head beneath the willow tree,
Wilt thou, sweet mourner! at my stone appear,
And sooth my parted spirit lingering near?
Oh, wilt thou come at evening hour to shed
The tears of Memory o'er my narrow bed;
With aching temples on thy hand reclined,
Muse on the last farewell I leave behind,
Breathe a deep sigh to winds that murmur low,
And think on all my love, and all my wo?"
    So speaks affection, ere the infant eye
Can look regard, or brighten in reply;
But when the cherub lip hath learnt to claim
A mother's ear by that endearing name;
Soon as the playful innocent can prove
A tear of pity, or a smile of love,

Or cons his murmuring task beneath her care,
Or lisps with holy look his evening prayer,
Or gazing, mutely pensive, sits to hear
The mournful ballad warbled in his ear ;
How fondly looks admiring Hope the while
At every artless tear, and every smile !
How glows the joyous parent to descry
A guileless bosom, true to sympathy !
   Where is the troubled heart consign'd to share
Tumultuous toils, or solitary care,
Unblest by visionary thoughts that stray
To count the joys of Fortune's better day?
Lo, nature, life, and liberty relume
The dim-eyed tenant of the dungeon gloom,
A long-lost friend, or hapless child restored,
Smiles at his blazing hearth and social board ;
Warm from his heart the tears of rapture flow,
And virtue triumphs o'er remember'd wo.
   Chide not his peace, proud Reason ! nor destroy
The shadowy forms of uncreated joy,
That urge the lingering tide of life, and pour
Spontaneous slumber on his midnight hour.
Hark ! the wild maniac sings, to chide the gale
That wafts so slow her lover's distant sail ;
She, sad spectatress, on the wintry shore,
Watch'd the rude surge his shroudless corse that bore
Knew the pale form, and, shrieking in amaze,
Clasp'd her cold hands, and fix'd her maddening gaze
Poor widow'd wretch ! 'twas there she wept in vain,
Till Memory fled her agonizing brain ;—
But Mercy gave, to charm the sense of wo,
Ideal peace, that truth could ne'er bestow ;
Warm on her heart the joys of Fancy beam,
And aimless Hope delights her darkest dream.
   Oft when yon moon has climb'd the midnight sky,
And the lone sea-bird wakes its wildest cry,
Piled on the steep, her blazing fagots burn
To hail the bark that never can return ;

And still she waits, but scarce forbears to weep
That constant love can linger on the deep.
　　And, mark the wretch, whose wanderings never knew
The world's regard, that sooths, though half untrue ;
Whose erring heart the lash of sorrow bore,
But found not pity when it err'd no more.
Yon friendless man, at whose dejected eye
Th' unfeeling proud one looks—and passes by,
Condemn'd on Penury's barren path to roam,
Scorn'd by the world, and left without a home—
Even he, at evening, should he chance to stray
Down by the hamlet's hawthorn-scented way,
Where, round the cot's romantic glade, are seen
The blossom'd bean-field; and the sloping green,
Leans o'er its humble gate, and thinks the while—
Oh! that for me some home like this would smile,
Some hamlet shade, to yield my sickly form
Health in the breeze, and shelter in the storm !
There should my hand no stinted boon assign
To wretched hearts with sorrow such as mine !—
That generous wish can sooth unpitied care,
And Hope half mingles with the poor man's prayer
　　Hope ! when I mourn, with sympathizing mind,
The wrongs of fate, the woes of human kind,
Thy blissful omens bid my spirit see
The boundless fields of rapture yet to be ;
I watch the wheels of Nature's mazy plan,
And learn the future by the past of man.
　　Come, bright Improvement ! on the car of Time,
And rule the spacious world from clime to clime ;
Thy handmaid arts shall every wild explore,
Trace every wave, and culture every shore.
On Erie's banks, where tigers steal along,
And the dread Indian chants a dismal song,
Where human fiends on midnight errands walk,
And bathe in brains the murderous tomahawk,
There shall the flocks on thymy pasture stray,
And shepherds dance at Summer's opening day.

Each wandering genius of the lonely glen
Shall start to view the glittering haunts of men,
And silent watch, on woodland heights around,
The village curfew as it tolls profound.
    In Libyan groves, where damned rites are done,
That bathe the rocks in blood, and veil the sun,
Truth shall arrest the murderous arm profane,
Wild Obi flies—the veil is rent in twain.
    Where barbarous hordes on Scythian mountains roam,
Truth, Mercy, Freedom, yet shall find a home ;
Where'er degraded Nature bleeds and pines,
From Guinea's coast to Sibir's dreary mines,
'Truth shall pervade th' unfathom'd darkness there,
And light the dreadful features of despair—
Hark ! the stern captive spurns his heavy load,
And asks the image back that Heaven bestow'd !
Fierce in his eye the fire of valor burns,
And, as the slave departs, the man returns.
    Oh ! sacred Truth ! thy triumph ceased a while,
And Hope, thy sister, ceased with thee to smile,
When leagued Oppression pour'd to Northern wars
Her whisker'd pandoors and her fierce hussars,
Waved her dread standard to the breeze of morn,
Peal'd her loud drum, and twang'd her trumpet horn ;
Tumultuous horror brooded o'er her van,
Presaging wrath to Poland—and to man !
    Warsaw's last champion from her height survey'd,
Wide o'er the fields, a waste of ruin laid,—
Oh ! Heaven ! he cried, my bleeding country save !
Is there no hand on high to shield the brave ?
Yet, though destruction sweep those lovely plains,
Rise, fellow-men ! our country yet remains !
By that dread name, we wave the sword on high !
And swear for her to live !—with her to die !
    He said, and on the rampart-heights array'd
His trusty warriors, few, but undismay'd ;
Firm-paced and slow, a horrid front they form,
Still as the breeze, but dreadful as the storm ;

Low murmuring sounds along their banners fly,
Revenge, or death,—the watchword and reply ;
Then peal'd the notes, omnipotent to charm,
And the loud tocsin toll'd their last alarm !—
    In vain, alas ! in vain, ye gallant few !
From rank to rank your volley'd thunder flew :—
Oh, bloodiest picture in the book of Time,
Sarmatia fell, unwept, without a crime ;
Found not a generous friend, a pitying foe,
Strength in her arms, nor mercy in her wo !
Dropp'd from her nerveless grasp the shatter'd spear,
Closed her bright eye, and curb'd her high career ;—
(Hope, for a season, bade the world farewell,
And Freedom shriek'd—as Kosciusko fell !
    The sun went down, nor ceased the carnage there,
Tumultuous Murder shook the midnight air—
On Prague's proud arch the fires of ruin glow,
His blood-dyed waters murmuring far below ;
The storm prevails, the rampart yields away,
Bursts the wild cry of horror and dismay !
Hark, as the smouldering piles with thunder fall,
A thousand shrieks for hopeless mercy call !
Earth shook—red meteors flash'd along the sky,
And conscious Nature shudder'd at the cry !
    Oh ! righteous Heaven ; ere Freedom found a grave,
Why slept the sword, omnipotent to save ?
Where was thine arm, O Vengeance ! where thy rod,
That smote the foes of Zion and of God ;
That crush'd proud Ammon, when his iron car
Was yoked in wrath, and thunder'd from afar ?
Where was the storm that slumber'd till the host
Of blood-stain'd Pharaoh left their trembling coast ;
Then bade the deep in wild commotion flow,
And heaved an ocean on their march below ?
    Departed spirits of the mighty dead !
Ye that at Marathon and Leuctra bled !
Friends of the world ! restore your swords to man,
Fight in his sacred cause, and lead the van !

Yet for Sarmatia's tears of blood atone,
And make her arm puissant as your own !
Oh ! once again to Freedom's cause return
The patriot TELL—the BRUCE OF BANNOCKBURN !

    Yes ! thy proud lords, unpitied land ! shall see
That man hath yet a soul—and dare be free !
A little while, along thy saddening plains,
The starless night of Desolation reigns ;
Truth shall restore the light by Nature given,
And, like Prometheus, bring the fire of Heaven .
Prone to the dust Oppression shall be hurl'd,
Her name, her nature, wither'd from the world !

    Ye that the rising morn invidious mark,
And hate the light—because your deeds are dark ;
Ye that expanding truth invidious view,
And think, or wish, the song of HOPE untrue ;
Perhaps your little hands presume to span
The march of Genius and the powers of man ;
Perhaps ye watch, at Pride's unhallow'd shrine,
Her victims, newly slain, and thus divine :—
" Here shall thy triumph, Genius, cease, and here
Truth, Science, Virtue, close your short career "

    Tyrants ! in vain ye trace the wizard ring ;
In vain ye limit Mind's unwearied spring :
What ! can ye lull the winged winds asleep,
Arrest the rolling world, or chain the deep ?
No !—the wild wave contemns your sceptred hand :
It roll'd not back when Canute gave command !

    Man ! can thy doom no brighter soul allow ?
Still must thou live a blot on Nature's brow ?
Shall War's polluted banner ne'er be furl'd ?
Shall crimes and tyrants cease but with the world !
What ! are thy triumphs, sacred Truth, belied ?
Why then hath Plato lived—or Sidney died ?—

    Ye fond adorers of departed fame,
Who warm at Scipio's worth, or Tully's name !
Ye that, in fancied vision, can admire
The sword of Brutus, and the Theban lyre !

Rapt in historic ardor, who adore
Each classic haunt, and well-remember'd shore,   .
Where Valor tuned, amidst her chosen throng,
The Thracian trumpet and the Spartan song;
Or, wandering thence, behold the later charms
Of England's glory, and Helvetia's arms!
See Roman fire in Hampden's bosom swell,
And fate and freedom in the shaft of Tell!
Say, ye fond zealots to the worth of yore,
Hath Valor left the world—to live no more?
No more shall Brutus bid a tyrant die,
And sternly smile with vengeance in his eye?
Hampden no more, when suffering Freedom calls,
Encounter Fate, and triumph as he falls?
Nor Tell disclose, through peril and alarm,
The might that slumbers in a peasant's arm?

Yes! in that generous cause, forever strong,
The patriot's virtue and the poet's song,
Still, as the tide of ages rolls away,
Shall charm the world, unconscious of decay!

Yes! there are hearts, prophetic HOPE may trust,
That slumber yet in uncreated dust,
Ordain'd to fire th' adoring sons of earth,
With every charm of wisdom and of worth;
Ordain'd to light, with intellectual day,
The mazy wheels of nature as they play,
Or, warm with Fancy's energy, to glow,
And rival all but Shakspeare's name below.

And say, supernal Powers! who deeply scan
Heaven's dark decrees, unfathom'd yet by man,
When shall the world call down, to cleanse her shame,
That embryo spirit, yet without a name,—
That friend of Nature, whose avenging hands
Shall burst the Libyan's adamantine bands?
Who, sternly marking on his native soil
The blood, the tears, the anguish, and the toil,
Shall bid each righteous heart exult, to see
Peace to the slave, and vengeance on the free!

Yet, yet, degraded men ! th' expected day
That breaks your bitter cup, is far away ;
Trade, wealth, and fashion, ask you still to bleed,
And holy men give Scripture for the deed ;
Scourged, and debased, no Briton stoops to save
A wretch, a coward ; yes, because a slave !—
Eternal Nature ! when thy giant hand
Had heaved the floods, and fixed the trembling land
When life sprang startling at thy plastic call,
Endless her forms, and man the lord of all !
Say, was that lordly form inspired by thee,
To wear eternal chains and bow the knee ?
Was man ordain'd the slave of man to toil,
Yoked with the brutes, and fetter'd to the soil ;
Weigh'd in a tyrant's balance with his gold ?
No !—Nature stamp'd us in a heavenly mould !
She bade no wretch his thankless labor urge,
Nor, trembling, take the pittance and the scourge .
No homeless Libyan, on the stormy deep,
To call upon his country's name, and weep !—
Lo ! once in triumph, on his boundless plain,
The quiver'd chief of Congo loved to reign ;
With fires proportion'd to his native sky,
Strength in his arm, and lightning in his eye ;
Scour'd with wild feet his sun-illumined zone,
The spear, the lion, and the woods, his own !
Or led the combat, bold without a plan,
An artless savage, but a fearless man !
The plunderer came !—alas ! no glory smiles
For Congo's chief, on yonder Indian isles ;
Forever fall'n !—no son of Nature now,
With Freedom charter'd on his manly brow !
Faint, bleeding, bound, he weeps the night away,
And when the sea-wind wafts the dewless day,
Starts, with a bursting heart, for evermore
To curse the sun that lights their guilty shore !
The shrill horn blew ; at that alarum knell
His guardian angel took a last farewell !

That funeral dirge to darkness hath resign'd
The fiery grandeur of a generous mind !
Poor fetter'd man ! I hear thee whispering low
Unhallow'd vows to Guilt, the child of Wo !
Friendless thy heart ; and canst thou harbor there
A wish but death—a passion but despair?
   The widow'd Indian, when her lord expires,
Mounts the dread pile, and braves the funeral fires !
So falls the heart at Thraldom's bitter sigh !
So Virtue dies, the spouse of Liberty !
   But not to Libya's barren climes alone,
To Chili, or the wild Siberian zone,
Belong the wretched heart and haggard eye,
Degraded worth, and poor misfortune's sigh !—
Ye orient realms, where Ganges' waters run !
Prolific fields ! dominions of the sun !
How long your tribes have trembled and obey'd !
How long was Timour's iron sceptre sway'd,
Whose marshall'd hosts, the lions of the plain,
From Scythia's northern mountains to the main,
Raged o'er your plunder'd shrines and altars bare,
With blazing torch and gory cimeter,—
Stunn'd with the cries of death each gentle gale,
And bathed in blood the verdure of the vale !
Yet could no pangs the immortal spirit tame,
When Brama's children perish'd for his name
The martyr smiled beneath avenging power,
And braved the tyrant in his torturing hour !
   When Europe sought your subject realms to gain,
And stretch'd her giant sceptre o'er the main,
Taught her proud barks the winding way to shape,
And braved the stormy Spirit of the Cape ;
Children of Brama ! then was Mercy nigh
To wash the stain of blood's eternal dye ?
Did Peace descend, to triumph and to save,
When freeborn Britons cross'd the Indian wave ?
Ah, no !—to more than Rome's ambition true,
The Nurse of Freedom gave it not to you !

She the bold route of Europe's guilt began,
And, in the march of nations, led the van !
　Rich in the gems of India's gaudy zone,
And plunder piled from kingdoms not their own,
Degenerate trade ! thy minions could despise
The heart-born anguish of a thousand cries ;
Could lock, with impious hands, their teeming store,
While famish'd nations died along the shore :
Could mock the groans of fellow-men, and bear
The curse of kingdoms peopled with despair ;
Could stamp disgrace on man's polluted name
And barter, with their gold, eternal shame !
　But hark ! as bow'd to earth the Bramin kneels,
From heavenly climes propitious thunder peals !
Of India's fate her guardian spirits tell,
Prophetic murmurs breathing on the shell,
And solemn sounds that awe the listening mind,
Roll on the azure paths of every wind.
　" Foes of mankind ! (her guardian spirits say,)
Revolving ages bring the bitter day,
When heaven's unerring arm shall fall on you,
And blood for blood these Indian plains bedew ;
Nine times have Brama's wheels of lightning hurl'd
His awful presence o'er the alarmed world ;
Nine times hath Guilt, through all his giant frame,
Convulsive trembled, as the Mighty came ;
Nine times hath suffering Mercy spared in vain—
But Heaven shall burst her starry gates again !
He comes ! dread Brama shakes the sunless sky
With murmuring wrath, and thunders from on high,
Heaven's fiery horse, beneath his warrior form,
Paws the light clouds, and gallops on the storm !
Wide waves his flickering sword ; his bright arms glow
Like summer suns, and light the world below !
Earth, and her trembling isles in Ocean's bed,
Are shook ; and Nature rocks beneath his tread !
　" To pour redress on India's injured realm,
The oppressor to dethrone, the proud to whelm ;

To chase destruction from her plunder'd shore
With arts and arms that triumph'd once before,
The tenth Avatar comes ! at Heaven's command
Shall Seriswattee wave her hallow'd wand !
And Camdeo bright, and Ganesa sublime,
Shall bless with joy their own propitious clime !—
Come, Heavenly Powers ! primeval peace restore !
Love !— Mercy !—Wisdom !—rule for evermore !"

END OF THE FIRST PART.

ANALYSIS.—PART II.

Apostrophe to the power of Love—its intimate connection with generous and social Sensibility—allusion to that beautiful passage in the beginning of the book of Genesis, which represents the happiness of Paradise itself incomplete, till love was superadded to its other blessings—the dreams of future felicity which a lively imagination is apt to cherish, when Hope is animated by refined attachment—this disposition to combine, in one imaginary scene of residence, all that is pleasing in our estimate of happiness, compared to the skill of the great artist who personified perfect beauty, in the picture of Venus, by an assemblage of the most beautiful features he could find—a summer and winter evening described, as they may be supposed to arise in the mind of one who wishes, with enthusiasm, for the union of friendship and retirement

Hope and Imagination inseparable agents—even in those contemplative moments when our imagination wanders beyond the boundaries of this world, our minds are not unattended with an impression that we shall some day have a wider and more distinct prospect of the universe, instead of the partial glimpse we now enjoy.

The last and most sublime influence of Hope is the concluding topic of the poem—the predominance of a belief in a future state over the terrors attendant on dissolution—the baneful influence of that skeptical philosophy which bars us from such comforts—allusion to the fate of a suicide—episode of Conrad and Ellenore—conclusion

PART. THE SECOND.

In joyous youth, what soul hath never known
Thought, feeling, taste, harmonious to its own?
Who hath not paused while Beauty's pensive eye
Ask'd from his heart the homage of a sigh?
Who hath not own'd, with rapture-smitten frame,
The power of grace, the magic of a name?
    There be, perhaps, who barren hearts avow,
Cold as the rocks on Torneo's hoary brow;
There be, whose loveless wisdom never fail'd,
In self-adoring pride securely mail'd:—
But, triumph not, ye peace-enamor'd few!
Fire, Nature, Genius, never dwelt with you!
For you no fancy consecrates the scene
Where rapture utter'd vows, and wept between;
'Tis yours, unmoved, to sever and to meet;
No pledge is sacred, and no home is sweet!
Who that would ask a heart to dulness wed,
The waveless calm, the slumber of the dead?
No; the wild bliss of Nature needs alloy,
And fear and sorrow fan the fire of joy!
And say, without our hopes, without our fears,
Without the home that plighted love endears,
Without the smile from partial beauty won,
Oh! what were man?—a world without a sun
    Till Hymen brought his love-delighted hour,
There dwelt no joy in Eden's rosy bower!
In vain the viewless seraph lingering there,
At starry midnight charm'd the silent air;

In vain the wild-bird caroll'd on the steep,
To hail the sun, slow wheeling from the deep ;
In vain, to sooth the solitary shade,
Aërial notes in mingling measure play'd ;
The summer wind that shook the spangled tree,
The whispering wave, the murmur of the bee ;—
Still slowly pass'd the melancholy day,
And still the stranger wist not where to stray.
The world was sad !—the garden was a wild !
And man, the hermit, sigh'd—till woman smiled !
   True, the sad power to generous hearts may bring
Delirious anguish on his fiery wing ;
Barr'd from delight by Fate's untimely hand,
By wealthless lot, or pitiless command ;
Or doom'd to gaze on beauties that adorn
The smile of triumph or the frown of scorn ;
While Memory watches o'er the sad review
Of joys that faded like the morning dew ;
Peace may depart—and life and nature seem
A barren path, a wildness, and a dream !
   But can the noble mind forever brood,
The willing victim of a weary mood,
On heartless cares that squander life away,
And cloud young Genius brightening into day ?—
Shame to the coward thought that e'er betray'd
The noon of manhood to a myrtle shade !—
If Hope's creative spirit cannot raise
One trophy sacred to thy future days,
Scorn the dull crowd that haunt the gloomy shrine,
Of hopeless love to murmur and repine !
But, should a sigh of milder mood express
Thy heart-warm wishes, true to happiness,
Should Heaven's fair harbinger delight to pour
Her blissful visions on thy pensive hour,
No tear to blot thy memory's pictured page,
No fears but such as fancy can assuage ;
Though thy wild heart some hapless hour may miss
The peaceful tenor of unvaried bliss,

(For love pursues an ever-devious race,
True to the winding lineaments of grace ;)
Yet still may Hope her talisman employ
To snatch from Heaven anticipated joy,
And all her kindred energies impart
That burn the brightest in the purest heart.
    When first the Rhodian's mimic art array'd
The queen of Beauty in her Cyprian shade,
The happy master mingled on his piece
Each look that charm'd him in the fair of Greece.
To faultless Nature true, he stole a grace
From every finer form and sweeter face ;
And as-he sojourn'd on the Ægean isles,
Woo'd all their love, and treasured all their smiles ;
Then glow'd the tints, pure, precious, and refined,
And mortal charms seem'd heavenly when combined
Love on the picture smiled !   Expression pour'd
Her mingling spirit there—and Greece adored !
    So thy fair hand, enamor'd Fancy ! gleans
The treasured pictures of a thousand scenes ;
Thy pencil traces on the lover's thought
Some cottage-home, from towns and toil remote
Where love and lore may claim alternate hours,
With Peace embosom'd in Idalian bowers !
Remote from busy Life's bewilder'd way,
O'er all his heart shall Taste and Beauty sway !
Free on the sunny slope or winding shore,
With hermit steps to wander and adore !
There shall he love, when genial morn appears,
Like pensive Beauty smiling in her tears,
To watch the brightening roses of the sky,
And muse on Nature with a poet's eye !—
And when the sun's last splendor lights the deep,
The woods and waves, and murmuring winds asleep
When fairy harps th' Hesperian planet hail,
And the lone cuckoo sighs along the vale,
His path shall be where streamy mountains swell
Their shadowy grandeur o'er the narrow dell,

Where mouldering piles and forests intervene,
Mingling with darker tints the living green ;
No circling hills his ravish'd eye to bound,
Heaven, Earth, and Ocean, blazing all around.
The moon is up—the watch-tower dimly burns--
And down the vale his sober step returns ;
But pauses oft, as winding rocks convey
The still sweet fall of music far away ;
And oft he lingers from his home awhile
To watch the dying notes !—and start, and smile!
Let Winter come ! let polar spirits sweep
The darkening world, and tempest-troubled deep !
Though boundless snows the wither'd heath deform,
And the dim sun scarce wanders through the storm,
Yet shall the smile of social love repay,
With mental light, the melancholy day !
And, when its short and sullen noon is o'er,
The ice-chain'd waters slumbering on the shore,
How bright the fagots in his little hall
Blaze on the hearth, and warm the pictured wall !
How blest he names, in Love's familiar tone,
The kind, fair friend, by nature mark'd his own ;
And, in the waveless mirror of his mind,
Views the fleet years of pleasure left behind,
Since when her empire o'er his heart began !
Since first he call'd her his before the holy man !
Trim the gay taper in his rustic dome,
And light the wintry paradise of home ;
And let the half-uncurtain'd window hail
Some way-worn man benighted in the vale !
Now, while the moaning night-wind rages high,
As sweep the shot-stars down the troubled sky,
While fiery hosts in Heaven's wide circle play,
And bathe in lurid light the milky-way,
Safe from the storm, the meteor, and the shower,
Some pleasing page shall charm the solemn hour—
With pathos shall command, with wit beguile,
A generous tear of anguish, or a smile—

Thy woes, Arion ! and thy simple tale,
O'er all the heart shall triumph and prevail !
Charm'd as they read the verse too sadly true,
How gallant Albert, and his weary crew,
Heaved all their guns, their foundering bark to save,
And toil'd—and shriek'd—and perish'd on the wave !
Yes, at the dead of night, by Lonna's steep,
The seaman's cry was heard along the deep ;
There on his funeral waters, dark and wild,
The dying father bless'd his darling child !
Oh ! Mercy, shield her innocence, he cried,
Spent on the prayer his bursting heart, and died !
Or they will learn how generous worth sublimes
The robber Moor, and pleads for all his crimes !
How poor Amelia kiss'd, with many a tear,
His hand, blood-stain'd, but ever, ever dear !
Hung on the tortured bosom of her lord,
And wept and pray'd perdition from his sword !
Nor sought in vain ! at that heart-piercing cry
The strings of Nature crack'd with agony !
He, with delirious laugh, the dagger hurl'd,
And burst the ties that bound him to the world !
Turn from his dying words, that smite with steel
The shuddering thoughts, or wind them on the wheel—
Turn to the gentler melodies that suit
Thalia's harp, or Pan's Arcadian lute ;
Or, down the stream of Truth's historic page,
From clime to clime descend, from age to age !
Yet there, perhaps, may darker scenes obtrude
Than Fancy fashions in her wildest mood ;
There shall he pause with horrent brow, to rate
What millions died—that Cæsar might be great !
Or learn the fate that bleeding thousands bore,
March'd by their Charles to Dnieper's swampy shore !
Faint in his wounds, and shivering in the blast,
The Swedish soldier sunk—and groan'd his last !
File after file the stormy showers benumb,
Freeze every standard-sheet, and hush the drum !

Horseman and horse confess'd the bitter pang,
And arms and warriors fell with hollow clang
Yet, ere he sunk in Nature's last repose,
Ere life's warm torrent to the fountain froze,
The dying man to Sweden turn'd his eye,
Thought of his home, and closed it with a sigh!
Imperial Pride look'd sullen on his plight,
And Charles beheld—nor shudder'd at the sight.

Above, below, in Ocean, Earth, and Sky,
Thy fairy worlds, Imagination, lie,
And Hope attends, companion of the way,
Thy dream by night, thy visions of the day!
In yonder pensile orb, and every sphere
That gems the starry girdle of the year;
In those unmeasured worlds, she bids thee tell,
Pure from their God, created millions dwell,
Whose names and natures, unreveal'd below,
We yet shall learn, and wonder as we know;
For, as Iona's saint, a giant form,
Throned on her towers, conversing with the storm,
(When o'er each Runic altar, weed-entwined,
The vesper clock tolls mournful to the wind,)
Counts every wave-worn isle, and mountain hoar,
From Kilda to the green Ierne's shore;
So, when thy pure and renovated mind
This perishable dust hath left behind,
Thy seraph eye shall count the starry train,
Like distant isles embosom'd in the main;
Rapt to the shrine where motion first began,
And light and life in mingling torrent ran;
From whence each bright rotundity was hurl'd,
The throne of God,—the centre of the world!

Oh! vainly wise, the moral Muse hath sung
That suasive Hope hath but a Syren tongue!
True; she may sport with life's untutor'd day,
Nor heed the solace of its last decay,
The guileless heart her happy mansion spurn,
And part, like Ajut—never to return!

But yet, methinks, when Wisdom shall assuage
The grief and passions of our greener age,
Though dull the close of life, and far away
Each flower that hail'd the dawning of the day ;
Yet o'er her lovely hopes, that once were dear,
The time-taught spirit, pensive, not severe,
With milder griefs her aged eye shall fill,
And weep their falsehood, though she loves them still !
　　Thus, with forgiving tears, and reconciled,
The king of Judah mourn'd his rebel child !
Musing on days, when yet the guiltless boy
Smiled on his sire, and fill'd his heart with joy !
My Absalom ! the voice of Nature cried,
Oh ! that for thee thy father could have died !
For bloody was the deed, and rashly done,
That slew my Absalom !—my son !—my son !
　　Unfading Hope ! when life's last embers burn,
When soul to soul, and dust to dust return !
Heaven to thy charge resigns the awful hour !
Oh ! then, thy kingdom comes ! Immortal Power !
What though each spark of earth-born rapture fly
The quivering lip, pale cheek, and closing eye !
Bright to the soul thy seraph hands convey
The morning dream of life's eternal day—
Then, then, the triumph and the trance begin,
And all the phœnix spirit burns within !
　　Oh ! deep-enchanting prelude to repose,
The dawn of bliss, the twilight of our woes !
Yet half I hear the panting spirit sigh,
It is a dread and awful thing to die !
Mysterious worlds, untravell'd by the sun !
Where Time's far wandering tide has never run,
From your unfathom'd shades, and viewless spheres,
A warning comes, unheard by other ears.
'Tis Heaven's commanding trumpet, long and loud,
Like Sinai's thunder, pealing from the cloud !
While Nature hears, with terror-mingled trust,
The shock that hurls her fabric to the dust :

And, like the trembling Hebrew, when he trod
The roaring waves, and call'd upon his God,
With mortal terrors clouds immortal bliss,
And shrieks, and hovers o'er the dark abyss!
   Daughter of Faith, awake, arise, illume
The dread unknown, the chaos of the tomb;
Melt, and dispel, ye spectre-doubts, that roll
Cimmerian darkness o'er the parting soul!
Fly, like the moon-eyed herald of Dismay,
Chased on his night-steed by the star of day!
The strife is o'er—the pangs of Nature close,
And life's last rapture triumphs o'er her woes.
Hark! as the spirit eyes, with eagle gaze,
The noon of Heaven undazzled by the blaze,
On heavenly winds that waft her to the sky,
Float the sweet tones of star-born melody;
Wild as that hallow'd anthem sent to hail
Bethlehem's shepherds in the lonely vale,
When Jordan hush'd his waves, and midnight still
Watch'd on the holy towers of Zion hill!
   Soul of the just! companion of the dead!
Where is thy home, and whither art thou fled!
Back to its heavenly source thy being goes,
Swift as the comet wheels to whence he rose;
Doom'd on his airy path awhile to burn,
And doom'd, like thee, to travel, and return.—
Hark! from the world's exploding centre driven,
With sounds that shook the firmament of Heaven,
Careers the fiery giant, fast and far,
On bickering wheels, and adamantine car,
From planet whirl'd to planet more remote,
He visits realms beyond the reach of thought;
But wheeling homeward, when his course is run,
Curbs the red yoke, and mingles with the sun!
So hath the traveller of earth unfurl'd
Her trembling wings, emerging from the world;
And o'er the path by mortal never trod,
Sprung to her source, the bosom of her God!

Oh! lives there, Heaven! beneath thy dread expanse,
One hopeless, dark idolater of Chance,
Content to feed, with pleasures unrefined,
The lukewarm passions of a lowly mind;
Who, mouldering earthward, 'reft of every trust,
In joyless union wedded to the dust,
Could all his parting energy dismiss,
And call this barren world sufficient bliss?—
There live, alas! of heaven-directed mien,
Of cultured soul, and sapient eye serene,
Who hail thee, Man! the pilgrim of a day,
Spouse of the worm, and brother of the clay,
Frail as the leaf in Autumn's yellow bower,
Dust in the wind, or dew upon the flower;
A friendless slave, a child without a sire,
Whose mortal life, and momentary fire,
Light to the grave his chance-created form,
As ocean-wrecks illuminate the storm;
And, when the gun's tremendous flash is o'er,
To night and silence sink for evermore!—
Are these the pompous tidings ye proclaim,
Lights of the world, and demi-gods of Fame?
Is this your triumph—this your proud applause,
Children of Truth, and champions of her cause?
For this hath Science search'd, on weary wing,
By shore and sea—each mute and living thing!
Launch'd with Iberia's pilot from the steep,
To worlds unknown and isles beyond the deep?
Or round the cope her living chariot driven,
And wheel'd in triumph through the signs of Heaven.
Oh! star-eyed Science, hast thou wander'd there,
To waft us home the message of despair?
Then bind the palm, thy sage's brow to suit,
Of blasted leaf, and death-distilling fruit!
Ah me! the laurell'd wreath that Murder rears,
Blood-nursed, and watered by the widow's tears,
Seems not so foul, so tainted, and so dread,
As waves the night-shade round the skeptic head.

What is the bigot's torch, the tyrant's chain?
I smile on death, if Heaven-ward Hope remain:
But, if the warring winds of Nature's strife
Be all the faithless charter of my life,
If Chance awaked, inexorable power,
This frail and feverish being of an hour;
Doom'd o'er the world's precarious scene to sweep,
Swift as the tempest travels on the deep,
To know Delight but by her parting smile,
And toil, and wish, and weep a little while;
Then melt, ye elements, that form'd in vain
This troubled pulse, and visionary brain!
Fade, ye wild flowers, memorials of my doom
And sink, ye stars, that light me to the tomb!
Truth, ever lovely,—since the world began,
The foe of tyrants, and the friend of man,—
How can thy words from balmy slumber start
Reposing Virtue, pillow'd on the heart!
Yet, if thy voice the note of thunder roll'd,
And that were true which Nature never told,
Let Wisdom smile not on her conquer'd field;
No rapture dawns, no treasure is reveal'd!
Oh! let her read, nor loudly, nor elate,
The doom that bars us from a better fate;
But, sad as angels for the good man's sin,
Weep to record, and blush to give it in!

    And well may Doubt, the mother of Dismay,
Pause at her martyr's tomb, and read the lay.
Down by the wilds of yon deserted vale,
It darkly hints a melancholy tale!
There, as the homeless madman sits alone,
In hollow winds he hears a spirit moan!
And there, they say, a wizard orgie crowds,
When the Moon lights her watch-tower in the clouds
Poor lost Alonzo! Fate's neglected child!
Mild be the doom of Heaven—as thou wert mild!
For oh! thy heart in holy mould was cast,
And all thy deeds were blameless, but the last.

Poor lost Alonzo! still I seem to hear
The clod that struck thy hollow-sounding bier!
When Friendship paid, in speechless sorrow drown'd,
Thy midnight rites, but not on hallow'd ground!
    Cease, every joy, to glimmer on my mind,
But leave—oh! leave the light of Hope behind!
What though my winged hours of bliss have been,
Like angel-visits, few and far between,
Her musing mood shall every pang appease,
And charm—when pleasures lose.the power to please!
Yes; let each rapture, dear to Nature, flee:
Close not the light of Fortune's stormy sea—
Mirth, Music, Friendship, Love's propitious smile,
Chase every care, and charm a little while,
Ecstatic throbs the fluttering heart employ,
And all her strings are harmonized to joy!—
But why so short is Love's delighted hour?
Why fades the dew on Beauty's sweetest flower?
Why can no hymned charm of music heal
The sleepless woes impassion'd spirits feel?
Can Fancy's fairy hands no veil create,
To hide the sad realities of fate?—
    No! not the quaint remark, the sapient rule,
Nor all the pride of Wisdom's worldly school,
Have power to sooth, unaided and alone,
The heart that vibrates to a feeling tone!
When stepdame Nature every bliss recalls,
Fleet as the meteor o'er the desert falls;
When, 'reft of all, yon widow'd sire appears
A lonely hermit in the vale of years;
Say, can the world one joyous thought bestow
To Friendship, weeping at the couch of Wo?
No! but a brighter sooths the last adieu,—
Souls of impassion'd mould, she speaks to you!
Weep not, she says, at Nature's transient pain,
Congenial spirits part to meet again!
    What plaintive sobs thy filial spirit drew,
What sorrow choked thy long and last adieu!

Daughter of Conrad? when he heard his kne l,
And bade his country and his child farewell!
Doom'd the long isles of Sydney-cove to see,
The martyr of his crimes, but true to thee ?
'Thrice the sad father tore thee from his heart,
And thrice return'd, to bless thee, and to part ;
Thrice from his trembling lips he murmur'd low
The plaint that own'd unutterable wo ;
Till Faith, prevailing o'er his sullen doom,
As bursts the morn on night's unfathom'd gloom,
Lured his dim eye to deathless hopes sublime,
Beyond the realms of Nature and of Time !

  "And weep not thus," he cried, " young Ellenore,
My bosom bleeds, but soon shall bleed no more !
Short shall this half-extinguish'd spirit burn,
And soon these limbs to kindred dust return !
But not, my child, with life's precarious fire,
The immortal ties of Nature shall expire ;
These shall resist the triumph of decay,
When time is o'er, and worlds have pass'd away
Cold in the dust this perish'd heart may lie,
But that which warm'd it once shall never die !
That spark unburied in its mortal frame,
With living light, eternal, and the same,
Shall beam on Joy's interminable years,
Unveil'd by darkness—unassuaged by tears!

  " Yet, on the barren shore and stormy deep,
One tedious watch is Conrad doom'd to weep ;
But when I gain the home without a friend,
And press the uneasy couch where none attend,
This last embrace, still cherish'd in my heart,
Shall calm the struggling spirit ere it part !
Thy darling form shall seem to hover nigh,
And hush the groan of life's last agony !

  " Farewell ! when strangers lift thy father's b er,
And place my nameless stone without a tear ;
When each returning pledge hath told my child
That Conrad's tomb is on the desert piled ;

And when the dream of troubled Fancy sees
Its lonely rank grass waving in the breeze ;
Who then will sooth thy grief, when mine is o'er ?
Who will protect thee, helpless Ellenore ?
Shall secret scenes thy filial sorrows hide,
Scorn'd by the world, to factious guilt allied ?
Ah ! no ; methinks the generous and the good
Will woo thee from the shades of solitude !
O'er friendless grief compassion shall awake,
And smile on innocence, for Mercy's sake !"

Inspiring thought of rapture yet to be,
The tears of Love were hopeless, but for thee !
If in that frame no deathless spirit dwell,
If that faint murmur be the last farewell,
If Fate unite the faithful but to part,
Why is their memory sacred to the heart ?
Why does the brother of my childhood seem
Restored awhile in every pleasing dream ?
Why do I joy the lonely spot to view,
By artless friendship bless'd when life was new ?

Eternal Hope ! when yonder spheres sublime
Peal'd their first notes to sound the march of Time,
Thy joyous youth began—but not to fade.—
When all the sister planets have decay'd ;
When wrapt in fire the realms of ether glow,
And Heaven's last thunder shakes the world below ;
Thou, undismay'd, shalt o'er the ruins smile,
And light thy torch at Nature's funeral pile.

8

THEODRIC:

A DOMESTIC TALE.

'Twas sunset, and the Ranz des Vaches was sung,
And lights were o'er th' Helvetian mountains flung,
That gave the glacier tops their richest glow,
And tinged the lakes like molten gold below.
Warmth flush'd the wonted regions of the storm,
Where, Phœnix-like, you saw the eagle's form,
That high in Heaven's vermilion wheel'd and soar'd,
Woods nearer frown'd, and cataracts dash'd and roar'd,
From heights browsed by the bounding bouquetin ;
Herds tinkling roam'd the long-drawn vales between,
And hamlets glitter'd white, and gardens flourish'd green,
'Twas transport to inhale the bright sweet air !
The mountain-bee was revelling in its glare,
And roving with his minstrelsy across
The scented wild weeds, and enamell'd moss.
Earth's features so harmoniously were link'd,
She seem'd one great glad form, with life instinct,
That felt Heaven's ardent breath, and smiled below
Its flush of love, with consentaneous glow.
  A Gothic church was near ; the spot around
Was beautiful, ev'n though sepulchral ground ;
For there nor yew nor cypress spread their gloom,
But roses blossom'd by each rustic tomb.
Amidst them one of spotless marble shone—
A maiden's grave—and 'twas inscribed thereon,
That young and loved she died whose dust was there :
  " Yes," said my comrade, " young she died, and fair
Grace form'd her, and the soul of gladness play'd

Once in the blue eyes of that mountain-maid :
Her fingers witch'd the chords they pass'd along,
And her lips seem'd to kiss the soul in song :
Yet woo'd, and worshipp'd as she was, till few
Aspired to hope, 'twas sadly, strangely true,
That heart, the martyr of its fondness, burn'd
And died of love that could not be return'd.

    Her father dwelt where yonder Castle shines
O'er clustering trees and terrace-mantling vines.
As gay as ever, the laburnum's pride
Waves o'er each walk where she was wont to glide,—
And still the garden whence she graced her brow,
As lovely blooms, though trode by strangers now.
How oft, from yonder window o'er the lake,
Her song of wild Helvetian swell and shake
Has made the rudest fisher bend his ear
And rest enchanted on his oar to hear !
Thus bright, accomplish'd, spirited, and bland,
Well-born, and wealthy for that simple land,
Why had no gallant, native youth the art
To win so warm—so exquisite a heart ?
She, midst these rocks inspired with feelings strong
By mountain-freedom—music—fancy—song,
Herself descended from the brave in arms,
And conscious of romance-inspiring charms,
Dreamt of Heroic beings ; hoped to find
Some extant spirit of chivalric kind ;
And scorning wealth, look'd cold ev'n on the claim
Of manly worth, that lack'd the wreath of fame.

    Her younger brother, sixteen summers old,
And much her likeness both in mind and mould,
Had gone, poor boy ! in soldiership to shine,
And bore an Austrian banner on the Rhine.
'Twas when, alas ! our Empire's evil star
Shed all the plagues, without the pride of war ;
When patriots bled, and bitterer anguish cross'd
Our brave, to die in battles foully lost.
The youth wrote home the rout of many a day ;

Yet still he said, and still with truth could say,
One corps had ever made a valiant stand,—
The corps in which he served,—Theodric's band.
His fame, forgotten chief, is now gone by,
Eclipsed by brighter orbs in Glory's sky ;
Yet once it shone, and veterans, when they show
Our fields of battle twenty years ago,
Will tell you feats his small brigade perform'd,
In charges nobly faced and trenches storm'd.
Time was, when songs were chanted to his fame,
And soldiers loved the march that bore his name :
The zeal of martial hearts was at his call,
And that Helvetian's, Udolph's, most of all.
'Twas touching, when the storm of war blew wild,
To see a blooming boy,—almost a child,—
Spur fearless at his leader's words and signs,
Brave death in reconnoitring hostile lines,
And speed each task, and tell each message clear,
In scenes where war-train'd men were stunn'd with fear
　Theodric praised him, and they wept for joy
In yonder house,—when letters from the boy
Thank'd Heaven for life, and more, to use his phrase,
Than twenty lives—his own Commander's praise.
Then follow'd glowing pages, blazoning forth
The fancied image of his leader's worth,
With such hyperbo'es of youthful styles
As made his parents dry their tears and smile .
But differently far his words impress'd
A wondering sister's well-believing breast ;—
She caught th' illusion, bless'd Theodric's name,
And wildly magnified his worth and fame ;
Rejoicing life's reality contain'd
One, heretofore, her fancy had but feign'd,
Whose love could make her proud!—and time and chance
　　To passion raised that day-dream of Romance.
　Once, when with hasty charge of horse and man
Our arrière-guard had check'd the Gallic van,

Theodric, visiting the outposts, found
His Udolph wounded, weltering on the ground :
Sore crush'd,—half-swooning, half-upraised·he lay,
And bent his brow, fair boy ! and grasp'd the clay.
His fate moved ev'n the common soldier's ruth—
Theodric succor'd him ; nor left the youth
To vulgar hands, but brought him to his tent,
And lent what aid a brother would have lent.

Meanwhile, to save his kindred half the smart
The war-gazette's dread blood-roll might impart,
He wrote th' event to them ; and soon could tell
Of pains assuaged and symptoms auguring well :
And last of all, prognosticating cure,
Enclosed the leech's vouching signature.

Their answers, on whose pages you might note
That tears had fall'n, while trembling fingers wrote,
Gave boundless thanks for benefits conferr'd,
Of which the boy, in secret, sent them word,
Whose memory Time, they said, would never blot ;
But which the giver had himself forgot.

In time, the stripling, vigorous and heal'd,
Resumed his barb and banner in the field,
And bore himself right soldier-like, till now
The third campaign had manlier bronzed his brow,
When peace, though but a scanty pause for breath,—
A curtain-drop between the acts of death,—
A check in frantic war's unfinish'd game,
Yet dearly bought, and direly welcome, came.
The camp broke up, and Udolph left his chief
As with a son's or younger brother's grief :
But journeying home, how rapt his spirits rose !
How light his footsteps crush'd St. Gothard's snows !
How dear seem'd ev'n the waste and wild Shreckhorn,
Though rapt in clouds, and frowning as in scorn
Upon a downward world of pastoral charms ;
Where, by the very smell of dairy-farms,
And fragrance from the mountain-herbage blown,
Blindfold his native hills he could have known !

His coming down yon lake,—his boat ı view
Of windows where love's fluttering kerchief flew,—
The arms spread out for him—the tears that burst,—
('Twas JULIA's, 'twas his sister's, met him first :)
Their pride to see war's medal at his breast,
And all their rapture's greeting, may be guess'd.
　　Ere long, his bosom triumph'd to unfold
A gift he meant their gayest room to hold,—
The picture of a friend in warlike dress ;
And who it was he first bade JULIA guess.
'Yes,' she replied, ' 'twas he methought in sleep,
When you were wounded, told me not to weep.'
The painting long in that sweet mansion drew
Regards its living semblance little knew.
　　Meanwhile THEODRIC, who had years before
Learnt England's tongue, and loved her classic lore,
A glad enthusiast now explored the land,
Where Nature, Freedom, Art, smile hand in hand.;
Her women fair ; her men robust for toil ;
Her vigorous souls, high-cultured as her soil ;
Her towns, where civic independence flings
The gauntlet down to senates, courts, and kings ;
Her works of art, resembling magic's powers ;
Her mighty fleets, and learning's beauteous bowers,—
These he had visited with wonder's smile,
And scarce endured to quit so fair an isle.
But how our fates from unmomentous things
May rise, like rivers out of little springs !
A trivial chance postponed his parting day,
And public tidings caused, in that delay,
An English Jubilee.　'Twas a glorious sight ;
At eve stupendous London, clad in light,
Pour'd out triumphant multitudes to gaze ;
Youth, age, wealth, penury, smiling in the blaze ·
Th' illumined atmosphere was warm and bland,
And Beauty's groups, the fairest of the land,
Conspicuous, as in some wide festive room,
In open chariots pass'd with pearl and plume.

Amidst them he remark'd a lovelier mien
Than e'er his thoughts had shaped, or eyes had seen ;
The throng detain'd her till he rein'd his steed,
And, ere the beauty pass'd, had time to read
The motto and the arms her carriage bore.
Led by that clue, he left not England's shore
Till he had known her ; and to know her well
Prolong'd, exalted, bound, enchantment's spell ;
For with affections warm, intense, refined,
She mix'd such calm and holy strength of mind,
That, l.ke Heaven's image in the smiling brook,
Celestial peace was pictured in her look.
Hers was the brow, in trials unperplex'd,
That cheer'd the sad, and tranquillized the vex'd ;
She studied not the meanest to eclipse,
And yet the wisest listen'd to her lips ;
She sang not, knew not Music's magic skill,
But yet her voice had tones that sway'd the will.
He sought—he won her—and resolved to make
His future home in England for her sake.
    Yet, ere they wedded, matters of concern
To Cæsar's Court commanded his return,
A season's space,—and on his Alpine way,
He reach'd those bowers, that rang with joy that day:
The boy was half beside himself,—the sire,
All frankness, honor, and Helvetian fire,
Of speedy parting would not hear him speak ;
And tears bedew'd and brighten'd Julia's cheek.
    Thus, loath to wound their hospitable pride,
A month he promised with them to abide ;
As blithe he trod the mountain-sward as they,
And felt his joy make ev'n the young more gay.
How jocund was their breakfast-parlor fann'd
By yon blue water's breath,—their walks how bland!
Fair Julia seem'd her brother's soften'd sprite—
A gem reflecting Nature's purest light,—
And with her graceful wit there was inwrought
A wildly sweet unworldliness of thought,

That almost child-like to his kindness drew,
And twin with UDOLPH in his friendsl ip grew.
But did his thoughts to love one moment range !—
No ! he who had loved CONSTANCE could not change :
Besides, till grief betray'd her undesign'd,
Th' unlikely thought could scarcely reach his mind,
That eyes so young on years like his should beam
Unwoo'd devotion back for pure esteem.
   True she sang to his very soul, and brought
Those trains before him of luxuriant thought,
Which only Music's Heaven-born art can bring,
To sweep across the mind with angel wing.
Once, as he smiled amidst that waking trance,
She paused o'ercome : he thought it might be chance,
And, when his first suspicions dimly stole,
Rebuked them back like phantoms from his soul.
But when he saw his caution gave her pain,
And kindness brought suspense's rack again,
Faith, honor, friendship, bound him to unmask
Truths which her timid fondness fear'd to ask.
   And yet with gracefully ingenuous power
Her spirit met th' explanatory hour ;—
Ev'n conscious beauty brighten'd in her eyes,
That told she knew their love no vulgar prize ;
And pride, like that of one more woman-grown,
Enlarged her mien, enrich'd her voice's tone.
'Twas then she struck the keys, and music made
That mock'd all skill her hand had e'er display'd :
Inspired and warbling, rapt from things around,
She look'd the very Muse of magic sound,
Painting in sound the forms of joy and wo,
Until the mind's eye saw them melt and glow.
Her closing strain composed and calm she play'd,
And sang no words to give its pathos aid ;
But grief seem'd lingering in its lengthen'd swell,
And like so many tears the trickling touches fell.
Of CONSTANCE then she heard THEODRIC speak,
And steadfast smoothness still possess'd her cheek.

But when he told her how he oft had plann'd
Of old a journey to their mountain-land,
That might have brought him hither years before,
'Ah! then,' she cried, ' you knew not England's shore
And, had you come,—and wherefore did you not?'
' Yes,' he replied, ' it would have changed our lot!'
Then burst her tears through pride's restraining bands,
And with her handkerchief, and both her hands,
She hid her voice and wept.—Contrition stung
THEODRIC for the tears his words had wrung.
' But no,' she cried, ' unsay not what you've said,
Nor grudge one prop on which my pride is stay'd
To think I could have merited your faith
Shall be my solace even unto death !'—
' JULIA,' THEODRIC said, with purposed look
Of firmness, ' my reply deserved rebuke ;
But by your pure and sacred peace of mind,
And by the dignity of womankind,
Swear that when I am gone you'll do your best
To chase this dream of fondness from your breast.'

Th' abrupt appeal electrified her thought ;—
She look'd to Heav'n as if its aid she sought,
Dried hastily the tear-drops from her cheek,
And signified the vow she could not speak.

Ere long he communed with her mother mild :
' Alas !' she said, ' I warn'd—conjured my child,
And grieved for this affection from the first,
But like fatality it has been nursed ;
For when her fill'd eyes on your picture fix'd,
And when your name in all she spoke was mix'd,
'Twas hard to chide an over-grateful mind !
Then each attempt a likelier choice to find
Made only fresh-rejected suitors grieve,
And UDOLPH's pride—perhaps her own—believe
That, could she meet, she might enchant ev'n you.
You came.—I augur'd the event, 'tis true,
But how was UDOLPH's mother to exclude
The guest that claim'd our boundless gratitude ?

And that unconscious you had cast a spell
On Julia's peace. my pride refused to tell:
Yet in my child's illusion I have seen,
Believe me well, how blameless you have been
Nor can it cancel, howsoe'er it end,
Our debt of friendship to our boy's best friend.'
At night he parted with the aged pair;
At early morn rose Julia to prepare
The last repast her hands for him should make·
And Udolph to convoy him o'er the lake.
The parting was to her such bitter grief,
That of her own accord she made it brief;
But, lingering at her window, long survey'd
His boat's last glimpses melting into shade.

Theodric sped to Austria, and achieved
His journey's object.   Much was he relieved
When Udolph's letters told that Julia's mind
Had borne his loss firm, tranquil, and resign'd.
He took the Rhenish route to England, high
Elate with hopes, fulfill'd their ecstasy,
And interchanged with Constance's own breath
The sweet eternal vows that bound their faith.

To paint that being to a grovelling mind
Were like portraying pictures to the blind.
'Twas needful ev'n infectiously to feel
Her temper's fond and firm and gladsome zeal,
To share existence with her, and to gain
Sparks from her love's electrifying chain
Of that pure pride, which, lessening to her breast
Life's ills, gave all its joys a treble zest,
Before the mind completely understood
That mighty truth—how happy are the good !

Ev'n when her light forsook him, it bequeath'd
Ennobling sorrow; and her memory breathed
A sweetness that survived her living days,
As odorous scents outlast the censer's blaze.

Or, if a trouble dimm'd their golden joy,
'Twas outward dross, and not infused alloy :

Their home knew but affection's looks and speech–
A little Heaven, above dissension's reach.
But midst her kindred there was strife and gall ;
Save one congenial sister, they were all
Such foils to her bright intellect and grace,
As if she had engross'd the virtue of her race.
Her nature strove th' unnatural feuds to heal,
Her wisdom made the weak to her appeal ;
And, tho' the wounds she cured were soon unclosed,
Unwearied still her kindness interposed.
   Oft on those errands though she went in vain,
And home, a blank without her, gave him pain,
He bore her absence for its pious end.—
But public grief his spirit came to bend ;
For war laid waste his native land once more,
And German honor bled at every pore.
Oh ! were he there, he thought, to rally back
One broken band, or perish in the wrack !
Nor think that CONSTANCE sought to move and melt
His purpose : like herself she spoke and felt :—
' Your fame is mine, and I will bear all wo
Except its loss !—but with you let me go
To arm you for, to embrace you from, the fight ;
Harm will not reach me—hazards will delight !'
He knew those hazards better ; one campaign
In England he conjured her to remain,
And she expressed assent, although her heart
In secret had resolved *they* should not part.
   How oft the wisest on misfortune's shelves
Are wreck'd by errors most unlike themselves !
That little fault, *that* fraud of love's romance,
That plan's concealment, wrought their whole mis-
      chance.
He knew it not preparing to embark,
But felt extinct his comfort's latest spark,
When, midst those number'd days, she made repair
Again to kindred worthless of her care.
'Tis true she said the tidings she would write

Would make her absence on his heart sit light ;
But, haplessly, reveal'd not yet her plan,
And left him in his home a lonely man.

Thus damp'd in thoughts, he mused upon the past
'Twas long since he had heard from UDOLPH last,
And deep misgivings on his spirit fell
That all with UDOLPH's household was not well.
'Twas that too true prophetic mood of fear
That augurs griefs inevitably near,
Yet makes them not less startling to the mind
When come.   Least look'd-for then of human kind,
His UDOLPH ('twas, he thought at first, his sprite,)
With mournful joy that morn surprised his sight.
How changed was UDOLPH ! . Scarce THEODRIC durst
Inquire his tidings,—he reveal'd the worst.
' At first,' he said, ' as JULIA bade me tell,
She bore her fate high-mindedly and well,
Resolved from common eyes her grief to hide,
And from the world's compassion saved our pride ;
But still her health gave way to secret wo, .
And long she pined—for broken hearts die slow !
Her reason went, but came returning, like ·
The warning of her death-hour—soon to strike ;
And all for which she now, poor sufferer ! sighs,
Is once to see THEODRIC ere she dies.
Why should I come to tell you this caprice ?
Forgive me ! for my mind has lost its peace.
I blame myself, and ne'er shall cease to blame,
That my insane ambition for the name
Of brother to THEODRIC, founded all
Those high-built hopes that crush'd her by their fall.
I made her slight her mother's counsel sage,
But now my parents droop with grief and age ;
And, though my sister's eyes mean no rebuke,
They overwhelm me with their dying look.
The journey's long, but you are full of ruth ;
And she who shares your heart, and knows its truth,
Has faith in your affection, far above

The fear of a poor dying object's love.'—
' She has, my UDOLPH,' he replied, ' 'tis true ;
And oft we talk of JULIA—oft of you.'
Their converse came abruptly to a close ;
For scarce could each his troubled looks compose,
When visitants, to CONSTANCE near akin,
(In all but traits of soul,) were usher'd in.
They brought not her, nor midst their kindred band
The sister who alone, like her, was bland ;
But said—and smiled to see it give him pain—
That CONSTANCE would a fortnight yet remain.
Vex'd by their tidings, and the haughty view
They cast on UDOLPH as the youth withdrew,
THEODRIC blamed his CONSTANCE's intent.—
The demons went, and left him as they went
To read, when they were gone beyond recall,
A note from her loved hand explaining all.
She said, that with their house she only stay'd
That parting peace might with them all be made ;
But pray'd for love to share his foreign life,
And shun all future chance of kindred strife.
He wrote with speed, his soul's consent to say
The letter miss'd her on her homeward way.
In six hours CONSTANCE was within his arms :
Moved, flush'd, unlike her wonted calm of charms,
And breathless—with uplifted hands outspread—
Burst into tears upon his neck, and said,—
' I knew that those who brought your message laugh'd
With poison of their own to point the shaft ;
And this my one kind sister thought, yet loath
Confess'd she fear'd 'twas true you had been wroth.
But here you are, and smile on me : my pain
Is gone, and CONSTANCE is herself again.'
His ecstasy, it may be guess'd, was much :
Yet pain's extreme and pleasure's seem'd to touch.
What pride ! embracing beauty's perfect mould ;
What terror ! lest his few rash words, mistold,
Had agonized her pulse to fever's heat :

But calm'd again so soon it healthful beat,
And such sweet tones were in her voice's sound,
Composed herself, she breathed composure round.
    Fair being! with what sympathetic grace
She heard, bewail'd, and pleaded JULIA's case;
Implored he would her dying wish attend,
' And go,' she said, ' to-morrow with your friend;
I'll wait for your return on England's shore,
And then we'll cross the deep, and part no more.'
    To-morrow both his soul's compassion drew
To JULIA's call, and CONSTANCE urged anew
That not to heed her now would be to bind
A load of pain for life upon his mind.
He went with UDOLPH—from his CONSTANCE went—
Stifling, alas! a dark presentiment
Some ailment lurk'd, ev'n whilst she smiled, to mock
His fears of harm from yester-morning's shock
Meanwhile a faithful page he singled out,
To watch at home, and follow straight his route,
If aught of threaten'd change her health should show
—With UDOLPH then he reach'd the house of wo
    That winter's eve how darkly Nature's brow
Scowl'd on the scenes it lights so lovely now!
The tempest, raging o'er the realms of ice,
Shook fragments from the rifted precipice;
And, whilst their falling echo'd to the wind,
The wolf's long howl in dismal discord join'd,
While white yon water's foam was raised in clouds
That whirl'd like spirits wailing in their shrouds:
Without was Nature's elemental din—
And beauty died, and friendship wept, within!
    Sweet JULIA, though her fate was finish'd half,
Still knew him—smiled on him with feeble laugh—
And bless'd him, till she drew her latest sigh!
But lo! while UDOLPH's bursts of agony,
And age's tremulous wailings, round him rose,
What accents pierced him deeper yet than those!
'Twas tidings, by his English messenger,

Of Constance—brief and terrible they were.
She still was living when the page set out
From home, but whether now was left in doubt.
Poor Julia ! saw he then thy death's relief—
Stunn'd into stupor more than wrung with grief ?
It was not strange ; for in the human breast
Two master-passions cannot co-exist,
And that alarm which now usurp'd his brain.
Shut out not only peace, but other pain.
'Twas fancying Constance underneath the shroud
That cover'd Julia made him first weep loud,
And tear himself away from them that wept.
Fast hurrying homeward, night nor day he slept,
Till, launch'd at sea, he dreamt that his soul's saint
Clung to him on a bridge of ice, pale, faint,
O'er cataracts of blood. Awake, he bless'd
The shore ; nor hope left utterly his breast,
Till reaching home, terrific omen ! there
The straw-laid street preluded his despair— .
The servant's look—the table that reveal'd
His letter sent to Constance last, still seal'd—
Though speech and hearing left him, told too clear
That he had now to suffer—not to fear.
He felt as if he ne'er should cease to feel—
A wretch live-broken on misfortune's wheel :
Her death's cause—he might make his peace with
        Heaven,
Absolved from guilt, but never self-forgiven.
   The ocean has its ebbings—so has grief ;
'Twas vent to anguish, if 'twas not relief,
To lay his brow ev'n on her death-cold cheek.
Then first he heard her one kind sister speak :
She bade him, in the name of Heaven, forbear
With self-reproach to deepen his despair :
' 'Twas blame,' she said, ' I shudder to relate,
But none of yours, that caused our darling's fate ;
Her mother (must I call her such ?) foresaw,
Should Constance leave the land, she would withdraw

Our House's charm against the world's neglect—
'The only gem that drew it some respect.
Hence, when you went, she came and vainly spoke
To change her purpose—grew incensed, and broke
With execrations from her kneeling child.
Start not ! your angel from her knee rose mild,
Fear'd that she should not long the scene outlive,
Yet bade ev'n you th' unnatural one forgive.
Till then her ailment had been slight, or none ;
But fast she droop'd, and fatal pains came on :
Foreseeing their event, she dictated
And sign'd these words for you.'   The letter said—
   ' Theodric, this is destiny above
Our power to baffle ; bear it then, my love !
Rave not to learn the usage I have borne,
For one true sister left me not forlorn ;
And though you're absent in another land,
Sent from me by my own well-meant command,
Your soul, I know, as firm is knit to mine
As these clasp'd hands in blessing you now join
Shape not imagined horrors in my fate—
Ev'n now my sufferings are not very great ;
And when your grief's first transports shall subside,
I call upon your strength of soul and pride
To pay my memory, if 'tis worth the debt,
Love's glorying tribute—not forlorn regret :
I charge my name with power to conjure up
Reflections balmy, not its bitter cup.
My pardoning angel, at the gates of Heaven,
Shall look not more regard than you have given
To me ; and our life's union has been clad
In smiles of bliss as sweet as life e'er had
Shall gloom be from such bright remembrance cast ?
Shall bitterness outflow from sweetness past ?
No ! imaged in the sanctuary of your breast,
There let me smile, amidst high thoughts at rest ;
And let contentment on your spirit shine,
As if its peace were still a part of mine :

For if you war not proudly with your pain,
For you I shall have worse than lived in vain.
But I conjure your manliness to bear
My loss with noble spirit—not despair :
I ask you by our love to promise this,
And kiss these words, where I have left a kiss,—
The latest from my living lips for yours.'—
    Words that will solace him while life endures :
For though his spirit from affliction's surge
Could ne'er to life, as life had been, emerge,
Yet still that mind whose harmony elate
Rang sweetness, ev'n beneath the crush of fate,—
That mind in whose regard all things were placed
In views that softened them, or lights that graced,
That soul's example could not but dispense
A portion of its own bless'd influence ;
Invoking him to peace, and that self-sway
Which Fortune cannot give, nor take away :
And though he mourn'd her long, 'twas with such wo
As if her spirit watch'd him still below."

TRANSLATIONS.

SONG OF HYBRIAS THE CRETAN

My wealth's a burly spear and brand,
And a right good shield of hides untann'd,
   Which on my arm I buckle :
With these I plough, I reap, I sow,
With these I make the sweet vintage flow,
   And all around me truckle.

But your wights that take no pride to wield
A massy spear and well-made shield,
   Nor joy to draw the sword :
Oh, I bring those heartless, hapless drones,
Down in a trice on their marrow-bones,
   To call me King and Lord.

FRAGMENT.

FROM THE GREEK OF ALCMAN.

The mountain summits sleep : glens, cliffs, and caves
   Are silent—all the black earth's reptile brood—
   The bees—the wild beasts of the mountain wood :
In depths beneath the dark red ocean's waves
   Its monsters rest, whilst wrapt in bower and spray
   Each bird is hush'd that stretch'd its pinions to the day

MARTIAL ELEGY.

FROM THE GREEK OF TYRTÆUS.

How glorious fall the valiant, sword in hand,
In front of battle for their native land!
But oh! what ills await the wretch that yields,
A recreant outcast from his country's fields!
The mother whom he loves shall quit her home,
An aged father at his side shall roam;
His little ones shall weeping with him go,
And a young wife participate his wo;
While scorn'd and scowl'd upon by every face,
They pine for food, and beg from place to place

Stain of his breed! dishonoring manhood's form,
All ills shall cleave to him :—Affliction's storm
Shall bind him wandering in the vale of years,
Till, lost to all but ignominious fears,
He shall not blush to leave a recreant's name,
And children, like himself, inured to shame.

But we will combat for our fathers' land,
And we will drain the life-blood where we stand,
To save our children :—fight ye side by side,
And serried close, ye men of youthful pride,
Disdaining fear, and deeming light the cost
Of life itself in glorious battle lost.

Leave not our sires to stem th' unequal fight,
Whose limbs are nerved no more with buoyant might
Nor, lagging backward, let the younger breast
Permit the man of age, (a sight unbless'd,)
To welter in the combat's foremost thrust,

His hoary head dishevell'd in the dust,
And venerable bosom bleeding bare.

But youth's fair form, though fallen, is ever fair
And beautiful in death the boy appears,
The hero boy that dies in blooming years:
In man's regret he lives, and woman's tears,
More sacred than in life, and lovelier far,
For having perish'd in the front of war.

----------◆----------

SPECIMENS OF TRANSLATION FROM MEDEA.

Σκαιους δε λεγων, κουδέν τι σοφους
Τους προσθε βροτους ουκ αν αμαρτοις.
                    Medea, v. 194, p. 33, Glasg edit.

TELL me, ye bards, whose skill sublime
First charm'd the ear of youthful Time,
With numbers wrapt in heavenly fire,
Who bade delighted Echo swell
The trembling transports of the lyre,
The murmur of the shell—
Why to the burst of Joy alone
Accords sweet Music's soothing tone?
Why can no bard, with magic strain,
In slumbers steep the heart of pain?
While varied tones obey your sweep,
The mild, the plaintive, and the deep,
Bends not despairing Grief to hear
Your golden lute, with ravish'd ear?
Has all your art no power to bind
The fiercer pangs that shake the mind,
And lull the wrath at whose command
Murder bares her gory hand?

When flush'd with joy, the rosy throng
Weave the light dance, ye swell the song !
Cease, ye vain warblers ! cease to charm .
The breast with other raptures warm !
Cease ! till your hand with magic strain
In slumbers steep the heart of pain !

SPEECH OF THE CHORUS,

IN THE SAME TRAGEDY,

**TO DISSUADE MEDEA FROM HER PURPOSE OF PUTTING HER CHIL-
DREN TO DEATH, AND FLYING FOR PROTECTION TO ATHENS.**

O HAGGARD queen ! to Athens dost thou guide
  Thy glowing chariot, steep'd in kindred gore ;
Or seek to hide thy foul infanticide
  Where Peace and Mercy dwell for evermore ?

The land where Truth, pure, precious, and sublime,
  Woos the deep silence of sequester'd bowers,
And warriors, matchless since the first of time,
  Rear their bright banners o'er unconquer'd towers !

Where joyous youth, to Music's mellow strain,
  Twines in the dance with nymphs forever fair,
While Spring eternal on the lilied plain,
  Waves amber radiance through the fields of air !

The tuneful Nine (so sacred legends tell)
  First waked their heavenly lyre these scenes among
Still in your greenwood bowers they love to dwell ;
  Still in your vales they swell the choral song !

But there the tuneful, chaste, Pierian fair,
  The guardian nymphs of green Parnassus, now
Sprung from Harmonia, while her graceful hair
  Waved in high auburn o'er her polish'd brow !

ANTISTROPHE I.

Where silent vales, and glades of green array,
    The murmuring wreaths of cool Cephisus lave,
There, as the muse hath sung, at noon of day,
    The queen of Beauty bow'd to taste the wave ;

And blest the stream, and breathed across the land
    The soft, sweet gale that fans yon summer bowers ;
And there the sister Loves, a smiling band,
    Crown'd with the fragrant wreaths of rosy flowers !

" And go," she cries, " in yonder valleys rove,
    With Beauty's torch the solemn scenes illume ;
Wake in each eye the radiant light of Love,
    Breathe on each cheek young Passion's tender bloom

Entwine, with myrtle chains, your soft control,
    To sway the hearts of Freedom's darling kind !
With glowing charms enrapture Wisdom's soul,
    And mould to grace ethereal Virtue's mind"

STROPHE II.

The land where Heaven's own hallow'd waters play,
    Where friendship binds the generous and the good,
Say, shall it hail thee from thy frantic way,
    Unholy woman ! with thy hands embrued

In thine own children's gore ?   Oh ! ere they bleed,
    Let Nature's voice thy ruthless heart appal !
Pause at the bold, irrevocable deed—
    The mother strikes—the guiltless babes shall fall !

Think what remorse thy maddening thoughts shall sting,
    When dying pangs their gentle bosoms tear !
Where shalt thou sink, when lingering echoes ring
    The screams of horror in thy tortured ear ?

No ! let thy bosom melt to Pity's cry,—
  In dust we kneel—by sacred Heaven implore—
O ! stop thy lifted arm, ere yet they die,
  Nor dip thy horrid hands in infant gore '-

ANTISTROPHE II.

Say, how shalt thou that barbarous soul assume,
  Undamp'd by horror at the daring plan?
Hast thou a heart to work thy children's doom ?
  Or hands to finish what thy wrath began?

When o'er each babe you look a last adieu,
  And gaze on Innocence that smiles asleep,
Shall no fond feeling beat to Nature true,
  Charm thee to pensive thought—and bid thee weep ?

When the young suppliants clasp their parent dear,
  Heave the deep sob, and pour the artless prayer,—
Ay ! thou shalt melt ;—and many a heart-shed tear
  Gush o'er the harden'd features of despair!

Nature shall throb in every tender string,—
  Thy trembling heart the ruffian's task deny ;—
Thy horror-smitten hands afar shall fling
  The blade, undrench'd in blood's eternal dye.

CHORUS.

  Hallow'd Earth ! with indignation
    Mark, oh mark, the murderous deed!
  Radiant eye of wide creation,
    Watch th' accursed infanticide !

  Yet, ere Colchia's rugged daughter
    Perpetrate the dire design,
  And consign to kindred slaughter
    Children of thy golden line !

O'CONNOR'S CHILD;

"THE FLOWER OF LOVE LIES BLEEDING"

I.

Oh! once the harp of Innisfail
Was strung full high to notes of gladness ;
But yet it often told a tale
Of more prevailing sadness.
Sad was the note, and wild its fall,
As winds that moan at night forlorn
Along the isles of Fion-Gall,
When, for O'Connor's child to mourn,
The harper told, how lone, how far
From any mansion's twinkling star,
From any path of social men,
Or voice, but from the fox's den,
The lady in the desert dwelt ;
And yet no wrongs, no fear she felt:
Say, why should dwell in place so wild,
O'Connor's pale and lovely child?

II.

Sweet lady! she no more inspires
Green Erin's hearts with beauty's power,
As, in the palace of her sires,
She bloom'd a peerless flower.
Gone from her hand and bosom, gone,
The royal brooch, the jewell'd ring,
That o'er her dazzling whiteness 'hone.
Like dews on lilies of the spring.

10

Yet why, though fall'n her brother's kerne,
Beneath De Bourgo's battle stern,
While yet in Leinster unexplored,
Her friends survive the English sword ;
Why lingers she from Erin's host,
So far on Galway's shipwreck'd coast :
Why wanders she a huntress wild—
O'Connor's pale and lovely child?

III.

And fix'd on empty space, why burn
Her eyes with momentary wildness ;
And wherefore do they then return
To more than woman's mildness?
Dishevell'd are her raven locks ;
On Connocht Moran's name she calls ;
And oft amidst the lonely rocks
She sings sweet madrigals.
Placed midst the fox-glove and the moss,
Behold a parted warrior's cross !
That is the spot where, evermore,
The lady, at her shieling door,
Enjoys that, in communion sweet,
The living and the dead can meet,
For, lo ! to love-lorn fantasy,
The hero of her heart is nigh.

IV.

Bright as the bow that spans the storm,
In Erin's yellow vesture clad,
A son of light—a lovely form,
He comes and makes her glad ;
Now on the grass-green turf he sits,
His tassell'd horn beside him laid ;
Now o'er the hills in chase he flits,
The hunter and the deer a shade !
Sweet mourner ! these are shadows vain
That cross the twilight of her brain ;

Yet she will tell you, she is blest,
Of Connocht Moran's tomb possess'd,
More richly than in Aghrim's bower,
When bards high praised her beauty's power,
And kneeling pages offer'd up
The mórat in a golden cup.

v.

" A hero's bride ! this desert bower,
It ill befits thy gentle breeding:
And wherefore dost thou love this flowei
To call—' My love lies bleeding?'
This purple flower my tears have nursed;
A hero's blood supplied its bloom:
I love it, for it was the first
That grew on Connocht Moran's tomb.
Oh ! hearken, stranger, to my voice !
This desert mansion is my choice !
And blest, though fatal, be the star
That led me to its wilds afar:
For here these pathless mountains free
Gave shelter to my love and me ;
And every rock and every stone
Bore witness that he was my own.

vi.

O'Connor's child, I was the bud
Of Erin's royal tree of glory ;
But wo to them that wrapt in blood
The tissue of my story !
Still as I clasp my burning brain,
A death-scene rushes on my sight ;
It rises o'er and o'er again,
The bloody feud—the fatal night,
When chafing Connocht Moran's scorn,
They call'd my hero basely born ;
And bade him choose a meaner bride
Than from O'Connor's house of pride

Their tribe, they said, their high degree,
Was sung in Tara's psaltery ;
Witness their Eath's victorious brand,
And Cathal of the bloody hand ;
Glory (they said) and power and honor
Were in the mansion of O'Connor :
But he, my loved one, bore in field
A humbler crest, a meaner shield

VII.

Ah, brothers ! what did it avail,
That fiercely and triumphantly
Ye fought the English of the pale,
And stemm'd De Bourgo's chivalry ?
And what was it to love and me,
That barons by your standard rode ;
Or beal-fires for your jubilee
Upon a hundred mountains glow'd ?
What though the lords of tower and dome
From Shannon to the North-sea foam,—
Thought ye your iron hands of pride
Could break the knot that love had tied ? /
No :—let the eagle change his plume,
The leaf its hue, the flower its bloom ;
But ties around this heart were spun,
That could not, would not, be undone !

VIII.

At bleating of the wild watch-fold
Thus sang my love—' Oh, come with me :
Our bark is on the lake, behold
Our steeds are fasten'd to the tree.
Come far from Castle-Connor's clans :—
Come with thy belted forestere,
And I, beside the lake of swans,
Shall hunt for thee the fallow-deer ;
And build thy hut, and bring thee home
The wild-fowl and the honey-comb ;

And berries from the wood provide,
And play my clarshech by thy side.
Then come, my love !'—How could I stay ?
Our nimble stag-hounds track'd the way,
And I pursued, by moonless skies,
The light of Connocht Moran's eyes.

IX.

And fast and far, before the star
Of day-spring, rush'd we through the glade,
And saw at dawn the lofty bawn
Of Castle-Connor fade.
Sweet was to us the hermitage
Of this unplough'd, untrodden shore ;
Like birds all joyous from the cage,
For man's neglect we loved it more,
And well he knew, my huntsman dear,
To search the game with hawk and spear ;
While I, his evening food to dress,
Would sing to him in happiness.
But, oh, that midnight of despair !
When I was doom'd to rend my hair:
The night, to me, of shrieking sorrow !
The night, to him, that had no morrow !

X.

When all was hush'd, at even tide,
I heard the baying of their beagle :
Be hush'd ! my Connocht Moran cried,
'Tis but the screaming of the eagle.
Alas ! 'twas not the eyrie's sound ;
Their bloody bands had track'd us out ;
Up-listening starts our couchant hound—
And, hark ! again, that nearer shout
Brings faster on the murderers.
Spare—spare him—Brazil—Desmond fierce
In vain—no voice the adder charms ;
Their weapons cross'd my sheltering arms ·

Another's sword has laid him low—
Another's and another's;
And every hand that dealt the blow—
Ah me! it was a brother's!
Yes, when his moanings died away,
Their iron hands had dug the clay,
And o'er his burial turf they trod,
And I behold—oh God! oh God!—
His life-blood oozing from the sod!

XI.

Warm in his death-wounds sepulchred,
Alas! my warrior's spirit brave
Nor mass nor ulla-lulla heard,
Lamenting, sooth his grave.
Dragg'd to their hated mansion back,
How long in thraldom's grasp I lay
I knew not, for my soul was black,
And knew no change of night or day
One night of horror round me grew;
Or if I saw, or felt, or knew,
'Twas but when those grim visages,
The angry brothers of my race,
Glared on each eye-ball's aching throb,
And check'd my bosom's power to sob,
Or when my heart with pulses drear
Beat like a death-watch to my ear.

XII.

But Heaven, at last, my soul's eclipse
Did with a vision bright inspire;
I woke and felt upon my lips
A prophetess's fire.
Thrice in the east a war-drum beat,
I heard the Saxon's trumpet sound,
And ranged, as to the judgment-seat,
My guilty, trembling brothers round.
Clad in the helm and shield they came;

For now De Bourgo's sword and flame
Had ravaged Ulster's boundaries,
And lighted up the midnight skies.
The standard of O'Connor's sway
Was in the turret where I lay ;
That standard, with so dire a look,
As ghastly shone the moon and pale,
I gave,—that every bosom shook
Beneath its iron mail.

XIII.

And go ! (I cried) the combat seek,
Ye hearts that unappalled bore
The anguish of a sister's shriek,
Go !—and return no more !
For sooner guilt the ordeal brand
Shall grasp unhùrt, than ye shall hold
The banner with victorious hand,
Beneath a sister's curse unroll'd.
O stranger ! by my country's loss !
And by my love ! and by the cross !
I swear I never could have spoke
The curse that sever'd nature's yoke :
But that a spirit o'er me stood,
And fired me with the wrathful mood ;
And phrensy to my heart was given,
To speak the malison of heaven.

XIV.

They would have cross'd themselves, all mute ;
They would have pray'd to burst the spell ;
But at the stamping of my foot
Each hand down powerless fell !
And go to Athunree ! (I cried)
High lift the banner of your pride !
But know that where its sheet unrolls,
The weight of blood is on your souls !
Go where the havoc of your kerne

Shall float as high as mountain fern!
Men shall no more your mansion know;
The nettles on your hearth shall grow!
Dead, as the green oblivious flood
That mantles by your walls, shall be
The glory of O'Connor's blood!
Away! away to Athunree!
Where, downward when the sun shall fall,
The raven's wing shall be your pall!
And not a vassal shall unlace
The visor from your dying face!

xv.

A bolt that overhung our dome
Suspended till my curse was given,
Soon as it pass'd these lips of foam,
Peal'd in the blood-red heaven.
Dire was the look that o'er their backs
The angry parting brothers threw:
But now, behold! like cataracts,
Come down the hills in view
O'Connor's plumed partisans;
Thrice ten Kilnagorvian clans
Were marching tó their doom:
A sudden storm their plumage toss'd,
A flash of lightning o'er them cross'd,
And all again was gloom!

xvi.

Stranger! I fled the home of grief,
At Conrocht Moran's tomb tc fall;
I found the helmet of my chief,
His bow still hanging on our wall,
And took it down, and vow'd to rove
This desert place a huntress bold;
Nor would I change my buried love
For any heart of living mould.
No! for I am a hero's child;

I'll hunt my quarry in the wild ;
And still my home this mansion make,
Of all unheeded and unheeding,
And cherish, for my warrior's sake—
' The flower of love lies bleeding.' "

I OCHIEL'S WARNING.

Wizard.—Lochiel.

WIZARD.

Lochiel, Lochiel ! beware of the day
When the Lowlands shall meet thee in battle array
For a field of the dead rushes red on my sight,
And the clans of Culloden are scatter'd in fight.
They rally, they bleed, for their kingdom and crown ,
Wo, wo to the riders that trample them down !
Proud Cumberland prances, insulting the slain,
And their hoof-beaten bosoms are trod to the plain.
But hark ! through the fast flashing lightning of war,
What steed to the desert flies frantic and far ?
'Tis thine, oh Glenullin ! whose bride shall await,
Like a love-lighted watch-fire, all night at the gate.
A steed comes at morning : no rider is there ;
But its bridle is red with the sign of despair.
Weep, Albin ! to death and captivity led !
Oh weep ! but thy tears cannot number the dead :
For a merciless sword on Culloden shall wave,
Culloden ! that reeks with the blood of the brave.

LOCHIEL.

Go, preach to the coward, thou death-telling seer !
Or, if gory Culloden so dreadful appear,

Draw, dotard, around thy old wavering sight,
This mantle, to cover the phantoms of fright

WIZARD.

Ha! laugh'st thou, Lochiel, my vision to scorn?
Proud bird of the mountain, thy plume shall be torn!
Say, rush'd the bold eagle exultingly forth,
From his home, in the dark rolling clouds of the north!
Lo! the death-shot of foemen outspeeding, he rode
Companionless, bearing destruction abroad;
But down let him stoop from his havoc on high!
Ah! home let him speed,—for the spoiler is nigh.
Why flames the far summit? Why shoot to the blast
Those embers, like stars from the firmament cast?
'Tis the fire-shower of ruin, all dreadfully driven
From his eyrie, that beacons the darkness of heaven.
Oh, crested Lochiel! the peerless in might,
Whose banners arise on the battlements' height,
Heaven's fire is around thee, to blast and to burn;
Return to thy dwelling! all lonely return!
For the blackness of ashes shall mark where it stood,
And a wild mother scream o'er her famishing brood.

LOCHIEL.

False Wizard, avaunt! I have marshall'd my clan,
Their swords are a thousand, their bosoms are one!
They are true to the last of their blood and their breath,
And like reapers descend to the harvest of death.
Then welcome be Cumberland's steed to the shock!
Let him dash his proud foam like a wave on the rock!
But wo to his kindred, and wo to his cause,
When Albin her claymore indignantly draws;
When her bonneted chieftains to victory crowd,
Clanronald the dauntless, and Moray the proud,
All plaided and plumed in their tartan array——

WIZARD.

—— Lochiel, Lochiel ! beware of the day ;
For, dark and despairing, my sight I may seal,
But man cannot cover what God would reveal ;
Tis the sunset of life gives me mystical lore,
And coming events cast their shadows before.
I tell thee, Culloden's dread echoes shall ring
With the bloodhounds that bark for thy fugitive king.
Lo ! anointed by Heaven with the vials of wrath,
Behold, where he flies on his desolate path !
Now in darkness and billows, he sweeps from my sight
Rise, rise ! ye wild tempests, and cover his flight !
'Tis finish'd. Their thunders are hush'd on the moors
Culloden is lost, and my country deplores,
But where is the iron-bound prisoner ? Where ?
For the red eye of battle is shut in despair.
Say, mounts he the ocean-wave, banish'd, forlorn,
Like a limb from his country cast bleeding and torn ?
Ah no ! for a darker departure is near ;.
The war-drum is muffled, and black is the bier ;
His death-bell is tolling : oh ! mercy, dispel
Yon sight, that it freezes my spirit to tell !
Life flutters convulsed in his quivering limbs,
And his blood-streaming nostril in agony swims.
Accursed be the fagots, that blaze at his feet,
Where his heart shall be thrown, ere it ceases to beat,
With the smoke of its ashes to poison the gale——

LOCHIEL.

—— Down, soothless insulter ! I trust not the tale :
For never shall Albin a destiny meet,
So black with dishonor, so foul with retreat.
Though my perishing ranks should be strew'd in their
  gore,
Like ocean-weeds heap'd on the surf-beaten shore,
Lochiel, untainted by flight or by chains,
While the kindling of life in his bosom remains,

Shall victor exult, or in death be laid low,
With his back to the field, and his feet to the foe!
And leaving in battle no blot on his name,
Look proudly to Heaven from the death-bed of fame.

BATTLE OF THE BALTIC.

I

Of Nelson and the North,
Sing the glorious day's renown
When to battle fierce came forth
All the might of Denmark's crown,
And her arms along the deep proudly shone,
By each gun the lighted brand,
In a bold determined hand,
And the Prince of all the land
Led them on.—

II.

Like leviathans afloat,
Lay their bulwarks on the brine;
While the sign of battle flew
On the lofty British line:
It was ten of April morn by the chime:
As they drifted on their path,
There was silence deep as death;
And the boldest held his breath,
For a time.—

III.

But the might of England flush'd
To anticipate the scene;

And her van the fleeter rush'd
O'er the deadly space between.
'Hearts of oak!" our captains cried; when
    each gun
From its adamantine lips
Spread a death-shade round the ships,
Like the hurricane eclipse
Of the sun.

IV.

Again   again! again!
And the havoc did not slack,
Till a feeble cheer the Dane
To our cheering sent us back ;—
Their shots along the deep slowly boom :—
Then ceased—and all is wail,
As they strike the shatter'd sail;
Or, in conflagration pale,
Light the gloom.—

V.

Out spoke the victor then,
As he hail'd them o'er the wave;
'Ye are brothers! ye are men!
And we conquer but to save :—
So peace instead of death let us bring;
But yield, proud foe, thy fleet,
With the crews, at England's feet,
And make submission meet
To our King.'—

VI.

Then Denmark bless'd our chief,
That he gave her wounds repose;
And the sounds of joy and grief
From her people wildly rose,
As death withdrew his shades from the day
While the sun look'd smiling bright

11

O'er a wide and woful sight,
Where the fires of funeral light
Died away.

VII

Now joy, Old England, raise !
For the tidings of thy might,
By the festal cities' blaze,
Whilst the wine-cup shines in light ;
And yet amidst that joy and uproar,
Let us think of them that sleep,
Full many a fathom deep,
By thy wild and stormy steep,
Elsinore !

VIII.

Brave hearts ! to Britain's pride
Once so faithful and so true,
On the deck of fame that died ;— .
With the gallant good Riou :*
Soft sigh the winds of Heaven o'er their grave !
While the billow mournful rolls
And the mermaid s song condoles,
Singing glory to the souls
Of the brave !—

* Captain Riou, justly entitled the gallant and the good, by
Lord Nelson, when he wrote home his dispatches.

YE MARINERS OF ENGLAND:

A NAVAL ODE.

I

Ye Mariners of England!
That guard our native seas;
Whose flag has braved, a thousand years,
The battle and the breeze!
Your glorious standard launch again
To match another foe!
And sweep through the deep,
While the stormy winds do blow;
While the battle rages loud and long,
And the stormy winds do blow.

II

The spirits of your fathers
Shall start from every wave!—
For the deck it was their field of fame,
And Ocean was their grave:
Where Blake and mighty Nelson fell,
Your manly hearts shall glow,
As ye sweep through the deep,
While the stormy winds do blow;
While the battle rages loud and long,
And the stormy winds do blow.

III.

Britannia needs no bulwarks,
No towers along the steep;
Her march is o'er the mountain-waves,
Her home is on the deep

With thunders from her native oak,
She quells the floods below,—
As they roar on the shore,
When the stormy winds do blow :
When the battle rages loud and long
And the stormy winds do blow.

IV.

The meteor flag of England
Shall yet terrific burn ;
Till danger's troubled night depart,
And the star of peace return.
Then, then, ye ocean-warriors !
Our song and feast shall flow
To the fame of your name,
When the storm has ceased to blow ;
When the fiery fight is heard no more
And the storm has ceased to blow

HOHENLINDEN

On Linden, when the sun was low
All bloodless lay th' untrodden snow,
And dark as winter was the flow
Of Iser, rolling rapidly.

But Linden saw another sight,
When the drum beat, at dead of night,
Commanding fires of death to light
The darkness of her scenery.

By torch and trumpet fast array'd,
Each horseman drew his battle-blade,

And furious every charger neigh'd,
To join the dreadful revelry

Then shook the hills with thunder riven,
Then rush'd the steed to battle driven,
And louder than the bolts of heaven,
Far flash'd the red artillery.

But redder yet that light shall glow
On Linden's hills of stained snow,
And bloodier yet the torrent flow
Of Iser, rolling rapidly.

'Tis morn, but scarce yon level sun
Can pierce the war-clouds, rolling dun,
Where furious Frank, and fiery Hun,
Shout in their sulph'rous canopy.

The combat deepens. On, ye brave,
Who rush to glory, or the grave !
Wave, Munich ! all thy banners wave,
And charge with all thy chivalry !

Few, few shall part where many meet !
The snow shall be their winding-sheet,
And every turf beneath their feet
Shall be a soldier's sepulchre.

----♦----

GLENARA.

O heard ye yon pibroch sound sad in the gale,
Where a band cometh slowly with weeping and wail ?
'Tis the chief of Glenara laments for his dear ;
And her sire, and the people, are call'd to her bier

Glenara came first with the mourners and shroud ;
Her kinsmen they follow'd, but mourn'd not aloud:
Their plaids all their bosoms were folded around :
They march'd all in silence,—they look'd on the ground

In silence they reach'd over mountain and moor,
To a heath, where the oak-tree grew lonely and hoar :
" Now here let us place the gray stone of her cairn :
Why speak ye no word !"—said Glenara the stern.

" And tell me, I charge you ! ye clan of my spouse,
Why fold ye your mantles, why cloud ye your brows ?"
So spake the rude chieftain :—no answer is made,
But each mantle unfolding a dagger display'd.

" I dreamt of my lady, I dreamt of her shroud,"
Cried a voice from the kinsmen, all wrathful and loud ;
" And empty that shroud, and that coffin did seem ·
Glenara ! Glenara ! now read me my dream !"

O ! pale grew the cheek of that chieftain, I ween,
When the shroud was unclosed, and no lady was seen ;
When a voice from the kinsmen spoke louder in scorn,
'Twas the youth who had loved the fair Ellen of Lorn :

" I dreamt of my lady, I dreamt of her grief,
I dreamt that her lord was a barbarous chief :·
On a rock of the ocean fair Ellen did seem ;
Glenara ! Glenara ! now read me my dream !"

In dust, low the traitor has knelt to the ground,
And the desert reveal'd where his lady was found ;
From a rock of the ocean that beauty is borne—
Now joy to the house of fair Ellen of Lorn !

EXILE OF ERIN.

THERE came to the beach a poor Exile of Erin,
  The dew on his thin robe was heavy and chill:
For his country he sigh'd, when at twilight repairing
  To wander alone by the wind-beaten hill.
But the day-star attracted his eye's sad devotion,
For it rose o'er his own native isle of the ocean,
Where once in the fire of his youthful emotion,
  He sang the bold anthem of Erin go bragh.

Sad is my fate! said the heart-broken stranger;
  The wild deer and wolf to a covert can flee,
But I have no refuge from famine and danger,
  A home and a country remain not to me.
Never again, in the green sunny bowers,
Where my forefathers lived, shall I spend the sweet
     hours,
Or cover my harp with the wild-woven flowers,
  And strike to the numbers of Erin go bragh !

Erin, my country! though sad and forsaken,
  In dreams I revisit thy sea-beaten shore ;
But, alas! in a far foreign land I awaken,
  And sigh for the friends who can meet mé no more !
Oh cruel fate ! wilt thou never replace me
In a mansion of peace—where no perils can chase me
Never again shall my brothers embrace me ?
  They died to defend me, or live to deplore !

Where is my cabin-door, fast by the wild wood ?
  Sisters and sire ! did ye weep for its fall ?

Where is the mother that look'd on my childhood?
　And where is the bosom-friend, dearer than all?
Oh! my sad heart! long abandon'd by pleasure,
Why did it dote on a fast-fading treasure?
Tears, like the rain drop, may fall without measure,
　But rapture and beauty they cannot recall.

Yet all its sad recollections suppressing,
　One dying wish my lone bosom can draw:
Erin! an exile bequeaths thee his blessing!
　Land of my forefathers! Erin go bragh!
Buried and cold, when my heart stills her motion,
Green be thy fields,—sweetest isle of the ocean!
And thy harp-striking bards sing aloud with devotion,—
　Erin mavournin—Erin go bragh!*

———◆———

LORD ULLIN'S DAUGHTER.

A CHIEFTAIN, to the Highlands bound,
　Cries, " Boatman, do not tarry!
And I'll give thee a silver pound
　To row us o'er the ferry."—

" Now who be ye, would cross Lochgyle,
　This dark and stormy water?"
" O, I'm the chief of Ulva's isle,
　And this Lord Ullin's daughter.—

And fast before her father's men
　Three days we've fled together,
For should he find us in the glen,
　My blood would stain the heather

* Ireland my darling—Ireland forever.

His horsemen hard behind us ride ;
  Should they our steps discover,
Then who will cheer my bonny bride
  When they have slain her lover ?"—

Outspoke the hardy Highland wight,
  " I'll go, my chief—I'm ready :—
It is not for your silver bright ;
  But for your winsome lady :

And by my word ! the bonny bird
  In danger shall not tarry ;
So though the waves are raging white,
  I'll row you o'er the ferry."—

By this the storm grew loud apace,
  The water-wraith was shrieking ;
And in the scowl of heaven each face
  Grew dark as they were speaking.

But still as wilder blew the wind,
  And as the night grew drearer,
Adown the glen rode armed men,
  Their trampling sounded nearer.—

" O haste thee, haste !" the lady cries,
  Though tempests round us gather ;
I'll meet the raging of the skies,
  But not an angry father."—

The boat has left a stormy land,
  A stormy sea before her,—
When, oh ! too strong for human hand,
  The tempest gather'd o'er her.—

And still they row'd amidst the roar
  Of waters fast prevailing :
Lord Ullin reach'd that fatal shore,
  His wrath was changed to wailing.—

For sore dismay'd, through storm and shade,
  His child he did discover :—
One lovely hand she stretch'd for aid,
  And one was round her lover.

"Come back ! come back !" he cried in grief,
  "Across this stormy water:
And I'll forgive your Highland chief,
  My daughter !—oh my daughter !"—

'Twas vain: the loud waves lash'd the shore,
  Return or aid preventing :—
The waters wild went o'er his child,
  And he was left lamenting.

ODE TO THE MEMORY OF BURNS

Soul of the Poet ! wheresoe'er,
Reclaim'd from earth, thy genius plume
Her wings of immortality :
Suspend thy harp in happier sphere,
And with thine influence illume
The gladness of our jubilee.

And fly like fiends from secret spell,
Discord and Strife, at Burns's name,
Exorcised by his memory ;
For he was chief of bards that swell
The heart with songs of social flame,
And high delicious revelry.

And Love's own strain to him was given,
To warble all its ecstasies

With Pythian words unsought, unwill'd,—
Love, the surviving. gift of Heaven,
The choicest sweet of Paradise,
In life's else bitter cup distill'd.

Who that has melted o'er his lay
To Mary's soul, in Heaven above,
But pictured sees, in fancy strong,
The landscape and the livelong day
'That smiled upon their mutual love?—
Who that has felt forgets the song?

Nor skill'd one flame alone to fan :
His country's high-soul'd peasantry
What patriot-pride he taught !—how much
To weigh the inborn worth of man !
And rustic life and poverty
Grow beautiful beneath his touch.

Him, in his clay-built cot, the muse
Entranced, and show'd him all the forms,
Of fairy-light and wizard gloom,
(That only gifted Poet views,)
The Genii of the floods and storms,
And martial shades from Glory's tomb.

On Bannock-field what thoughts arouse
'The swain whom Burns's song inspires?
Beat not his Caledonian veins,
As o'er the heroic turf he ploughs,
With all the spirit of his sires,
And all their scorn of death and chains?

And see the Scottish exile tann'd
By many a far and foreign clime,
Bend o'er his home-born verse, and weep

In memory of his native land,
With love that scorns the lapse of time,
And ties that stretch beyond the deep.

Encamp'd by Indian rivers wild,
The soldier resting on his arms,
In Burns's carol sweet recalls
The scenes that bless'd him when a child
And glows and gladdens at the charms
Of Scotia's woods and waterfalls.

O deem not, midst this worldly strife,
An idle art the Poet brings:
Let high Philosophy control,
And sages calm, the stream of life,
'Tis he refines its fountain-springs,
The nobler passions of the soul.

It is the muse that consecrates
The native banner of the brave,
Unfurling at the trumpet's breath,
Rose, thistle, harp; 'tis she elates
To sweep the field or ride the wave,
A sunburst in the storm of death.

And thou, young hero, when thy pal!
Is cross'd with mournful sword and plume,
When public grief begins to fade,
And only tears of kindred fall,
Who but the Bard shall dress thy tomb,
And greet with fame thy gallant shade?

Such was the soldier—Burns, forgive
That sorrows of mine own intrude
In strains to thy great memory due.
In verse like thine, oh! could he live,

The friend I mourn'd—the brave, the good—
Edward that died at Waterloo !*

Farewell, high chief of Scottish song !
That couldst alternately impart
Wisdom and rapture in thy page,
And brand each vice with satire stiong,
Whose lines are mottoes of the heart,
Whose truths electrify the sage.

Farewell ! and ne'er may Envy dare
To wring one baleful poison drop
From the crush'd laurels of thy bust :
But while the lark sings sweet in air,
Still may the grateful pilgrim stop,
Tc bless the spot that holds thy dust.

LINES

At the silence of twilight's contemplative hour,
  I have mused in a sorrowful mood,
On the wind-shaken weeds that embosom the bower,
  Where the home of my forefathers stood.
All ruin'd and wild is their roofless abode,
  And lonely the dark raven's sheltering tree :
And travell'd by few is the grass-cover'd road,
Where the hunter of deer and the warrior trode,
  To his hills that encircle the sea.

* Major Edward Hodge, of the 7th Hussars, who fell at the head of his squadron in the attack of the Polish Lancers.

12

Yet wandering, I found on my ruinous walk,
  By the dial-stone aged and green,
One rose of the wilderness left on its stalk,
  To mark where a garden had been.
Like a brotherless hermit, the last of its race,
  All wild in the silence of nature, it drew,
From each wandering sun-beam, a lonely embrace,
For the night-weed and thorn overshadow'd the place,
  Where the flower of my forefathers grew.·

Sweet bud of the wilderness! emblem of all
  That remains in this desolate heart!
The fabric of bliss to its centre may fall,
  But patience shall never depart!
Though the wilds of enchantment, all vernal and bright,
  In the days of delusion by fancy combined
With the vanishing phantoms of love and delight,
Abandon my soul, like a dream of the night,
  And leave but a desert behind.

Be hush'd, my dark spirit! for wisdom condemns
  When the faint and the feeble deplore ;
Be strong as the rock of the ocean that stems
  A thousand wild waves on the shore !
Through the perils of chance, and the scowl of disdain,
  May thy front be unalter'd, thy courage elate !
Yea ! even the name I have worshipp'd in vain
Shall awake not the sigh of remembrance again :
  To bear is to conquer our fate.

THE SOLDIER'S DREAM.

Our bugles sang truce—for the night-cloud had lower'd
  And the sentinel stars set their watch in the sky;
And thousands had sunk on the ground overpower'd,
  The weary to sleep, and the wounded to die.

When reposing that night on my pallet of straw,
  By the wolf-scaring fagot that guarded the slain;
At the dead of the night a sweet vision I saw,
  And thrice ere the morning I dreamt it again.

Methought from the battle-field's dreadful array,
  Far, far I had roam'd on a desolate track:
'Twas Autumn,—and sunshine arose on the way
  To the home of my fathers, that welcomed me back

I flew to the pleasant fields traversed so oft
  In life's morning march, when my bosom was young;
I heard my own mountain-goats bleating aloft,
  And knew the sweet strain that the corn-reapers
    sung.

Then pledged we the wine-cup, and fondly I swore,
  From my home and my weeping friends never to
    part;
My little ones kiss'd me a thousand times o'er,
  And my wife sobb'd aloud in her fulness of heart.

Stay, stay with us,—rest, thou art weary and worn;
  And fain was their war-broken soldier to stay;—
But sorrow return'd with the dawning of morn,
  And the voice in my dreaming ear melted away.

TO THE RAINBOW.

TRIUMPHAL arch, that fill'st the sky
  When storms prepare to part,
I ask not proud Philosophy
  To teach me what thou art—

Still seem, as to my childhood's sight,
  A midway station given
For happy spirits to alight
  Betwixt the earth and heaven.

Can all that Optics teach, unfold
  Thy form to please me so,
As when I dreamt of gems and gold
  Hid in thy radiant bow?

When Science from Creation's face
  Enchantment's veil withdraws,
What lovely visions yield their place
  To cold material laws!

And yet, fair bow, no fabling dreams,
  But words of the Most High,
Have told why first thy robe of beams
  Was woven in the sky.

When o'er the green undeluged earth
  Heaven's covenant thou didst shine,
How came the world's gray fathers forth
  To watch thy sacred sign.

And when its yellow lustre smiled
  O'er mountains yet untrod,
Each mother held aloft her child
  To bless the bow of God.

Methinks. thy jubilee to keep,
  The first made anthem rang
On earth deliver'd from the deep,
  And the first poet sang.

Nor ever shall the Muse's eye
  Unraptured greet thy beam :
Theme of primeval prophecy,
  Be still the prophet's theme !

The earth to thee her incense yields,
  The lark thy welcome sings,
When glittering in the freshen'd fields
  The snowy mushroom springs.

How glorious is thy girdle cast
  O'er mountain, tower, and town,
Or, mirror'd in the ocean vast,
  A thousand fathoms down !

As fresh in yon horizon dark,
  As young thy beauties seem,
As when the eagle from the ark
  First sported in thy beam.

For, faithful to its sacred page,
  Heaven still rebuilds thy span,
Nor lets the type grow pale with age
  That first spoke peace to man.

THE LAST MAN

ALL worldly shapes shall melt in gloom,
  The sun himself must die,
Before this mortal shall assume
  Its Immortality!

I saw a vision in my sleep,
That gave my spirit strength to sweep
  Adown the gulf of Time!
I saw the last of human mould,
That shall Creation's death behold,
  As Adam saw her prime!

The Sun's eye had a sickly glare,
  The Earth with age was wan,
The skeletons of nations were
  Around that lonely man!
Some had expired in fight,—the brands
Still rusted in their bony hands;
  In plague and famine some!
Earth's cities had no sound nor tread;
And ships were drifting with the dead
  To shores where all was dumb!

Yet, prophet-like, that lone one stood,
  With dauntless words and high,
That shook the sere leaves from the wood
  As if a storm pass'd by,
Saying, We are twins in death, proud Sun,
Thy face is cold, thy race is run,

'Tis Mercy bids thee go.
For thou ten thousand thousand years
Hast seen the tide of human tears,
    That shall no longer flow.

What though beneath thee man put forth
    His pomp, his pride, his skill ;
And arts that made fire, flood and earth,
    The vassals of his will ;—
Yet mourn I not thy parted sway,
Thou dim discrowned king of day ·
    For all these trophied arts
And triumphs that beneath thee sprang,
Heal'd not a passion or a pang
    Entail'd on human hearts.

Go, let oblivion's curtain fall
    Upon the stage of men,
Nor with thy rising beams recall
    Life's tragedy again.
Its piteous pageants bring not back,
Nor waken flesh, upon the rack
    Of pain anew to writhe ;
Stretch'd in disease's shapes abhorr'd
Or mown in battle by the sword,
    Like grass beneath the scythe

Ev'n I am weary in yon skies
    To watch thy fading fire ;
Test of all sumless agonies,
    Behold not me expire.
My lips that speak thy dirge of death—
Their rounded gasp and gurgling breath
    To see thou shalt not boast.
The eclipse of Nature spreads my pall,—
The majesty of Darkness shall
    Receive my parting ghost !

This spirit shall return to Him
  Who gave its heavenly spark ;
Yet think not, Sun, it shall be dim
  When thou thyself art dark !
No ! it shall live again, and shine
In bliss unknown to beams of thine,
  By Him recall'd to breath,
Who captive led captivity,
Who robb'd the grave of Victory,—
  And took the sting from Death !

Go, Sun, while Mercy holds me up
  On Nature's awful waste
To drink this last and bitter cup
  Of grief that man shall taste—
Go, tell the night that hides thy face,
Thou saw'st the last of Adam's race,
  On Earth's sepulchral clod,
The darkening universe defy
To quench his Immortality,
  Or shake his trust in God !

————◆————

A DREAM.

WELL may sleep present us fictions,
  Since our waking moments teem
With such fanciful convictions
  As make life itself a dream.—
Half our daylight faith's a fable ;
  Sleep disports with shadows too,
Seeming in their turn as stable
  As the world we wake to view.
Ne'er by day did Reason's mint

A DREAM.

Give my thoughts a clearer print
Of assured reality,
Than was left by Phantasy
Stamp'd and color'd on my sprite,
In a dream of yesternight.

In a bark, methought, lone steering,
  I was cast on Ocean's strife;
This, 'twas whisper'd in my hearing,
  Meant the sea of life.
Sad regrets from past existence
  Came, like gales of chilling breath;
Shadow'd in the forward distance
  Lay the land of Death.
Now seeming more, now less remote,
On that dim-seen shore, methought,
I beheld two hands a space
Slow unshroud a spectre's face;
And my flesh's hair upstood,—
'Twas mine own similitude.—

But my soul revived at seeing
  Ocean, like an emerald spark,
Kindle, while an air-dropp'd being
  Smiling steer'd my bark.
Heaven-like—yet he look'd as human
  As supernal beauty can,
More compassionate than woman,
  Lordly more than man.
And as some sweet clarion's breath
Stirs the soldier's scorn of death—
So his accents bade me brook
The spectre's eyes of icy look,
Till it shut them—turn'd its head,
Like a beaten foe, and fled.

" Types not this," I said, " fair spirit!
  That my death-hour is not come?

Say, what days shall I inherit?--
   Tell my soul their sum."
" No," he said, " yon phantom's aspect,
   Trust me, would appal thee worse,
Held in clearly measured prospect :—
   Ask not for a curse !
Make not, for I overhear
Thine unspoken thoughts as clear
As thy mortal ear could catch
The close-brought tickings of a watch—
Make not the untold request
That's now revolving in thy breast.

'Tis to live again, remeasuring
   Youth's years, like a scene rehearsed,
In thy second lifetime treasuring
   Knowledge from the first.
Hast thou felt, poor self-deceiver !
   Life's career so void of pain,
As to wish its fitful fever
   New begun again?
Could experience, ten times thine,
Pain from Being disentwine—
Threads by Fate together spun?
Could thy flight Heaven's lightning shun !
No, nor could thy foresight's glance
'Scape the myriad shafts of Chance.

Wouldst thou bear again Love's trouble—
   Friendship's death-dissever'd ties;
Toil to grasp or miss the bubble
   Of Ambition's prize?
Say thy life's new guided action
   Flow'd from Virtue's fairest springs—
Still would Envy and Detraction
   Double not their stings?
Worth itself is but a charter
To be mankind's distinguish'd martyr "

—I caught the moral, and cried, "Hail!
Spirit! let us onward sail
Envying, fearing, hating none—
Guardian Spirit, steer me on!"

VALEDICTORY STANZAS

TO

J. P. KEMBLE, ESQ.

COMPOSED FOR A PUBLIC MEETING HELD JUNE, 18

PRIDE of the British stage,
    A long and last adieu!
Whose image brought th' heroic age
    Revived to Fancy's view.
Like fields refresh'd with dewy light
    When the sun smiles his last,
Thy parting presence makes more bright
    Our memory of the past;
And memory conjures feelings up
    That wine or music need not swell,
As high we lift the festal cup
    To Kemble—fare thee well!

His was the spell o'er hearts
    Which only Acting lends,—
The youngest of the sister Arts,
    Where all their beauty blends:
For ill can Poetry express
    Full many a tone of thought sublime,

And Painting, mute and motionless,
 Steals but a glance of time.
But by the mighty actor brought,
 Illusion's perfect triumphs come,—
Verse ceases to be airy thought,
 And Sculpture to be dumb.

Time may again revive,
 But ne'er eclipse the charm,
When Cato spoke in him alive,
 Or Hotspur kindled warm.
What soul was not resign'd entire
 To the deep sorrows of the Moor,—
What English heart was not on fire
 With him at Agincourt?
And yet a majesty possess'd
 His transport's most impetuous tone,
And to each passion of the breast
 The Graces gave their zone.

High were the task—too high,
 Ye conscious bosoms here !
In words to paint your memory
 Of Kemble and of Lear ;
But who forgets that white discrowned head,
 Those bursts of Reason's half-extinguish'd glare,
Those tears upon Cordelia's bosom shed,
 In doubt more touching than despair,
 If 'twas reality he felt ?
  Had Shakspeare's self amidst you been,
 Friends, he had seen you melt,
  And triumph'd to have seen !

And there was many an hour
 Of blended kindred fame,
When Siddons's auxiliar power
 And sister magic came.
Together at the Muse's side

The tragic paragons had grown—
They were the children of her pride,
  The columns of her throne,
And undivided favor ran
  From heart to heart in their applause,
Save for the gallantry of man,
  In lovelier woman's cause.

Fair as some classic dome,
  Robust and richly graced,
Your KEMBLE's spirit was the home
  Of genius and of taste ;
Taste like the silent dial's power,
  That when supernal light is given,
Can measure inspiration's hour,
  And tell its height in heaven.
At once ennobled and correct,
  His mind survey'd the tragic page,
And what the actor could effect,
  The scholar could presage.

These were his traits of worth :—
  And must we lose them now !—
And shall the scene no more show forth
  His sternly pleasing brow !
Alas, the moral brings a tear !—
  'Tis all a transient hour below ;
And we that would detain thee here,
  Ourselves as fleetly go !
Yet shall our latest age
  This parting scene review :—
Pride of the British stage,
  A long and last adieu !

GERTRUDE OF WYOMING.

PART I.

ADVERTISEMENT.

Most of the popular histories of England, as well as of the American war, give an authentic account of the desolation of Wyoming, in Pennsylvania, which took place in 1778, by an incursion of the Indians. The Scenery and Incidents of the following Poem are connected with that event. The testimonies of historians and travellers concur in describing the infant colony as one of the happiest spots of human ex istence, for the hospitable and innocent manners of the in habitants, the beauty of the country, and the luxuriant fer- tility of the soil and climate. In an evil hour, the junction of European with Indian arms converted this terrestrial para- dise into a frightful waste. Mr. Isaac Weld informs us, that the ruins of many of the villages, perforated with balls, and bearing marks of conflagration, were still preserved by the recent inhabitants, when he travelled through America in 1796

PART THE FIRST.

I.

On Susquehanna's side, fair Wyoming!
Although the wild-flower on thy ruin'd wall,
And roofless homes, a sad remembrance bring
Of what thy gentle people did befall;
Yet thou wert once the loveliest land of all
That see the Atlantic wave their morn restore.
Sweet land! may I thy lost delights recall,
And paint thy Gertrude in her bowers of yore,
Whose beauty was the love of Pennsylvania's shore!

II.

Delightful Wyoming! beneath thy skies,
The happy shepherd swains had naught to do
But feed their flocks on green declivities,
Or skim perchance thy lake with light canoe,
From morn till evening's sweeter pastime grew,
With timbrel, when beneath the forests brown,
Thy lovely maidens would the dance renew;
And aye those sunny mountains half-way down
Would echo flagelet from some romantic town.

III.

Then, where of Indian hills the daylight takes
His leave, how might you the flamingo see
Disporting like a meteor on the lakes—
And playful squirrel on his nut-grown tree:

And every sound of life was full of glee,
From merry mock-bird's song, or hum of men ;
While hearkening, fearing naught their revelry,
The wild deer arch'd his neck from glades, and then,
Unhunted, sought his woods and wilderness again.

IV.

And scarce had Wyoming of war or crime
Heard, but in transatlantic story rung,
For here the exile met from every clime,
And spoke in friendship every distant tongue ;
Men from the blood of warring Europe sprung
Were but divided by the running brook ;
And happy where no Rhenish trumpet sung,
On plains no sieging mine's volcano shook,
The blue-eyed German changed his sword to pruning-
      hook.

V.

Nor far some Andalusian saraband
Would sound to many a native roundelay—
But who is he that yet a dearer land
Remembers, over hills and far away ?
Green Albin !* what though he no more survey
Thy ships at anchor on the quiet shore,
Thy pellochs† rolling from the mountain bay,
Thy lone sepulchral cairn upon the moor,
And distant isles that hear the loud Corbrechtan‡ roar !

VI.

Alas ! poor Caledonia's mountaineer,
That want's stern edict e'er, and feudal grief,
Had forced him from a home he loved so dear !
Yet found he here a home, and glad relief,

* Scotland.
† The Gaelic appellation for the porpoise.
‡ The great whirlpool of the Western Hebrides.

And plied the beverage from his own fair sheaf,
That fired his Highland blood with mickle glee :
And England sent her men, of men the chief,
Who taught those sires of Empire yet to be,
To plant the tree of life,—to plant fair Freedom's tree

VII.

Here was not mingled in the city's pomp
Of life's extremes the grandeur and the gloom ;
Judgment awoke not here her dismal tromp,
Nor seal'd in blood a fellow-creature's doom,
Nor mourn'd the captive in a living tomb.
One venerable man, beloved of all,
Sufficed, where innocence was yet in bloom,
To sway the strife, that seldom might befall :
And Albert was their judge in patriarchal hall.

VIII.

How reverend was the look, serenely aged,
He bore, this gentle Pennsylvanian sire,
Where all but kindly fervors were assuaged,
Undimm'd by weakness' shade, or turbid ire !
And though, amidst the calm of thought entire,
Some high and haughty features might betray
A soul impetuous once, 'twas earthly fire
That fled composure's intellectual ray,
As Ætna's fires grow dim before the rising day.

IX.

I boast no song in magic wonders rife,
But yet, oh Nature ! is there naught to prize,
Familiar in thy bosom scenes of life ?
And dwells in daylight truth's salubrious skies
No form with which the soul may sympathize ?—
Young, innocent, on whose sweet forehead mild
The parted ringlet shone in simplest guise,
An inmate in the home of Albert smiled,
Or blest his noonday walk—she was his only child.

X.

The rose of England bloom'd on Gertrude's cheek—
What though these shades had seen her birth, her sire
A Briton's independence taught to seek
Far western worlds ; and there his household fire
The light of social love did long inspire,
And many a halcyon day he lived to see
Unbroken but by one misfortune dire,
When fate had reft his mutual heart—but she
Was gone—and Gertrude climb'd a widow'd father's
    knee.

XI.

A loved bequest,—and I may half impart—
To them that feel the strong paternal tie,
How like a new existence to his heart
That living flower uprose beneath his eye,
Dear as she was from cherub infancy,
From hours when she would round his garden play,
To time when as the ripening years went by,
Her lovely mind could culture well repay,
And more engaging grew, from pleasing day to day.

XII.

I may not paint those thousand infant charms ;
(Unconscious fascination, undesigned !)
The orison repeated in his arms,
For God to bless her sire and all mankind ;
The book, the bosom on his knee reclined,
Or how sweet fairy-lore he heard her con,
(The playmate ere the teacher of her mind :)
All uncompanion'd else her heart had gone
Till now, in Gertrude's eyes, their ninth blue summer
   . shone.

XIII.

And summer was the tide, and sweet the hour,
When sire and daughter saw, with fleet descent,
An Indian from his bark approach their bower,
Of buskin'd limb, and swarthy lineament ;

The red wild feathers on his brow were blent,
And bracelets bound the arm that help'd to light
A boy, who seem'd, as he beside him went,
Of Christian vesture, and complexion bright,
Led by his dusky guide, like morning brought by night.

XIV.

Yet pensive seem'd the boy for one so young—
The dimple from his polish'd cheek had fled;
When, leaning on his forest-bow unstrung,
Th' Oneida warrior to the planter said,
And laid his hand upon the stripling's head,
" Peace be to thee! my words this belt approve;
The paths of peace my steps have hither led:
This little nursling, take him to thy love,
And shield the bird unfledged, since gone the parent dove

XV.

Christian! I am the foeman of thy foe;
Our wampum league thy brethren did embrace:
Upon the Michigan, three moons ago,
We launch'd our pirogues for the bison chase,
And with the Hurons planted for a space,
With true and faithful hands, the olive-stalk;
But snakes are in the bosoms of their race,
And though they held with us a friendly talk,
The hollow peace-tree fell beneath their tomahawk!

XVI.

It was encamping on the lake's far port,
A cry of Areouski* broke our sleep,
Where storm'd an ambush'd foe thy nation's fort,
And rapid, rapid whoops came o'er the deep;
But long thy country's war-sign on the steep
Appear'd through ghastly intervals of light,
And deathfully their thunders seem'd to sweep,
Till utter darkness swallow'd up the sight,
As if a shower of blood had quench'd the fiery fight!

* The Indian God of War.

XVII.

It slept—it rose again—on high their tower
Sprung upwards like a torch to light the skies,
Then down again it rain'd an ember shower,
And louder lamentations heard we rise :
As when the evil Man'tou that dries
Th' Ohio woods, consumes them in his ire,
In vain the desolated panther flies,
And howls amidst his wilderness of fire :
Alas ! too late, we reach'd and smote those Hurons
    dire !

XVIII.

But as the fox beneath the nobler hound,
So died their warriors by our battle-brand ;
And from the tree we, with her child, unbound
A lonely mother of the Christian land :—
Her lord—the captain of the British band—
Amidst the slaughter of his soldiers lay.
Scarce knew the widow our delivering hand ;
Upon her child she sobb'd, and swoon'd away,
Or shriek'd unto the God to whom the Christians pray

XIX.

Our virgins fed her with their kindly bowls
Of fever balm and sweet sagamité :
But she was journeying to the land of souls,
And lifted up her dying head to pray
That we should bid an ancient friend convey
Her orphan to his home of England's shore ;
And take, she said, this token far away,
To one that will remember us of yore,
When he beholds the ring that Waldegrave's Julia wore.

XX.

And I, the eagle of my tribe, have rush'd
With this lorn dove."—A sage's self-command
Had quell'd the tears from Albert's heart that gush'd ;
But yet his cheek—his agitated hand—

That shower'd upon the stranger of the land
No common boon, in grief but ill beguiled
A soul that was not wont to be unmann'd;
" And stay," he cried, " dear pilgrim of the wild,
Preserver of my old, my boon companion's child!—

XXI.

Child of a race whose name my bosom warms,
On earth's remotest bounds how welcome here!
Whose mother oft, a child, has fill'd these arms,
Young as thyself, and innocently dear,
Whose grandsire was my early life's compeer.
Ah, happiest home of England's happy clime!
How beautiful ev'n now thy scenes appear,
As in the noon and sunshine of my prime!
How gone like yesterday these thrice ten years of time!

XXII.

And Julia! when thou wert like Gertrude now,
Can I forget thee, favorite child of yore?
Or thought I, in thy father's house, when thou
Wert lightest hearted on his festive floor,
And first of all his hospitable door
To meet and kiss me at my journey's end?
But where was I when Waldegrave was no more?
And thou didst pale thy gentle head extend
In woes, that ev'n the tribe of deserts was thy friend!*

XXIII.

He said—and strain'd unto his heart the boy;—
Far differently, the mute Oneida took
His calumet of peace, and cup of joy;
As monumental bronze unchanged his look;
A soul that pity touch'd, but never shook;
Train'd from his tree-rock'd cradle to his bier
The fierce extreme of good and ill to brook
Impassive—fearing but the shame of fear—
A stoic of the woods—a man without a tear.

XXIV.

Yet deem not good.1ess on the savage stock
Of Outalissi's heart disdain'd to grow ;
As lives the oak unwither'd on the rock
By storms above, and barrenness below ;
He scorn'd his own, who felt another's wo :
And ere the wolf-skin on his back he flung,
Or laced his moccasins, in act to go,
A song of parting to the boy he sung,
Who slept on Albert's couch, nor heard his friendly
    tongue.

XXV.

" Sleep, wearied one ! and in the dreaming land
Shouldst thou to-morrow with thy mother meet,
Oh ! tell her spirit, that the white man's hand
Hath pluck'd the thorns of sorrow from thy feet ;
While I in lonely wilderness shall greet
Thy little foot-prints—or by traces know
The fountain, where at noon I thought it sweet
To feed thee with the quarry of my bow,
And pour'd the lotus-horn, or slew the mountain roe

XXVI.

Adieu ! sweet scion of the rising sun !
But should affliction's storms thy blossom mock,
Then come again—my own adopted one !
And I will graft thee on a noble stock :
The crocodile, the condor of the rock,
Shall be the pastime of thy sylvan wars ;
And I will teach thee, in the battle's shock,
To pay with Huron blood thy father's scars,
And gratulate his soul rejoicing in the stars !"

XXVII.

So finish'd he the rhyme (howe'er uncouth)
That true to nature's fervid feelings ran ;
(And song is but the eloquence of truth :)
Then forth uprose that lone way-faring man ;

But dauntless he, nor chart, nor journey's plan
In woods required, whose trained eye was keen,
As eagle of the wilderness, to scan
His path by mountain, swamp, or deep ravine,
Or ken far friendly huts on good savannas green.

XXVIII.

Old Albert saw him from the valley's side—
His pirogue launch'd—his pilgrimage begun—
Far, like the red-bird's wing he seem'd to glide ;
Then dived, and vanish'd in the woodlands dun.
Oft, to that spot by tender memory won,
Would Albert climb the promontory's height,
If but a dim sail glimmer'd in the sun ;
But never more, to bless his longing sight,
Was Outalissi hail'd, with bark and plumage bright.

END OF THE FIRST PART.

PART THE SECOND

I.

A valley from the river shore withdrawn
Was Albert's home, two quiet woods between
Whose lofty verdure overlook'd his lawn ;
And waters to their resting place serene
Came freshening, and reflecting all the scene
(A mirror in the depth of flowery shelves ;)
So sweet a spot of earth, you might (I ween)
Have guess'd some congregation of the elves,
To sport by summer moons, had shaped it for themselves

Yet wanted not the eye far scope to muse,
Nor vistas open'd by the wandering stream ;
Both where at evening Alleghany views,
Through ridges burning in her western beam,
Lake after lake interminably gleam :
And past those settlers' haunts the eye might roam
Where earth's unliving silence all would seem ,
Save where on rocks the beaver built his dome,
Or buffalo remote low'd far from human home.

III.

But silent not that adverse eastern path,
Which saw Aurora's hills th' horizon crown ;
There was the river heard, in bed of wrath,
(A precipice of foam from mountains brown,)

Like tumults heard from some far distant town
But softening in approach he left his gloom,
And murmur'd pleasantly, and laid him down
To kiss those easy curving banks of bloom,
That lent the windward air an exquisite perfume.

IV.

It seem'd as if those scenes sweet influence had
On Gertrude's soul, and kindness like their own
Inspired those eyes affectionate and glad,
That seem'd to love whate'er they look'd upon ;
Whether with Hebe's mirth her features shone,
Or if a shade more pleasing them o'ercast,
(As if for heavenly musing meant alone ;)
Yet so becomingly th' expression past,
That each succeeding look was lovelier than the last.

V.

Nor guess I, was that Pennsylvanian home,
With all its picturesque and balmy grace,
And fields that were a luxury to roam,
Lost on the soul that look'd from such a face!
Enthusiast of the woods ! when years apace
Had bound thy lovely waist with woman's zone,
The sunrise path, at morn, I see thee trace
To hills with high magnolia overgrown,
And joy to breathe the groves, romantic and alone.

VI.

The sunrise drew her thoughts to Europe forth,
That thus apostrophized its viewless scene :
" Land of my father's love, my mother's birth !
The home of kindred I have never seen !
We know not other—oceans are between :
Yet say, far friendly hearts ! from whence we came,
Of us does oft remembrance intervene ?
My mother sure—my sire a thought may claim ;-
But Gertrude is 'o you an unregarded name.

14

VII.

And yet, loved England! when thy name I trace
In many a pilgrim's tale and poet's song,
How can I choose but wish for one embrace
Of them, the dear unknown, to whom belong
My mother's looks,—perhaps her likeness strong?
Oh, parent! with what reverential awe,
From features of thine own related throng,
An image of thy face my soul could draw!
And see thee once again whom I too shortly saw!"

VIII.

Yet deem not Gertrude sigh'd for foreign joy;
To sooth a father's couch her only care,
And keep his reverend head from all annoy:
For this, methinks, her homeward steps repair,
Soon as the morning wreath had bound her hair;
While yet the wild deer trod in spangling dew,
While boatman caroll'd to the fresh-blown air,
And woods a horizontal shadow threw,
And early fox appear'd in momentary view.

IX.

Apart there was a deep untrodden grot,
Where oft the reading hours sweet Gertrude wore;
Tradition had not named its lonely spot;
But here (methinks) might India's sons explore
Their fathers' dust, or lift, perchance of yore,
Their voice to the great Spirit:—rocks sublime
To human art a sportive semblance bore,
And yellow lichens color'd all the clime,
Like moonlight battlements, and towers decay'd by time.

X.

But high in amphitheatre above,
Gay tinted woods their massy foliage threw:
Breathed but an air of heaven, and all the grove
As if instinct with living spirit grew,

Rolling its verdant gulfs of every hue ;
And now suspended was the pleasing din,
Now from a murmur faint it swell'd anew,
Like the first note of organ heard within
Cathedral aisles,—ere yet its symphony begin.

XI.

It was in tnis lone valley she would charm
The lingering noon, where flowers a couch had strown;
Her cheek reclining, and her snowy arm
On hillock by the pine-tree half o'ergrown :
And aye that volume on her lap is thrown,
Which every heart of human mould endears ;
With Shakspeare's self she speaks and smiles alone,
And no intruding visitation fears,
To shame the unconscious laugh, or stop her sweetest
    tears.

XII.

And naught within the grove was heard or seen
But stock-doves plaining through its gloom profound,
Or winglet of the fairy humming-bird,
Like atoms of the rainbow fluttering round ;
When lo ! there enter'd to its inmost ground
A youth, the stranger of a distant land ;
He was, to weet, for eastern mountains bound ;
But late th' equator suns his cheek had tann'd,
And California's gales his roving bosom fann'd.

XIII.

A steed, whose rein hung loosely o'er his arm,
He led dismounted ; ere his leisure pace,
Amid the brown leaves, could her ear alarm,
Close he had come, and worshipp'd for a space
Those downcast features :—she her lovely face
Uplift on one, whose lineaments and frame
Wore youth and manhood's intermingled grace:
Iberian seemed his boot—his robe the same,
And well the Spanish p'ume his lofty looks became.

XIV.

For Albert's home he sought—her finger fair
Has pointed where the father's mansion stood.
Returning from the copse he soon was there ;
And soon has Gertrude hied from dark green wood ;
Nor joyless, by the converse, understood
Between the man of age and pilgrim young,
That gay congeniality of mood,
And early liking from acquaintance sprung ;
Full fluently conversed their guest in England's tougne

XV.

And well could he his pilgrimage of taste
Unfold,—and much they loved his fervid strain,
While he each fair variety retraced
Of climes, and manners, o'er the eastern main.
Now happy Switzer's hills,—romantic Spain,—
Gay lilied fields of France,—or, more refined,
The soft Ausonia's monumental reign ;
Nor less each rural image he design'd
Than all the city's pomp and home of human kind.

XVI.

Anon some wilder portraiture he draws ;
Of Nature's savage glories he would speak,—
The loneliness of earth that overawes,—
Where, resting by some tomb of old Cacique,
The lama-driver on Peruvia's peak,
Nor living voice nor motion marks around ;
But storks that to the boundless forest shriek,
Or wild-cane arch high flung o'er gulf profound,
That fluctuates when the storms of El Dorado sound.

XVII.

Pleased with his guest, the good man still would ply
Each earnest question, and his converse court ;
But Gertrude, as she eyed him, knew not why
A strange and troubling wonder stopp'd her short.

"In England thou hast been,—and, by report,
An orphan's name (quoth Albert) may'st have known.
Sad tale!—when latest fell our frontier fort,—
One innocent—one soldier's child—alone
Was spared, and brought to me, who loved him as my
    own.

XVIII.

Young Henry Waldegrave! three delightful years
These very walls his infant sports did see,
But most I loved him when his parting tears
Alternately bedew'd my child and me:
His sorest parting, Gertrude, was from thee;
Nor half its grief his little heart could hold;
By kindred he was sent for o'er the sea,
They tore him from us when but twelve years old,
And scarcely for his loss have I been yet consoled!"

XIX.

His face the wanderer hid—but could not hide
A tear, a smile, upon his cheek that dwell;
"And speak! mysterious stranger!" (Gertrude cried)
"It is!—it is!—I knew—I knew him well!
'Tis Waldegrave's self, of Waldegrave come to tell!"
A burst of joy the father's lips declare;
But Gertrude speechless on his bosom fell;
At once his open arms embraced the pair,
Was never group more blest in this wide world of care

XX.

"And will ye pardon then (replied the youth)
Your Waldegrave's feigned name, and false attire:
I durst not in the neighborhood, in truth,
The very fortunes of your house inquire;
Lest one that knew me might some tidings dire
Impart, and I my weakness all betray;
For had I lost my Gertrude and my sire,
I meant but o'er your tombs to weep a day,
Unknown I meant to weep, unknown to pass away.

XXI.

But here ye live, ye bloom,—in each dear face,
The changing hand of time I may not blame;
For there, it hath but shed more reverend grace,
And here, of beauty perfected the frame
And well I know your hearts are still the same—
They could not change—ye look the very way,
As when an orphan first to you I came. ·
And have ye heard of my poor guide, I pray ?
Nay, wherefore weep ye, friends, on such a joyous day !"

XXII.

" And art thou here ? or is it but a dream ?
And wilt thou, Waldegrave, wilt thou leave us more ?"—
" No, never ! thou that yet dost lovelier seem
Than aught on earth—than ev'n thyself of yore—
I will not part thee from thy father's shore ;
But we shall cherish him with mutual arms,
And hand in hand again the path explore,
Which every ray of young remembrance warms,
While thou shalt be my own, with all thy truth and
    charms !"

XXIII.

At morn, as if beneath a galaxy
Of over-arching groves in blossoms white,
Where all was odorous scent and harmony,
And gladness to the heart, nerve, ear, and sight:
There, if, oh, gentle Love ! I read aright
The utterance that seal'd thy sacred bond,
'Twas listening to these accents of delight
She hid upon his breast those eyes, beyond
Expression's power to paint, all languishingly fond—

XXIV.

" Flower of my life, so lovely, and so lone !
Whom I would rather in this desert meet,
Scorning, and scorn'd by fortune's power, than own
Her pomp and splendors lavish'd at my feet !

Turn not from me thy breath, more exquisite
Than odors cast on heaven's own shrine—to please—
Give me thy love, than luxury more sweet,
And more than all the wealth that loads the breeze,
When Coromandel's ships return from Indian seas."

XXV.

Then would that home admit them—happier far
Than grandeur's most magnificent saloon,
While, here and there, a solitary star
Flush'd in the darkening firmament of June ;
And silence brought the soul-felt hour, full soon,
Ineffable, which I may not portray ;
For never did the hymenean moon
A paradise of hearts more sacred sway,
In all that slept beneath her soft voluptuous ray

END OF THE SECOND PART.

PART THE THIRD.

I.

O Love ! in such a wilderness as this,
Where transport and security entwine,
Here is the empire of thy perfect bliss,
And here thou art a god indeed divine.
Here shall no forms abridge, no hours confine,
The views, the walks, that boundless joy inspire !
Roll on, ye days of raptured influence, shine !
Nor, blind with ecstasy's celestial fire,
Shall love behold the spark of earth-born time expire.

II.

Three little moons, how short ! amidst the grove
And pastoral savannas they consume !
While she, beside her buskin'd youth to rove,
Delights, in fancifully wild costume,
Her lovely brow to shade with Indian plume ;
And forth in hunter-seeming vest they fare ;
But not to chase the deer in forest gloom,
'Tis but the breath of heaven—the blessed air—
And interchange of hearts unknown, unseen to share.

III.

What though the sportive dog oft round them note,
Or fawn, or wild bird bursting on the wing ;
Yet who, in love's own presence, would devote
To death those gentle throats that wake the spring,
Or writhing from the brook its victim bring ?

No!—nor let fear one little warbler rouse ;
But, fed by Gertrude's hand, still let them sing,
Acquaintance of her path, amidst the boughs,
That shade ev'n now her love, and witness'd first her
    vows.

IV.

Now labyrinths, which but themselves can pierce,
Methinks, conduct them to some pleasant ground,
Where welcome hills shut out the universe,
And pines their lawny walk encompass round,
There, if a pause delicious converse found, .
'Twas but when o'er each heart th' idea stole,
(Perchance awhile in joy's oblivion drown'd)
That come what may, while life's glad pulses roll,
Indissolubly thus should soul be knit to soul.

V.

And in the visions of romantic youth,
What years of endless bliss are yet to flow !
But mortal pleasure, what art thou in truth?
The torrent's smoothness, ere it dash below !
And must I change my song? and must I show, .
Sweet Wyoming ! the day when thou wert doom'd,
Guiltless, to mourn thy loveliest bowers laid low !
When where of yesterday a garden bloom'd,
Death overspread his pall, and blackening ashes gloom'd .

VI.

Sad was the year, by proud oppression driven,
When Transatlantic Liberty arose,
Not in the sunshine and the smile of heaven,
But wrapt in whirlwinds, and begirt with woes,
Amidst the strife of fratricidal foes ;
Her birth star was the light of burning plains ;[*]
Her baptism is the weight of blood that flows
From kindred hearts—the blood of British veins—
And famine tracks her steps, and pestilential pains.

* Alluding to the miseries that attended the American civil war

VII.

Yet, ere the storm of death had raged remote,
Or siege unseen in heaven reflects its beams,
Who now each dreadful circumstance shall note,
That fills pale Gertrude's thoughts, and nightly dreams!
Dismal to her the forge of battle gleams
Portentous light! and music's voice is dumb;
Save where the fife its shrill reveillé screams,
Or midnight streets re-echo to the drum,
That speaks of maddening strife, and blood-stain'd fields
　　　to come.

VIII.

It was in truth a momentary pang;
Yet how comprising myriad shapes of wo!
First when in Gertrude's ear the summons rang,
A husband to the battle doom'd to go!
" Nay meet not thou (she cries) thy kindred foe!
But peaceful let us seek fair England's strand!"
" Ah, Gertrude, thy beloved heart, I know,
Would feel like mine the stigmatizing brand!
Could I forsake the cause of Freedom's holy band!

IX.

But shame—but flight—a recreant's name to prove,
To h'de in exile ignominious fears;
Say, ev'n if this I brook'd, the public love
Thy father's bosom to his home endears:
And how could I his few remaining years,
My Gertrude, sever from so dear a child?"
So, day by day, her boding heart he cheers.
At last that heart to hope is half beguiled,
And, pale through tears suppress'd, the mournful beauty
　　　smiled.

X.

Night came,—and in their lighted bower, full late,
The joy of converse had endured—when, hark!
Abrupt and loud, a summons shook their gate;
And heedless of the dog's obstrep'rous bark,

A form had rush'd amidst them from the dark,
And spread his arms,—and fell upon the floor:
Of aged strength his limbs retain'd the mark;
But desolate he look'd, and famish'd poor,
As ever shipwreck'd wretch lone left on desert shore.

XI.

Uprisen, each wond'ring brow is knit and arch'd:
A spirit from the dead they deem him first:
To speak he tries; but quivering, pale, and parch'd,
From lips, as by some powerless dream accursed,
Emotions unintelligible burst;
And long his filmed eye is red and dim;
At length the pity-proffer'd cup his thirst
Had half assuaged, and nerved his shuddering limb,
When Albert's hand he grasp'd;—but Albert knew not
    him—

XII.

" And hast thou then forgot," (he cried forlorn,
And eyed the group with half indignant air,)
" Oh! hast thou, Christian chief, forgot the morn
When I with thee the cup of peace did share?
Then stately was this head, and dark this hair,
That now is white as Appalachia's snow;
But, if the weight of fifteen years' despair,
And age hath bow'd me, and the torturing foe,
Bring me my boy—and he will his deliverer know!"—

XIII.

It was not long, with eyes and heart of flame,
Ere Henry to his loved Oneida flew:
" Bless thee, my guide!"—but backward, as he came,
The chief his old bewilder'd head withdrew,
And grasp'd his arm, and look'd and look'd him through
'Twas strange—nor could the group a smile control—
The long, the doubtful scrutiny to view:
At last delight o'er all his features stole,
" It is—my own," he cried, and clasp'd him to his soul

XIV.

"Yes! thou recall'st my pride of years, for then
The bowstring of my spirit was not slack,
When, spite of woods, and floods, and ambush'd men,
I bore thee like the quiver on my back,
Fleet as the whirlwind hurries on the rack ;
Nor foeman then, nor cougar's crouch I fear'd,*
For I was strong as mountain cataract :
And dost thou not remember how we cheer'd,
Upon the last hill-top, when white men's huts appear'd

XV.

Then welcome be my death-song, and my death !
Since I have seen thee, and again embraced."
And longer had he spent his toil-worn breath ;
But with affectionate and eager haste,
Was every arm outstretch'd around their guest,
To welcome and to bless his aged head.
Soon was the hospitable banquet placed ;
And Gertrude's lovely hands a balsam shed
On wounds with fever'd joy that more profusely bled.

XVI.

"But this is not a time,"—he started up,
And smote his breast with wo-denouncing hand—
"This is no time to fill the joyous cup,
The Mammoth comes,—the foe,—the Monster Brandt,—
With all his howling desolating band ;—
These eyes have seen their blade and burning pine
Awake at once, and silence half your land.
Red is the cup they drink ; but not with wine :
Awake, and watch to-night, or see no morning shine !

XVII.

Scorning to wield the hatchet for his bribe,
Gainst Brandt himself I went to battle forth :
Accursed Brandt ! he left of all my tribe
Nor man, nor child, nor thing of living birth :

* Cougar, the American tiger.

No! not the dog that watch'd my household hearth,
Escaped that night of blood, upon our plains!
All perish'd!—I alone am left on earth!
To whom nor relative nor blood remains,
No!—not a kindred drop that runs in human veins.

XVIII.

But go!—and rouse your warriors;—for, if right
These old bewilder'd eyes could guess, by signs
Of striped and starred banners, on yon height
Of eastern cedars, o'er the creek of pines—
Some fort embattled by your country shines:
Deep roars th' innavigable gulf below
Its squared rock, and palisaded lines.
Go! seek the light its warlike beacons show;
Whilst I in ambush wait, for vengeance, and the foe!"

XIX.

Scarce had he utter'd—when Heaven's verge extreme
Reverberates the bomb's descending star,—
And sounds that mingled laugh,—and shout,—and
To freeze the blood, in one discordant jar,   [scream,—
Rung to the pealing thunderbolts of war.
Whoop after whoop with rack the ear assail'd;
As if unearthly fiends had burst their bar;
While rapidly the marksman's shot prevail'd :—
And aye, as if for death, some lonely trumpet wail'd.

XX.

Then look'd they to the hills, where fire o'erhung
The bandit groups, in one Vesuvian glare;
Or swept, far seen, the tower, whose clock unrung
Told legible that midnight of despair.
She faints,—she falters not,—th' heroic fair,—
As he the sword and plume in haste array'd.
One short embrace—he clasp'd his dearest care—
But hark! what nearer war-drum shakes the glade?
Joy, joy! Columbia's friends are trampling through the
    shade!

XXI.

Then came of every race the mingled swarm,
Far rung the groves and gleam'd the midnight grass,
With flambeau, javelin, and naked arm ;
As warriors wheel'd their culverins of brass,
Sprung from the woods, a bold athletic mass,
Whom virtue fires, and liberty combines :
And first the wild Moravian yagers pass,
His plumed host the dark Iberian joins—
And Scotia's sword beneath the Highland thistle shines

XXII.

And in, the buskin'd hunters of the deer,
To Albert's home, with shout and cymbal throng :—
Roused by their warlike pomp, and mirth, and cheer,
Old Outalissi woke his battle song,
And, beating with his war-club cadence strong,
Tells how his deep-stung indignation smarts,
Of them that wrapt his house in flames, ere long,
To whet a dagger on their stony hearts,
And smile avenged ere yet his eagle spirit parts —

XXIII.

Calm, opposite the Christian father rose,
Pale on his venerable brow its rays
Of martyr light the conflagration throws ;
One hand upon his lovely child he lays,
And one th' uncover'd crowd to silence sways ;
While, though the battle flash is faster driven,—
Unawed, with eye unstartled by the blaze,
He for his bleeding country prays to Heaven,—
Prays that the men of blood themselves may be forgiven

XXIV.

Short time is now for gratulating speech :
And yet, beloved Gertrude, ere began
Thy country's flight, yon distant towers to reach,
Look'd not on thee the rudest partisan

With brow relax'd to love ?   And murmurs ran,
As round and round their willing ranks they drew,
From beauty's sight to shield the hostile van.
Grateful, on them a placid look she threw,
Nor wept, but as she bade her mother's grave adieu !

. XXV.

Past was the flight, and welcome seem'd the tower,
That like a giant standard-bearer frown'd
Defiance on the roving Indian power,
Beneath, each bold and promontory mound
With embrasure emboss'd, and armor crown'd,
And arrowy frize, and wedged ravelin,
. Wove like a diadem its tracery round
The lofty summit of that mountain green ;
Here stood secure the group, and eyed a distant scene,—

XXVI.

A scene of death ! where fires beneath the sun,
And blended arms, and white pavilions glow ;
And for the business of destruction done,
Its requiem the war-horn seem'd to blow :
There, sad spectatress of her country's wo !
The lovely Gertrude, safe from present harm,
Had laid her cheek, and clasp'd her hands of snow
On Waldegrave's shoulder, half within his arm
Enclosed, that felt her heart, and hush'd its wild alarm.

XXVII.

But short that contemplation—sad and short
The pause to bid each much-loved scene adieu !
Beneath the very shadow of the fort,
Where friendly swords were drawn, and banners flew ;
Ah ! who could deem that foot of Indian crew
Was near ?—yet there, with lust of murd'rous deeds,
Gleam'd like a basilisk, from woods in view,
The ambush'd foeman's eye—his volley speeds,
And Albert—Albert falls the dear old father bleeds !

XXVIII.

And tranced in giddy horror Gertrude swoon'd ;
Yet, while she clasps him lifeless to her zone,
Say, burst they, borrow'd from her father's wound,
These drops ?—Oh, God ! the life-blood is her own !
And faltering, on her Waldegrave's bosom thrown—
" Weep not, O Love !"—she cries, " to see me bleed—
Thee, Gertrude's sad survivor, thee alone
Heaven's peace commiserate ; for scarce I heed
These wounds ;—yet thee to leave is death, is death
       indeed !

XXIX.

Clasp me a little longer on the brink
Of fate ! while I can feel thy dear caress ;
And when this heart hath ceased to beat—oh ! think,
And let it mitigate thy wo's excess,
That thou hast been to me all tenderness,
And friend to more than human friendship just.
Oh ! by that retrospect of happiness,
And by the hopes of an immortal trust,
God shall assuage thy pangs—when I am laid in dust !

XXX.

Go, Henry, go not back, when I depart,
The scene thy bursting tears too deep will move,
Where my dear father took thee to his heart,
And Gertrude thought it ecstasy to rove
With thee, as with an angel, through the grove
Of peace, imagining her lot was cast
In heaven ; for ours was not like earthly love.
And must this parting be our very last ?
No ! I shall love thee still, when death itself is past.—

XXXI.

Half could I bear, methinks, to leave this earth,—
And thee, more loved than aught beneath the sun,
If I had lived to smile but on the birth
Of one dear pledge ;—but shall there then be none,

In future times—no gentle little one,
To clasp thy neck, and look, resembling me?
Yet seems it, even while life's last pulses run,
A sweetness in the cup of death to be,
Lord of my bosom's love! to die beholding thee!"

XXXII.

Hush'd were his Gertrude's lips! but still their bland
And beautiful expression seem'd to melt
With love that could not die! and still his hand
She presses to the heart no more that felt.
Ah, heart! where once each fond affection dwelt,
And features yet that spoke a soul more fair.
Mute, gazing, agonizing as he knelt,—
Of them that stood encircling his despair,
He heard some friendly words;—but knew not what
    they were.

XXXIII.

For now, to mourn their judge and child, arrives
A faithful band.   With solemn rites between
'Twas sung, how they were lovely in their lives,
And in their deaths had not divided been.
Touch'd by the music, and the melting scene,
Was scarce one tearless eye amidst the crowd:—
Stern warriors, resting on their swords, were seen
To veil their eyes, as pass'd each much-loved shroud—
While woman's softer soul in wo dissolved aloud.

XXXIV.

Then mournfully the parting bugle bid
Its farewell, o'er the grave of worth and truth;
Prone to the dust, afflicted Waldegrave hid
His face on earth;—him watch'd, in gloomy ruth,
His woodland guide: but words had none to sooth
The grief that knew not consolation's name:
Casting his Indian mantle o'er the youth,
He watch'd, beneath its folds, each burst that came
Convulsive, ague-like, across his shuddering frame!

XXXV.

" And I could weep :"—th' Oneida chief
His descant wildly thus begun :
" But that I may not stain with grief
The death-song of my father's son,
Or bow this head in wo !
For by my wrongs, and by my wrath !
To-morrow Areouski's breath,
(That fires yon heaven with storms of death,)
Shall light us to the foe :
And we shall share, my Christian boy !
The foeman's blood, the avenger's joy !

XXXVI.

But thee, my flower, whose breath was given
By milder genii o'er the deep,
The spirits of the white man's heaven
Forbid not thee to weep :—
Nor will the Christian host,
Nor will thy father's spirit grieve,
To see thee, on the battle's eve,
Lamenting, take a mournful leave
Of her who loved thee most :
She was the rainbow to thy sight !
Thy sun—thy heaven—of lost delight !

XXXVII.

To-morrow let us do or die !
But when the bolt of death is hurl'd,
Ah ! whither then with thee to fly,
Shall Outalissi roam the world ?
Seek we thy once-loved home ?
The hand is gone that cropp'd its flowers.
Unheard their clock repeats its hours !
Cold is the hearth within their bowers !
And should we thither roam,
Its echoes, and its empty tread,
Would sound like voices from the dead !

XXXVIII.

Or shall we cross yon mountains blue,
Whose streams my kindred nation quaff'd,
And by my side, in battle true,
A thousand warriors drew the shaft?
Ah! there, in desolation cold,
The desert serpent dwells alone,
Where grass o'ergrows each mouldering bone,
And stones themselves to ruin grown,
Like me, are death-like old.
Then seek we not their camp,—for there—
The silence dwells of my despair!

XXXIX.

But hark, the trump!—to-morrow thou
In glory's fires shalt dry thy tears:
Ev'n from the land of shadows now
My father's awful ghost appears,
Amidst the clouds that round us roll;
He bids my soul for battle thirst—
He bids me dry the last—the first—
The only tears that ever burst
From Outalissi's soul;
Because I may not stain with grief
The death-song of an Indian chief!"

LINES

WRITTEN AT THE REQUEST OF THE HIGHLAND SOCIETY IN
LONDON, WHEN MET TO COMMEMORATE THE 21ST
OF MARCH, THE DAY OF VICTORY IN EGYPT.

———

PLEDGE to the much-loved land that gave us birth!
  Invincible romantic Scotia's shore!
Pledge to the memory of her parted worth!
  And first, amidst the brave, remember Moore!

And be it deem'd not wrong that name to give,
  In festive hours, which prompts the patriot's sigh!
Who would not envy such as Moore to live?
  And died he not as heroes wish to die?

Yes, though too soon attaining glory's goal,
  To us his bright career too short was given;
Yet in a mighty cause his phœnix soul
  Rose on the flames of victory to Heaven!

How oft (if beats in subjugated Spain
  One patriot heart) in secret shall it mourn
For him!—How oft on far Corunna's plain
  Shall British exiles weep upon his urn!

Peace to the mighty dead;—our bosom thanks
  In sprightlier strains the living may inspire!
Joy to the chiefs that lead old Scotia's ranks,
  Of Roman garb and more than Roman fire!

Triumphant be the thistle still unfurl'd,
  Dear symbol wild ! on Freedom's hills it grows,
Where Fingal stemm'd the tyrants of the world,
  And Roman eagles found unconquer'd foes.

Joy to the band* this day on Egypt's coast,
  Whose valor tamed proud France's tricolor,
And wrench'd the banner from her bravest host,
  Baptized Invincible in Austria's gore !

Joy for the day on red Vimeira's strand,
  When, bayonet to bayonet opposed,
First of Britannia's host her Highland band
  Gave but the death-shot once, and foremost closed !

Is there a son of generous England here
  Or fervid Erin ?—he with us shall join,
To pray that in eternal union dear,
  The rose, the shamrock, and the thistle twine !

Types of a race who shall th' invader scorn,
  As rocks resist the billows round their shore ;
Types of a race who shall to time unborn
  Their country leave unconquer'd as of yore !

* The 42d regiment.

STANZAS

TO THE MEMORY OF THE SPANISH PATRIOTS LATEST
KILLED IN RESISTING THE REGENCY AND
THE DUKE OF ANGOULEME

BRAVE men who at the Trocadero fell—
Beside your cannons conquer'd not, though slain,
There is a victory in dying well
For Freedom,—and ye have not died in vain ;
For come what may, there shall be hearts in Spain
To honor, ay embrace your martyr'd lot,
Cursing the Bigot's and the Bourbon's chain,
And looking on your graves, though trophied not,
As holier hallow'd ground than priests could make the
    spot !

What though your case be baffled—freemen cast
In dungeons—dragg'd to death, or forced to flee ;
Hope is not wither'd in affliction's blast—
The patriot's blood 's the seed of Freedom's tree ;
And short your orgies of revenge shall be,
Cowl'd Demons of the Inquisitorial cell !
Earth shudders at your victory,—for ye
Are worse than common fiends from Heaven that fell,
The baser, ranker sprung, *Autochthones* of Hell !

Go to your bloody rites again—bring back
The hall of horrors and the assessor's pen,
Recording answers shriek'd upon the rack ;
Smile o'er the gaspings of spine-broken men ;—
Preach, perpetrate damnation in your den ;—

Then let your altars, ye blasphemers! peal
With thanks to Heaven, that let you loose again,
To practise deeds with torturing fire and steel
No eye may search—no tongue may challenge or reveal

Yet laugh not in your carnival of crime
Too proudly, ye oppressors!—Spain was free,
Her soil has felt the foot-prints, and her clime
Been winnow'd by the wings of Liberty ;
And these even parting scatter as they flee
Thoughts—influences, to live in hearts unborn,
Opinions that shall wrench the prison-key
From Persecution—show her mask off-torn,
And tramp her bloated head beneath the foot of Scorn

Glory to them that die in this great cause ;
Kings, Bigots, can inflict no brand of shame,
Or shape of death, to shroud them from applause :—
No !—manglers of the martyr's earthly frame !
Your hangmen fingers cannot touch his fame.
Still in your prostrate land there shall be some
Proud hearts, the shrines of Freedom's vestal flame.
Long trains of ill may pass unheeded, dumb,
But vengeance is behind, and justice is to come.

--------◆--------

SONG OF THE GREEKS

Again to the battle, Achaians !
Our hearts bid the tyrants defiance ;
Our land, the first garden of Liberty's tree—
It has been, and shall yet be, the land of the free :
For the cross of our faith is replanted,
The pale dying crescent is daunted,

And we march that the foot-prints of Mahomet's slaves
May be wash'd out in blood from our forefathers' graves
Their spirits are hovering o'er us,
And the sword shall to glory restore us.

Ah! what though no succor advances,
Nor Christendom's chivalrous lances
Are stretch'd in our aid—be the combat our own!
And we'll perish or conquer more proudly alone ;
For we've sworn by our Country's assaulters,
By the virgins they dragg'd from our altars,
By our massacred patriots, our children in chains,
By our heroes of old, and their blood in our veins,
That, living, we shall be victorious,
Or that, dying, our deaths shall be glorious.

A breath of submission we breathe not ;
The sword that we've drawn we will sheath not !
Its scabbard is left where our martyrs are laid,
And the vengeance of ages has whetted its blade.
Earth may hide—waves ingulf—fire consume us,
But they shall not to slavery doom us :
If they rule, it shall be o'er our ashes and graves ;
But we've smote them already with fire on the waves,
And new triumphs on land are before us,
To the charge !—Heaven's banner is o'er us.

This day shall ye blush for its story,
Or brighten your lives with its glory.
Our women, oh, say, shall they shriek in despair,
Or embrace us from conquest with wreaths in their hair ?
Accursed may his memory blacken,
If a coward there be that would slacken
Till we've trampled the turban, and shown ourselves
    worth
Being sprung from and named for the godlike of earth.
Strike home, and the world shall revere us
As heroes descended from heroes.

Old Greece lightens up with emotion
Her inlands, her isles of the Ocean ;
Fanes rebuilt and fair towns shall with jubilee ring,
And the Nine shall new-hallow their Helicon's spring :
Our hearths shall be kindled in gladness,
That were cold and extinguish'd in sadness ;
Whilst our maidens shall dance with their white-waving
    arms,
Singing joy to the brave that deliver'd their charms,
When the blood of yon Mussulman cravens,
Shall have purpled the beaks of our ravens.

ODE TO WINTER.

When first the fiery-mantled sun
His heavenly race began to run ;
Round the earth and ocean blue,
His children four the Seasons flew.
First, in green apparel dancing,
    The young Spring smiled with angel grace ;
Rosy Summer next advancing,
    Rush'd into her sire's embrace :—
Her bright-hair'd sire, who bade her keep
    Forever nearest to his smiles,
On Calpe's olive-shaded steep,
    On India's citron-cover'd isles :
More remote and buxom-brown,
    The Queen of vintage bow'd before his throne
A rich pomegranate gemm'd her crown,
    A ripe sheaf bound her zone.
But howling Winter fled afar,
To hills that prop the polar star,

And loves on deer-borne car to ride
With barren Darkness by his side,
Round the shore where loud Lofoden
   Whirls to death the roaring whale,
Round the hall where Runic Odin
   Howls his war-song to the gale ;
Save when adown the ravaged globe
   He travels on his native storm,
Deflowering Nature's grassy robe,
   And trampling on her faded form :—·
Till light's returning lord assume
   The shaft that drives him to his polar field,
Of power to pierce his raven plume
   And crystal-cover'd shield.

Oh, sire of storms ! whose savage ear
The Lapland drum delights to hear,
When Phrensy with her blood-shot eye
Implores thy dreadful deity,
Archangel ! power of desolation !
   Fast descending as thou art,
Say, hath mortal invocation
   Spells to touch thy stony heart?
Then sullen Winter, hear my prayer,
And gently rule the ruin'd year ;
Nor chill the wanderer's bosom bare,
Nor freeze the wretch's falling tear ;—
To shuddering Want's unmantled bed
Thy horror-breathing agues cease to lead,
And gently on the orphan head
Of innocence descend.—

But chiefly spare, O king of clouds !
The sailor on his airy shrouds ;
When wrecks and beacons strew the steep,
And spectres walk along the deep.
Milder yet thy snowy breezes
   Pour on yonder tented shores,
Where the Rhine's broad billow freezes,

Or the dark-brown Danube roars.
Oh, winds of Winter! list ye there
  To many a deep and dying groan ;
Or start, ye demons of the midnight air,
  At shrieks and thunders louder than your own.
Alas ! ev'n your unhallow'd breath·
  May spare the victim fallen low ;
But man will ask no truce to death,—
  No bounds to humau wo.*

LINES

SPOKEN BY MRS. BARTLEY AT DRURY-LANE THEATRE, ON
THE FIRST OPENING OF THE HOUSE AFTER THE
DEATH OF THE PRINCESS CHARLOTTE, 1817.

BRITONS ! although our task is but to show
The scenes and passions of fictitious wo,
Think not we come this night without a part
In that deep sorrow of the public heart,
Which like a shade hath darken'd every place,
And moisten'd with a tear the manliest face !
The bell is scarcely hush'd in Windsor's piles,
That toll'd a requiem from the solemn aisles,
For her, the royal flower, low laid in dust,
That was your fairest hope, your fondest trust.
Unconscious of the doom, we dreamt, alas !
That ev'n these walls, ere many months should pass,

* This ode was written in Germany, at the close of 1800, before the conclusion of hostilities.

Which but return sad accents for her now,
Perhaps had witness'd her benignant brow,
Cheer'd by the voice you would have raised on high,
In bursts of British love and loyalty.
But, Britain! now thy chief, thy people mourn,
And Claremont's home of love is left forlorn:—
There, where the happiest of the happy dwelt,
The 'scutcheon glooms, and royalty hath felt
A wound that every bosom feels its own,—
The blessing of a father's heart o'erthrown—
The most beloved and most devoted bride
Torn from an agonized husband's side,
Who " long as Memory holds her seat" shall view
That speechless, more than spoken last adieu,
When the fix'd eye long look'd connubial faith,
And beam'd affection in the trance of death.
Sad was the pomp that yesternight beheld,
As with the mourner's heart the anthem swell'd ;
While torch succeeding torch illumed each high
And banner'd arch of England's chivalry.
The rich plumed canopy, the gorgeous pall,
The sacred march, and sable-vested wall,—
These were not rites of inexpressive show,
But hallow'd as the types of real wo !
Daughter of England ! for a nation's sighs,
A nation's heart went with thine obsequies !—
And oft shall time revert a look of grief
On thine existence, beautiful and brief.
Fair spirit ! send thy blessing from above
On realms where thou art canonized by love !
Give to a father's, husband's bleeding mind,
The peace that angels lend to human kind ;
To us who in thy loved remembrance feel
A sorrowing, but a soul-ennobling zeal—
A loyalty that touches all the best
And loftiest principles of England's breast !   .
Still may thy name speak concord from the tomb—
Still in the Muse's breath thy memory bloom !

They shall describe thy life—thy form portray ;
But all the love that mourns thee swept away,
'Tis not in language or expressive arts
To paint—ye feel it, Britons. in your hearts!　　•

LINES ON THE GRAVE OF A SUICIDE.

By strangers left upon a lonely shore,
　　Unknown, unhonor'd, was the friendless dead
For child to weep, or widow to deplore,
　　There never came to his unburied head :—
　　All from his dreary habitation fled.
Nor will the lantern'd fisherman at eve
　　Launch on that water by the witches' tower,
Where hellebore and hemlock seem to weave
　　Round its dark vaults a melancholy bower
　　For spirits of the dead at night's enchanted hour.

They dread to meet thee, poor unfortunate!
　　Whose crime it was, on Life's unfinish'd road,
To feel the step-dame buffetings of fate,
　• And render back thy being's heavy load.
　　Ah! once, perhaps, the social passions glow'd
In thy devoted bosom—and the hand
　　That smote its kindred heart, might yet be prone
To deeds of mercy.　Who may understand
　　Thy many woes, poor suicide, unknown?—
　　He who thy being gave shall judge of thee alone.

REULLURA *

Star of the morn and eve,
  Reullura shone like thee,
And well for her might Aodh grieve,
  The dark-attired Culdee.
Peace to their shades! the pure Culdee
  Were Albyn's earliest priests of God,
Ere yet an island of her seas
  By foot of Saxon monk was trod,
Long ere her churchmen by bigotry
Were barr'd from wedlock's holy tie.
'Twas then that Aodh, famed afar,
  In Iona preach'd the word with power,
And Reullura, beauty's star,
  Was the partner of his bower.

But, Aodh, the roof lies low,
  And the thistle-down waves bleaching,
And the bat flits to and fro
  Where the Gaël once heard thy preaching;
And fallen is each column'd aisle
  Where the chiefs and the people knelt.
'Twas near that temple's goodly pile
  That honor'd of men they dwelt.
For Aodh was wise in the sacred law,
And bright Reullura's eyes oft saw
  The veil of fate uplifted.
Alas, with what visions of awe
  Her soul in that hour was gifted—
When pale in the temple and faint,

* Reullura, in Gaëlic, signifies "beautiful star."

With Aodh she stood alone
By the statue of an aged Saint!
   Fair sculptured was the stone,
It bore a crucifix;
   Fame said it once had graced
A Christian temple, which the Picts
   In the Britons' land laid waste:
The Pictish men, by St. Columb taught,
Had hither the holy relic brought.
Reullura eyed the statue's face,
   And cried, " It is, he shall come,
Even he, in this very place,
   To avenge my martyrdom.

For, wo to the Gaël people!
   Ulvfagre is on the main,
And Iona shall look from tower and steeple
   On the coming ships of the Dane;
And, dames and daughters, shall all your locks
   With the spoiler's grasp entwine?
No! some shall have shelter in caves and rocks,
   And the deep sea shall be mine.
Baffled by me shall the Dane return,
And here shall his torch in the temple burn,
Until that holy man shall plough
   The waves from Innisfail.
His sail is on the deep e'en now,
   And swells to the southern gale."

" Ah! knowest thou not, my bride,"
   The holy Aodh said,
" That the Saint whose form we stand beside
   Has for ages slept with the dead?"
" He liveth, he liveth," she said again,
   " For the span of his life tenfold extends
Beyond the wonted years of men.
   He sits by the graves of well-loved friends
That died ere thy grandsire's grandsire's birth;

The oak is decay'd with age on earth,
Whose acorn-seed had been planted by him;
  And his parents remember the day of dread
When the sun on the cross look'd dim,
  And the graves gave up their dead.
Yet preaching from clime to clime,
  He hath roam'd the earth for ages,
And hither he shall come in time
  When the wrath of the heathen rages,
In time a remnant from the sword—
  Ah! but a remnant to deliver;
Yet, blest be the name of the Lord!
  His martyrs shall go into bliss forever.
Lochlin,* appall'd, shall put up her steel,
And thou shalt embark on the bounding keel;
Safe shalt thou pass through her hundred ships,
  With the Saint and a remnant of the Gaël,
And the Lord will instruct thy lips
  To preach in Innisfail."†

The sun, now about to set,
  Was burning o'er Tiree,
And no gathering cry rose yet
  O'er the isles of Albyn's sea,
Whilst Reullura saw far rowers dip
  Their oars beneath the sun,
And the phantom of many a Danish ship,
  Where ship there yet was none.
And the shield of alarm was dumb,
Nor did their warning till midnight come,
When watch-fires burst from across the main
  From Rona, and Uist, and Skye,
To tell that the ships of the Dane
  And the red-hair'd slayers were nigh.

Our islemen arose from slumbers,
  And buckled on their arms;

    * Denmark.   † Ireland.

But few, alas! were their numbers
  In Lochlin's mailed swarms.
And the blade of the bloody Norse
  Has fill'd the shores of the Gaël
With many a floating corse,
  And with many a woman's wail.
They have lighted the islands with ruin's torch,
And the holy men of Iona's church
In the temple of God lay slain ;
  All but Aodh, the last Culdee,
But bound with many an iron chain,
  Bound in that church was he.
And where is Aodh's bride?
  Rocks of the ocean flood !
Plunged she not from your heights in pride,
  And mock'd the men of blood ?
Then Ulvfagre and his bands
  In the temple lighted their banquet up,
And the print of their blood-red hands
  Was left on the altar cup.
'Twas then that the Norseman to Aodh said,
" Tell where thy church's treasure's laid,
Or I'll hew thee limb from limb."
  As he spoke the bell struck three,
And every torch grew dim
  That lighted their revelry.

But the torches again burnt bright,
  And brighter than before,
When an aged man of majestic height
  Enter'd the temple door.
Hush'd was the revellers' sound,.
  They were struck as mute as the dead,
And their hearts were appall'd by the very sound
  Of his footsteps' measured tread.
Nor word was spoken by one beholder,
While he flung his white robe back o'er his shoul-
  der,

And stretching his arms—as eath
  Unriveted Aodh's bands,
As if the gyves had been a wreath
  Of willows in his hands.

All saw the stranger's similitude
  To the ancient statue's form ;
The Saint before his own image stood,
  And grasp'd Ulvfagre's arm.
Then uprose the Danes at last to deliver
  Their chief, and shouting with one accord,
They drew the shaft from its rattling quiver,
  They lifted the spear and sword,
And levell'd their spears in rows.
But down went axes and spears and bows,
When the Saint with his crosier sign'd,
  The archer's hand on the string was stopp'd,
And down, like reeds laid flat by the wind,
  Their lifted weapons dropp'd.
The Saint then gave a signal mute,
  And though Ulvfagre will'd it not,
He came and stood at the statue's foot,
  Spell-riveted to the spot,
Till hands invisible shook the wall,
  And the tottering image was dash'd
Down from its lofty pedestal.
  On Ulvfagre's helm it crash'd—
Helmet, and skull, and flesh, and brain,
It crush'd as millstones crush the grain.
Then spoke the Saint, whilst all and each
  Of the Heathen trembled round,
And the pauses amidst his speech
  Were as awful as the sound :

" Go back, ye wolves, tc your dens," (he cried,)
  " And tell the nations abroad,
How the fiercest of your herd has died
  That slaughter'd the flock of God.

Gather him bone by bone,
  And take with you o'er the flood
The fragments of that avenging stone
  That drank his heathen blood.
These are the spoils from Iona's sack,
  The only spoils ye shall carry back;
For the hand that uplifteth spear or sword
  Shall be wither'd by palsy's shock,
And I come in the name of the Lord
  To deliver a remnant of his flock."

A remnant was call'd together,
  A doleful remnant of the Gaël,
And the Saint in the ship that had brought him
        hither
  Took the mourners to Innisfail.
Unscathed they left Iona's strand,
  When the opal morn first flush'd the sky,
For the Norse dropp'd spear, and bow, and brand,
  And look'd on them silently;
Safe from their hiding-places came
Orphans and mothers, child and dame:
But, alas! when the search for Reullura spread,
  No answering voice was given,
For the sea had gone o'er her lovely head,
  And her spirit was in Heaven

THE TURKISH LADY.

'Twas the hour when rites unholy
  Call'd each Paynim voice to prayer,
And the star that faded slowly
  Left to dews the freshen'd air

Day her sultry fires had wasted,
    Calm and sweet the moonlight rose;
Ev'n a captive spirit tasted
    Half oblivion of his woes.

Then 'twas from an Emir's palace
    Came an Eastern lady bright:
She, in spite of tyrants jealous,
    Saw and loved an English knight,

" Tell me, captive, why in anguish
    Foes have dragg'd thee here to dwell,
Where poor Christians as they languish
    Hear no sound of Sabbath bell ?"—

" 'Twas on Transylvania's Bannat,
    When the Crescent shone afar,
Like a pale disastrous planet
    O'er the purple tide of war- -

In that day of desolation,
    Lady, I was captive made ;
Bleeding for my Christian nation
    By the walls of high Belgrade."

" Captive ! could the brightest jewel
    From my turban set thee free ?"
" Lady, no !—the gift were cruel,
    Ransom'd, yet if reft of thee.

Say, fair princess ! would it grieve thee
    Christian climes should we behold ?"—
" Nay, bold knight ! I would not leave thee
    Were thy ransom paid in gold !"

Now in Heaven's blue expansion
    Rose the midnight star to view,

When to quit her father's mansion
Thrice she wept, and bade adieu!

" Fly we then, while none discover!
    Tyrant barks, in vain ye ride!"—
Soon at Rhodes the British lover
    Clasp'd his blooming Eastern bride.

THE BRAVE ROLAND.

THE brave Roland!—the brave Roland!—
False tidings reach'd the Rhenish strand
    That he had fallen in fight;
And thy faithful bosom swoon'd with pain,
O loveliest maiden of Allémayne!
    For the loss of thine own true knight.

But why so rash has she ta'en the veil,
In yon Nonnenwerder's cloisters pale?
    For her vow had scarce been sworn,
And the fatal mantle o'er her flung,
When the Drachenfels to a trumpet rung—
    'Twas her own dear warrior's horn!

Wo! wo! each heart shall bleed—shall break!
She would have hung upon his neck,
    Had he come but yester-even;
And he had clasp'd those peerless charms
That shall never, never fill his arms,
    Or meet him but in heaven.

Yet Roland the brave—Roland the true—
He could not bid that spot adieu;
17

It was dear still 'midst his woes;
For he loved to breathe the neighboring air,
And to think she bless'd him in her prayer,
    When the Halleluiah rose.

There's yet one window of that pile,
Which he built above the Nun's green isle;
    Thence sad and oft look'd he
(When the chant and organ sounded slow)
On the mansion of his love below,
    For herself he might not see.

She died!—He sought the battle-plain;
Her image fill'd his dying brain,
    When he fell and wish'd to fall:
And her name was in his latest sigh,
When Roland, the flower of chivalry,
    Expired at Roncevall.

THE SPECTRE BOAT.

A BALLAD.

LIGHT rued false Ferdinand to leave a lovely maid for,
    lorn,
Who broke her heart and died to hide her blushing
    cheek from scorn.
One night he dreamt he woo'd her in their wonted
    bower of love,
Where the flowers sprang thick around them, and the
    birds sang sweet above.

But the scene was swiftly changed into a churchyard's
dismal view,
And her lips grew black beneath his kiss, from love's
delicious hue.
What more he dreamt, he told to none; but shuddering,
pale, and dumb,
Look'd out upon the waves, like one that knew his
hour was come.

'Twas now the dead watch of the night—the helm was
lash'd a-lee,
And the ship rode where Mount Ætna lights the deep
Levantine sea;
When beneath its glare a boat came, row'd by a woman
in her shroud,
Who, with eyes that made our blood run cold, stood up
and spoke aloud :—

" Come, Traitor, down, for whom my ghost still wanders unforgiven !.
Come down, false Ferdinand, for whom I broke my
peace with heaven !"
It was vain to hold the victim, for he plunged to meet
her call,
Like the bird that shrieks and flutters in the gazing
serpent's thrall. .

You may guess the boldest mariner shrunk daunted
from the sight,
For the Spectre and her winding-sheet shone blue with
hideous light ;
Like a fiery wheel the boat spun with the waving of
her hand,
And round they went, and down they went, as the
cock crew from the land

—

Oh, how hard it is to find
The one just suited to our mind;
  And if that one should be
False, unkind, or found too late,
What can we do but sigh at fate,
  And sing Wo's me—Wo's me!

Love's a boundless burning waste,
Where Bliss's stream we seldom taste,
  And still more seldom flee
Suspense's thorns, Suspicion's stings;
Yet somehow Love a something brings
  That's sweet—ev'n when we sigh ' Wo's me!'

———◆———

THE LOVER TO HIS MISTRESS

ON HER BIRTH-DAY.

If any white-wing'd Power above
  My joys and griefs survey,
The day when thou wert born, my love—
  He surely bless'd that day.

I laugh'd (till taught by thee) when told
  Of Beauty's magic powers,
That ripen'd life's dull ore to gold,
  And changed its weeds to flowers.

My mind had lovely shapes portray'd ;
  But thought I earth had one
Could make even Fancy's visions fade
  Like stars before the sun ?

I gazed, and felt upon my lips
  The unfinish'd accents hang :
One moment's bliss, one burning kiss
  To rapture changed each pang.

And though as swift as lightning's flash
  Those tranced moments flew,
Not all the waves of time shall wash
  Their memory from my view.

But duly shall my raptured song,
  And gladly shall my eyes
Still bless this day's return, as long
  As thou shalt see it rise.

ADELGITHA.

The ordeal's fatal trumpet sounded,
  And sad pale Adelgitha came,
When forth a valiant champion bounded,
  And slew the slanderer of her fame.

She wept, deliver'd from her danger ;
  But when he knelt to claim her glove—
" Seek not," she cried, " oh ! gallant stranger,
  For hapless Adelgitha's love.

" For he is in a foreign far land
    Whose arm should now have set me free ;
And I must wear the willow garland
    For him that's dead, or false to me."

" Nay ! say not that his faith is tainted !"—
    He raised his visor—At the sight
She fell into his arms and fainted ;
    It was indeed her own true knight !

----◆----

LINES

ON RECEIVING A SEAL WITH THE CAMPBELL CREST, FROM
K. M—, BEFORE HER MARRIAGE.

THIS wax returns not back more fair
    Th' impression of the gift you send,
Than stamp'd upon my thoughts I bear
    The image of your worth, my friend !—

We are not friends of yesterday ;—
    But poets' fancies are a little
Disposed to heat and cool, (they say,)—
    By turns impressible and brittle.

Well ! should its frailty e'er condemn
    My heart to prize or please you less,
Your type is still the sealing gem,
    And *mine* the waxen brittleness.

What transcripts of my weal and wo
    This little signet yet may lock,—
What utterances to friend or foe,
    In reason's calm or passion's shock !

What scenes of life's yet curtain'd page
  May own its confidential die,
Whose stamp awaits th' unwritten page,
  And feelings of futurity!—

Yet wheresoe'er my pen I lift
  To date the epistolary sheet,
The blest occasion of the gift
  Shall make its recollection sweet;

Sent when the star that rules your fates
  Hath reach'd its influence most benign—
When every heart congratulates,
  And none more cordially than mine.

So speed my song—mark'd with the crest
  That erst the advent'rous Norman wore,
Who won the Lady of the West,
  The daughter of Macaillan Mor.

Crest of my sires! whose blood it seal'd
  With glory in the strife of swords,
Ne'er may the scroll that bears it yield
  Degenerate thoughts or faithless words!

Yet little might I prize the stone,
  If it but typed the feudal tree
From whence, a scatter'd leaf, I'm blown
  In Fortune's mutability.

No!—but it tells me of a heart
  Allied by friendship's living tie;
A prize beyond the herald's art—
  Our soul-sprung consanguinity!

KATH'RINE! to many an hour of mine
  Light wings and sunshine you have lent;
And so adieu, and still be thine
  The all-in-all of life—Content

THE DIRGE OF WALLACE.

THEY lighted a taper at the dead of night,
   And chanted their holiest hymn ;
But her brow and her bosom were damp with affright—
   Her eye was all sleepless and dim !
And the lady of Elderslie wept for her lord,
   .When a death-watch beat in her lonely room,
When her curtain had shook of its own accord,
And the raven had flapp'd at her window-board—
   To tell of her warrior's doom.

" Now, sing ye the death-song and loudly pray
   For the soul of my knight so dear ;
And call me a widow this wretched day,
   Since the warning of God is here.
For a nightmare rides on my strangled sleep :—
   The lord of my bosom is doom'd to die ;
His valorous heart they have wounded deep ;
And the blood-red tears shall his country weep
   For Wallace of Elderslie !"

Yet knew not his country that ominous hour,
   Ere the loud matin bell was rung, ·
That a trumpet of death on an English tower
   Had the dirge of her champion sung !
When his dungeon light look'd dim and red
   On the high-born blood of a martyr slain,
No anthem was sung at his holy death-bed ;
No weeping there was when his bosom bled—
   And his heart was rent in twain !

Oh, it was not thus when his oaken spear
  Was true to that knight forlorn,
And hosts of a thousand were scatter'd, like deer
  At the blast of the hunter's horn ;
When he strode on the wreck of each well-fought field
  With the yellow-hair'd chiefs of his native land ;
For his lance was not shiver'd on helmet or shield—
And the sword that seem'd fit for Archangel to wield
  Was light in his terrible hand !

Yet bleeding aud bound, though the Wallace wight
  For his long-loved country die,
The bugle ne'er sung to a braver knight
  Than William of Elderslie !
But the day of his glory shall never depart ;
  His head unentomb'd shall with glory be palm'd :
From its blood streaming altur his spirit shall start ;
Tho' the raven has fed on his mouldering heart,
  A nobler was never embalm'd !

CHAUCER AND WINDSOR.

Long shalt thou flourish, Windsor ! bodying forth
Chivalric times, and long shall live around
Thy Castle—the old oaks of British birth,
Whose gnarled roots, tenacious and profound,
As with a lion's talons grasp the ground.
But should thy towers in ivied ruin rot,
There's one, thine inmate once, whose strain renown'd
Would interdict thy name to be forgot ;
For Chaucer loved thy bow'rs and trode this very spot.

Chaucer! our Helicon's first fountain-stream,
Our morning star of song—that led the way
To welcome the long-after coming beam
Of Spenser's light and Shakspeare's perfect day.
Old England's fathers live in Chaucer's lay,
As if they ne'er had died. He group'd and drew
Their likeness with a spirit of life so gay,
That still they live and breathe in Fancy's view,
Fresh beings fraught with truth's imperishable hue.

GILDEROY.

The last, the fatal hour is come,
 That bears my love from me:
I hear the dead note of the drum,
 I mark the gallows' tree!

The bell has toll'd; it shakes my heart;
 The trumpet speaks thy name;
And must my Gilderoy depart
 To bear a death of shame?

No bosom trembles for thy doom;
 No mourner wipes a tear;
The gallows' foot is all thy tomb,
 The sledge is all thy bier.

Oh, Gilderoy! bethought we then
 So soon, so sad to part,
When first in Roslin's lovely glen
 You triumph'd o'er my heart?

Your locks they glitter'd to the sheen,
  Your hunter garb was trim ;
And graceful was the riband green
  That bound your manly limb !

Ah ! little thought I to deplore
  Those limbs in fetters bound ;
Or hear, upon the scaffold floor,
  The midnight hammer sound.

Ye cruel, cruel, that combined
  The guiltless to pursue ;
My Gilderoy was ever kind,
  He could not injure you !

A long adieu ! but where shall fly
  Thy widow all forlorn,
When every mean and cruel eye
  Regards my wo with scorn ?

Yes ! they will mock thy widow's tears,
  And hate thine orphan boy ;
Alas ! his infant beauty wears
  The form of Gilderoy.

Then will I seek the dreary mound
  That wraps thy mouldering clay,
And weep and linger on the ground,
  And sigh my heart away.

STANZAS

ON THE THREATENED INVASION

1803.

———

Our bosoms we'll bare for the glorious strife,
  And our oath is recorded on high,
To prevail in the cause that is dearer than life,
  Or crush'd in its ruins to die !
Then rise, fellow freemen, and stretch the right hand,
And swear to prevail in your dear native land !

'Tis the home we hold sacred is laid to our trust—
  God bless the green Isle of the brave !
Should a conqueror tread on our forefathers' dust,
  It would rouse the old dead from their grave !
Then rise, fellow freemen, and stretch the right hand,
And swear to prevail in your dear native land !

In a Briton's sweet home shall a spoiler abide,
  Profaning its loves and its charms ?
Shall a Frenchman insult the loved fair at our side ?
  To arms ! oh, my Country, to arms !
Then rise, fellow freemen, and stretch the right hand
And swear to prevail in your dear native land !

Shall a tyrant enslave us, my countrymen !—No !
  His head to the sword shall be given—
A death-bed repentance be taught the proud foe,
  And his blood be an offering to Heaven !
Then rise, fellow freemen, and stretch the right hand,
And swear to prevail in your dear native land !

THE RITTER BANN

The Ritter Bann from Hungary
　Came back, renown'd in arms,
But scorning jousts of chivalry,
　And love and ladies' charms.

While other knights held revels, he
　Was wrapp'd in thoughts of gloom,
And in Vienna's hostelrie
　Slow paced his lonely room.

There enter'd one whose face he knew,—
　Whose voice, he was aware,
He oft at mass had listen'd to,
　In the holy house of prayer.

'T was the Abbot of St. James's monks,
　A fresh and fair old man :
His reverend air arrested even
　The gloomy Ritter Bann.

But seeing with him an ancient dame
　Come clad in Scotch attire,
The Ritter's color went and came,
　And loud he spoke in ire.

" Ha ! nurse of her that was my bane,
　Name not her name to me ;
I wish it blotted from my brain :
　Art poor ?—take alms, and flee."

18

" Sir Knight," the abbot interposed,
  " This case your ear demands ;"
And the crone cried, with a cross enclosed
  In both her trembling hands :

" Remember, each his sentence waits ;
  And he that shall rebut
Sweet Mercy's suit, on him the gates
  Of Mercy shall be shut.

You wedded undispensed by Church
  Your cousin Jane in Spring ;—
In Autumn, when you went to search
  For churchmen's pardoning,

Her house denounced your marriage-band,
  Betroth'd her to De Grey,
And the ring you put upon her hand
  Was wrench'd by force away.

Then wept your Jane upon my neck,
  Crying, ' Help me, nurse, to flee
To my Howel Bann's Glamorgan hills ;'
  But word arrived—ah me !—

You were not there ; and 'twas their threat,
  By foul means or by fair,
To-morrow morning was to set
  The seal on her despair.

1 had a son, a sea-boy, in
  A ship at Hartland Bay ;
By his aid from her cruel kin
  I bore my bird away.

To Scotland from the Devon's
  Green myrtle shores we fled ;
And the Hand that sent the ravens
  To Elijah, gave us bread.

She wrote you by my son, but he
   From England sent us word
You had gone into some far countrie,
   In grief and gloom he heard.

For they that wrong'd you, to elude
   Your wrath, defamed my child ;
And you—ay, blush, Sir, as you should—
   Believed, and were beguiled.

To die but at your feet, she vow'd
   To roam the world ; and we
Would both have sped and begg'd our bread,
   But so it might not be.

For when the snow-storm beat our roof,
   She bore a boy, Sir Bann,
Who grew as fair your likeness proof
   As child e'er grew like man.

'Twas smiling on that babe one morn
   While heath bloom'd on the moor,
Her beauty struck young Lord Kinghorn
   As he hunted past our door.

She shunn'd him, but he raved of Jane,
   And roused his mother's pride :
Who came to us in high disdain,—
   ' And where's the face,' she cried,

' Has witch'd my boy to wish for one
   So wretched for his wife ?—
Dost love thy husband ?   Know, my son
   Has sworn to seek his life.'

Her anger sore dismay'd us,
   For our mite was wearing scant,
And, unless that dame would aid us,
   There was none to aid our want.

So I told her, weeping bitterly,
   What all our woes had been ;
And, though she was a stern ladie,
   The tears stood in her een.

And she housèd us both, when, cheerfully,
   My child to her had sworn,
That even if made a widow, she
   Would never wed Kinghorn."——

Here paused the nurse, and then began
   The abbot, standing by :—
" Three months ago a wounded man
   To our abbey came to die.

He heard me long, with ghastly eyes
   And hand obdurate clench'd,
Speak of the worm that never dies,
   And the fire that is not quench'd.

At last by what this scroll attests
   He left atonement brief,
For years of anguish to the breasts
   His guilt had wrung with grief.

' There lived,' he said, ' a fair young dame
   Beneath my mother's roof ;
I loved her, but against my flame
   Her purity was proof.

I feign'd repentance, friendship pure ;
   That mood she did not check,
But let her husband's miniature
   Be copied from her neck,

As means to search him • my deceit
   Took care to him was borne
Naught but his picture's counterfeit,
   And Jane's reported scorn.

The treachery took : she waited wild ;
  My slave came back and lied
Whate'er I wish'd ; she clasp'd her child,
  And swoon'd, and all but died.

I felt her tears for years and years
  Quench not my flame, but stir ;
The very hate I bore her mate
  Increased my love for her.

Fame told us of his glory, while
  Joy flush'd the face of Jane ;
And while she bless'd his name, her smile
  Struck fire into my brain.

No fears could damp ; I reach'd the camp,
  Sought out its champion ;
And if my broad-sword fail'd at last,
  'Twas long and well laid on.

This wound's my meed, my name's Kinghorn,
  My foe's the Ritter Bann.'——
The wafer to his lips was borne,
  And we shrived the dying man.

He died not till you went to fight
  The Turks at Warradein ;
But I see my tale has changed you pale."—
  The abbot went for wine ;

And brought a little page who pour'd
  It out, and knelt and smiled ;—
The stunn'd knight saw himself restored
  To childhood in his child ;

And stoop'd and caught him to his breast,
  Laugh'd loud and wept anon,
And with a shower of kisses press'd
  The darling little one.

"And where went Jane?"—"To a nunnery,
   Sir—
Look not again so pale—
Kinghorn's old dame grew harsh to her."—
   "And she has ta'en the veil!"—

"Sit down, Sir," said the priest, "I bar
   Rash words."—They sat all three,
And the boy play'd with the knight's broad star,
   As he kept him on his knee.

"Think ere you ask her dwelling-place,"
   The abbot further said;
"Time draws a veil o'er beauty's face
   More deep than cloister's shade.

Grief may have made her what you can
   Scarce love perhaps for life."
"Hush, abbot," cried the Ritter Bann,
   "Or tell me where's my wife."

The priest undid two doors that hid
   The inn's adjacent room,
And there a lovely woman stood,
   Tears bathed her beauty's bloom.

One moment may with bliss repay
   Unnumber'd hours of pain;
Such was the throb and mutual sob
   Of the Knight embracing Jane.

SONG.

"MEN OF ENGLAND."

Men of England! who inherit
  Rights that cost your sires their blood!
Men whose undegenerate spirit
  Has been proved on field and flood:—

By the foes you've fought uncounted,
  By the glorious deeds ye've done,
Trophies captured—breaches mounted,
  Navies conquer'd—kingdoms won!

Yet, remember, England gathers
  Hence but fruitless wreaths of fame,
If the freedom of your fathers
  Glow not in your hearts the same.

What are monuments of bravery,
  Where no public virtues bloom?
What avail in lands of slavery,
  Trophied temples, arch, and tomb?

Pageants!—Let the world revere us
  For our people's rights and laws,
And the breasts of civic heroes
  Bared in Freedom's holy cause.

Yours are Hampden's, Russell's glory,
    Sidney's matchless shade is yours,—
Martyrs in heroic story,
    Worth a hundred Agincourts !

We're the sons of sires that baffled
    Crown'd and mitred tyranny ;—
They defied the field and scaffold
    For their birthrights—so will we.

SONG.

Drink ye to her that each loves best,
    And if you nurse a flame
That's told but to her mutual breast,
    We will not ask her name.

Enough, while memory tranced and glad
    Paints silently the fair,
That each should dream of joys he's had,
    Or yet may hope to share.

Yet far, far hence be jest or boast
    From hallow'd thoughts so dear ;
But drink to her that each loves most,
    As she would love to hear.

THE HARPER.

On the green banks of Shannon, when Sheelah was
    nigh,
No blithe Irish lad was so happy as I ;
No harp like my own could so cheerily play,
And wherever I went was my poor dog Tray.

When at last I was forced from my Sheelah to part,
She said, (while the sorrow was big at her heart,)
Oh ! remember your Sheelah when far, far away:
And be kind, my dear Pat, to our poor dog Tray.

Poor dog ! he was faithful and kind, to be sure,
And he constantly loved me, although I was poor ;
When the sour-looking folks sent me heartless away,
I had always a friend in my poor dog Tray.

When the road was so dark, and the night was so cold
And Pat and his dog were grown weary and old,
How snugly we slept in my old coat of gray,
And he lick'd me for kindness—my poor dog Tray.

Though my wallet was scant, I remember'd his case,
Nor refused my last crust to his pitiful face ;
But he died at my feet on a cold winter day,
And I play'd a sad lament for my poor dog Tray.

Where now shall I go, poor, forsaken, and blind ?
Can I find one to guide me, so faithful, and kind ?
To my sweet native village, so far, far away,
I can never more return with my poor dog Tray.

THE WOUNDED HUSSAR.

Alone to the banks of the dark-rolling Danube
    Fair Adelaide hied when the battle was o'er:—
" Oh whither," she cried, " hast thou wander'd, my
        lover,
    Or here dost thou welter and bleed on the shore?

What voice did I hear? 'twas my Henry that sigh'd!"
    All mournful she hasten'd, nor wander'd she far,
When bleeding, and low, on the heath she descried,
    By the light of the moon, her poor wounded Hussar !

From his bosom that heaved, the last torrent was stream-
        ing,
    And pale was his visage, deep mark'd with a scar!
And dim was that eye, once expressively beaming,
    That melted in love, and that kindled in war !

How smit was poor Adelaide's heart at the sight !
    How bitter she wept o'er the victim of war !
" Hast thou come, my fond Love, this last sorrowful
        night,
    To cheer the lone heart of your wounded Hussar ?"

" Thou shalt live," she replied, " Heaven's mercy re-
        lieving
    Each anguishing wound, shall forbid me to mourn !"—
" Ah, no ! the last pang of my bosom is heaving !
    No light of the morn shall to Henry return !

Thou charmer of life, ever tender and true !
  Ye babes of my love, that await me afar !"—
His faltering tongue scarce could murmur adieu,
  When he sunk in her arms—the poor wounded Hussar.

LOVE AND MADNESS.

AN ELEGY.

WRITTEN IN 1795.

Hark ! from the battlements of yonder tower*
The solemn bell has toll'd the midnight hour !
Roused from drear visions of distemper'd sleep,
Poor B———k wakes—in solitude to weep !

  " Cease, Memory, cease (the friendless mourner cried,
To probe the bosom too severely tried !
Oh ! ever cease, my pensive thoughts, to stray
Through the bright fields of Fortune's better day,
When youthful Hope, the music of the mind,
Tuned all its charms, and E———n was kind !

  Yet, can I cease, while glows this trembling frame,
In sighs to speak thy melancholy name ?
I hear thy spirit wail in every storm !
In midnight shades I view thy passing form !
Pale as in that sad hour when doom'd to feel,
Deep in thy perjured heart, the bloody steel !

* Warwick Castle.

Demons of Vengeance ! ye at whose command
I grasp'd the sword with more than woman's hand,
Say ye, did Pity's trembling voice control,
Or horror damp the purpose of my soul ?
No ! my wild heart sat smiling o'er the plan,
Till Hate fulfill'd what baffled Love began !

Yes ; let the clay-cold breast that never knew
One tender pang to generous Nature true,
Half-mingling pity with the gall of scorn,
Condemn this heart, that bled in love forlorn !

And ye, proud fair, whose soul no gladness warms,
Save Rapture's homage to your conscious charms !
Delighted idols of a gaudy train,
Ill can your blunter feelings guess the pain,
When the fond faithful heart, inspired to prove
Friendship refined, the calm delight of Love,
Feels all its tender strings with anguish torn,
And bleeds at perjured Pride's inhuman scorn !

Say, then, did pitying Heaven condemn the deed,
When Vengeance bade thee, faithless lover ! bleed ?
Long had I watch'd thy dark foreboding brow,
What time thy bosom scorn'd its dearest vow !
Sad, though I wept the friend, the lover changed,
Still thy cold look was scornful and estranged,
Till from thy pity, love, and shelter thrown,
I wander'd hopeless, friendless, and alone !

Oh ! righteous Heaven ! 'twas then my tortured soul
First gave to wrath unlimited control !
Adieu the silent look ! the streaming eye !
The murmur'd plaint ! the deep heart-heaving sigh !
Long-slumbering Vengeance wakes to better deeds ;
He shrieks, he falls, the perjured lover bleeds !
Now the last laugh of agony is o'er,
And pale in blood he sleeps, to wake no more !

'Tis done! the flame of hate no longer burns:
Nature relents, but, ah! too late returns!
Why does my soul this gush of fondness feel?
Trembling and faint, I drop the guilty steel!
Cold on my heart the hand of terror lies,
And shades of horror close my languid eyes!

Oh! 'twas a deed of Murder's deepest grain!
Could B———k's soul so true to wrath remain?
A friend long true, a once foud lover fell!—
Where Love was foster'd could not Pity dwell?

Unhappy youth! while yon pale crescent glows
To watch on silent Nature's deep repose,
Thy sleepless spirit, breathing from the tomb,
Foretells my fate, and summons me to come!
Once more I see thy sheeted spectre stand,
Roll the dim eye, and wave the paly hand!

Soon may this fluttering spark of vital flame
Forsake its languid melancholy frame!
Soon may these eyes their trembling lustre close,
Welcome the dreamless night of long repose!
Soon may this wo-worn spirit seek the bourne,
Where, lull'd to slumber, Grief forgets to mourn!"

HALLOWED GROUND

WHAT's hallow'd ground? Has earth a clod
Its Maker meant not should be trod
By man, the image of his God
    Erect and free,
Unscourged by Superstition's rod
    To bow the knee?

'That's hallow'd ground—where, mourn'd and miss'd,
The lips repose our love has kiss'd :—
But where's their memory's mansion? Is't
    Yon churchyard's bowers?
No! in ourselves their souls exist,
    A part of ours.

A kiss can consecrate the ground
Where mated hearts are mutual bound :
The spot where love's first links were wound,
    That ne'er are riven,
Is hallow'd down to earth's profound,
    And up to Heaven!

For time makes all but true love old ;
The burning thoughts that then were told
Run molten still in memory's mould ;
    And will not cool,
Until the heart itself be cold
    In Lethe's pool

What hallows ground where heroes sleep ?
'Tis not the sculptured piles you heap !
In dews that heavens far distant weep
      Their turf may bloom ;
Or Genii twine beneath the deep
      Their coral tomb :

But strew his ashes to the wind
Whose sword or voice has served mankind—
And is he dead, whose glorious mind
      Lifts thine on high ?—
To live in hearts we leave behind,
      Is not to die.

Is't death to fall for Freedom's right ?
He's dead alone that lacks her light !
And murder sullies in Heaven's sight
      The sword he draws :—
What can alone ennoble fight ?
      A noble cause !

Give that ! and welcome War to brace
Her drums ! and rend Heaven's reeking space !
The colors planted face to face,
      The charging cheer,
Though Death's pale horse lead on the chase,
      Shall still be dear.

And place our trophies where men kneel
To Heaven !—but Heaven rebukes my zeal !
The cause of Truth and human weal,
      O God above !
Transfer it from the sword's appeal
      To Peace and Love.

Peace, Love ! the cherubim that join
Their spread w'ngs o'er Devotion's shrine,

Prayers sound in vain, and temples shine,
    Where they are not—
The heart alone can make divine
    Religion's spot.

To incantations dost thou trust,
And pompous rites in domes august?
See mouldering stones and metal's rust
    Belie the vaunt,
That men can bless one pile of dust
    With chime or chaunt.

The ticking wood-worm mocks thee, man!
Thy temples—creeds themselves grow wan!
But there's a dome of nobler span,
    A temple given
Thy faith, that bigots dare not ban—
    Its space is Heaven!

Its roof star-pictured Nature's ceiling,
Where trancing the rapt spirit's feeling,
And God himself to man revealing,
    The harmonious spheres
Make music, though unheard their pealing
    By mortal ears.

Fair stars! are not your beings pure?
Can sin, can death your worlds obscure?
Else why so swell the thoughts at your
    Aspect above?
Ye must be Heavens that make us sure
    Of heavenly love!

And in your harmony sublime
I read the doom of distant time;
That man's regenerate soul from crime
    Shall yet be drawn,
And reason on his mortal clime
    Immortal dawn.

What's hallow'd ground ?   'Tis what gives birth
To sacred thoughts in souls of worth !—
Peace ! Independence ! Truth ! go forth
    Earth's compass round ;
And your high priesthood shall make earth
    All hallow'd ground.

SONG.

WITHDRAW not yet those lips and fingers
   Whose touch to mine is rapture's spell ;
Life's joy for us a moment lingers,
   And death seems in the word—Farewell.
The hour that bids us part and go,
It sounds not yet,—oh ! no, no, no !

Time, whilst I gaze upon thy sweetness,
   Flies like a courser nigh the goal ;
To-morrow where shall be his fleetness,
   When thou art parted from my soul ?
Our hearts shall beat, our tears shall flow,
But not together—no, no, no !

CAROLINE

PART I

I'LL bid the hyacinth to blow,
   I'll teach my grotto green to be;
And sing my true love, all below
   The holly bower and myrtle tree

There all his wild-wood sweets to bring,
   The sweet South wind shall wander by,
And with the music of his wing
   Delight my rustling canopy.

Come to my close and clustering bower,
   Thou spirit of a milder clime,
Fresh with the dews of fruit and flower,
   Of mountain heath, and moory thyme.

With all thy rural echoes come,
   Sweet comrade of the rosy day,
Wafting the wild bee's gentle hum,
   Or cuckoo's plaintive roundelay.

Where'er thy morning breath has play'd,
   Whatever isles of ocean fann'd,
Come to my blossom-woven shade,
   Thou wandering wind of fairy-land.

For sure from some enchanted isle,
   Where Heaven and Love their sabbath hold,
Where pure and happy spirits smile,
   Of beauty's fairest, brightest mould:

From some green Eden of the deep,
  Where Pleasure's sigh alone is heaved,
Where tears of rapture lovers weep,
  Endear'd, undoubting, undeceived ;

From some sweet paradise afar,
  Thy music wanders, distant, lost—
Where Nature lights her leading star,
  And love is never, never cross'd.

Oh gentle gale of Eden bowers,
  If back thy rosy feet should roam,
To revel with the cloudless Hours
  In Nature's more propitious home,

Name to thy loved Elysian grovès,
  That o'er enchanted spirits twine,
A fairer form than cherub loves,
  And let the name be CAROLINE.

CAROLINE.

PART II.

TO THE EVENING STAR.

GEM of the crimson-color'd Even,
  Companion of retiring day,
Why at the closing gates of Heaven,
  Beloved star dost thou delay?

So fair thy pensile beauty burns,
  When soft the tear of twilight flows ;
So due thy plighted love returns,
  To chambers brighter than the rose :

To Peace, to Pleasure, and to Love,
   So kind a star thou seem'st to be,
Sure some enamor'd orb above
   Descends and burns to meet with thee

Thine is the breathing, blushing hour,
   When all unheavenly passions fly,
Chased by the soul-subduing power
   Of Love's delicious witchery.

O! sacred to the fall of day,
   Queen of propitious stars, appear,
And early rise, and long delay,
   When Caroline herself is here!

Shine on her chosen green resort,
   Whose trees the sunward summit crown,
And wanton flowers, that well may court
   An angel's feet to tread them down.

Shine on her sweetly-scented road,
   Thou star of evening's purple dome,
That lead'st the nightingale abroad,
   And guid'st the pilgrim to his home.

Shine, where my charmer's sweeter breath
   Embalms the soft exhaling dew,
Where dying winds a sigh bequeath
   To kiss the cheek of rosy hue.

Where, winnow'd by the gentle air,
   Her silken tresses darkly flow,
And fall upon her brow so fair,
   Like shadows on the mountain snow.

Thus, ever thus, at day's decline,
   In converse sweet, to wander far,
O bring with thee my Caroline,
   And thou shalt be my Ruling Star!

THE BEECH TREE'S PETITION.

O LEAVE this barren spot to me !
Spare, woodman, spare the beechen tree!
Though bush or flow'ret never grow
My dark unwarming shade below ;
Nor summer bud perfume the dew
Of rosy blush, or yellow hue !
Nor fruits of autumn, blossom-born,
My green and glossy leaves adorn ;
Nor murmuring tribes from me derive
Th' ambrosial amber of the hive ;
Yet leave this barren spot to me :
Spare, woodman, spare the beechen tree !

    Thrice twenty summers I have seen
The sky grow bright, the forest green ;
And many a wintry wind have stood
In bloomless, fruitless solitude,
Since childhood in my pleasant bower
First spent its sweet and sportive hour,
Since youthful lovers in my shade
Their vows of truth and rapture made;
And on my trunk's surviving frame
Carved many a long-forgotten name.
Oh ! by the sighs of gentle sound,
First breathed upon this sacred ground ;
By all that Love has whisper'd here,
Or Beauty heard with ravish'd ear;
As Love's own altar honor me :
Spare, woodman, spare the beechen tree !

FIELD FLOWERS

Yᴇ field flowers! the gardens eclipse you, 'tis true,
Yet, wildings of Nature, I dote upon you,
    For ye waft me to summers of old,
When the earth teem'd around me with fairy delight,
And when daisies and buttercups gladden'd my sight,
    Like treasures of silver and gold.

I love you for lulling me back into dreams
Of the blue Highland mountains and echoing streams,
    And of birchen glades breathing their balm,
While the deer was seen glancing in sunshine remote,
And the deep mellow crush of the wood-pigeon's note
    Made music that sweeten'd the calm.

Not a pastoral song has a pleasanter tune
Than ye speak to my heart, little wildings of June·
    Of old ruinous castles ye tell,
Where I thought it delightful your beauties to find,
When the magic of Nature first breathed on my mind
    And your blossoms were part of her spell.

Even now what affections the violet awakes;
What loved little islands, twice seen in their lakes,
    · Can the wild water-lily restore;
What landscapes I read in the primrose's looks,
And what pictures of pebbled and minnowy brooks,
    In the vetches that tangled their shore.

Earth's cultureless buds, to my heart ye were dear,
Ere the fever of passion, or ague of fear
   Had scathed my existence's bloom ;
Once I welcome you more, in life's passionless stage,
With the visions of youth to revisit my age,
   And I wish you to grow on my tomb.

SONG.

TO THE EVENING STAR.

Star that bringest home the bee,
And sett'st the weary laborer free !
If any star shed peace, 'tis thou,
   That send'st it from above,
Appearing when Heaven's breath and brow
   Are sweet as hers we love.

Come to the luxuriant skies,
Whilst the landscape's odors rise,
Whilst far-off lowing herds are heard,
   And songs, when toil is done,
From cottages whose smoke unstirr'd
   Curls yellow in the sun.

Star of love's soft interviews,
Parted lovers on thee muse ;
Their remembrancer in Heaven
   Of thrilling vows thou art,
Too delicious to be riven
   By absence from the heart.

STANZAS TO PAINTING

O THOU by whose expressive art
   Her perfect image Nature sees
In union with the Graces start,
   And sweeter by reflection please !

In whose creative hand the hues
   Fresh from yon orient rainbow shine,
I bless thee, Promethéan Muse !
   And call thee brightest of the Nine !

Possessing more than vocal power,
   Persuasive more than poet's tongue ;
Whose lineage, in a raptured hour,
   From Love, the Sire of Nature, sprung ;

Does Hope her high possession meet ?
   Is joy triumphant, sorrow flown ?
Sweet is the trance, the tremor sweet,
   When all we love is all our own.

But oh ! thou pulse of pleasure dear,
   Slow throbbing, cold, I feel thee part ;
Lone absence plants a pang severe,
   Or death inflicts a keener dart.

Then for a beam of joy to light
   In memory's sad and wakeful eye !
Or banish from the noon of night
   Her dreams of deeper agony.

Shall Song its witching cadence roll?
  Yea, even the tenderest air repeat,
That breathed when soul was knit to soul,
  And heart to heart responsive beat?

What visions rise! to charm, to melt!
  The lost, the loved, the dead are near!
Oh, hush that strain too deeply felt!
  And cease that solace too severe!

But thou, serenely silent art!
  By heaven and love wast taught to lend
A milder solace to the heart,
  The sacred image of a friend.

All is not lost! if, yet possess'd,
  To me that sweet memorial shine:—
If close and closer to my breast
  I hold that idol all divine.

Or, gazing through luxurious tears,
  Melt o'er the loved departed form,
Till death's cold bosom half appears
  With life, and speech, and spirit warm.

She looks! she lives! this trancèd hour,
  Her bright eye seems a purer gem
Than sparkles on the throne of power,
  Or glory's wealthy diadem.

Yes, Genius, yes! thy mimic aid
  A treasure to my soul has given,
Where beauty's canonizèd shade
  Smiles in the sainted hues of heaven.

No spectre forms of pleasure fled,
  Thy softening, sweetening tints restore;
For thou canst give us back the dead,
  E'en in the loveliest looks they wore.
20

Then blest be Nature's guardian Muse,
   Whose hand her perish'd grace redeems!
Whose tablet of a thousand hues
   The mirror of creation seems.

From Love began thy high descent;
   And lovers, charm'd by gifts of thine,
Shall bless thee mutely eloquent;
   And call thee brightest of the Nine!

LINES

INSCRIBED ON THE MONUMENT LATELY FINISHED BY
MR. CHANTREY,

Which has been erected by the Widow of Admiral Sir G. Camp
bell, K. C. B., to the memory of her Husband.

To him, whose loyal, brave, and gentle heart,
Fulfill'd the hero's and the patriot's part,—
Whose charity, like that which Paul enjoin'd,
Was warm, beneficent, and unconfined,—
This stone is rear'd: to public duty true,
The seaman's friend, the father of his crew—
Mild in reproof, sagacious in command,
He spread fraternal zeal throughout his band,
And led each arm to act, each heart to feel,
What British valor owes to Britain's weal.
These were his public virtues:—but to trace
His private life's fair purity and grace,
To paint the traits that drew affection strong
From friends, an ample and an ardent throng,

And, more, to speak his memory's grateful claim
On her who mourns him most, and bears his name—
O'ercomes the trembling hand of widow'd grief,
O'ercomes the heart, unconscious of relief,
Save in religion's high and holy trust,
Whilst placing their memorial o'er his dust.

———◆———

THE MAID'S REMONSTRANCE.

Never wedding, ever wooing,
Still a love-lorn heart pursuing,
Read you not the wrong you're doing
    In my cheek's pale hue?
All my life with sorrow strewing,
    Wed, or cease to woo.

Rivals banish'd, bosoms plighted,
Still our days are disunited;
Now the lamp of hope is lighted,
    Now half quench'd appears,
Damp'd, and wavering, and benighted,
    Midst my sighs and tears.

Charms you call your dearest blessing,
Lips that thrill at your caressing,
Eyes a mutual soul confessing,
    Soon you'll make them grow
Dim, and worthless your possessing
    Not with age, but wo!

STANZAS

ON THE BATTLE OF NAVARINO.

———

HEARTS of oak that have bravely deliver'd the brave,
And uplifted old Greece from the brink of the grave,
'Twas the helpless to help, and the hopeless to save,
  That your thunderbolts swept o'er the brine:
And as long as yon sun shall look down on the wave
  The light of your glory shall shine.

For the guerdon ye sought with your bloodshed and toil,
Was it slaves, or dominion, or rapine, or spoil?
No! your lofty emprise was to fetter and foil
  The uprooter of Greece's domain!
When he tore the last remnant of food from her soil,
  Till her famish'd sank pale as the slain!

Yet, Navarin's heroes! does Christendom breed
The base hearts that will question the fame of your deed?
Are they men?—let ineffable scorn be their meed,
  And oblivion shadow their graves!—
Are they women?—to Turkish serails let them speed;
  And be mothers of Mussulman slaves.

Abettors of massacre! dare ye deplore
That the death-shriek is silenced on Hellas's shore?
That the mother aghast sees her offspring no more
  By the hand of Infanticide grasp'd?
And that stretch'd on yon billows distain'd by their gore
  Missolonghi's assassins have gasp'd?

Prouder scene never hallow'd war's pomp to the mind,
Than when Christendom's pennons woo'd social the
    wind,
And the flower of her brave for the combat combined.
   Their watch-word, humanity's vow:
Not a sea-boy that fought in that cause, but mankind
   Owes a garland to honor his brow!

Nor grudge, by our side, that to conquer or fall,
Came the hardy rude Russ, and the high-mettled Gaul:
For whose was the genius, that plann'd at its call,
   Where the whirlwind of battle should roll?
All were brave! but the star of success over all
   Was the light of our Codrington's soul.

That star of thy day-spring, regenerate Greek!
Dimm'd the Saracen's moon, and struck pallid his cheek
In its fast flushing morning thy Muses shall speak
   When their lore and their lutes they reclaim:
And the first of their songs from Parnassus's peak
   Shall be " *Glory to Codrington's name.*"

ABSENCE.

'Tis not the loss of love's assurance,
   It is not doubting what thou art,
But 'tis the too, too long endurance
   Of absence, that afflicts my heart.

The fondest thoughts two hearts can cherish,
   When each is lonely doom'd to weep,
Are fruits on desert isles that perish,
   Or riches buried in the deep.

What though, untouch'd by jealous madness,
    Our bosom's peace may fall to wreck ;
Th' undoubting heart, that breaks with sadness,
    Is but more slowly doom'd to break.

Absence ! is not the soul torn by it
    From more than light, or life, or breath ?
'Tis Lethe's gloom, but not its quiet,—
    The pain without the peace of death !

LINES

ON REVISITING A SCOTTISH RIVER.

AND call they this Improvement?—to have changed,
My native Clyde, thy once romantic shore,
Where Nature's face is banish'd and estranged,
And Heaven reflected in thy wave no more ;
Whose banks, that sweeten'd May-day's breath before,
Lie sere and leafless now in summer's beam,
With sooty exhalations cover'd o'er ;
And for the daisied greensward, down thy stream
Unsightly brick-lanes smoke, and clanking engines
    gleam.

Speak not to me of swarms the scene sustains ;
One heart free tasting Nature's breath and bloom
Is worth a thousand slaves to Mammon's gains.
But whither goes that wealth, and gladdening whom ?
See, left but life enough and breathing-room
The hunger and the hope of life to feel,
Yon pale Mechanic bending o'er his loom,
And Childhood's self as at Ixion's wheel,
From morn till midnight task'd to earn its little meal.

Is this Improvement?—where the human breed
Degenerates as they swarm and overflow,
Till Toil grows cheaper than the trodden weed,
And man competes with man, like foe with foe,
Till Death, that thins them, scarce seems public wo?
Improvement!—smiles it in the poor man's eyes,
Or blooms it on the cheek of Labor?—No—
To gorge a few with Trade's precarious prize,
We banish rural life, and breathe unwholesome skies.

Nor call that evil slight; God has not given
This passion to the heart of man in vain,
For Earth's green face, th' untainted air of Heaven,
And all the bliss of Nature's rustic reign.
For not alone our frame imbibes a stain
From fœtid skies; the spirit's healthy pride
Fades in their gloom—And therefore I complain,
That thou no more through pastoral scenes shouldst
    glide,
My Wallace's own stream, and once romantic Clyde!

THE "NAME UNKNOWN;"

IN IMITATION OF KLOPSTOCK.

PROPHETIC pencil! wilt thou trace
A faithful image of the face,
  Or wilt thou write the 'Name Unknown,'
Ordain'd to bless my charmed soul,
And all my future fate control,
  Unrivall'd and alone?

Delicious Idol of my thought!
Though sylph or spirit hath not taught
   My boding heart thy precious name;
Yet musing on my distant fate,
To 'charms unseen I consecrate
   A visionary flame.

Thy rosy blush, thy meaning eye,
Thy virgin voice of melody,
   Are ever present to my heart;
Thy murmur'd vows shall yet be mine,
My thrilling hand shall meet with thine,
   And never, never part!

Then fly, my days, on rapid wing,
Till Love the viewless treasure bring;
   While I, like conscious Athens, own
A power in mystic silence seal'd,
A guardian angel unreveal'd,
   And bless the ' Name Unknown!'

LINES

ON THE CAMP HILL, NEAR HASTINGS,

In the deep blue of eve,
Ere the twinkling of stars had begun,
   Or the lark took his leave
Of the skies and the sweet setting sun,

I climb'd to yon heights,
Where the Norman encamp'd him of old,
   With his bowmen and knights,
And his banner all burnish'd with gold.

At the Conqueror's side
There his minstrelsy sat harp in hand,
    In pavilion wide ;
And they chanted the deeds of Roland.

    Still the ramparted ground
With a vision my fancy inspires,
    And I hear the trump sound,
As it marshall'd our Chivalry's sires.

    On each turf of that mead
Stood the captors of England's domains,
    That ennobled her breed
And high-mettled the blood of her veins.

    Over hauberk and helm
As the sun's setting splendor was thrown,
    Thence they look'd o'er a realm—
And to-morrow beheld it their own.

* * *

FAREWELL TO LOVE.

I HAD a heart that doted once in passion's boundless pain,
And though the tyrant I abjured, I could not break his
    chain ;
But now that Fancy's fire is quench'd, and ne'er can
    burn anew,
I've bid to Love, for all my life, adieu ! adieu ! adieu !

I've known, if ever mortal knew, the spells of Beauty's
    thrall,
And if my song has told them not, my soul has felt
    them all ;

But Passion robs my' peace no more, and Beauty's
    witching sway
Is now to me a star that's fallen—a dream that's pass'd
    away.

Hail ! welcome tide of life, when no tumultuous billows
    roll,
How wondrous to myself appears this halcyon calm of
    soul !
The wearied bird blown o'er the deep would sooner quit
    its shore,
Than I would cross the gulf again that time has brought
    me o'er.

Why say they Angels feel the flame ?—Oh, spirits of
    the skies !
Can love like ours, that dotes on dust, in heavenly
    bosoms rise ?—
Ah no ; the hearts that best have felt its power, the best
    can tell,
That peace on earth itself begins, when Love has bid
    farewell.

LINES ON POLAND.

AND have I lived to see thee sword in hand
Uprise again, immortal Polish Land !—
Whose flag brings more than chivalry to mind,
And leaves the tri-color in shade behind ;
A theme for uninspired lips too strong ;
That swells my heart beyond the power of song:—

Majestic men, whose deeds have dazzled faith,
Ah! yet your fate's suspense arrests my breath;
Whilst envying bosoms bared to shot and steel,
I feel the more that fruitlessly I feel.

Poles! with what indignation I endure
Th' half-pitying, servile mouths that call you poor;
Poor! is it England mocks you with her grief,
Who hates, but dares not chide, th' *Imperial Thief?*
France with her soul beneath a Bourbon's thrall,
And Germany that has no soul at all,—
States, quailing at the giant overgrown,
Whom dauntless Poland grapples with alone!
No, ye are rich in fame e'en whilst ye bleed:
We cannot aid you—*we* are poor indeed!

In Fate's defiance—in the world's great eye,
Poland has won her immortality;
The Butcher, should he reach her bosom now,
Could not tear Glory's garland from her brow;
Wreath'd, filleted, the victim falls renown'd,
And all her ashes will be holy ground!

But turn, my soul, from presages so dark:
Great Poland's spirit is a deathless spark
That's fann'd by Heaven to mock the Tyrant's rage
She, like the eagle, will renew her age,
And fresh historic plumes of Fame put on,—
Another Athens after Marathon,—
Where eloquence shall fulmine, arts refine,
Bright as her arms that now in battle shine.
Come—should the heavenly shock my life destroy,
And shut its flood-gates with excess of joy;
Come but the day when Poland's fight is won—
And on my grave-stone shine the morrow's sun—
The day that sees Warsaw's cathedral glow,
With endless ensigns ravish'd from the foe,—
Her women lifting their fair hands with thanks,

Her pious warriors kneeling in their ranks,
The 'scutcheon'd walls of high heraldic boast,
The odorous altars' elevated host,
The organ sounding through the aisle's long glooms,
The mighty dead seen sculptured o'er their tombs;
(John, Europe's saviour—Poniatowski's fair
Resemblance—Kosciusko's shall be there;)
The taper'd pomp—the hallelujah's swell,
Shall o'er the soul's devotion cast a spell,
Till visions cross the rapt enthusiast's glance,
And all the scene becomes a waking trance.
Should Fate put far—far off that glorious scene,
And gulfs of havoc interpose between,
Imagine not, ye men of every clime,
Who act, or by your sufferance share the crime—
Your brother Abel's blood shall vainly plead
Against the " *deep damnation*" of the deed.
Germans, ye view its horror and disgrace
With cold phosphoric eyes and phlegm of face.
Is Allemagne profound in science, lore,
And minstrel art?—her shame is but the more
To doze and dream by governments oppress'd,
The spirit of a book-worm in each breast.
Well can ye mouth fair Freedom's classic line,
And talk of Constitutions o'er your wine:
But all your vows to break the tyrant's yoke
Expire in Bacchanalian song and smoke:
Heavens! can no ray of foresight pierce the lead
And mystic mtaphysics of your heads,
To show the self-same grave, Oppression delves
For Poland's rights, is yawning for yourselves!

See, whilst the Pole, the vanguard aid of France,
Has vaulted on his barb and couch'd the lance,
France turns from her abandon'd friends afresh,
And sooths the Bear that prowls for patriot flesh;
Buys, ignominious purchase! short repose,
With dying curses and the groans of those

That served, and loved, and put in her their trust.
Frenchmen! the dead accuse you from the dust—
Brows laurell'd—bosoms mark'd with many a scar
For France—that wore her Legion's noblest star,
Cast dumb reproaches from the field of Death
On Gallic honor: and this broken faith
Has robb'd you more of Fame—the life of life—
Than twenty battles lost in glorious strife!

And what of England—Is she steep'd so low
In poverty, crest-fallen, and palsied so,
That we must sit much wroth, but timorous more,
With Murder knocking at our neighbor's door!—
Not Murder mask'd and cloak'd, with hidden knife,
Whose owner owes the gallows life for life;
But *Public Murder!*—that with pomp and gaud,
And royal scorn of Justice, walks abroad
To wring more tears and blood than e'er were wrung
By all the culprits Justice ever hung! .
We read the diadem'd Assassin's vaunt,
And wince, and wish we had not hearts to pant
With useless indignation—sigh, and frown,
But have not hearts to throw the gauntlet down.

If but a doubt hung o'er the grounds of fray,
Or trivial rapine stopp'd the world's highway;
Were this some common strife of States embroil'd;—
Britannia on the spoiler and the spoil'd
Might calmly look, and, asking time to breathe,
Still honorably wear her olive wreath.
But this is Darkness combating with Light:
Earth's adverse Principles for empire fight:
Oppression, that has belted half the globe,
Far as his knout could reach or dagger probe,
Holds reeking o'er our brother-freemen slain
That dagger—shakes it at us in disdain;
Talks big to Freedom's states of Poland's thrall,
And, trampling one, contemns them one and all.

My country ! colors not thy once proud brow
At this affront ?—Hast thou not fleets enow
With Glory's streamer, lofty as the lark,
Gay fluttering o'er each thunder-bearing bark,
To warm the insulter's seas with barbarous blood,
And interdict his flag from Ocean's flood ?
Ev'n now far off the sea-cliff, where I sing,
I see, my Country and my Patriot King !
Your ensign glad the deep.   Becalm'd and slow
A war-ship rides ; while Heaven's prismatic bow
Uprisen behind her on th' horizon's base,
Shines flushing through the tackle, shrouds, and stays,
And wraps her giant form in one majestic blaze.
My soul accepts the omen ; Fancy's eye
Has sometimes a veracious augury :
The Rainbow types Heaven's promise to my sight ;
The Ship, Britannia's interposing Might !

But if there should be none to aid you, Poles,
Ye'll but to prouder pitch wind up your souls,
Above example, pity, praise, or blame,
To sow and reap a boundless field of Fame.
Ask aid no more from Nations that forget
Your championship—old Europe's mighty debt.
Though Poland (Lazarus-like) has burst the gloom,
She rises not a beggar from the tomb :
In Fortune's frown, on Danger's giddiest brink,
Despair and Poland's name must never link.-
All ills have bounds—plague, whirlwind, fire, and flood
Ev'n Power can spill but bounded sums of blood.
States caring not what Freedom's price may be,
May late or soon, but must at last be free ;
For body-killing tyrants cannot kill
The public soul—the hereditary will
That downward as from sire to son it goes,
By shifting bosoms more intensely glows :
Its heir-loom is the heart, and slaughter'd men
Fight fiercer in their orphans o'er again.

Poland recasts—though rich in heroes old—.
Her men in more and more heroic mould :
Her eagle ensign best among mankind
Becomes, and types her eagle-strength of mind :
Her praise upon my faltering lips expires :
Resume it, younger bards, and nobler lyres !

MARGARET AND DORA.

Margaret's beauteous—Grecian arts
Ne'er drew form completer,
Yet why, in my heart of hearts,
Hold I Dora's sweeter ?

Dora's eyes of heavenly blue,
Pass all painting's reach,
Ring-dove's notes are discord to
The music of her speech.

Artists ! Margaret's smile receive,
And on canvass show it ;
But for perfect worship leave
Dora to her poet.

A THOUGHT SUGGESTED BY THE NEW YEAR.

The more we live, more brief appear
   Our life's succeeding stages:
A day to childhood seems a year,
   And years like passing ages.

The gladsome current of our youth,
   Ere passion yet disorders,
Steals, lingering like a river smooth
   Along its grassy borders.

But, as the care-worn cheek grows wan,
   And sorrow's shafts fly thicker,
Ye stars, that measure life to man,
   Why seem your courses quicker?

When joys have lost their bloom and breath,
   And life itself is vapid,
Why, as we reach the Falls of death,
   Feel we its tide more rapid?

It may be strange—yet who would change,
   Time's course to slower speeding;
When one by one our friends have gone,
   And left our bosoms bleeding?

Heaven gives our years of fading strength
   Indemnifying fleetness;
And those of Youth, a *seeming length*,
   Proportion'd to their sweetness.

SONG.

How delicious is the winning
Of a kiss at Love's beginning,
When two mutual hearts are sighing
For the knot there's no untying !

Yet, remember, 'midst your wooing,
Love has bliss, but Love has ruing ;
Other smiles may make you fickle,
Tears for other charms may trickle.

Love he comes, and Love he tarries,
Just as fate or fancy carries ;
Longest stays, when sorest chidden ;
Laughs and flies, when press'd and bidden.

Bind the sea to slumber stilly,
Bind its odor to the lily,
Bind the aspen ne'er to quiver,
Then bind Love to last forever !

Love's a fire that needs renewal
Of fresh beauty for its fuel ;
Love's wing moults when caged and captured,
Only free, he soars enraptured.

Can you keep the bee from ranging,
Or the ring-dove's neck from changing ;
No ! nor fetter'd Love from dying,
In the knot there's no untying.

THE POWER OF RUSSIA.

So all this gallant blood has gush'd in vain !
And Poland by the Northern Condor's beak
And talons torn, lies prostrated again.
O, British patriots, that were wont to speak
Once loudly on this theme, now hush'd or meek !
O, heartless men of Europe—Goth and Gaul
Cold, adder-deaf to Poland's dying shriek ;—
That saw the world's last land of heroes fall—
The brand of burning shame is on you all—all—all !

But this is not the drama's closing act !
Its tragic curtain must uprise anew.
Nations, mute accessories to the fact !
That Upas-tree of power, whose fostering dew
Was Polish blood, has yet to cast o'er you
The lengthening shadow of its head elate—
A deadly shadow, darkening Nature's hue.
To all that's hallow'd, righteous, pure, and great,
Wo ! wo ! when they are reach'd by Russia's withering
    hate.

Russia, that on his throne of adamant,
Consults what nation's breast shall next be gored :
He on Polonia's Golgotha will plant
His standard fresh ; and, horde succeeding horde,
On patriot tomb-stones he will whet the sword,
For more stupendous slaughters of the free.
Then Europe's realms, when their best blood is pour'd,
Shall miss thee, Poland ! as they bend the knee,
All—all in grief, but none in glory likening thee.

Why smote ye not the Giant whilst he reel'd?
O, fair occasion, gone forever by !
To have lock'd his lances in their northern field,
Innocuous as the phantom chivalry
That flames and hurtles from yon boreal sky !
Now wave thy pennon, Russia, o'er the land
Once Poland ; build thy bristling castles high ;
Dig dungeons deep ; for Poland's wrested brand
Is now a weapon new to widen thy command—

An awful width ! Norwegian woods shall build
His fleets ; the Swede his vassal, and the Dane ;
The glebe of fifty kingdoms shall be till'd
To feed his dazzling, desolating train,
Camp'd sumless, 'twixt the Black and Baltic main
Brute hosts, I own ; but Sparta could not write,
And Rome, half-barbarous, bound Achaia's chain :
So Russia's spirit, midst Sclavonic night,
Burns with a fire more dread than all your polish'd
        light.

But Russia's limbs (so blinded statesmen say)
Are crude, and too colossal to cohere.
O, lamentable weakness ! reckoning weak
The stripling Titan, strengthening year by year
What implement lacks he for war's career,
That grows on earth, or in its floods and mines,
(Eighth sharer of the inhabitable sphere)
Whom Persia bows to, China ill confines,
And India's homage waits, when Albion's star de-
        clines?

But time will teach the Russ, ev'n conquering War
Has handmaid arts: ay, ay, the Russ will woo
All sciences that speed Bellona's car,
All murder's tactic arts, and win them too ;
But never holier Muses shall imbue

His breast, that's made of nature's basest clay
The sabre, knout, and dungeon's vapor blue
His laws and ethics: far from him away
Are all the lovely Nine, that breathe but Freedom's day

Say, ev'n his serfs, half-humanized, should learn
Their human rights,—will Mars put out his flame
In Russian bosoms? no, he'll bid them burn
A thousand years for naught but martial fame,
Like Romans:—yet forgive me, Roman name!
Rome could impart what Russia never can ;
Proud civic rights to salve submission's shame.
Our strife is coming ; but in Freedom's van
The Polish eagle's fall is big with fate to man.

Proud bird of old ! Mohammed's moon recoil'd
Before thy swoop: had we been timely bold,
That swoop, still free, had stunn'd the Russ, and
    foil'd
Earth's new oppressors, as it foil'd her old.
Now thy majestic eyes are shut and cold:
And colder still Polonia's children find
The sympathetic hands, that we outhold.
But, Poles, when we are gone, the world will mind,
Ye bore the brunt of fate, and bled for humankind.

So hallow'dly have ye fulfill'd your part,
My pride repudiates ev'n the sigh that blends
With Poland's name—name written on my heart.
My heroes, my grief-consecrated friends!
Your sorrow, in nobility, transcends
Your conqueror's joy: his cheek may blush ; but
    shame
Can tinge not yours, though exile's tear descends ;
Nor would ye change your conscience, cause, and
    name,
For his, with all his wealth, and all his felon fame.

Thee, Niemciewitz, whose song of stirring power
The Czar forbids to sound in Polish lands ;
Thee, Czartoryski, in thy banish'd bower,
The patricide, who in thy palace stands,
May envy ; proudly may Polonia's bands
Throw down their swords at Europe's feet in scorn,
Saying—" Russia from the metal of these brands
Shall forge the fetters of your sons unborn ;
Our setting star is your misfortunes' rising morn."

LINES

ON LEAVING A SCENE IN BAVARIA.

ADIEU the woods and water's side,
   Imperial Danube's rich domain!
Adieu the grotto, wild and wide,
   The rocks abrupt, and grassy plain!
   For pallid Autumn once again
Hath swell'd each torrent of the hill ;
   Her clouds collect, her shadows sail,
   And watery winds that sweep the vale,
Grow loud and louder still.

But not the storm, dethroning fast
   Yon monarch oak of massy pile
Nor river roaring to the blast
   Around its dark and desert isle ;
   Nor church-bell tolling to beguile
The cloud-born thunder passing by,
   Can sound in discord to my soul :
   Roll on, ye mighty waters, roll !
And rage, thou darken'd sky !

Thy blossoms now no longer bright;
  Thy wither'd woods no longer green;
Yet, Eldurn shore, with dark delight
  I visit thy unlovely scene !
  For many a sunset hour serene
My steps have trod thy mellow dew;
  When his green light the glow-worm gave,
  When Cynthia from the distant wave
Her twilight anchor drew,

And plough'd, as with a swelling sail,
  The billowy clouds and starry sea ;
Then while thy hermit nightingale
  Sang on his fragrant apple-tree,—
  Romantic, solitary, free,
The visitant of Eldurn's shore,
  On such a moonlight mountain stray'd,
  As echo'd to the music made
By Druid harps of yore.

Around thy savage hills of oak,
  Around thy waters bright and blue,
No hunter's horn the silence broke,
  No dying shriek thine echo knew ;
  But safe, sweet Eldurn woods, to you
The wounded wild deer ever ran,
  Whose myrtle bound their grassy cave,
  Whose very rocks a shelter gave
From blood-pursuing man.

Oh heart effusions, that arose
  From nightly wanderings cherish'd here;
To him who flies from many woes,
  Even homeless deserts can be dear !
  The last and solitary cheer
Of those that own no earthly home,
  Say—is it not, ye banish'd race,
  In such a loved and lonely place
Companionless to roam ?

Yes! I have loved thy wild abode,
  Unknown, unplough'd, untrodden shore;
Where scarce the woodman finds a road,
  And scarce the fisher plies an oar;
  For man's neglect I love thee more;
That art nor avarice intrude
  To tame thy torrent's thunder-shock,
  Or prune thy vintage of the rock
Magnificently rude.

Unheeded spreads thy blossom'd bud
  Its milky bosom to the bee;
Unheeded falls along the flood
  Thy desolate and aged tree.
  Forsaken scene, how like to thee
The fate of unbefriended Worth!
  Like thine her fruit dishonor'd falls;
  Like thee in solitude she calls
A thousand treasures forth.

Oh! silent spirit of the place,
  If, lingering with the ruin'd year,
Thy hoary form and awful face
  I yet might watch and worship here!
  Thy storm were music to mine ear,
Thy wildest walk a shelter given
  Sublimer thoughts on earth to find,
  And share, with no unhallow'd mind,
The majesty of heaven.

What though the bosom friends of Fate,—
  Prosperity's unweaned brood,—
Thy consolations cannot rate,
  O self-dependent solitude!
  Yet with a spirit unsubdued,
Though darken'd by the clouds of Care,
  To worship thy congenial gloom,
  A pilgrim to the Prophet's tomb
The Friendless shall repair.

On him the world hath never smiled
  Or look'd but with accusing eye ;—
All-silent goddess of the wild,
  To thee that misanthrope shall fly !
  I hear his deep soliloquy,
I mark his proud but ravaged form,
  As stern he wraps his mantle round,
  And bids, on winter's bleakest ground,
Defiance to the storm.

Peace to his banish'd heart, at last,
  In thy dominions shall descend,
And, strong as beechwood in the blast,
  His spirit shall refuse to bend ;
  Enduring life without a friend,
The world and falsehood left behind,
  Thy votary shall bear elate,
  (Triumphant o'er opposing Fate,)
His dark inspired mind.

But dost thou, Folly, mock the Muse
  A wanderer's mountain walk to sing,
Who shuns a warring world, nor woos
  The vulture cover of its wing ?
  Then fly, thou cowering, shivering thing,
Back to the fostering world beguiled,
  To waste in self-consuming strife
  The loveless brotherhood of life,
Reviling and reviled !

Away, thou lover of the race
  That hither chased yon weeping deer !
If Nature's all majestic face
  More pitiless than man's appear ;
  Or if the wild winds seem more drear
Than man's cold charities below,
  Behold around his peopled plains,
  Where'er the social savage reigns,
Exuberance of wo !

His art and honors wouldst thou seek
　Emboss'd on grandeur's giant walls?
Or hear his moral thunders speak
　Where senates light their airy halls,
　Where man his brother man enthralls;
Or sends his whirlwind warrants forth
　To rouse the slumbering fiends of war,
　To dye the blood-warm waves afar,
And desolate the earth?

From clime to clime pursue the scene,
　And mark in all thy spacious way,
Where'er the tyrant man has been,
　There Peace, the cherub, cannot stay;
　In wilds and woodlands far away
She builds her solitary bower,
　Where only anchorites have trod,
　Or friendless men, to worship God,
Have wander'd for an hour.

In such a far forsaken vale,—
　And such, sweet Eldurn vale, is thine,—
Afflicted nature shall inhale
　Heaven-borrow'd thoughts and joys divine;
　No longer wish, no more repine
For man's neglect or woman's scorn;—
　Then wed thee to an exile's lot,
　For if the world hath loved thee not
Its absence may be borne.

22

THE DEATH-BOAT OF HELIGOLAND.

Can restlessness reach the cold sepulchred head?—
Ay, the quick have their sleep-walkers, so have the
    dead.
There are brains, though they moulder, that dream in
    the tomb,
And that maddening forehear the last trumpet of doom,
Till their corses start sheeted to revel on earth,
Making horror more deep by the semblance of mirth
By the glare of new-lighted volcanoes they dance,
Or at mid-sea appal the chill'd mariner's glance.
Such, I wot, was the band of cadaverous smile
Seen ploughing the night-surge of Heligo's isle.

The foam of the Baltic had sparkled like fire,
And the red moon look'd down with an aspect of ire;
But her beams on a sudden grew sick-like and gray,
And the mews that had slept clang'd and shriek'd far
    away—
And the buoys and the beacons extinguish'd their light
As the boat of the stony-eyed dead came in sight,
High bounding from billow to billow; each form
Had its shroud like a plaid flying loose to the storm;
With an oar in each pulseless and icy-cold hand,
Fast they plough'd, by the lee-shore of Heligoland,
Such breakers as boat of the living ne'er cross'd;
Now surf-sunk for minutes again they uptoss'd,
And with livid lips shouted reply o'er the flood
To the challenging watchman that curdled his blood—

"We are dead—we are bound from our graves in the
    west,
First to Hecla, and then to————" Unmeet was the
    rest
For man's ear.   The old abbey bell thunder'd its clang,
And their eyes gleam'd with phosphorous light as it
    rang:
Ere they vanish'd, they stopp'd, and gazed silently grim,
'Till the eye could define them, garb, feature, and limb.

Now who were those roamers?—of gallows or wheel
Bore they marks, or the mangling anatomist's steel?
No, by magistrates' chains 'mid their grave-clothes you
    saw,
They were felons too proud to have perish'd by law;
But a riband that hung where a rope should have been,
'Twas the badge of their faction, its hue was not green,
Show'd them men who had trampled and tortured and
    driven
To rebellion the fairest Isle breathed on by Heaven,—
Men whose heirs would yet finish the tyrannous task,
If the Truth and the Time had not dragg'd off their
    mask.
They parted—but not till the sight might discern
A scutcheon distinct at their pinnace's stern,
Where letters emblazon'd in blood-color'd flame,
Named their faction—I blot not my page with its name.

———◆———

SONG.

When Love came first to Earth, the Spring
    Spread rose-beds to receive him,
And back he vow'd his flight he'd wing
    To Heaven, if she should leave him—

But Spring departing, saw his faith
 Pledged to the next new-comer—
He revell'd in the warmer breath
 And richer bowers of Summer.

Then sportive Autumn claim'd by rights
 An Archer for her lover,
And even in Winter's dark cold nights
 A charm he could discover.

Her routs and balls, and fireside joy,
 For this time were his reasons—
In short, Young Love's a gallant boy,
 That likes all times and seasons.

SONG.

Earl March look'd on his dying child,
 And smit with grief to view her—
The youth, he cried, whom I exiled,
 Shall be restored to woo her.

She's at the window many an hour
 His coming to discover:
And *he* look'd up to Ellen's bower,
 And *she* look'd on her lover—

But ah! so pale, he knew her not,
 Though her smile on him was dwelling,
And am I then forgot—forgot?—
 It broke the heart of Ellen.

In vain he weeps, in vain he sighs,
  Her cheek is cold as ashes;
Nor love's own kiss shall wake those eyes
  To lift their silken lashes.

SONG.

When Napoleon was flying
  From the field of Waterloo,
A British soldier dying
  To his brother bade adieu!

" And take," he said, " this token
  To the maid that owns my faith
With the words that I have spoken
  In affection's latest breath."

Sore mourn'd the brother's heart,
  When the youth beside him fell;
But the trumpet warn'd to part,
  And they took a sad farewell.

There was many a friend to lose him,
  For that gallant soldier sigh'd;
But the maiden of his bosom
  Wept when all their tears were dried

LINES TO JULIA M——.

SENT WITH A COPY OF THE AUTHOR'S POEMS.

Since there is magic in your look
And in your voice a witching charm,
As all our hearts consenting tell,
Enchantress, smile upon my book,
And guard its lays from hate and harm
By Beauty's most resistless spell.

The sunny dew-drop of thy praise,
Young day-star of the rising time,
Shall with its odoriferous morn
Refresh my sere and wither'd bays.
Smile, and I will believe my rhyme
Shall please the beautiful unborn.

Go forth, my pictured thoughts, and rise
In traits and tints of sweeter tone,
When Julia's glance is o'er ye flung ;
Glow, gladden, linger in her eyes,
And catch a magic not your own,
Read by the music of her tongue.

DRINKING SONG OF MUNICH

Sweet Iser ! were thy sunny realm
And flowery gardens mine,
Thy waters I would shade with elm
To prop the tender vine ;

My golden flagons I would fill
With rosy draughts from every hill ;
  And under every myrtle bower,
My gay companions should prolong
The laugh, the revel, and the song,
  To many an idle hour.

Like rivers crimson'd with the beam
  Of yonder planet bright,
Our balmy cups should ever stream
  Profusion of delight ;
No care should touch the mellow heart,
And sad or sober none depart ;
  For wine can triumph over wo,
And Love and Bacchus, brother powers,
Could build in Iser's sunny bowers
  A paradise below

LINES

ON THE DEPARTURE OF EMIGRANTS FOR NEW SOUTH WALES.

On England's shore I saw a pensive band,
With sails unfurl'd for earth's remotest strand,
Like children parting from a mother, shed
Tears for the home that could not yield them bread ;
Grief mark'd each face receding from the view,
'Twas grief to nature honorably true.
And long, poor wanderers o'er the ecliptic deep,
The song that names but home shall make you weep ;

Oft shall ye fold your flocks by stars above
In that far world, and miss the stars ye love ;
Oft when its tuneless birds scream round forlorn,
Regret the lark that gladdens England's morn,
And, giving England's names to distant scenes,
Lament that earth's extension intervenes.

But cloud not yet too long, industrious train,
Your solid good with sorrow nursed in vain :
For has the heart no interest yet as bland
As that which binds us to our native land ?
The deep-drawn wish, when children crown our hearth
To hear the cherub-chorus of their mirth,
Undamp'd by dread that want may e'er unhouse,
Or servile misery knit those smiling brows :
The pride to rear an independent shed,
And give the lips we love unborrow'd bread :
To see a world, from shadowy forests won,
In youthful beauty wedded to the sun ;
To skirt our home with harvests widely sown,
And call the blooming landscape all our own,
Our children's heritage, in prospect long.
These are the hopes, high-minded hopes and strong,
That beckon England's wanderers o'er the brine,
To realms where foreign constellations shine ;
Where streams from undiscover'd fountains roll,
And winds shall fan them from th' Antarctic pole.
And what though doom'd to shores so far apart
From England's home, that ev'n the homesick heart
Quails, thinking, ere that gulf can be recross'd,
How large a space of fleeting life is lost :
Yet there, by time, their bosoms shall be changed,
And strangers once shall cease to sigh estranged,
But jocund in the year's long sunshine roam,
That yields their sickle twice its harvest-home.

There, marking o'er his farm's expanding ring
New fleeces whiten and new fruits upspring,

The gray-hair'd swain, his grandchild sporting round,
Shall walk at eve his little empire's bound,
Emblazed with ruby vintage, ripening corn,
And verdant rampart of acacian thorn,
While, mingling with the scent his pipe exhales,
The orange-grove's and fig-tree's breath prevails;
Survey with pride beyond a monarch's spoil,
His honest arm's own subjugated soil;
And summing all the blessings God has given,
Put up his patriarchal prayer to Heaven,
That when his bones shall here repose in peace,
The scions of his love may still increase,
And o'er a land where life has ample room,
In health and plenty innocently bloom.

Delightful land, in wildness ev'n benign,
The glorious past is ours, the future thine
As in a cradled Hercules, we trace
The lines of empire in thine infant face.
What nations in thy wide horizon's span
Shall teem on tracts untrodden yet by man!
What spacious cities with their spires shall gleam,
Where now the panther laps a lonely stream,
And all but brute or reptile life is dumb!
Land of the free! thy kingdom is to come,
Of states, with laws from Gothic bondage burst,
And creeds by charter'd priesthoods unaccursed:
Of navies, hoisting their emblazon'd flags,
Where shipless seas now wash unbeacon'd crags;
Of hosts review'd in dazzling files and squares,
Their pennon'd trumpets breathing native airs,—
For minstrels thou shalt have of native fire,
And maids to sing the songs themselves inspire:—
Our very speech, methinks, in after time,
Shall catch th' Ionian blandness of thy clime;
And whilst the light and luxury of thy skies
Give brighter smiles to beauteous woman's eyes,
The Arts, whose soul is love, shall all spontaneous rise

Untrack'd in deserts lies the marble mine,
Undug the ore that midst thy roofs shall shine ;
Unborn the hands—but born they are to be—
Fair Australasia, that shall give to thee
Proud temple-domes, with galleries winding high,
So vast in space, so just in symmetry,
They widen to the contemplating eye,
With colonnaded aisles in long array,
And windows that enrich the flood of day
O'er tesselated pavements, pictures fair,
And niched statues breathing golden air.
Nor there, whilst all that's seen bids Fancy swell,
Shall Music's voice refuse to seal the spell ;
But choral hymns shall wake enchantment round,
And organs yield their tempests of sweet sound.

Meanwhile, ere Arts triumphant reach their goal,
How blest the years of pastoral life shall roll !
Ev'n should some wayward hour the settler's mind
Brood sad on scenes forever left behind,
Yet not a pang that England's name imparts,
Shall touch a fibre of his children's hearts ;
Bound to that native land by nature's bond,
Full little shall their wishes rove beyond
Its mountains blue, and melon-skirted streams,
Since childhood loved and dreamt of in their dreams.
How many a name, to us uncouthly wild,
Shall thrill that region's patriotic child,
And bring as sweet thoughts o'er his bosom's chords,
As aught that's named in song to us affords !
Dear shall that river's margin be to him,
Where sportive first he bathed his boyish limb,
Or petted birds, still brighter than their bowers,
Or twined his tame young kangaroo with flowers.
But more magnetic yet to memory
Shall be the sacred spot, still blooming nigh,
The bower of love, where first his bosom burn'd,
And smiling passion saw its smile return'd.

Go forth and prosper then, emprising band :
May He, who in the hollow of his hand
The ocean holds, and rules the whirlwind's sweep,
Assuage its wrath, and guide you on the deep !

LINES

ON REVISITING CATHCART.

Oh ! scenes of my childhood, and dear to my heart,
Ye green waving woods on the margin of Cart,
How blest in the morning of life I have stray'd,
By the stream of the vale and the grass-cover'd glade !

Then, then every rapture was young and sincere,
Ere the sunshine of bliss was bedimm'd by a tear,
And a sweeter delight every scene seem'd to lend,
That the mansion of peace was the home of a FRIEND

Now the scenes of my childhood and dear to my heart
All pensive I visit, and sigh to depart ;
Their flowers seem to languish, their beauty to cease,
For a *stranger* inhabits the mansion of peace.

But hush'd be the sigh that untimely complains,
While Friendship and all its enchantment remains,
While it blooms like the flower of a winterless clime,
Untainted by chance, unabated by time.

THE CHERUBS.

Two spirits reach'd this world of ours :
The lightning's locomotive powers
   Were slow to their agility :
In broad daylight they moved incog,
Enjoying, without mist or fog,
   Entire invisibility.

The one, a simple cherub lad,
Much interest in our planet had,
   Its face was so romantic ;
He couldn't persuade himself that man
Was such as heavenly rumors ran,
   A being base and frantic.

The elder spirit, wise and cool,
Brought down the youth as to a school ;
   But strictly on condition,
Whatever they should see or hear,
With mortals not to interfere ;
   'Twas not in their commission.

They reach'd a sovereign city proud,
Whose emperor pray'd to God aloud,
   With all his people kneeling,
And priests perform'd religious rites :
" Come," said the younger of the sprites,
   " This shows a pious feeling."

YOUNG SPIRIT.

" Ar'n't these a decent godly race ?"

OLD SPIRIT.

" The dirtiest thieves on Nature's face."

YOUNG SPIRIT.

" But hark, what cheers they're giving
Their emperor !—And is he a thief ?"

OLD SPIRIT

" Ay, and a cut-throat too ;—in brief,
  THE GREATEST SCOUNDREL LIVING."

YOUNG SPIRIT.

" But say, what were they praying for,
This people and their emperor ?"

OLD SPIRIT.

" Why, but for God's assistance
To help their army, late sent out :
And what that army is about,
  You'll see at no great distance."

On wings outspeeding mail or post,
Our sprites o'ertook the Imperial host,
  In massacres it wallow'd :
A noble nation met its hordes,
But broken fell their cause and swords,
  Unfortunate, though hallow'd.

They saw a late bombarded town,
Its streets still warm with blood ran down ;
  Still smoked each burning rafter ;
And hideously, 'midst rape and sack,
The murderer's laughter answer'd back
  His prey's convulsive laughter.
  23

They saw the captive eye the dead,
With envy of his gory bed,—
   Death's quick reward of bravery :
They heard the clank of chains, and then
Saw thirty thousand bleeding men
   Dragg'd manacled to slavery.

"Fie ! fie !" the younger heavenly spark
Exclaim'd :—" we must have miss'd our mark,
   And enter'd hell's own portals :
Earth can't be stain'd with crimes so black ;
Nay, sure, we've got among a pack
   Of fiends, and not of mortals."

"No," said the elder ; "no such thing :
Fiends are not fools enough to wring
   The necks of one another :—
They know their interests too well :
Men fight ; but every devil in hell
   Lives friendly with his brother.

And I could point you out some fellows,
On this ill-fated planet Tellus,
   In royal power that revel ;
Who, at the opening of the book
Of judgment, may have cause to look
   With envy at the devil."

Name but the devil, and he'll appear,
Old Satan in a trice was near,
   With smutty face and figure :
But spotless spirits of the skies,
Unseen to e'en his saucer eyes,
   Could watch the fiendish nigger.

"Halloo !" he cried, "I smell a trick :
A mortal supersedes Old Nick,
   The scourge of earth appointed :

He robs me of my trade, outrants
The blasphemy of hell, and vaunts
   Himself the Lord's anointed.

Folks make a fuss about my mischief:
D—d fools, they tamely suffer this chief
   To play his pranks unbounded."
The cherubs flew ; but saw from high,
At human inhumanity,
   The devil himself astounded.

———◆———

SENEX'S SOLILOQUY ON HIS YOUTH-
FUL IDOL.

PLATONIC friendship at your years,
   Says Conscience, should content ye
Nay, name not fondness to her ears,
   The darling's scarcely twenty.

Yes, and she'll loathe me unforgiven,
   To dote thus out of season ;
But beauty is a beam from heaven,
   That dazzles blind our reason.

I'll challenge Plato from the skies,
   Yes, from his spheres harmonic,
To look in M—y C——'s eyes,
   And try to be Platonic.

TO SIR FRANCIS BURDETT,

ON HIS SPEECH DELIVERED IN PARLIAMENT, AUGUST 7
1832, RESPECTING THE FOREIGN POLICY OF
GREAT BRITAIN.

———

Burdett, enjoy thy justly foremost fame,
   Through good and ill report—through calm and
       storm—
For forty years the pilot of reform !
But that which shall afresh entwine thy name
   With patriot laurels never to be sere,
Is that thou hast come nobly forth to chide
Our slumbering statesmen for their lack of pride—
   Their flattery of Oppressors, and their fear—
When Britain's lifted finger, and her frown,
Might call the nations up, and cast their tyrants down.

Invoke the scorn—Alas ! too few inherit
   The scorn for despots cherish'd by our sires,
   That baffled Europe's persecuting fires,
And shelter'd helpless states !—Recall that spirit,
   And conjure back Old England's haughty mind—
Convert the men who waver now, and pause
   Between their love of self and human kind ;
And move, Amphion-like, those hearts of stone—
The hearts that have been deaf to Poland's dying groan !

Tell them, we hold the Rights of Man too dear,
   To bless ourselves with lonely freedom blest ;
   But could we hope, with sole and selfish breast,
To breathe untroubled Freedom's atmosphere ?—

Suppose we wish'd it ?   England could not stand
A lone oasis in the desert ground
Of Europe's slavery ; from the waste around
    Oppression's fiery blast and whirling sand
Would reach and scathe us !   No ; it may not be :
Britannia and the world conjointly must be free !

Burdett, demand why Britons send abroad
    Soft greetings to th' infanticidal Czar,
    The Bear on Poland's babes that wages war
Once, we are told, a mother's shriek o'erawed
    A lion, and he dropp'd her lifted child ;
But Nicholas, whom neither God nor law,
Nor Poland's shrieking mothers overawe,
Outholds to us his friendship's gory clutch :
Shrink, Britain—shrink, my king and country, from the
        touch !

He prays to Heaven for England's king, he says—
    And dares he to the God of mercy kneel,
    Besmear'd with massacres from head to heel ?
No ; Moloch is his god—to him he prays ;
    And if his weird-like prayers had power to bring
An influence, their power would be to curse.
His hate is baleful, but his love is worse—
    A serpent's slaver deadlier than its sting !
Oh, feeble statesmen—ignominious times,
That lick the tyrant's feet, and smile upon his crimes !

ODE TO THE GERMANS.

The Spirit of Britannia
  Invokes across the main,
Her sister Allemannia
  To burst the Tyrant's chain:
By our kindred blood, she cries,
Rise, Allemannians, rise,
  And hallow'd thrice the band
Of our kindred hearts shall be,
  When your land shall be the land
    Of the free—of the free!

With Freedom's lion-banner
  Britannia rules the waves;
Whilst your Broad stone of honor*
  Is still the camp of slaves.
For shame, for glory's sake,
Wake, Allemannians, wake,
  And thy tyrants now that whelm
Half the world shall quail and flee,
  When your realm shall be the realm
    Of the free—of the free!

Mars owes to you his thunder†
  That shakes the battle-field,
Yet to break your bonds asunder
  No martial bolt has peal'd.
Shall the laurell'd land of art
Wear shackles on her heart?

Ehrenbreitstein signifies, in German, "*the broad stone o.
honor.*"
  † Germany invented gunpowder, clock-making, and printing

No ! the clock ye framed to tell
By its sound, the march of time ;
  Let it clang oppression's knell
     O'er your clime—o'er your clime !

The press's magic letters,
  That blessing ye brought forth,—
Behold ! it lies in fetters
  On the soil that gave it birth :
But the trumpet must be heard,
And the charger must be spurr'd ;
  For your father Armin's Sprite
Calls down from heaven, that ye
  Shall gird you for the fight,
     And be free !—and be free !

———◆———

LINES

ON A PICTURE OF A GIRL IN THE ATTITUDE OF PRAYER,

By the Artist Gruse, in the possession of Lady Stepney.

———

Was man e'er doom'd that beauty made
  By mimic art should haunt him ;
Like Orpheus, I adore a shade
  And dote upon a phantom.

Thou maid that in my inmost thought
  Art fancifully sainted,
Why liv'st thou not—why art thou naught
  But canvass sweetly painted ?

Whose looks seem lifted to the skies,
  . Too pure for love of mortals—
As if they drew angelic eyes
    To greet thee at heaven's portals.

Yet loveliness has here no grace,
    Abstracted or ideal—
Art ne'er but from a living face
    Drew looks so seeming real.

What wert thou, maid?—thy life—thy name
    Oblivion hides in mystery ;
Though from thy face my heart could frame
    A long romantic history.

Transported to thy time I seem,
    Though dust thy coffin covers—
And hear the songs, in fancy's dream,
    Of thy devoted lovers.

How witching must have been thy breath—
    How sweet the living charmer—
Whose every semblance after death
    Can make the heart grow warmer !

Adieu, the charms that vainly move
    My soul in their possession—
That prompt my lips to speak of love,
    Yet rob them of expression.

Yet thee, dear picture, to have praised
    Was but a poet's duty ;
And shame to him that ever gazed
    Impassive on thy beauty.

LINES

ON THE VIEW FROM ST. LEONARD'S.

Hail to thy face and odors, glorious Sea!
'Twere thanklessness in me to bless thee not,
Great beauteous Being! in whose breath and smile
My heart beats calmer, and my very mind
Inhales salubrious thoughts.   How welcomer
Thy murmurs than the murmurs of the world!
Though like the world thou fluctuatest, thy din
To me is peace, thy restlessness repose.
Ev'n gladly I exchange yon spring-green lanes
With all the darling field-flowers in their prime,
And gardens haunted by the nightingale's
Long trills and gushing ecstasies of song,
For these wild headlands, and the sea-mew's clang—

With thee beneath my windows, pleasant Sea,
I long not to o'erlook earth's fairest glades
And green savannas—Earth has not a plain
So boundless or so beautiful as thine;
The eagle's vision cannot take it in:
The lightning's wing, too weak to sweep its space,
Sinks half-way o'er it like a wearied bird:
It is the mirror of the stars, where all
Their hosts within the concave firmament,
Gay marching to the music of the spheres,
Can see themselves at once.
                              Nor on the stage
Of rural landscape are there lights and shades
Of more harmonious dance and play than thine.

How vividly this moment brightens forth,
Between gray parallel and leaden breadths,
A belt of hues that stripes thee many a league,
Flush'd like the rainbow, or the ringdove's neck,
And giving to the glancing sea-bird's wing
The semblance of a meteor.

      Mighty Sea!
Chameleon-like thou changest, but there's love
In all thy change, and constant sympathy
With yonder Sky—thy Mistress; from her brow
Thou tak'st thy moods and wear'st her colors on
Thy faithful bosom; morning's milky white,
Noon's sapphire, or the saffron glow of eve;
And all thy balmier hours, fair Element,
Have such divine complexion—crisped smiles,
Luxuriant heavings, and sweet whisperings,
That little is the wonder Love's own Queen
From thee of old was fabled to have sprung—
Creation's common! which no human power
Can parcel or enclose; the lordliest floods
And cataracts that the tiny hands of man
Can tame, conduct, or bound, are drops of dew
To thee that couldst subdue the Earth itself,
And brook'st commandment from the heavens alone
For marshalling thy waves—

      Yet, potent Sea!
How placidly thy moist lips speak ev'n now
Along yon sparkling shingles. Who can be
So fanciless as to feel no gratitude
That power and grandeur can be so serene,
Soothing the home-bound navy's peaceful way,
And rocking ev'n the fisher's little bark
As gently as a mother rocks her child?—

The inhabitants of other worlds behold
Our orb more lucid for thy spacious share
On earth's rotundity; and is he not
A blind worm in the dust, great Deep, the man

Who sees not or who seeing has no joy
In thy magnificence?   What though thou art
Unconscious and material, thou canst reach
The inmost immaterial mind's recess,
And with thy tints and motion stir its chords
To music, like the light on Memnon's lyre !

The Spirit of the Universe in thee
Is visible ; thou hast in thee the life—
The eternal, graceful, and majestic life
Of nature, and the natural human heart
Is therefore bound to thee with holy love

Earth has her gorgeous towns: the earth-circling sea
Has spires and mansions more amusive still—
Men's volant homes that measure liquid space
On wheel or wing.   The chariot of the land
With pain'd and panting steeds and clouds of dust
Has no sight-gladdening motion like these fair
Careerers with the foam beneath their bows,
Whose streaming ensigns charm the waves by day
Whose carols and whose watch-bells cheer the night,
Moor'd as they cast the shadows of their masts
In long array, or hither flit and yond
Mysteriously with slow and crossing lights,
Like spirits on the darkness of the deep.

There is a magnet-like attraction in
These waters to the imaginative power
That links the viewless with the visible,
And pictures things unseen.   To realms beyond
Yon highway of the world my fancy flies,
When by her tall and triple mast we know
Some noble voyager that has to woo
The trade-winds and to stem the ecliptic surge.
The coral groves—the shores of conch and pearl,
Where she will cast her anchor and reflect
Her cabin-window lights on warmer waves,

And under planets brighter than our own :
The nights of palmy isles, that she will see
Lit boundless by the fire-fly—all the smells
Of tropic fruits that will regale her—all
The pomp of nature, and the inspiriting
Varieties of life she has to greet,
Come swarming o'er the meditative mind.

True, to the dream of Fancy, Ocean has
His darker tints ; but where's the element
That checkers not its usefulness to man
With casual terror ?   Scathes not Earth sometimes
Her children with Tartarean fires, or shakes
Their shrieking cities, and, with one last clang
Of bells for their own ruin, strews them flat
As riddled ashes—silent as the grave?
Walks not Contagion on the Air itself?
I should—old Ocean's Saturnalian days
And roaring nights of revelry and sport
With wreck and human wo—be loath to sing;
For they are few and all their ills weigh light
Against his sacred usefulness, that bids
Our pensile globe revolve in purer air.
Here Morn and Eve with blushing thanks receive
Their freshening dews, gay fluttering breezes cool
Their wings to fan the brow of fever'd climes,
And here the Spring dips down her emerald urn
For showers to glad the earth.

                    Old Ocean was
Infinity of ages ere we breathed
Existence—and he will be beautiful
When all the living world that sees him now
Shall roll unconscious dust around the sun.
Quelling from age to age the vital throb
In human hearts, Death shall not subjugate
The pulse that swells in *his* stupendous breast,
Or interdict his minstrelsy to sound

In thundering concert with the quiring winds ;
But long as Man to parent Nature owns
Instinctive homage, and in times beyond
The power of thought to reach, bard after bard
Shall sing thy glory, Beatific Sea.

THE DEAD EAGLE.

WRITTEN AT ORAN.

Fallen as he is, this king of birds still seems
Like royalty in ruins.   Though his eyes
Are shut, that look undazzled on the sun,
He was the sultan of the sky, and earth
Paid tribute to his eyry.   It was perch'd
Higher than human conqueror ever built
His banner'd fort.   Where Atlas' top looks o'er
Zahara's desert to the equator's line :
From thence the winged despot mark'd his prey,
Above th' encampments of the Bedouins, ere
Their watchfires were extinct, or camels knelt
To take their loads, or horsemen scour'd the plain,
And there he dried his feathers in the dawn,
Whilst yet th' unwaken'd world was dark below.

There's such a charm in natural strength and power,
That human fancy has forever paid
Poetic homage to the bird of Jove.
Hence, 'neath his image, Rome array'd her turms
And cohorts for the conquest of the world.
And figuring his flight, the mind is fill'd
With thoughts that mock the pride of wingless man.

True the carr'd aeronaut can mount as high ;
But what's the triumph of his volant art ?
A rash intrusion on the realms of air.
His helmless vehicle, a silken toy,
A bubble bursting in the thunder-cloud ;
His course has no volition, and he drifts
The passive plaything of the winds.   Not such
Was this proud bird : he clove the adverse storm,
And cuff'd it with his wings.   He stopp'd his fligh;
As easily as the Arab reins his steed,
And stood at pleasure 'neath Heaven's zenith, like
A lamp suspended from its azure dome.
Whilst underneath him the world's mountains lay
Like molehills, and her streams like lucid threads
Then downward, faster than a falling star,
He near'd the earth, until his shape distinct
Was blackly shadow'd on the sunny ground ;
And deeper terror hush'd the wilderness,
To hear his nearer whoop.   Then, up again
He soar'd and wheel'd.   There was an air of scorn
In all his movements, whether he threw round
His crested head to look behind him ; or
Lay vertical and sportively display'd
The inside whiteness of his wing declined,
In gyres and undulations full of grace,
An object beautifying Heaven itself.

He—reckless who was victor, and above
The hearing of their guns—saw fleets engaged
In flaming combat.   It was naught to him
What carnage, Moor or Christian, strew'd their decks.
But if his intellect had match'd his wings,
Methinks he would have scorn'd man's vaunted power
To plough the deep ; his pinions bore him down
To Algiers the warlike, or the coral groves,
That blush beneath the green of Bona's waves ;
And traversed in an hour a wider space
Than yonder gallant ship, with all her sails

Wooing the winds, can cross from morn till eve.
His bright eyes were his compass, earth his chart,
His talons anchor'd on the stormiest cliff,
And on the very light-house rock he perch'd,
When winds churn'd white the waves.

        The earthquake's self
Disturb'd not him that memorable day,
When, o'er yon table-land, where Spain had built
Cathedrals, cannon'd forts, and palaces,
A palsy-stroke of Nature shook Oran,
Turning her city to a sepulchre,
And strewing into rubbish all her homes ;
Amidst whose traceable foundations now,
Of streets and squares, the hyæna hides himself.
That hour beheld him fly as careless o'er
The stifled shrieks of thousands buried quick,
As lately when he pounced the speckled snake,
Coil'd in yon mallows and wide nettle fields
That mantle o'er the dead old Spanish town.

Strange is the imagination's dread delight
In objects link'd with danger, death, and pain !
Fresh from the luxuries of polish'd life,
The echo of these wilds enchanted me ;
And my heart beat with joy when first I heard
A lion's roar come down the Lybian wind,
Across yon long, wide, lonely inland lake,
Where boat ne'er sails from homeless shore to shore.

And yet Numidia's landscape has its spots
Of pastoral pleasantness—though far between,
The village planted near the Maraboot's
Round roof has aye its feathery palm trees
Pair'd, for in solitude they bear no fruits.
Here nature's hues all harmonize—fields white
With alasum, or blue with bugloss—banks
Of glossy fennel, blent with tulips wild,

And sunflowers, like a garment prank'd with gold ;
Acres and miles of opal asphodel
Where sports and couches the black-eyed gazelle.
Here, too, the air's harmonious—deep-toned doves
Coo to the fife-like carol of the lark ;
And when they cease, the holy nightingale
Winds up his long, long shakes of ecstasy,
With notes that seem but the protracted sounds
Of glassy runnels bubbling over rocks.

———◆———

SONG.

To Love in my heart, I exclaim'd t'other morning,
Thou hast dwelt here too long, little lodger, take warn
      ing ;
Thou shalt tempt me no more from my life's sobe
      duty,
To go gadding, bewitch'd by the young eyes of beauty
  For weary's the wooing, ah ! weary,
When an old man will have a young dearie.

The god left my heart, at its surly reflections,
But came back on pretext of some sweet recollections,
And he made me forget what I ought to remember.
That the rose-bud of June cannot bloom in November.
  Ah ! Tom, 'tis all o'er with thy gay days—
Write psalms, and not songs for the ladies.

But time's been so far from my wisdom enriching,
That the longer I live, beauty seems more bewitching
And the only new lore my experience traces,
Is to find fresh enchantment in magical faces.
  How weary is wisdom, how weary !
When one sits by a smiling young dearie !

And should she be wroth that my homage pursues her,
I will turn and retort on my lovely accuser ;
Who's to blame, that my heart by your image is
      haunted—
It is you, the enchantress—not I, the enchanted.
  Would you have me behave more discreetly,
Beauty, look not so killingly sweetly.

———◆———

LINES

WRITTEN IN A BLANK LEAF OF LA PEROUSE'S VOYAGES.

LOVED Voyager ! his pages had a zest
More sweet than fiction to my wondering breast,
When, rapt in fancy, many a boyish day
I track'd his wanderings o'er the watery way,
Roam'd round the Aleutian isles in waking dreams,
Or pluck'd the *fleur-de-lys* by Jesso's streams—
Or gladly leap'd on that far Tartar strand,
Where Europe's anchor ne'er had bit the sand,
Where scarce a roving wild tribe cross'd the plain,
Or human voice broke nature's silent reign ;
But vast and grassy deserts feed the bear,
And sweeping deer-herds dread no hunter's snare.
Such young delight his real records brought,
His truth so touch'd romantic springs of thought,
That all my after-life—his fate and fame
Entwined romance with La Perouse's name.—
Fair were his ships, expert his gallant crews,
And glorious was th' emprise of La Perouse,—

Humanely glorious!   Men will weep for him,
When many a guilty martial fame is dim :
He plough'd the deep to bind no captive's chain—
Pursued no rapine—strew'd no wreck with slain ,
And, save that in the deep themselves lie low,
His heroes pluck'd no wreath from human wo.
'Twas his the earth's remotest bound to scan,
Conciliating with gifts barbaric man—
Enrich the world's contemporaneous mind,
And amplify the picture of mankind.
Far on the vast Pacific—midst those isles,
O'er which the earliest morn of Asia smiles,
He sounded and gave charts to many a shore
And gulf of Ocean new to nautic lore ;
Yet he that led Discovery o'er the wave,
Still fills himself an undiscover'd grave.
He came not back,—Conjecture's cheek grew pale,
Year after year—in no propitious gale,
His lilied banner held its homeward way,
And Science sadden'd at her martyr's stay.

An age elapsed—no wreck told where or when
The chief went down with all his gallant men,
Or whether by the storm and wild sea flood
He perish'd, or by wilder men of blood
The shuddering Fancy only guess'd his doom,
And Doubt to Sorrow gave but deeper gloom.
An age elapsed—when men were dead or gray,
Whose hearts had mourn'd him in their youthful day;
Fame traced on Mannicolo's shore at last,
The boiling surge had mounted o'er his mast.
The islesmen told of some surviving men,
But Christian eyes beheld them ne'er again.
Sad bourne of all his toils—with all his band—
To sleep, wreck'd, shroudless, on a savage strand !
Yet what is all that fires a hero's scorn
.f death ?—the hope to live in hearts unborn :
Life to the brave is not its fleeting breath,

But worth—foretasting fame, that follows death.
That worth had La Perouse—that meed he won ;
He sleeps—his life's long stormy watch is done.
In the great deep, whose boundaries and space
He measured, Fate ordain'd his resting-place ;
But bade his fame, like th' Ocean rolling o'er
His relics—visit every earthly shore.
Fair Science on that Ocean's azure robe,
Still writes his name in picturing the globe,
And paints—(what fairer wreath cou.d glory twine ?)
His watery course—a world-encircling line.

PILGRIM OF GLENCOE.*

THE sunset sheds a horizontal smile
O'er Highland frith and Hebridean isle,
While, gay with gambols of its finny shoals,
The glancing wave rejoices as it rolls
With streamer'd busses, that distinctly shine
All downward, pictured in the glassy brine ;
Whose crews, with faces brightening in the sun,
Keep measure with their oars, and all in one
Strike up th' old Gaelic song.—Sweep, rowers, sweep !
The fisher's glorious spoils are in the deep.

Day sinks—but twilight owes the traveller soon,
To reach his bourne, a round unclouded moon,
Bespeaking long undarken'd hours of time ;
False hope—the Scots are steadfast—not their clime.

A war-worn soldier from the western land,
Seek's Cona's vale by Ballihoula's strand ;
The vale, by eagle-haunted cliffs o'erhung,
Where Fingal fought and Ossian's harp was strung—

* I received the substance of the tradition on which this Poem
is founded, in the first instance, from a friend in London, who
wrote to Matthew N. Macdonald, Esq., of Edinburgh. He had
the kindness to send me a circumstantial account of the tradition ; and that gentleman's knowledge of the Highlands, as well
as his particular acquaintance with the district of Glencoe, leave
me no doubt of the incident having really happened. I have
not departed from the main facts of the tradition as reported to
me by Mr. Macdonald ; only I have endeavored to color the per-
sonages of the story, and to make them as distinctive as possible.

Our veteran's forehead, bronzed on sultry plains,
Had stood the brunt of thirty fought campaigns;
He well could vouch the sad romance of wars,
And count the dates of battles by his scars;
For he had served where o'er and o'er again
Britannia's oriflamme had lit the plain
Of glory—and victorious stamp'd her name
On Oudenarde's and Blenheim's fields of fame.
Nine times in battle-field his blood had stream'd,
Yet vivid still his veteran blue eye gleam'd;
Full well he bore his knapsack—unoppress'd,
And march'd with soldier-like erected crest:
Nor sign of ev'n loquacious age he wore,
Save when he told his life's adventures o'er;
Some tired of these; for terms to him were dear
Too tactical by far for vulgar ear';
As when he talk'd of rampart and ravine,
And trenches fenced with gabion and fascine—
But when his theme possess'd him all and whole,
He scorn'd proud puzzling words and warm'd the soul;
Hush'd groups hung on his lips with fond surprise,
That sketch'd old scenes—like pictures to their eyes:—
The wide war-plain, with banners glowing bright,
And bayonets to the furthest stretch of sight;
The pause, more dreadful than the peal to come
From volleys blazing at the beat of drum—
Till all the field of thundering lines became
Two level and confronted sheets of flame.
Then to the charge, when Marlbro's hot pursuit
Trode France's gilded lilies underfoot;
He came and kindled—and with martial lung
Would chant the very march their trumpets sung.—

Th' old soldier hoped, ere evening's light should fail,
To reach a home, south-east of Cona's vale;
But looking at Bennevis, capp'd with snow,
He saw its mists come curling down below,
And spread white darkness o'er the sunset glow;—

Fast rolling like tempestuous Ocean's spray,
Or clouds from troops in battle's fiery day—
So dense, his quarry 'scaped the falcon's sight.
The owl alone exulted, hating light.

Benighted thus our pilgrim groped his ground,
Half 'twixt the river's and the cataract's sound.
At last a sheep-dog's bark inform'd his ear
Some human habitation might be near;
Anon sheep-bleatings rose from rock to rock,—
'Twas Luath hounding to their fold the flock.
Ere long the cock's obstreperous clarion rang,
And next, a maid's sweet voice, that spinning sang:
At last amidst the greensward (gladsome sight!)
A cottage stood, with straw-roof golden bright.

He knock'd, was welcomed in; none ask'd his name,
Nor whither he was bound nor whence he came;
But he was beckon'd to the stranger's seat,
Right side the chimney fire of blazing peat
Blest Hospitality makes not her home
In wallèd parks and castellated dome;
She flies the city's needy greedy crowd,
And shuns still more the mansions of the proud;—
The balm of savage or of simple life,
A wild flower cut by culture's polish'd knife!

The house, no common sordid shieling cot,
Spoke inmates of a comfortable lot,
The Jacobite white rose festoon'd their door;
The windows sash'd and glazed, the oaken floor,
The chimney graced with antlers of the deer,
The rafters hung with meat for winter cheer,
And all the mansion, indicated plain
Its master a superior shepherd swain.

Their supper came—the table soon was spread
With eggs and milk and cheese and barley bread.

The family were three—a father hoar,
Whose age you'd guess at seventy years or more,
His son look'd fifty—cheerful like her lord,
His comely wife presided at the board ;
All three had that peculiar courteous grace
Which marks the meanest of the Highland race ;
Warm hearts that burn alike in weal and wo,
As if the north-wind fann'd their bosoms' glow !
But wide unlike their souls : old Norman's eye
Was proudly savage ev'n in courtesy.
His sinewy shoulders—each, though aged and lean
Broad as the curl'd Herculean head between,—
His scornful lip, his eyes of yellow fire,
And nostrils that dilated quick with ire,
With ever downward-slanting shaggy brows,
Mark'd the old lion you would dread to rouse.

Norman, in truth, had led his earlier life
In raids of red revenge and feudal strife ;
Religious duty in revenge he saw,
Proud Honor's right and Nature's honest law.
First in the charge and foremost in pursuit,
Long-breath'd, deep-chested, and in speed of foot
A match for stags—still fleeter when the prey
Was man, in persecution's evil day ;
Cheer'd to that chase by brutal bold Dundee,
No Highland hound had lapp'd more blood than he.
Oft had he changed the covenanter's breath
From howls of psalmody to howls of death ;
And though long bound to peace, it irk'd him still
His dirk had ne'er one hated foe to kill.

Yet Norman had fierce virtues, that would mock
Cold-blooded tories of the modern stock
Who starve the breadless poor with fraud and cant ;—
He slew and saved them from the pangs of want.
Nor was his solitary lawless charm
Mere dauntlessness of soul and strength of arm ;

He had his moods of kindness now and then,
And feasted ev'n well-manner'd lowland men
Who blew not up his Jacobitish flame,
Nor prefaced with "pretender" Charles's name.
Fierce, but by sense and kindness not unwon,
He loved, respected ev'n, his wiser son ;
And brook'd from him expostulations sage,
When all advisers else were spurn'd with rage.

Far happier times had moulded Ronald's mind,
By nature too of more sagacious kind.
His breadth of brow, and Roman shape of chin,
Squared well with the firm man that reign'd within.
Contemning strife as childishness, he stood
With neighbors on kind terms of neighborhood,
And whilst his father's anger naught avail'd,
His rational remonstrance never fail'd.
Full skilfully he managed farm and fold,
Wrote, cipher'd, profitably bought and sold ;
And, bless'd with pastoral leisure, deeply took
Delight to be inform'd, by speech or book,
Of that wide world beyond his mountain home,
Where oft his curious fancy loved to roam.
Oft while his faithful dog ran round his flock,
He read long hours when summer warm'd the rock :
Guests who could tell him aught were welcomed
        warm,
Ev'n pedlers' news had to his mind a charm ;
That like an intellectual magnet-stone
Drew truth from judgments simpler than his own.

His soul's proud instinct sought not to enjoy
Romantic fictions, like a minstrel boy ;
Truth, standing on her solid square, from youth
He worshipp'd—stern uncompromising truth.
His goddess kindlier smiled on him, to find
A votary of her light in land so blind ;
She bade majestic History unroll

Broad views of public welfare to his soul,
Until he look'd on clannish feuds and foes
With scorn, as on the wars of kites and crows;
Whilst doubts assail'd him, o'er and o'er again,
If men were made for kings or kings for men.
At last, to Norman's horror and dismay,
He flat denied the Stuarts' right to sway.

No blow-pipe ever whiten'd furnace fire,
Quick as these words lit up his father's ire;
Who envied even old Abraham for his faith,
Ordain'd to put his only son to death.
He started up—in such a mood of soul
The white bear bites his showman's stirring pole;
He danced too, and brought out, with snarl and howl,
"O Dia! Dia! and Dioul! Dioul!"*
But sense foils fury—as the blowing whale
Spouts, bleeds, and dyes the waves without avail—
Wears out the cable's length that makes him fast,
But, worn himself, comes up harpoon'd at last—
E'en so, devoid of sense, succumbs at length
Mere strength of zeal to intellectual strength.
His son's close logic so perplex'd his pate,
Th' old hero rather shunn'd than sought debate;
Exhausting his vocabulary's store
Of oaths and nick-names, he could say no more,
But tapp'd his mull,† roll'd mutely in his chair,
Or only whistled Killicranky's air.

Witch legends Ronald scorn'd—ghost, kelpie, wraith,
And all the trumpery of vulgar faith;
Grave matrons ev'n were shock'd to hear him slight
Authenticated facts of second-sight—
Yet never flinch'd his mockery to confound
The brutal superstition reigning round.

* God and the devil—a favorite ejaculation of Highland saints.
† Snuff-horn.

Reserved himself, still Ronald loved to scan
Men's natures—and he liked the old hearty man,
So did the partner of his heart and life—
Who pleased her Ronald, ne'er displeased his wife.
His sense, 'tis true, compared with Norman's son,
Was common-place—his tales too long outspun:
Yet Allan Campbell's sympathizing mind
Had held large intercourse with human kind;
Seen much, and gayly graphically drew
The men of every country, clime, and hue;
Nor ever stoop'd, though soldier-like his strain,
To ribaldry of mirth or oath profane.
All went harmonious till the guest began
To talk about his kindred, chief and clan,
And, with his own biography engross'd,
Mark'd not the changed demeanor of each host;
Nor how old choleric Norman's cheek became
Flush'd at the Campbell and Breadalbane name
Assigning, heedless of impending harm,
Their steadfast silence to his story's charm,
He touch'd a subject perilous to touch—
Saying, " Midst this well-known vale I wonder'd much
To lose my way.   In boyhood, long ago,
I roam'd, and loved each pathway of Glencoe;
Trapp'd leverets, pluck'd wild berries on its braes,
And fish'd along its banks long summer days.
But times grew stormy—bitter feuds arose,
Our clan was merciless to prostrate foes.
I never palliated my chieftain's blame,
But mourn'd the sin, and redden'd for the shame
Of that foul morn (Heaven blot it from the year!)
Whose shapes and shrieks still haunt my dreaming
ear.
What could I do? a serf—Glenlyon's page,
A soldier sworn at nineteen years of age;
T'have breathed one grieved remonstrance to our chief,

Tho pit or gallows* would have cured my grief.
Forced, passive as the musket in my hand,
I march'd—when, feigning royalty's command,
Against the clan Macdonald, Stairs's lord
Sent forth exterminating fire and sword;
And troops at midnight through the vale defiled,
Enjoin'd to slaughter woman, man, and child.
My clansmen many a year had cause to dread
The curse that day entail'd upon their head;
Glenlyon's self confess'd th' avenging spell—
I saw it light on him.
                              " It so befell :—
A soldier from our ranks to death was brought,
By sentence deem'd too dreadful for his fault;
All was prepared—the coffin and the cart
Stood near twelve muskets, levell'd at his heart.
The chief, whose breast for ruth had still some room,
Obtain'd reprieve a day before his doom ;—
But of the awarded boon surmised no breath.
The sufferer knelt, blindfolded, waiting death,—
And met it.   Though Glenlyon had desired
The musketeers to watch before they fired ;
If from his pocket they should see he drew
A handkerchief—their volley should ensue ;
But if he held a paper in its place,
It should be hail'd the sign of pardoning grace :—
He, in a fatal moment's absent fit,
Drew forth the handkerchief, and not the writ ;
Wept o'er the corpse and wrung his hands in wo,
Crying ' Here's thy curse again—Glencoe ! Glencoe.' "

Though thus his guest spoke feelings just and clear,
The cabin's patriarch lent impatient ear ;
Wroth that, beneath his roof, a living man

---

* To hang their vassals, or starve them to death in a dungeon, was a privilege of the Highland chiefs who had hereditary
jurisdictions.

Should boast the swine-blood of the Campbell clan ;
He hasten'd to the door—call'd out his son
To follow ; walk'd a space, and thus begun :—
" You have not, Ronald, at this day to learn
The oath I took beside my father's cairn,
When you were but a babe a twelvemonth born ;
Sworn on my dirk—by all that's sacred, sworn
To be revenged for blood that cries to Heaven—
Blood unforgiveable, and unforgiven :
But never power, *since then*, have I possess'd
To plant my dagger in a Campbell's breast.
Now, here's a self-accusing partisan,
Steep'd in the slaughter of Macdonald's clan
I scorn his civil speech and sweet-lipp'd show
Of pity—he is still our house's foe :
I'll perjure not myself—but sacrifice
The caitiff ere to-morrow's sun arise
Stand ! hear me—you're my son, the deed is just
And if I say—it must be done—it must :
A debt of honor which my clansmen crave,
Their very dead demand it from the grave."
Conjuring then their ghosts, he humbly pray'd
Their patience till the blood-debt should be paid.
But Ronald stopp'd him.—" Sir, Sir, do not dim
Your honor by a moment's angry whim ;
Your soul's too just and generous, were you cool,
To act at once th' assassin and the fool.
Bring me the men on whom revenge is due,
And I will dirk them willingly as you !
But all the real authors of that black
Old deed are gone—you cannot bring them back,
And this poor guest, 'tis palpable to judge,
In all his life ne'er bore our clan a grudge ;
Dragg'd when a boy against his will to share
That massacre, he loath'd the foul affair.
Think, if your harden'd heart be conscience-proof,
To stab a stranger underneath your roof
One who has broken bread within your gate—

Reflect—before reflection comes too late,—
Such ugly consequences there may be
As judge and jury, rope and gallows-tree.
The days of dirking snugly are gone by,
Where could you hide the body privily
When search is made for't ?"
                                    " Plunge it in yon flood,
That Campbells crimson'd with our kindred blood.'
" Ay, but the corpse may float—"
                                    " Pshaw ! dead men tell
No tales—nor will it float if leaded well.
I am determined !"—What could Ronald do ?
No house within ear-reach of his halloo,
Though that would but have publish'd household
      shame,
He temporized with wrath he could not tame,
And said, " Come in, till night put off the deed,
And ask a few more questions ere he bleed."
They enter'd ; Norman with portentous air
Strode to a nook behind the stranger's chair,
And, speaking naught, sat grimly in the shade,
With dagger in his clutch beneath his plaid.
His son's own plaid, should Norman pounce his prey
Was coil'd thick round his arm, to turn away
Or blunt the dirk.   He purposed leaving free
The door, and giving Allan time to flee,
Whilst he should wrestle with (no safe emprise)
His father's maniac strength and giant size.
Meanwhile he could nowise communicate
The impending peril to his anxious mate ;
But she, convinced no trifling matter now
Disturb'd the wonted calm of Ronald's brow,
Divined too well the cause of gloom that lower'd,
And sat with speechless terror overpower'd.
Her face was pale, so lately blithe and bland,
The stocking knitting-wire shook in her hand.
But Ronald and the guest resumed their thread
Of converse, still its theme that day of dread

" Much," said the veteran, "much as I bemoan
That deed, when half a hundred years have flown
Still on one circumstance I can reflect
That mitigates the dreadful retrospect.
A mother with her child before us flew,
I had the hideous mandate to pursue ;
But swift of foot, outspeeding bloodier men.
I chased, o'ertook her in the winding glen,
And show'd her palpitating, where to save
Herself and infant in a secret cave ;
Nor left them till I saw that they could mock
Pursuit and search within that sheltering rock."
" Heavens !" Ronald cried, in accents gladly wild,
" That woman was my mother—I the child !
Of you unknown by name she late and air,*
Spoke, wept, and ever bless'd you in her prayer,
Ev'n to her death ; describing you withal
A well-look'd florid youth, blue-eyed and tall."
They rose, exchanged embrace : the old lion then
Upstarted, metamorphosed, from his den ;
Saying, " Come and make thy home with us for life
Heaven-sent preserver of my child and wife.
I fear thou'rt poor, that Hanoverian thing
Rewards his soldiers ill."—" God save the king !"
With hand upon his heart, old Allan said,
" I wear his uniform, I eat his bread,
And whilst I've tooth to bite a cartridge, all
For him and Britain's fame I'll stand or fall."
" Bravo !" cried Ronald.   " I commend your zeal,"
Quoth Norman, " and I see your heart is leal ;
But I have pray'd my soul may never thrive
If thou shouldst leave this house of ours alive.
Nor shalt thou ; in this home protract thy breath
Of easy life, nor leave it till thy death."

* Scotch for late and early.

'The following morn arose serene as glass,
And red Bennevis shone like molten brass ;
While sunrise open'd flowers with gentle force,
The guest and Ronald walk'd in long discourse
" Words fail me," Allan said, " to thank aright
Your father's kindness shown me yesternight ;
Yet scarce I'd wish my latest days to spend
A fireside fixture with the dearest friend :
Besides, I've but a fortnight's furlough now,
To reach Macallin More,* beyond Lochawe.
I'd fain memorialize the powers that be,
To deign remembrance of my wounds and`me ;
My life-long service never bore the brand
Of sentence—lash—disgrace or reprimand.
And so I've written, though in meager style,
A long petition to his Grace Argyle ;
I mean, on reaching Innerara's shore,
To leave it safe within his castle door."
" Nay," Ronald said, " the letter that you bear
Intrust it to no lying varlet's care ;
But say a soldier of King George demands
Access, to leave it in the Duke's own hands.
But show me, first, the epistle to your chief,
'Tis naught, unless succinctly clear and brief ;
Great men have no great patience when they read,
And long petitions spoil the cause they plead."

That day saw Ronald from the field full soon
Return ; and when they all had dined at noon,
He conn'd the old man's memorial—lopp'd its length,
And gave it style, simplicity, and strength ;
'Twas finish'd in an hour—and in the next
Transcribed by Allan in perspicuous text.
At evening, he and Ronald shared once more
A long and pleasant walk by Cona's shore.
" I'd press you," quoth his host—(" I need not say

* The Duke of Argyle.

How warmly) ever more with us to stay ;
But Charles intends, 'tis said, in these same parts
To try the fealty of our Highland hearts
'Tis my belief, that he and all his line
Have—saving to be hang'd—no right divine ;
From whose mad enterprise can only flow
To thousands slaughter, and to myriads wo.
Yet have they stirr'd my father's spirit sore,,
He flints his pistols—whets his old claymore—
And longs as ardently to join the fray
As boy to dance who hears the bagpipe play.
Though calm one 'day, the next, disdaining rule,
He'd gore your red coat like an angry bull:
I told him, and he own'd it might be so,
Your tempers never could in concert flow.
But ' Mark,' he added, ' Ronald ! from our door
Let not this guest depart forlorn and poor ;
Let not your souls the niggardness evince
Of lowland pedler, or of German prince ;
He gave you life—then feed him as you'd feed
Your very father were he cast in need.'
He gave—you'll find it by your bed to-night,
A leathern purse of crowns, all sterling bright :
You see I do you kindness not by stealth.
My wife—no advocate of squandering wealth—
Vows that it would be parricide, or worse,
Should we neglect you—here's a silken purse,
Some golden pieces through the network shine,
'Tis proffer'd to you from her heart and mine.
But come ! no foolish delicacy, no.!
We own, but cannot cancel what we owe-
This sum shall duly reach you once a year."
Poor Allan's furrow'd face, and flowing tear,
Confess'd sensations which he could not speak.
Old Norman bade him farewell kindly meek.

At morn, the smiling dame rejoiced to pack
With viands full the old soldier's haversack.

He fear'd not hungry grass* with such a load,
And Ronald saw him miles upon his road.

A march of three days brought him to Lochfyne
Argyle, struck with his manly look benign,
And feeling interest in the veteran's lot,
Created him a sergeant on the spot—
An invalid, to serve not—but with pay
(A mighty sum to him,) twelve pence a day
"But have you heard not," said Macallin More,
"Charles Stuart's landed on Eriska's shore,
And Jacobites are arming?"—"What! indeed!
Arrived! then I'm no more an invalid;
My new-got halbert I must straight employ
In battle."—"As you please, old gallant boy:
Your gray hairs well might plead excuse, 'tis true,
But now's the time we want such men as you."
In brief, at Innerara Allan stay'd,
And join'd the banners of Argyle's brigade.

Meanwhile, th' old choleric shepherd of Glencoe
Spurn'd all advice, and girt himself to go.
What was't to him that foes would poind their fold,
Their lease, their very beds beneath them sold!
And firmly to his text he would have kept,
Though Ronald argued and his daughter wept.
But midst the impotence of tears and prayer,
Chance snatch'd them from proscription and despair
Old Norman's blood was headward wont to mount
Too rapid from his heart's impetuous fount;
And one day, whilst the German rats he cursed,
An artery in his wise sensorium burst.
The lancet saved him: but how changed, alas,
From him who fought at Killiecrankie's pass!

* When the hospitable Highlanders load a parting guest with
provisions, they tell him he will need them, as he has to go
over a great deal of *hungry grass.*

Tame as a spaniel, timid as a child,
He mutter'd incoherent words and smiled ;
He wept at kindness, roll'd a vacant eye,
And laugh'd full often when he meant to cry
Poor man ! whilst in this lamentable state,
Came Allan back one morning to his gate,
Hale and unburden'd by the woes of eild,
And fresh with credit from Culloden's field.
'Twas fear'd at first, the sight of him might touch
The old Macdonald's morbid mind too much ;
But no ! though Norman knew him and disclosed,
Ev'n rallying memory, he was still composed ;
Ask'd all particulars of the fatal fight,
And only heaved a sigh for Charles's flight ;
Then said, with but one moment's pride of air,
It might not have been so had I been there !
Few days elapsed till he reposed beneath
His gray cairn, on the wild and lonely heath ;
Son, friends, and kindred of his dust took leave,
And Allan, with the crape bound round his sleeve.

Old Allan now hung up his sergeant's sword,
And sat, a guest for life, at Ronald's board.
He waked no longer at the barrack's drum,
Yet still you'd see, when peep of day was come,
Th' erect tall red-coat, walking pastures round,
Or delving with his spade the garden ground.
Of cheerful temper, habits strict and sage,
He reach'd, enjoy'd a patriarchal age—
Loved to the last by the Macdonalds.　Near
Their house, his stone was placed with many a tear
And Ronald's self, in stoic virtue brave,
Scorn'd not to weep at Allan Campbell's grave.

THE CHILD AND HIND.*

Come, maids and matrons, to caress
Wiesbaden's gentle hind ;
And, smiling, deck its glossy neck
With forest flowers entwined.

Your forest flowers are fair to show,
And landscapes to enjoy ;
But fairer is your friendly doe
That watch'd the sleeping boy

* I wish I had preserved a copy of the Wiesbaden newspaper in which this anecdote of the " Child and Hind" is recorded ; but I have unfortunately lost it. The story, however, is a matter of fact ; it took place in 1838 : every circumstance mentioned in the following ballad literally happened
I was in Wiesbaden eight months ago, and was shown the
very tree under which the boy was found sleeping with a
bunch of flowers in his little hand. A similar occurrence is
told by tradition, of Queen Genevova's child being preserved
by being suckled by a female deer, when that Princess—an
early Christian—and now a Saint in the Romish calendar,
was chased to the desert by her heathen enemies. The spot
assigned to the traditionary event is not a hundred miles from
Wiesbaden, where a chapel still stands to her memory.

I could not ascertain whether the Hind that watched my
hero " Wilhelm," suckled him or not ;. but it was generally
believed that she had no milk to give him, and that the boy
must have been for two days and a half entirely without food
unless it might be grass or leaves. If this was the case, the
circumstance of the Wiesbaden deer watching the child, was
a still more wonderful token of instinctive fondness than that
of the deer in the Genevova tradition, who was naturally
anxious to be relieved of her milk.

'Twas after church—on Ascension day—
When organs ceased to sound,
Wiesbaden's people crowded gay
The deer-park's pleasant ground.

There, where Elysian meadows smile,
And noble trees upshoot,
The wild thyme and the chamomile
Smell sweetly at their root ;

The aspen quivers nervously,
The oak stands stilly bold—
And climbing bindweed hangs on high
His bells of beaten gold.*

Nor stops the eye till mountains shine
That bound a spacious view,
Beyond the lordly, lovely Rhine,
In visionary blue.

There, monuments of ages dark
Awaken thoughts sublime ;
Till, swifter than the steaming bark,
We mount the stream of time.

The ivy there old castles shades
That speak traditions high
Of minstrels—tournaments—crusades,
And mail-clad chivalry.

Here came a twelve years' married pair—
And with them wander'd free
Seven sons and daughters, blooming fair,
A gladsome sight to see.

* There is only one kind of bindweed that is yellow, and that
is the flower here mentioned, the Panicolatus Convolvulus.

Their Wilhelm, little innocent,
The youngest of the seven,
Was beautiful as painters paint
The cherubim of Heaven.

By turns he gave his hand, so dear,
To parent, sister, brother ;
And each, that he was safe and near,
Confided in the other.

But Wilhelm loved the field-flowers bright
With love beyond all measure ;
And cull'd them with as keen delight
As misers gather treasure.

Unnoticed, he contrived to glide
Adown a greenwood alley
By lilies lured—that grew beside
A streamlet in the valley ;

And there, where under beech and birch
The rivulet meander'd,
He stray'd, till neither shout nor search
Could track where he had wander'd.

Still louder, with increasing dread,
They call'd his darling name ;
But 'twas like speaking to the dead—
An echo only came.

Hours pass'd till evening's beetle roams,
And blackbird's songs begin ;
Then all went back to happy homes,
Save Wilhelm's kith and kin.

The night came on—all others slept
Their cares away till morn ;
But sleepless, all night watch'd and wept
That family forlorn.

26

Betimes the town-crier had been sent
  With loud bell, up and down ;
And told th' afflicting accident
  Throughout Wiesbaden's town :

The father, too, ere morning smiled,
  Had all his wealth uncoffer'd ;
And to the wight would bring his child,
  A thousand crowns had offer'd.

Dear friends, who would have blush'd to take
  That guerdon from his hand,
Soon join'd in groups—for pity's sake,
  The child-exploring band.

The news reach'd Nassau's Duke : ere earth
  Was gladden'd by the lark,
He sent a hundred soldiers forth
  To ransack all his park.

Their side-arms glitter'd through the wood,
  With bugle-horns to sound ;
Would that on errand half so good
  The soldier oft were found !

But though they roused up beast and bird
  From many a nest and den,
No signal of success was heard
  From all the hundred men.

A second morning's l'ght expands,
  Unfound the infant fair ;
And Wilhelm's household wring their hands,
  Abandon'd to despair.

But, haply, a poor artisan
  Search'd ceaselessly, till he
Found safe asleep the little one,
  Beneath a beechen tree.

His hand still grasp'd a bunch of flowers ;
And (true, though wondrous) near,
To sentry his reposing hours,
There stood a female deer—

Who dipp'd her horns at all that pass'd*
The spot where Wilhelm lay ;
Till force was had to hold her fast,
And bear the boy away.

Hail ! sacred love of childhood—hail !
How sweet it is to trace
Thine instinct in Creation's scale,
Ev'n 'neath the human race

To this poor wanderer of the wild
Speech, reason were unknown—
And yet she watch'd a sleeping child
As if it were her own ·

And thou, Wiesbaden's artisan,
Restorer of the boy,
Was ever welcomed mortal man
With such a burst of joy ?

The father's ecstasy—the mother's
Hysteric bosom's swell ;
The sisters' sobs—the shout of brothers,
I have not power to tell.

The working man, with shoulders broad,
Took blithely to his wife
The thousand crowns ; a pleasant load,
That made him rich for life.

* The female deer has no such antlers as the male, and sometimes no horns at all ; but I have observed many with short
ones suckling their fawns.

And Nassau's Duke the favorite took
Into his deer-park's centre,
To share a field with other pets
Where deer-slayer cannot enter.

There, whilst thou cropp'st thy flowery food
Each hand shall pat thee kind ;
And man shall never spill thy blood—
Wiesbaden's gentle hind.

———◆———

NAPOLEON AND THE BRITISH SAILOR *

I LOVE contemplating—apart
    From all his homicidal glory,
The traits that soften to our heart
    Napoleon's glory !

'Twas when his banners at Boulogne
    Arm'd in our island every freeman,
His navy chanced to capture one
    Poor British seaman.

They suffer'd him—I know not how,
    Unprison'd on the shore to roam ;
And aye was bent his longing brow
    On England's home.

* This anecdote has been published in several public journals,
with French and British.   My belief in its authenticity was confirmed by an Englishman long resident at Boulogne lately telling
me, that he remembered the circumstance to have been generally talked of in the place

His eye, methinks! pursued the flight
  Of birds to Britain half-way over;
With envy *they* could reach the white
  Dear cliffs of Dover.

A stormy midnight watch, he thought,
  Than this sojourn would have been dearer,
If but the storm his vessel brought
  To England nearer.

At last, when care had banish'd sleep,
  He saw one morning—dreaming—doting,
An empty hogshead from the deep
  Come shoreward floating;

He hid it in a cave, and wrought
  The live-long day laborious; lurking
Until he launch'd a tiny boat
  By mighty working

Heaven help us! 'twas a thing beyond
  Description wretched; such a wherry
Perhaps ne'er ventured on a pond,
  Or cross'd a ferry.

For ploughing in the salt-sea field,
  It would have made the boldest shudder;
Untarr'd, un, impass'd, and unkeel'd,
  No sail--no rudder.

From neighb'ring woods he interlaced
  His sorry skiff with wattled willows;
And thus equipp'd he would have pass'd
  The foaming billows—

But Frenchmen caught him on the beach,
  His little Argus sorely jeering;
Till tidings of him chanced to reach
  Napoleon's hearing.

. With folded arms Napoleon stood,
    Serene alike in peace and danger ;
And, in his wonted attitude,
    Address'd the stranger :—

" Rash man, that wouldst yon Channel pass.
    On twigs and staves so rudely fashion'd ;
Thy heart with some sweet British lass
    Must be impassion'd."

" I have no sweetheart," said the lad ;
    " But—absent long from one another—
Great was the longing that I had
    To see my mother."

" And so thou shalt," Napoleon said,
    " Ye've both my favor fairly won ;
A noble mother must have bred
    So brave a son."

He gave the tar a piece of gold,
    And, with a flag of truce, commanded
He should be shipp'd to England Old,
    And safely landed.

Our sailor oft could scantly shift
    To find a dinner, plain and hearty ;
But *never* changed the coin and gift
    Of Bonaparté.

THE JILTED NYMPH.

A SONG,

TO THE SCOTCH TUNE OF "WOO'D AND MARRIED AND A'.

I'M jilted, forsaken, outwitted ;
    Yet think not I'll whimper or brawl—
The lass is alone to be pitied
    Who ne'er has been courted at all :
Never by great or small,
Woo'd or jilted at all ;
    Oh, how unhappy's the lass
Who has never been courted at all !

My brother call'd out the dear faithless,
    In fits I was ready to fall,
Till I found a policeman who, scatheless,
    Swore them both to the peace at Guildhall ;
Seized them, seconds and all—
Pistols, powder and ball ;
    I wish'd him to die my devoted,
But not in a duel to sprawl.

What though at my heart he has tilted,
    What though I have met with a fall ?
Better be courted and jilted,
    Than never be courted at all.
Woo'd and jilted and all,
Still I will dance at the ball ;
    And waltz and quadrille
    With light heart and heel,
With proper young men, and tall.

But lately I've met with a suitor,
　Whose heart I have gotten in thrall,
And I hope soon to tell you in future
　That I'm woo'd, and married and all;
Woo'd and married and all,
What greater bliss can befall?
　And you all shall partake of my bridal cake,
When I'm woo'd and married, and all.

BENLOMOND.

Hadst thou a genius on thy peak,
　What tales, white-headed Ben,
Couldst thou of ancient ages speak,
　That mock th' historian's pen!

Thy long duration makes our lives
　Seem but so many hours;
And likens, to the bees' frail hives,
　Our most stupendous towers.

Temples and towers thou'st seen begun,
　New creeds, new conquerors' sway;
And, like their shadows in the sun,
　Hast seen them swept away.

Thy steadfast summit, heaven-allied,
　(Unlike life's little span,)
Looks down, a Mentor on the pride
　Of perishable man.

THE PARROT.

A DOMESTIC ANECDOTE.

The foLowing incident, so strongly illustrating the power
of memory and association in the lower animals, is not a fiction. I heard it many years ago in the Island of Mull, from
the family to whom the bird belonged.

THE deep affections of the breast,
   That Heaven to living things imparts,
Are not exclusively possess'd
   By human hearts.

A parrot, from the Spanish Main,
   Full young, and early caged, came o'er
With bright wings, to the bleak domain
   Of Mulla's shore.

To spicy groves where he had won
   His plumage of resplendent hue,
His native fruits, and skies, and sun,
   He bade adieu.

For these he changed the smoke of turf,
   A heathery land and misty sky,
And turn'd on rocks and raging surf
   His golden eye.

But, petted, in our climate cold
   He lived and chatter'd many a day;
Until with age, from green and gold
   His wings grew gray.

At last, when blind and seeming dumb,
  He scolded, laugh'd, and spoke no more,
A Spanish stranger chanced to come
  To Mulla's shore ;

He hail'd the bird in Spanish speech,
  The bird in Spanish speech replied,
Flapp'd round his cage with joyous screech,
  Dropp'd down, and died

ON GETTING HOME

THE PORTRAIT OF A FEMALE CHILD,

SIX YEARS OLD.

PAINTED BY EUGENIO LATILLA.

Type of the Cherubim above,
Come, live with me, and be my love !
Smile from my wall, dear roguish sprite,
By sunshine and by candle-light ;
For both look sweetly on thy traits :
Or, were the Lady Moon to gaze,
She'd welcome thee with lustre bland,
Like some young fay from Fairyland.
Cast in simplicity's own mould,
How canst thou be so manifold
In sportively distracting charms ?
Thy lips—thine eyes—thy little arms
That wrap thy shoulders and thy head,
In homeliest shawl of netted thread,

Brown woollen net-work; yet it seeks
Accordance with thy lovely cheeks,
And more becomes thy beauty's bloom
Than any shawl from Cashmere's loom.

Thou hast not, to adorn thee, girl,
Flower, link of gold, or gem or pearl—
I would not let a ruby speck
The peeping whiteness of thy neck
Thou need'st no casket, witching elf,
No gawd—thy toilet is thyself;
Not ev'n a rose-bud from the bower,
Thyself a magnet—gem and flower.

My arch and playful little creature,
Thou hast a mind in every feature;
Thy brow, with its disparted locks,
Speaks language that translation mocks;
Thy lucid eyes so beam with soul,
They on the canvass seem to roll—
Instructing both my head and heart
To idolize the painter's art.
He marshals minds to Beauty's feast—
He is Humanity's high priest
Who proves, by heavenly forms on earth,
How much this world of ours is worth.
Inspire me, child, with visions fair!
For children, in Creation, are
The only things that could be given
Back, and alive—unchanged—to Heaven.

SONG OF THE COLONISTS DEPARTING FOR NEW ZEALAND

Steer, helmsman, till you steer our way,
  By stars beyond the line ;
We go to found a realm, one day,
  Like England's self to shine.

CHORUS.

Cheer up—cheer up—our course we'll keep,
  With dauntless heart and hand ;
And when we've plough'd the stormy deep,
  We'll plough a smiling land :—

A land, where beauties importune
  The Briton to its bowers,
To sow but plenteous seeds, and prune
  Luxuriant fruits and flowers.
      Chorus.—Cheer up—cheer up, &c.

There, tracts uncheer'd by human words,
  Seclusion's wildest holds,
Shall hear the lowing of our herds,
  And tinkling of our folds.
      Chorus.—Cheer up—cheer up, &c.

Like rubies set in gold, shall blush
  Our vineyards girt with corn ;
And wine, and oil, and gladness gush
  From Amalthea's horn.
      Chorus.—Cheer up—cheer up, &c.

Britannia's pride is in our hearts,
   Her blood is in our veins—
We'll girdle earth with British arts,
   Like Ariel's magic chains.

CHORUS.

Cheer up—cheer up—our course we'll keep,
   With dauntless heart and hand ;
And when we've plough'd the stormy deep,
   We'll plough a smiling land.

MOONLIGHT.

The kiss that would make a maid's cheek flush
   Wroth, as if kissing were a sin
   Amidst the Argus eyes and din
     And tell-tale glare of noon,
Brings but a murmur and a blush,
   Beneath the modest moon.

Ye days, gone—never to come back,
   When love return'd entranced me so,
   That still its pictures move and glow
     In the dark chamber of my heart ;
Leave not my memory's future track—
   I will not let you part.

"Twas moonlight, when my earliest love
   First on my bosom dropp'd her head ;
A moment then concentrated
27

The bliss of years, as if the spheres
Their course had faster driven,
And carried Enoch-like above,
A living man to Heaven.

'Tis by the rolling moon we measure,
The date between our nuptial night
And that b'est hour which brings to light
The fruit of bliss—the pledge of faith;
When we impress upon the treasure
A father's earliest kiss.

The Moon's the Earth's enamor'd bride;
True to him in her very changes,
To other stars she never ranges:
Though, cross'd by him, sometimes she dips
Her light, in short offended pride,
And faints to an eclipse.

The fairies revel by her sheen;
'Tis only when the Moon's above
The fire-fly kindles into love,
And flashes light to show it:
The nightingale salutes her Queen
Of Heaven, her heav'nly poet.

Then ye that love—by moonlight gloom
Meet at my grave, and plight regard.
Oh! could I be the Orphéan bard
Of whom it is reported,
That nightingales sung o'er his tomb,
Whilst lovers came and courted.

CORA LINN, OR THE FALLS OF THE CLYDE.

WRITTEN ON REVISITING IT IN 1837.

The time I saw thee, Cora, last,
'Twas with congenial friends ;
And calmer hours of pleasure past—
My memory seldom sends.

It was as sweet an Autumn day
As ever shone on Clyde,
And Lanark's orchards all the way,
Put forth their golden pride ;

Ev'n hedges, busk'd in bravery,
Look'd rich that sunny morn ;
The scarlet hip and blackberry
So prank'd September's thorn.

In Cora's glen the calm how deep !
The trees on loftiest hill
Like statues stood, or things asleep,
All motionless and still.

The torrent spoke, as if his noise
Bade earth be quiet round,
And give his loud and lonely voice
A more commanding sound.

His foam, beneath the yellow light
Of noon, came down like one
Continuous sheet of jaspers bright,
Broad rolling by the sun.

Dear Linn ! let loftier falling floods
Have prouder names than thine ;
And king of all, enthroned in woods,
Let Niagara shine

Barbarian, let him shake his coasts
With reeking thunders far,
Extended like th' array of hosts
In broad, embattled war !

His voice appals the wilderness .
Approaching thine, we feel
A solemn, deep melodiousness,
That needs no louder peal.

More fury would but disenchant
Thy dream-inspiring din ;
Be thou the Scottish Muse's haunt,
Romantic Cora Linn.

LINES

SUGGESTED BY THE STATUE OF ARNOLD VON WINKELRIED,*

STANZ-UNDERWALDEN.

—

INSPIRING and romantic Switzers' land,
Though mark'd with majesty by Nature's hand,
What charm ennobles most thy landscape's face ?—
Th' heroic memory of thy native race—
Who forced tyrannic hosts to bleed or flee,
And made their rocks the ramparts of the free ;
Their fastnesses roll'd back th' invading tide
Of conquest, and their mountains taught them pride
Hence they have patriot names—in fancy's eye,
Bright as their glaciers glittering in the sky ;
Patriots who make the pageantries of kings
Like shadows seem and unsubstantial things.
Their guiltless glory mocks oblivion's rust,
Imperishable, for their cause was just.

Heroes of old ! to whom the Nine have strung
Their lyres, and spirit-stirring anthems sung ;
Heroes of chivalry ! whose banners grace
The aisles of many a consecrated place,
Confess how few of you can match in fame
The martyr Winkelried's immortal name !†

---

* For an account of this patriotic Swiss and his heroic death
at the battle of Sempach, see Dr. Beattie's "Switzerland Illustrated," vol. ii., pp. 111–115.

† The advocates of classical learning tell us that, without
classic historians, we should never become acquainted with the

SONG ON OUR QUEEN.

SET TO MUSIC BY CHARLES NEATE, ESQ.

———

VICTORIA's sceptre o'er the deep
    Has touch'd, and broken slavery's chain ;
Yet, strange magician ! she enslaves
    Our hearts within her own domain.

Her spirit is devout, and burns
    With thoughts averse to bigotry ;
Yet she, herself the idol, turns
    Our thoughts into idolatry.

most splendid traits of human character ; but one of those traits
patriotic self-devotion, may surely be heard of elsewhere, without learning Greek and Latin. There are few, who have read
modern history, unacquainted with the noble voluntary death
of the Switzer Winkelried. Whether he was a peasant or man
of superior birth, is a point not quite settled in history, though I
am inclined to suspect that he was simply a peasant. But this
is certain, that in the battle of Sempach, perceiving that there
was no other means of breaking the heavy-armed lines of the
Austrians than by gathering as many of their spears as he could
grasp together, he opened a passage for his fellow combatants,
who, with hammers and hatchets, hewed down the mailed
men-at-arms, and won the victory

LINES ON MY NEW CHILD-SWEETHEART

I HOLD it a religious duty
To love and worship children's beauty ;
They've least the taint of earthly clod,
They're freshest from the hand of God ;
With heavenly looks they make us sure
The heaven that made them must be pure ;
We love them not in earthly fashion,
But with a beatific passion.
I chanced to, yesterday, behold
A maiden child of beauty's mould ;
'Twas near, more sacred was the scene,
The palace of our patriot Queen.
The little charmer to my view
Was sculpture brought to life anew,
Her eyes had a poetic glow, . .
Her pouting mouth was Cupid's bow :
And through her frock I could descry
Her neck and shoulders' symmetry.
'Twas obvious from her walk and gait
Her limbs were beautifully straight ;
I stopp'd th' enchantress, and was told,
Though tall, she was but four years old.
Her guide so grave an aspect wore
I could not ask a question more ;
But follow'd her.   The little one
Threw backward ever and anon
Her lovely neck, as if to say,
" I know you love me, Mister Grey ;"

For by its instinct childhood's eye
Is shrewd in physiognomy ;
They well distinguish fawning art
From sterling fondness of the heart.

And so she flirted, like a true,
Good woman, till we bade adieu.
'Twas then I with regret grew wild,
Oh, beauteous, interesting child !
Why ask'd I not thy home and name ?
My courage fail'd me—more's the shame.
But where abides this jewel rare ?
Oh, ye that own her, tell me where !
For sad it makes my heart and sore
To think I ne'er may meet her more.

TO THE UNITED STATES OF NORTH AMERICA.

United States, your banner wears
　　Two emblems—one of fame ;
Alas, the other that it bears
　　Reminds us of your shame.

Your standard's constellation types
　　White freedom by its stars ;
But what's the meaning of the stripes ?
　　They mean your negroes' scars.

THE LAUNCH OF A FIRST-RATE

WRITTEN ON WITNESSING THE SPECTACLE.

———

ENGLAND hails thee with emotion,
   Mightiest child of naval art,
Heaven resounds thy welcome !   Ocean
   . Takes thee smiling to his heart.

Giant oaks of bold expansion
   O'er seven hundred acres fell,
All to build thy, noble mansion,
   Where our hearts of oak shall dwell.

'Midst those trees the wild deer bounded,
   Ages long ere we were born,
And our great-grandfathers sounded
   Many a jovial hunting-horn.

Oaks that living did inherit
   Grandeur from our earth and sky,
Still robust, the native spirit.
   In your timbers shall not die.

Ship to shine in martial story,
   Thou shalt cleave the ocean's path,
Freighted with Britannia's glory
   And the thunders of her wrath.

Foes shall crowd their sails and fly thee,
   Threat'ning havoc to their deck,

When afar they first descry thee,
    Like the coming whirlwind's speck

Gallant bark ! thy pomp and beauty
    Storm or battle ne'er shall blast,
Whilst our tars in pride and duty
    Nail thy colors to the mast.

EPISTLE FROM ALGIERS,

TO HORACE SMITH.

DEAR HORACE ! be melted to tears,
    For I'm melting with heat as I rhyme ;
Though the name of this place is All-jeers,
    'Tis no joke to fall in with its clime.

With a shaver* from France who came o'er,
    To an African inn I ascend ;
I am cast on a barbarous shore,
    Where a barber alone is my friend.

Do you ask me the sights and the news
    Of this wonderful city to sing ?
Alas ! my hotel has its mews,
    But no muse of the Helicon's spring.

* On board the vessel from Marseilles to Algiers I met with
a fellow-passenger whom I supposed to be a physician from
his dress and manners, and the attentions which he paid
me to alleviate the sufferings of my sea-sickness. He turned
out to be a perruquier and barber in Algeria—but his voca
tion did not lower him in my estimation—for he continued
his attentions till he passed my baggage through the customs
and helped me, when half dead with exhaustion, to the best
hotel.

My windows afford me the sight
  Of a people all diverse in hue ;
They are black, yellow, olive, and white,
  Whilst I in my sorrow look blue.

Here are groups for the painter to take,
  Whose figures jocosely combine,—
The Arab disguised in his haik,*
  And the Frenchman disguised in his wine

In his breeches of petticoat size
  You may say as the Mussulman goes,   .
That his garb is a fair compromise
  'Twixt a kilt and a pair of small-clothes.

The Mooresses, shrouded in white,
  Save two holes for their eyes to give room,
Seem like corpses in sport or in spite
  That have slyly whipp'd out of their tomb.

The old Jewish dames make me sick :
  If I were the devil—I declare
Such hags should not mount a broom-stick
  In my service to ride through the air.

But hipp'd and undined as I am,
  My hippogriff's course I must rein-
For the pain of my thirst is no sham,
  Though I'm bawling aloud for champagne.

Dinner's brought ; but the wines have no pith—
  They are flat as the statutes at law ;
And for all that they bring me, dear Smith !
  Would a glass of brown stout they could draw

O'er each French trashy dish as I bend,
  My heart feels a patriot's grief !

* A mantle worn by the natives.

And the round tears, O England' descend
　When I think on a round of thy beef.

Yes, my soul sentimentally craves
　British beer.—Hail, Britannia, hail!
To thy flag on the foam of the waves,
　And the foam on thy flagons of ale.

'Yet I own, in this hour of my drought,
　A dessert has most welcomely come ;
Here are peaches that melt in the mouth,
　And grapes blue and big as a plum.

There are melons too, luscious and great,
　But the slices I eat shall be few,
For from melons incautiously eat
　. Melancholic effects may ensue.

Horrid pun! you'll exclaim ; but be calm,
　Though my letter bears date, as you view
From the land of the date-bearing palm
　I will palm no more puns upon you.

TO A YOUNG LADY

WHO ASKED ME TO WRITE SOMETHING ORIGINAL FOR
HER ALBUM.

AN original something, fair maid, you would win me
To write—but how shall I begin ?
For I fear I have nothing original in me—
Excepting Original Sin.

FRAGMENT OF AN ORATORIO,

FROM THE BOOK OF JOB.

———

Having met my illustrious friend the Composer Neukomm, at Algiers, several years ago, I commenced this intended Oratorio at his desire, but he left the place before I proceeded farther in the poem ; and it has been thus left unfinished.

———

CRUSH'D by misfortune's yoke,
Job lamentably spoke—
" My boundless curse be on
The day that I was born ;
Quench'd be the star that shone
Upon my natal morn.
In the grave I long
To shroud my breast ;
Where the wicked cease to wrong,
And the weary are at rest."
Then Eliphaz rebuked his wild despair :
" What Heaven ordains, 'tis meet that man
    should bear.
Lately, at midnight drear,
A vision shook my bones with fear
A spirit pass'd before my face,
And yet its form I could not trace ;
It stopp'd—it stood—it chill'd my blood,
The hair upon my flesh uprose
With freezing dread !
Deep silence reign'd, and, at its close,
I heard a voice that said—

' Shall mortal man be more pure and just
Than God, who made him from the dust ?
Hast thou not learnt of old, how fleet
Is the triumph of the hypocrite ;
How soon the wreath of joy grows wan
On the brow of the ungodly man ?
By the fire of his conscience he perisheth
In an unblown flame :
The Earth demands his death,
And the Heavens reveal his shame.' "

JOB.

Is this your consolation ?
Is it thus that ye condole
With the depth of my desolation,
And the anguish of my soul ?
But I will not cease to wail
The bitterness of my bale.—
Man that is born of woman,
Short and evil is his hour ;
He fleeth like a shadow,
He fadeth like a flower.
My days are pass'd—my hope and trust
Is but to moulder in the dust.

CHORUS.

Bow, mortal, bow, before thy God,
Nor murmur at his chastening rod :
Fragile being of earthly clay,
Think on God's eternal sway !
Hark ! from the whirlwind forth
Thy Maker speaks—" Thou child of earth,
Where wert thou when I laid
Creation's corner-stone ?
When the sons of God rejoicing made,
And the morning stars together sang and shone ?

Hadst thou power to bid above
Heaven's constellations glow ;
Or shape the forms that live and move
On Nature's face below ?
Hast thou given the horse his strength and pride '
He paws the valley with nostril wide,
He smells far off the battle ;
He neighs at the trumpet's sound—
And his speed devours the ground,
As he sweeps to where the quivers rattle,
And the spear and shield shine bright,
'Midst the shouting of the captains
And the thunder of the fight.

NOTES

NOTES.

P. 5, l. 37.

And such thy strength-inspiring aid .hat bore
The hardy Byron to his native shore—

The following picture of his own distress, given by
Byron in his simple and interesting narrative, justifies
the description in page 5.

After relating the barbarity of the Indian cacique to
his child, he proceeds thus :—" A day or two after we
put to sea again, and crossed the great bay I mentioned
we had been at the bottom of when we first hauled
away to the westward. The land here was very low
and sandy, and something like the mouth of a river
which discharged itself into the sea, and which had
been taken no notice of by us before, as it was so shal-
low that the Indians were obliged to take every thing
out of their canoes, and carry them over land. We
rowed up the river four or five leagues, and then took
into a branch of it that ran first to the eastward, and
then to the northward : here it became much narrower,
and the stream excessively rapid, so that we gained but
little way, though we wrought very hard. At night we
landed upon its banks, and had a most uncomfortable
lodging, it being a perfect swamp, and we had nothing
to cover us, though it rained excessively. The Indians
were little better off than we, as there was no wood
here to make their wigwams ; so that all they could do
was to prop up the bark, which they carry in the bot-

tom of their canoes, and shelter themselves as well as they could to the leeward of it. Knowing the difficulties they had to encounter here, they had provided themselves with some seal; but we had not a morsel to eat, after the heavy fatigues of the day, excepting a sort of root we saw the Indians make use of, which was very disagreeable to the taste. We labored all next day against the stream, and fared as we had done the day before. The next day brought us to the carrying place. Here was plenty of wood, but nothing to be got for sustenance. We passed this night, as we had frequently done, under a tree; but what we suffered at this time is not easy to be expressed. I had been three days at the oar without any kind of nourishment except the wretched root above mentioned. I had no shirt, for it had rotted off by bits. All my clothes consisted of a short grieko, (something like a bear-skin,) a piece of red cloth which had once been a waistcoat, and a ragged pair of trousers, without shoes or stockings."

P. 6, l. 18.

—— *a Briton and a friend!*

Don Patricio Gedd, a Scotch physician in one of the Spanish settlements, hospitably relieved Byron and his wretched associates, of which the Commodore speaks in the warmest terms of gratitude.

P. 6, l. 32.

Or yield the lyre of Heaven another string.

The seven strings of Apollo's harp were the symbolical representation of the seven planets. Herschel, by discovering an eighth, might be said to add another string to the instrument.

P. 6, l. 33.

The Swedish sage.

Linnæus.

P. 7, l. 15

Deep from his vaults, the Loxian murmurs flow.

Loxias is the name frequently given to Apollo by Greek writers; it is met with more than once in the Choephorœ of Æschylus.

P 8, l. 9.

Unlocks a generous store at thy command,
Like Horeb's rocks beneath the prophet's hand.

See Exodus, chap. xvii. 3, 5, 6.

P. 12, l. 8.

Wild Obi flies—

Among the negroes of the West Indies, Obi, or Orhiah, is the name of a magical power, which is believed by them to affect the object of its malignity with dismal calamities. Such a belief must undoubtedly have been deduced from the superstitious mythology of their kinsmen on the coast of Africa. I have, therefore, personified Obi as the evil spirit of the African, although the history of the African tribes mentions the evil spirit of their religious creed by a different appellation.

P. 12, l. 12.

—— Sibir's dreary mines.

Mr. Bell of Antermony, in his Travels through Siberia, informs us that the name of the country is universally pronounced Sibir by the Russians.

P. 12, l. 26.

Presaging wrath to Poland—and to man!

The history of the partition of Poland, of the massacre in the suburbs of Warsaw, and on the bridge of Prague, the triumphant entry of Suwarrow into the Polish capital, and the insult offered to human nature, by the blasphemous thanks offered up to Heaven, for victories obtained over men fighting in the sacred cause of liberty, by murderers and oppressors, are events generally known.

The shrill horn blew.

The negroes in the West Indies are summoned to
their morning work by a shell or horn.

P. 17, l. 18.

How long was Timour's iron sceptre sway'd.

To elucidate this passage, I shall subjoin a quotation
from the preface to Letters from a Hindoo Rajah, a
work of elegance and celebrity.

" The impostor of Mecca had established, as one of
the principles of his doctrine, the merit of extending it
either by persuasion, or the sword, to all parts of the
earth.   How steadily this injunction was adhered to by
his followers, and with what success it was pursued, is
well known to all who are in the least conversant in
history.

" The same overwhelming torrent which had inun-
dated the greater part of Africa, burst its way into the
very heart of Europe, and covering many kingdoms of
Asia with unbounded desolation, directed its baneful
course to the flourishing provinces of Hindostan.   Here
these fierce and hardy adventurers, whose only improvement had been in the science of destruction, who added
the fury of fanaticism to the ravages of war, found the
great end of their conquest opposed by objects which
neither the ardor of their persevering zeal, nor savage
barbarity, could surmount.   Multitudes were sacrificed
by the cruel hand of religious persecution, and whole
countries were deluged in blood, in the vain hope, that
by the destruction of a part the remainder might be
persuaded, or terrified, into the profession of Mahomed-
ism.   But all these sanguinary efforts were ineffectual ;
and at length, being fully convinced, that though they
might extirpate, they could never hope to convert, any
number of the Hindoos, they relinquished the impracti-
cable idea with which they had entered upon their
career of conquest, and contented themselves with the

acquirement of the civil dominion and almost universal empire of Hindostan."—*Letters from a Hindoo Rajah, by Eliza Hamilton.*

P. 17, l. 32.

And braved the stormy Spirit of the Cape.

See the description of the Cape of Good Hope, translated from CAMÖENS, by MICKLE.

P. 18, l. 8.

While famish'd nations died along the shore.

The following account of British conduct, and its consequences, in Bengal, will afford a sufficient idea of the fact alluded to in this passage.

After describing the monopoly of salt, betel nut, and tobacco, the historian proceeds thus:—" Money in this current came but by drops ; it could not quench the thirst of those who waited in India to receive it. An expedient, such as it was, remained to quicken its pace. The natives could live with little salt, but could not want food. Some of the agents saw themselves well situated for collecting the rice into stores ; they did so. They knew the Gentoos would rather die than violate the principles of their religion by eating flesh. The alternative would therefore be between giving what they had, or dying. The inhabitants sunk ;—they that cultivated the land, and saw the harvest at the disposal of others, planted in doubt—scarcity ensued. Then the monopoly was easier managed—sickness ensued. In some districts the languid living left the bodies of their numerous dead unburied."—*Short History of the English Transactions in the East Indies,* p. 145.

P. 18, l. 23.

Nine times have Brama's wheels of lightning hurl'd
His awful presence o'er the alarmed world.

Among the sublime fictions of the Hindoo mythology, it is one article of belief, that the Deity Brama has descended nine times upon the world in various forms, and that he is yet to appear a tenth time, in the figure of a warrior upon a white horse, to cut off all incorrigible offenders. Avatar is the word used to express his de scent.

P. 19, l. 4.

Shall Seriswattee wave her hallow'd wand!
And Camdeo bright, and Ganesa sublime.

Camdeo is the God of Love in the mythology of the Hindoos. Ganesa and Seriswattee correspond to the pagan deities, Janus and Minerva.

P. 22, l. 26.

The noon of manhood to a myrtle shade!—

Sacred to Venus is the myrtle shade.—DRYDEN

P. 25, l. 1.

Thy woes, Arion!

Falconer, in his poem, "The Shipwreck," speaks of himself by the name of Arion.
See Falconer's "Shipwreck," Canto III.

P. 25, l. 14.

The robber Moor!

See Schiller's tragedy of "The Robbers," Scene v.

P. 25, l. 32.

What millions died—that Cæsar might be great!

The carnage occasioned by the wars of Julius Cæsar has been usually estimated at two millions of men.

P. 25, l. 33.

Or learn the fate that bleeding thousands bore,
March'd by their Charles to Dnieper's swampy shore.

"In this extremity," (says the biographer of Charles XII. of Sweden, speaking of his military exploits before the battle of Pultowa,) "the memorable winter of 1709, which was still more remarkable in that part of Europe than in France, destroyed numbers of his troops ; for Charles resolved to brave the seasons as he had done his enemies, and ventured to make long marches during this mortal cold. It was in one of these marches that two thousand men fell down dead with cold before his eyes."

P. 26, l. 19.

—— As Iona's saint.

The natives of the island of Iona have an opinion, that on certain evenings every year, the tutelary saint Columba is seen on the top of the church spires counting the surrounding islands, to see that they have not been sunk by the power of witchcraft.

P. 26, l. 38.

And part, like Ajut—never to return !

See the history of Ajut and Anningait in " The Rambler."

P. 34, l. 3.

That gave the glacier tops their richest glow.

The sight of the glaciers of Switzerland, I am told, has often disappointed travellers who had perused the accounts of their splendor and sublimity given by Bourrit and other describers of Swiss scenery. Possibly Bourrit, who had spent his life in an enamored familiarity with the beauties of Nature in Switzerland, may have leaned to the romantic side of description. One can pardon a man for a sort of idolatry of those imposing objects of Nature which heighten our ideas of the bounty of Nature or Providence, when we reflect that the glaciers— those seas of ice—are not only sublime, but useful they are the inexhaustible reservoirs which supply the principal rivers of Europe ; and their annual melting is in proportion to the summer heat which dries up those rivers and makes them need that supply,

That the picturesque grandeur of the glaciers should

somotimes disappoint the traveller, will not seem sur.
prising to any one who has been much in a 'mountainous country, and recollects that the beauty of Nature
in such countries is not only variable, but capriciously
dependent on the weather and sunshine. There are
about four hundred different glaciers,* according to the
computation of M. Bourrit, between Mont Blanc and
the frontiers of the Tyrol. · The full effect of the most
lofty and picturesque of them can, of course, only be
produced by the richest and warmest light of the atmosphere ; and the very heat which illuminates them
must have a changing influence on many of their ap-
pearances. I imagine it is owing to this circumstance,
namely, the casualty and changeableness of the appearance of some of the glaciers, that the impressions made
by them on the minds of other and more transient travellers have been less enchanting than those described by ·
M. Bourrit. On one occasion M. Bourrit seems even
to speak of a past phenomenon, and certainly one
which no other spectator attests in the same terms,
when he says, that there once existed, between the
Kandel Steig. and Lauterbrun, " a passage amidst singular glaciers, sometimes resembling magical towns
of ice, with pilasters, pyramids, columns, and obe-
lisks, reflecting to the sun the most brilliant hues of
the finest gems."—M. Bourrit's description of the Glacier
of the Rhone is quite enchanting :—" To form an idea,"
he says, " of this superb spectacle, figure in your mind
a scaffolding of transparent ice, filling a space of two
miles, rising to the clouds, and darting flashes of light
like the sun. Nor were the several parts less magnificent and surprising. One might see, as it were, the
streets and buildings of a city, erected in the form of an
amphitheatre, and embellished with pieces of water,
cascades, and torrents. The effects were as prodigious
as the immensity and the height ;—the most beautiful

---

* Occupying, if taken together, a surface of 130 square leagues

azure—the most splendid white—the regular appearance
of a thousand pyramids of ice, are more easy to be imagined than described."—*Bourrit,* iii. 163.

P. 34, l. 9.

From heights browsed by the bounding bouquetin.

Laborde, in his " Tableau de la Suisse," gives a curious account of this animal, the wild sharp cry and
elastic movements of which must heighten the picturesque appearance of its haunts.—" Nature," says Laborde, " has destined it to mountains covered with snow :
if it is not exposed to keen cold, it becomes blind. Its
agility in leaping much surpasses that of the chamois,
and would appear incredible to those who have not seen
it. There is not a mountain so high or steep to which
it will not trust itself, provided it has room to place its
feet ; it can scramble along the highest wall, if its surface be rugged."

P. 34, l, 15.

—— *enamell'd moss.*

The moss of Switzerland, as well as that of the Tyrol,
is remarkable for a bright smoothness, approaching to
the appearance of enamel.

P. 37, l. 33.

How dear seem'd ev'n the waste and wild Shreck-horn.

The Shreck-horn means, in German, the Peak of
Terror.

P. 37, l. 38.

Blindfold his native hills he could have known !

I have here availed myself of a striking expression of
the Emperor Napoleon respecting his recollections of
Corsica, which is recorded in Las Cases's History of the
Emperor's Abode at St. Helena.

P. 57, l. 1.

Innisfail, the ancient name of Ireland.

P. 58, l. 1.

Kerne, the plural of Kern, an Irish foot-soldier In this sense the word is used by Shakspeare. Gainsford, in his Glories of England, says, " They (the Irish) are desperate in revenge, and their kerne think no man dead *until his head be off.*"

P. 58, l. 20.

Shieling, a rude cabin or hut.

P. 58, l. 26

In Erin's yellow vesture clad

Yellow, dyed from saffron, was the favorite color of the ancient Irish. When the Irish chieftains came to make terms with Queen Elizabeth's lord-lieutenant, we are told by Sir John Davis, that they came to court in saffron-colored uniforms.

P. 59, l. 6

Môrat, a drink made of the juice of mulberry mixed with honey.

P. 60, l. 1.

Their tribe, they said, their high degree,
Was sung in Tara's psaltery.

The pride of the Irish in ancestry was so great, that one of the O'Neals being told that Barrett of Castlemone had been there only four hundred years, he replied,—that he hated the clown as if he had come there but yesterday.

Tara was the place of assemblage and feasting of the petty princes of Ireland. Very splendid and fabulous descriptions are given by the Irish historians of the pomp and luxury of those meetings. The psaltery of Tara was the grand national register of Ireland. The grand epoch of political eminence in the early history of the Irish is the reign of their great and favorite monarch, Ollam Fodlah, who reigned, according to Keating, about nine hundred and fifty years before the Christian æra. Under him was instituted the great Fes at Tara, which it is pretended was a triennial convention of the states, or a parliament; the members of which were the Druids, and other learned men, who represented the people in that assembly. Very minute accounts are given by Irish annalists of the magnificence and order of these entertainments; from which, if credible, we might collect the earliest traces of heraldry that occur in history. To preserve order and regularity in the great number and variety of the members who met on such occasions, the Irish historians inform us that when the banquet was ready to be served up, the shield-bearers of the princes, and other members of the convention, delivered in their shields and targets, which were readily distinguished by the coats of arms emblazoned upon them. These were arranged by the grand marshal and principal herald, and hung upon the walls on the right side of the table; and upon entering the apartments, each member took his seat under his respective shield or target, without the slightest disturbance. The concluding days of the meeting, it is allowed by the Irish antiquaries, were spent in very free excess of conviviality; but the first six, they say, were devoted to the examination and settlement of the annals of the kingdom. These were publicly rehearsed. When they had passed the approbation of the assembly, they were transcribed into the authentic chronicles of the nation, which was called the Register, or Psalter of Tara.

Col. Vallancey gives a translation of an old Irish fragment, found in Trinity College, Dublin, in which the palace of the above assembly is thus described as it existed in the reign of Cormac:—

" In the reign of Cormac, the palace of Tara was nine hundred feet square; the diameter of the surrounding rath, seven dice or casts of a dart; it contained one hundred and fifty apartments; one hundred and fifty dormitories, or sleeping-rooms for guards, and sixty men

in each : the height was twenty-seven cubits ; there
were one hundred and fifty common drinking-horns,
twelve doors, and one thousand guests daily, besides
princes, orators, and men of science, engravers of gold
and silver, carvers, modellers, and nobles." The Irish
description of the banqueting-hall is thus translated :
" Twelve stalls or divisions in each wing ; sixteen at-
tendants on each side, and two to each table ; one hun
dred guests in all."

P. 60, 1. 12.

And stemm'd De Bourgo's chivalry.

The house of O'Connor had a right to boast of their
victories over the English. It was a chief of the O'Con
nor race who gave a check to the English champion
De Courcy, so famous for his personal strength, and for
cleaving a helmet at one blow of his sword, in the presence of the kings of France and England, when the
French champion declined the combat with him.
Though ultimately conquered by the English under De
Bourgo, the O'Connors had also humbled the pride of
that name on a memorable occasion, viz. : when Walter de Bourgo, an ancestor of that De Bourgo who won
the battle of Athunree, had become so insolent as to
make excessive demands upon the territories of Connaught, and to bid defiance to all the rights and proper-
ties reserved by the Irish chiefs. Eath O'Connor, a
near descendant of the famous Cathal, surnamed of the
Bloody Hand, rose against the usurper, and defeated the
English so severely, that their general died of chagrin
after the battle.

P. 60, 1. 15.

Or beal-fires for your jubilee.

The month of May is to this day called Mi Beal
tiennie, *i. e.* the month of Beal's fire, in the original language of Ireland, and hence I believe the name of the
Beltan festival in the Highlands. These fires were

lighted on the summits of mountains (the Irish antiquaries say) in honor of the sun ; and are supposed, by those
conjecturing gentlemen, to prove the origin of the Irish
from some nation who worshipped Baal or Belus. Many
hills in Ireland still retain the name of Cnoc Greine, *i. e.*
the Hill of the Sun ; and on all are to be seen the ruins
of druidical altars.

P. 61, l. 2.

And play my clarshech by thy side.

The clarshech, or harp, the principal musical instrument of the Hibernian bards, does not appear to be of
Irish origin, nor indigenous to any of the British islands.
The Britons undoubtedly were not acquainted with it
during the residence of the Romans in their country, as
in all their coins, on which musical instruments are represented, we see only the Roman lyre, and not the British teylin, or harp.

P. 61, l. 9.

And saw at dawn the lofty bawn.

Bawn, from the Teutonic Bawen—to construct and
secure with branches of trees, was so called because the
primitive Celtic fortifications were made by digging a
ditch, throwing up a rampart, and on the latter fixing
stakes, which were interlaced with boughs of trees.
This word is used by Spenser ; but it is inaccurately
called by Mr. Todd, his annotator, an eminence.

P. 63, l. 25

To speak the malison of heaven.

If the wrath which I have ascribed to the heroine
of this little piece should seem to exhibit her character
as too unnaturally stripped of patriotic and domestic
affections, I must beg leave to plead the authority
of Corneille in the representation of a similar passion : I
allude to the denunciation of Camille, in the tragedy of
Horace. When Horace, accompanied by a soldier bear-

ing the three swords of the Curiatii, meets his sister, and invites her to congratulate him on his victory, she expresses only her grief, which he attributes at first only to her feelings for the loss of her two brothers; but when she bursts forth into reproaches against him as the murderer of her lover, the last of the Curiatii, he exclaims:

> ' O ciel! qui vit jamais une pareille rage!
> Crois-tu donc que je sois insensible à l'outrage,
> Que je souffre en mon sang ce mortel déshonneur?
> Aime, aime cette mort qui fait notre bonheur;
> Et préfère du moins au souvenir d'un homme
> Ce que doit ta naissance aux intérêts de Rome."

At the mention of Rome, Camille breaks out into this apostrophe:

> "Rome, l'unique objet de mon ressentiment!
> Rome, à qui vient ton bras d'immoler mon amant!
> Rome qui t'a vu naître et que ton cœur adore!
> Rome enfin que je haïs parce qu'elle t'honore!
> Puissent tous ses voisins ensemble conjurés
> Saper ses fondements encor mal assurés;
> Et si ce n'est assez de toute l'Italie,
> Que l'Orient contre elle à l'Occident s'allie;
> Que cent peuples unis des bouts de l'univers
> Passent pour la détruire et les monts et les mers;
> Qu'elle-même sur soi renverse ses murailles,
> Et de ses propres mains déchire ses entrailles;
> Que le courroux du ciel allumé par mes vœux
> Fasse pleuvoir sur elle un déluge de feux!
> Puissé-je de mes yeux y voir tomber ce foudre,
> Voir ses maisons en cendre, et tes lauriers en poudre,
> Voir le dernier Romain à son dernier soupir,
> Moi seule en être cause, et mourir de plaisir!"

P. 63, l. 30.

And go to Athunree! (I cried.)

In the reign of Edward the Second, the Irish presented to Pope John the Twenty-second a memorial of their sufferings under the English, of which the language exhibits all the strength of despair. " Ever since the English (say they) first appeared upon our coasts, they entered our territories under a certain specious pretence

cf charity, and external hypocritical show of religion,
endeavoring at the same time, by every artifice malice
could suggest, to extirpate us root and branch, and
without any other right than that of the strongest ; they
have so far succeeded by base fraudulence, and cunning,
that they have forced us to quit our fair and ample hab-
itations and inheritances, and to take refuge like wild
beasts in the mountains, the woods, and the morasses of
the country ;—nor even can the caverns and dens protect us against their insatiable avarice.   They pursue us
even into these frightful abodes ; endeavoring to dispos-
sess us of the wild uncultivated rocks, and arrogate to
themselves the PROPERTY OF EVERY PLACE on-which we
can stamp the figure of our feet."

The greatest effort ever made by the ancient Irish to
regain their native independence, was made at the time
when they called over the brother of Robert Bruce from
Scotland. William De Bourgo, brother to the Earl of
Ulster, and Richard de Bermingham, were sent against
the main body of the native insurgents, who were headed
rather than commanded by Felim O'Connor.   The important battle which decided the subjection of Ireland,
took place on the 10th of August, 1315.   It was the
bloodiest that ever was fought between the two nations,
and continued throughout the whole day, from the rising
to the setting sun   The Irish fought with inferior dis-
cipline, but with great enthusiasm.   They lost ten thousand men, among whom were twenty-nine chiefs of
Connaught.   Tradition states that, after this terrible
day, the O'Connor family, like the Fabian, were so
nearly exterminated, that throughout all Connaught not
one of the name remained, except Felim's brother, who
was capable of bearing arms.

P. 65

Lochiel, the chief of the warlike clan of the Camerons,
and descended from ancestors distinguished in their narrow sphere for great personal prowess, was a man wor-

thy of a better cause and fate than that in which he
embarked, the enterprise of the Stuarts in 1745. His
memory is still fondly cherished among the Highlanders,
by the appellation of the "*gentle Lochiel;*" for he was
famed for his social virtues as much as his martial and
magnanimous (though mistaken) loyalty. His influence was so important among the Highland chiefs, that
it depended on his joining with his clan whether the
standard of Charles should be raised or not in 1745
Lochiel was himself too wise a man to be blind to the
consequences of so hopeless an enterprise, but his sensibility to the point of honor overruled his wisdom.
Charles appealed to his loyalty, and he could not brook
the reproaches of his Prince. When Charles landed at
Borrodale, Lochiel went to meet him, but on his way
called at his brother's house, (Cameron of Fassafern,)
and told him on what errand he was going ; adding,
however, that he meant to dissuade the Prince from his
enterprise. Fassafern advised him in that case to communicate his mind by letter to Charles. " No," said
Lochiel, " I think it due to my Prince to give him my
reasons in person for refusing to join his standard."—
" Brother," replied Fassafern, " I know you better than
you know yourself: if the Prince once sets eyes on you,
he will make you do what he pleases." The interview
accordingly took place ; and Lochiel, with many arguments, but in vain, pressed the Pretender to return to
France, and reserve himself and his friends for a more
favorable occasion, as he had come, by his own ac-
knowledgment, without arms, or money, or adherents:
or, at all events, to remain concealed till his friends
should meet and deliberate what was best to be done.
Charles, whose mind was wound up to the utmost impatience, paid no regard to this proposal, but answered,
" that he was determined to put all to the hazard."
" In a few days," said he, " I will erect the royal standard, and proclaim to the people of Great Britain, that
Charles Stuart is come over to claim the crown of his

ancestors, and to win it, or perish in the attempt
Lochiel, who my father has often told me was our firm-
est friend, may stay at home and learn from the news-
papers the fate of his Prince."—" No," said Lochiel,
" I will share the fate of my Prince, and so shall every
man over whom nature or fortune hath given me any
power."

The other chieftains who followed Charles embraced
his cause with no better hopes. It engages our sympathy most strongly in their behalf, that no motive, but
their fear to be reproached with cowardice or disloyalty,
impelled them to the hopeless adventure. Of this we
have an example in the interview of Prince Charles
with Clanronald, another leading chieftain in the rebel
army.

"Charles," says Home, "almost reduced to despair,
in his discourse with Boisdale, addressed the two Highlanders with great emotion, and, summing up his arguments for taking arms, conjured them to assist their
Prince, their countryman, in his utmost need. Clanronald and his friend, though well-inclined to the cause,
positively refused, and told him that to take up arms
without concert or support was to pull down certain ruin
on their own heads. Charles persisted, argued, and implored. During this conversation (they were on ship-
board) the parties walked backwards and forwards on
the deck ; a Highlander stood near them, armed at all
points, as was then the fashion of his country. He was
a younger brother of Kinloch Moidart, and had come
off to the ship to inquire for news, not knowing who
was aboard. When he gathered from their discourse
that the stranger was the Prince of Wales ; when he
heard his chief and his brother refuse to take arms with
their Prince ; his color went and came, his eyes sparkled,
he shifted his place, and grasped his sword. Charles
observed his demeanor, and turning briskly to him,
called out, ' Will you assist me ?'—' I will, I will,' said
Ronald : ' though no other man in the Highlands should

draw a sword, I am ready to die for you .' Charles, with a profusion of thanks to his champion, said, he wished all the Highlanders were like him. Without further deliberation, the two Macdonalds declared that they would also join, and use their utmost endeavors to engage their countrymen to take arms."—*Home's Hist Rebellion*, p. 40.

P. 65, l. 20.

Weep, Albin!

The Gaelic appellation of Scotland, more particularly the Highlands.

P. 67, l. 8

Lo, anointed by Heaven with the vials of wrath,
Behold, where he flies on his desolate path!

The lines allude to the many hardships of the royal sufferer.

An account of the second sight, in Irish called Taish, is thus given in Martin's Description of the Western Isles of Scotland.

" The second sight is a singular faculty of seeing an otherwise invisible object, without any previous means used by the person who sees it for that end. The vision makes such a lively impression upon the seers, that they neither see nor think of any thing else except the vision as long as it continues ; and then they appear pensive or jovial according to the object which was represented to them.

" At the sight of a vision the eyelids of the person are erected, and the eyes continue staring until the object vanishes. This is obvious to others who are standing by when the persons happen to see a vision ; and occurred more than once to my own observation, and to others that were with me.

" There is one in Skie, of whom his acquaintance observed, that when he sees a vision the inner part of his eyelids turns so far upwards, that, after the object disappears, he must draw them down with his fingers, and sometimes employ others to draw them down, which he finds to be much the easier way.

" This faculty of the second sight does not lineally descend in a family, as some have imagined; for I know several parents who are endowed with it, and their children are not; and *vice versâ*. Neither is it acquired by any previous compact. And after strict inquiry, I could never learn from any among them, that this faculty was communicable to any whatsoever. The seer knows neither the object, time, nor place of a vision before it appears; and the same object is often seen by different persons living at a considerable distance from one another. The true way of judging as to the time and circumstances is by observation; for several persons of judgment who are without this faculty are more capable to judge of the design of a vision than a novice that is a seer. If an object appear in the day or night, it will come to pass sooner or later accordingly.

" If an object is seen early in a morning, which is not frequent, it will be accomplished in a few hours afterwards; if at noon, it will probably be accomplished that very day; if in the evening, perhaps that night; if after candles be lighted, it will be accomplished that night; the 'atter always an accomplishment by weeks, months, and sometimes years, according to the time of the night the vision is seen.

" When a shroud is seen about one, it is a sure prognostic of death. The time is judged according to the height of it about the person; for if it is not seen above the middle, death is not to be expected for the space of a year, and perhaps some months longer: and as it is frequently seen to ascend higher towards the head, death is concluded to be at hand within a few days, if not hours, as daily experience confirms. Examples of this kind were shown me, when the person of whom the observations were then made was in perfect health.

" It is ordinary with them to see houses, gardens, and

trees in places void of all these, and this in process of
time is wont to be accomplished; as at Mogslot, in
the Isle of Skie, where there were but a few sorry low
houses, thatched with straw; yet in a few years the
vision, which appeared often, was accomplished by the
building of several good houses in the very spot represented to the seers, and by the planting of orchards
there.

" To see a spark of fire is a forerunner of a dead
child, to be seen in the arms of those persons; of which
there are several instances. To see a seat empty at
the time of sitting in it, is a presage of that person's
death quickly after it.

" When a novice, or one that has lately obtained the
second sight, sees a vision in the night-time without
doors, and comes near a fire, he presently falls into a
swoon.

" Some find themselves as it were in a crowd of people, having a corpse, which they carry along with them;
and after such visions the seers come in sweating, and
describe the vision that appeared. If there be any of
their acquaintance among them, they give an account
of their names, as also of the bearers; but they know
nothing concerning the corpse."

Horses and cows (according to the same credulous
author) have certainly sometimes the same faculty; and
he endeavors to prove it by the signs of fear which the
animals exhibit, when second-signted persons see visions
in the same place.

" The seers (he continues) are generally illiterate and
well-meaning people, and altogether void of design: nor
could I ever learn that any of them ever made the least
gain by it; neither is it reputable among them to have
that faculty. Besides, the people of the Isles are not so
credulous as to believe implicitly before the thing pre-
dicted is accomplished; but when it is actually accomplished afterwards, it is not in their power to deny it
without offering violence to their own sense and reason

Besides, if the seers were deceivers, can it be reasonable to imagine that all the islanders who have not the
second sight should combine together, and offer violence
to their understandings and senses, to enforce themselves
to believe a lie from age to age? There are several persons
among them whose title and education raise them above
the suspicion of concurring with an impostor, merely to
gratify an illiterate, contemptible set of persons ; nor can
reasonable persons believe that children, horses, and
cows, should be pre-engaged in a combination in favor
of the second sight."—*Martin's Description of the
Western Isles of Scotland*, pp. 3, 11.

P. 96, l. 2.

From merry mock-bird's song.

The mocking-bird is of the form of, but larger than,
the thrush ; and the colors are a mixture of black, white,
and gray. What is said of the nightingale by its greatest admirers is what may with more propriety apply to
this bird, who, in a natural state, sings with very superior taste. Towards evening I have heard one begin
softly, reserving its breath to swell certain notes, which,
by this means, had a most astonishing effect. A gentleman in London had one of these birds for six years.
During the space of a minute he was heard to imitate
the woodlark, chaffinch, blackbird, thrush, and sparrow.
In this country (America) I have frequently known the
mocking-birds so engaged in this mimicry, that it was
with much difficulty I could ever obtain an opportunity
of hearing their own natural note. Some go so far as
to say, that they have neither peculiar notes, nor favorite imitations. This may be denied. Their few natural
notes resemble those of the (European) nightingale
Their song, however, has a greater compass and volume
than the nightingale's, and they have the faculty of
varying all intermediate notes in a manner which is
truly delightful.—*Ashe's Travels in America*, vol. ii.
p. 73.

P. 96, l. 23.

And distant isles that hear the loud Corbrechtan roar!

The Corybrechtan, or Corbrechtan, is a whirlpool on the western coast of Scotland, near the island of Jura, which is heard at a prodigious distance. Its name signifies the whirlpool of the Prince of Denmark; and there is a tradition that a Danish prince once undertook, for a wager, to cast anchor in it. He is said to have used woollen instead of hempen ropes, for greater strength, but perished in the attempt. On the shores of Argyleshire, I have often listened with great delight to the sound of this vortex, at the distance of many leagues. When the weather is calm, and the adjacent sea scarcely heard on these picturesque shores, its sound, which is like the sound of innumerable chariots, creates a magnificent and fine effect.

P. 98, l. 31.

Of buskin'd limb, and swarthy lineament.

In the Indian tribes there is a great similarity in their color, stature, &c. They are all, except the Snake Indians, tall in stature, straight, and robust. It is very seldom they are deformed, which has given rise to the supposition that they put to death their deformed children. Their skin is of a copper color; their eyes large, bright, black, and sparkling, indicative of a subtle and discerning mind: their hair is of the same color, and prone to be long, seldom or never curled. Their teeth are large and white; I never observed any decayed among them, which makes their breath as sweet as the air they inhale.—*Travels through America by Captains Lewis and Clarke, in 1804–5–6.*

P. 99, l. 11.

" Peace be to thee! my words this belt approve.

The Indians of North America accompany every formal address to strangers, with whom they form or recognise a treaty of amity, with a present of a string, or belt, of wampum. Wampum (says Cadwallader Colden) is made of the large whelk shell, *buccinum,* and shaped like long beads: it is the current money of the Indians.—*History of the Five Indian Nations,* p. 34, *New York edition.*

P. 99, l. 12.

The paths of peace my steps have hither led.

In relating an interview of Mohawk Indians with the Governor of New York, Colden quotes the following passage as a specimen of their metaphorical manner: " Where shall I seek the chair of peace? Where shall I find it but upon our path? and whither doth our path lead us but unto this house?"

P. 99, l. 16.

Our wampum league thy brethren did embrace.

When they solicit the alliance, offensive or defensive, of a whole nation, they send an embassy with a large belt of wampum and a bloody hatchet, inviting them to come and drink the blood of their enemies. The wampum made use of on these and other occasions, before their acquaintance with the Europeans, was nothing but small shells which they picked up by the sea-coasts, and on the banks of the lakes; and now it is nothing but a kind of cylindrical beads, made of shells, white and black, which are esteemed among them as silver and gold are among us. The black they call the most valuable, and both together are their greatest riches and ornaments; these among them answering all the end that money does amongst us. They have the art of stringing, twisting, and interweaving them into their belts, collars, blankets, and moccasins, &c. in ten thousand different sizes, forms, and figures, so as to be ornaments for every part of dress, and expressive to them of all their important transactions. They dye the wampum of various colors and shades, and mix and dispose them with great ingenuity and order, and so as to be significant among themselves of almost every thing they please; so that by these their words are kept, and their thoughts communicated to one another, as ours are by writing. The belts that pass from one nation to another in all treaties, declarations, and important transactions, are very carefully preserved in the cabins of their chiefs, and serve not only as a kind of record or history, but as a public treasure.—*Major Rogers's Account of North America.*

P. 100, l. 5.

As when the evil Manitou——

It is certain the Indians acknowledge one Supreme Being, or Giver of Life, who presides over all things; that is, the Great Spirit, and they look up to him as the source of good, from whence no evil can proceed. They also believe in a bad Spirit, to whom they ascribe great power; and suppose that through his power all the evils which befall mankind are inflicted. To him, therefore, they pray in their distresses, begging that he would either avert their troubles, or moderate them when they are no longer avoidable.

They hold also that there are good Spirits of a lower degree, who have their particular departments, in which they are constantly contributing to the happiness of mortals. These they suppose to preside over all the extraordinary productions of Nature, such as those lakes, rivers, and mountains that are of an uncommon magnitude; and likewise the beasts, birds, fishes, and even vegetables or stones, that exceed the rest of their species in size or singularity.—*Clarke's Travels among the Indians.*

The Supreme Spirit of Good is called by the Indians Kitchi Manitou; and the Spirit of Evil, Matchi Manitou.

P. 100, l. 20.

Of fever-balm and sweet sagamité:

The fever-balm is a medicine used by these tribes; it

is a decoction of a bush called the Fever Tree Sagamité is a kind of soup administered to their sick

P. 100, l. 28.

And I, the eagle of my tribe, have rush'd
With this lorn dove.

The testimony of all travellers among the American
Indians who mention their hieroglyphics, authorizes me
in putting this figurative language in the mouth of Outalissi. The dove is among them, as elsewhere, an
emblem of meekness; and the eagle that of a bold,
noble, and liberal mind. When the Indians speak of a
warrior who soars above the multitude in person and
endowments, they say, "he is like the eagle, who de-
stroys his enemies, and gives protection and abundance
to the weak of his own tribe."

P. 101, l. 25.

Far differently, the mute Oneida took, &c.

They are extremely circumspect and deliberate in
every word and action; nothing hurries them into any
intemperate wrath, but that inveteracy to their enemies
which is rooted in every Indian's breast. In all other
instances they are cool and deliberate, taking care to
suppress the emotions of the heart. If an Indian has
discovered that a friend of his is in danger of being cut
off by a lurking enemy, he does not tell him of his danger in direct terms as though he were in fear, but he
first coolly asks him which way he is going that day,
and having his answer, with the same indifference tells
him that he has been informed that a noxious beast lies
on the route he is going. This hint proves sufficient,
and his friend avoids the danger with as much caution
as though every design and motion of his enemy had
been pointed out to him.

If an Indian has been engaged for several days in the
chase, and by accident continued long without food,
when he arrives at the hut of a friend, where he knows

that his wants will be immediately supplied, he takes care not to show the least symptoms of impatience, or betray the extreme hunger that he is tortured with; but on being invited in, sits contentedly down, and smokes his pipe with as much composure as if his appetite was cloyed and he was perfectly at ease. He does the same if among strangers. This custom is strictly adhered to by every tribe, as they esteem it a proof of fortitude, and think the reverse would entitle them to the appellation of old women.

If you tell an Indian that his children have greatly signalized themselves against an enemy, have taken many scalps, and brought home many prisoners, he does not appear to feel any strong emotions of pleasure on the occasion; his answer generally is,—" They have done well," and he makes but very little inquiry about the matter; on the contrary, if you inform him that his children are slain or taken prisoners, he makes no complaints: he only replies, " It is unfortunate:"— and for some time asks no questions about how it happened.—*Lewis and Clarke's Travels.*

P. 101, l. 26.

His calumet of peace, &c.

Nor is the calumet of less importance or less revered than the wampum in many transactions relative both to peace and war. The bowl of this pipe is made of a kind of soft red stone, which is easily wrought and hollowed out; the stem is of cane, alder, or some kind of light wood, painted with different colors, and decorated with the heads, tails, and feathers of the most beautiful birds. The use of the calumet is to smoke either tobacco, or some bark, leaf, or herb, which they often use instead of it, when they enter into an alliance on any serious occasion or solemn engagements; this being among them the most sacred oath that can be taken, the violation of which is esteemed most infamous, and deserving of severe punishment from Heaven. When they treat of war, the whole pipe and all its ornaments are red : sometimes it is red only on one side, and by the disposition of the feathers, &c., one acquainted with their customs will know at first sight what the nation who presents it intends or desires. Smoking the calumet is also a religious ceremony on some occasions, and in all treaties is considered as a witness between the parties, or rather as an instrument by which they invoke the sun and moon to witness their sincerity, and to be as it were a guarantee of the treaty between them. This custom of the Indians, though to appearance somewhat ridiculous, is not without its reasons ; for as they find that smoking tends to disperse the vapors of the brain, to raise the spirits, and to qualify them for thinking and judging properly, they introduced it into their councils, where, after their resolves, the pipe was considered as a seal of their decrees, and as a pledge of their performance thereof it was sent to those they were consulting, in alliance or treaty with ;—so that smoking among them at the same pipe, is equivalent to our drinking together and out of the same cup.—*Major Rogers's Account of North America*, 1766.

The lighted calumet is also used among them for a purpose still more interesting than the expression of social frien lship. The austere manners of the Indians forbid any appearance of gallantry between the sexes in the daytime ; but at night' the young lover goes a calumetting, as his courtship is called. As these people live in a state of equality, and without fear of internal violence or theft in their own tribes, they leave their doors open by night as well as by day. The lover takes advantage of this liberty, lights his calumet, enters the cabin of his mistress, and gently presents it to her. If she extinguish it, she admits his addresses ; but if she suffer it to burn unnoticed, he retires with a disappointed and throbbing heart.—*Ashe's Travels.*

P. 101, l. 29.

Train'd from his tree-rock'd cradle to his bier.

An Indian child, as soon as he is born, is swathed with clothes, or skins; and being laid on his back, is bound down on a piece of thick board, spread over with soft moss. The board is somewhat larger and broader than the child, and bent pieces of wood, like pieces of hoops, are placed over its face to protect it, so that if the machine were suffered to fall the child probably would not be injured. When the women have any business to transact at home, they hang the boards on a tree, if there be one at hand, and set them a swinging from side to side, like a pendulum, in order to exercise the children.—*Weld*, vol. ii. p. 246.

P. 101, l. 30.

The fierce extreme of good and ill to brook
Impassive ———

Of the active as well as passive fortitude of the Indian character, the following is an instance related by Adair in his Travels:—

A party of the Senekah Indians came to war against the Katahba, bitter enemies to each other.—In the woods the former discovered a sprightly warrior belonging to the latter, hunting in their usual light dress: on his perceiving them, he sprang off for a hollow rock four or five miles distant, as they intercepted him from running homeward. He was so extremely swift and skilful with the gun, as to kill seven of them in the running fight before they were able to surround and take him. They carried him to their country in sad triumph; but though he had filled them with uncommon grief and shame for the loss of so many of their kindred, yet the love of martial virtue induced them to treat him, during their long journey, with a great deal more civility than if he had acted the part of a coward. The women and children, when they met him at their several towns, beat him and whipped him in as severe a manner as the occasion required, according to their law of justice, and at last he was formally condemned to die by the fiery torture.—It might reasonably be imagined that what he had for some time gone through, by being fed with a scanty hand, a tedious march, lying at night on the bare ground, exposed to the changes of the weather, with his arms and legs extended in a pair of rough stocks, and suffering such punishment on his entering into their hostile towns, as a prelude to those sharp torments for which he was destined, would have so impaired his health, and affected his imagination, as to have sent him to his long sleep, out of the way of any more sufferings.—Probably this would have been the case with the major part of white people under similar circumstances; but I never knew this with any of the Indians; and this cool-headed, brave warrior did not deviate from their rough lessons of martial virtue, but acted his part so well as to surprise and sorely vex his numerous enemies:—for when they were taking him, unpinioned, in their wild parade, to the place of torture, which lay near to a river, he suddenly dashed down those who stood in his way, sprang off, and plunged into the water, swimming underneath like an otter, only rising to take breath, till he reached the opposite shore. He now ascended the steep bank, but though he had good reason to be in a hurry, as many of the enemy were in the water, and others running, very like bloodhounds, in pursuit of him, and the bullets flying around him from the time he took to the river, yet his heart did not allow him to leave them abruptly, without taking leave in a formal manner, in return for the extraordinary favors they had done, and intended to do him. After slapping a part of his body in defiance to them, (continues the author,) he put up the shrill war-whoop, as his last salute, till some more convenient opportunity offered, and darted off in the manner of a beast broke loose from its torturing enemies. He continued his speed, so as to run by about midnight of the same day as far as his eager pursuers were two days in reaching. Tnere he rested till he happily discovered five of those Indians who had pursued him :—he lay hid a little way off their camp, till they were sound asleep. Every circumstance of his situation occurred to him, and inspired him with heroism. He was naked, torn, and hungry, and his enraged enemies were come up with him ;—but there was now every thing to relieve his wants, and a fair opportunity to save his life, and get great honor and sweet revenge by cutting them off. Resolution, a convenient spot, and sudden surprise, would effect the main object of all his wishes and hopes. He accordingly crept, took one of tneir tomahawks, and killed them all on the spot,— clothed himself, took a choice gun, and as much ammunition and provisions as he could well carry in a running march. He set off afresh with a light heart, and did not sleep for several successive nights, only when he reclined, as usual, a little before day, with his back to a tree. As it were by instinct, when he found he was free from the pursuing enemy, he made directly to the very place where he had killed seven of his enemies, and was taken by them for the fiery torture. He digged them up, burnt their bodies to ashes, and went home in safety with singular triumph. Other pursuing enemies came, on the evening of the second day, to the camp of their dead people, when the sight gave them a greater shock than they had ever known before. In their chilled war-council they concluded, that as he had done such surprising things in his defence before he was captivated, and since that in his naked condition, and now was well-armed, if they continued the pursuit he would spoil them all, for he surely was an enemy-wizard,—and therefore they returned home.—*Adair's General Observations on the American Indians,* p. 334

It is surprising (says the same author) to see the long-continued speed of the Indians. Though some of us have often run the swiftest of them out of sight for about the distance of twelve miles, yet afterwards, without any seeming toil, they would stretch on, leave us out of sight, and outwind any horse.—*Ibid*, p. 318.

If an Indian were driven out into the extensive woods, with only a knife and a tomahawk, or a small hatchet, it is not to be doubted but he would fatten even where a wolf would starve. He would soon collect fire by rubbing two dry pieces of wood together, make a bark hut, earthen vessels, and a bow and arrows; then kill wild game, fish, fresh-water tortoises, gather a plentiful variety of vegetables, and live in affluence.—*Ibid*, p. 410.

P. 102, l. 7.

Moccasins are a sort of Indian buskins.

P. 102, l. 10.

Sleep, wearied one! and in the dreaming land
Shouldst thou to-morrow with thy mother meet,

There is nothing (says Charlevoix) in which these barbarians carry their superstitions farther than in what regards dreams; but they vary greatly in their manner of explaining themselves on this point. Sometimes it is the reasonable soul which ranges abroad, while the sensitive continues to animate the body. Sometimes it is the familiar genius who gives salutary counsel with respect to what is going to happen. Sometimes it is a visit made by the soul of the object of which he dreams. But in whatever manner the dream is conceived, it is always looked upon as a thing sacred, and as the most ordinary way in which the gods make known their will to men. Filled with this idea, they cannot conceive how we should pay no regard to them. For the most part they look upon them either as a desire of the soul, inspired by some genius, or an order from him, and in consequence of this principle they hold it a religious duty to obey them. An Indian having dreamt of having a

finger cut off, had it really cut off as soon as he awoke,
having first prepared himself for this important action
by a feast. Another having dreamt of being a prisoner, and in the hands of his enemies, was much at a
loss what to do. He consulted the jugglers, and by
their advice caused himself to be tied to a post, and
burnt in several parts of the body.—*Charlevoix, Jour
.nal of a Voyage to North America*

P. 102, l. 18.

From a flower shaped like a horn, which Chateau
briand presumes to be of the lotus kind, the Indians in
their travels through the desert often find a draught of
dew purer than any other water.

P. 102, l. 23.
The crocodile, the condor of the rock.

The alligator, or American crocodile, when full-grown
(says Bertram) is a very large and terrible creature, and
of prodigious strength, activity, and swiftness in the
water. I have seen them twenty feet in length, and
some are supposed to be twenty-two or twenty-three
feet in length. Their body is as large as that of a
horse, their shape usually resembles that of a lizard,
which is flat, or cuneiform, being compressed on each
side, and gradually diminishing from the abdomen to the
extremity, which, with the whole body, is covered with
horny plates, or squamæ, impenetrable when on the body
of the live animal, even to a rifle-ball, except about
their head, and just behind their forelegs or arms, where,
it is said, they are only vulnerable. The head of a full-
grown one is about three feet, and the mouth opens
nearly the same length. Their eyes are small in proportion, and seem sunk in the head, by means of the
prominency of the brows ; the nostrils are large, inflated,
and prominent on the top, so that the head on the water
resembles, at a distance, a great chunk of wood floating
about : only the upper jaw moves, which they raise

almost perpendicular, so as to form a right angle with the lower one. In the fore-part of the upper jaw, on each side, just under the nostrils, are two very large, thick, strong teeth, or tusks, not very sharp, but rather the shape of a cone: these are as white as the finest polished ivory, and are not covered by any skin or lips, but always in sight, which gives the creature a frightful appearance; in the lower jaw are holes opposite to these teeth to receive them; when they clap their jaws together, it causes a surprising noise, like that which is made by forcing a heavy plank with violence upon the ground, and may be heard at a great distance.—But what is yet more surprising to a stranger, is the incredibly loud and terrifying roar which they are capable of making, especially in breeding time. It most resembles very heavy distant thunder, not only shaking the air and waters, but causing the earth to tremble; and when hundreds are roaring at the same time, you can scarcely be persuaded but that the whole globe is violently and dangerously agitated. An old champion, who is, perhaps, absolute sovereign of a little lake or lagoon, (when fifty less than himself are obliged to content themselves with swelling and roaring in little coves round about,) darts forth from the reedy coverts, all at once, on the surface of the waters in a right line, at first seemingly as rapid as lightning, but gradually more slowly, until he arrives at the centre of the lake, where he stops. He now swells himself by drawing in wind and water through his mouth, which causes a loud sonorous rattling in the throat for near a minute; but it is immediately forced out again through his mouth and nostrils with a loud noise, brandishing his tail in tne air, and the vapor running from his nostrils like smoke At other times, when swollen to an extent ready to burst, his head and tail lifted up, he spins or twirls round on the surface of the water. He acts his part like an Indian chief, when rehearsing the feats of war.—*Bertram's Travels in North America*

P. 102, l. 31.

Then forth uprose that lone way-faring man.

They discover an amazing sagacity, and acquire,
with the greatest readiness, any thing that depends upon
the attention of the mind.   By experience, and an acute
observation, they attain many perfections to which the
Americans are strangers.   For instance, they will cross
a forest or a plain, which is two hundred miles in breadth,
so as to reach with great exactness the point at which
they intend to arrive, keeping, during the whole of that
space, in a direct line, without any material deviations ;
and this they will do with the same ease, let the weather
be fair or cloudy.   With equal acuteness they will point
to that part of the heavens the sun is in, though it be
intercepted by clouds or fogs.   Besides this, they are
able to pursue, with incredible facility, the traces of
man or beast, either on leaves or grass ; and on this
account it is with great difficulty they escape discovery.
They are indebted for these talents not only to nature,
but to an extraordinary command of the intellectual
qualities, which can only be acquired by an unremitted
attention, and by long experience.   They are, in general, very happy in a retentive memory.   They can
recapitulate every particular that has been treated of
in council, and remember the exact time when they
were held.   Their belts of wampum preserve the substance of the treaties they have concluded with the
neighboring tribes for ages back, to which they will
appeal and refer with as much perspicuity and readiness as Europeans can to their written records.

The Indians are totally unskilled in geography, as well
as all the other sciences, and yet they draw on their
birch-bark very exact charts or maps of the countries
they are acquainted with.   The latitude and longitude
only are wanting to make them tolerably complete.

Their sole knowledge in astronomy consists in being
able to point out the polar star, by which they regulate
their course when they travel in the night.

They reckon the distance of places not by miles or leagues, but by a day's journey, which, according to the best calculation I could make, appears to be about twenty English miles. These they also divide into halves and quarters, and will demonstrate them in their maps with great exactness by the hieroglyphics just mentioned, when they regulate in council their war-parties, or their most distant hunting excursions.—*Lewis and Clarke's Travels.*

Some of the French missionaries have supposed that the Indians are guided by instinct, and have pretended that Indian children can find their way through a forest as easily as a person of maturer years; but this is a most absurd notion. It is unquestionably by a close attention to the growth of the trees, and position of the sun, that they find their way. On the northern side of a tree there is generally the most moss; and the bark on that side, in general, differs from that on the opposite one. The branches toward the south are, for the most part, more luxuriant than those on the other sides of trees, and several other distinctions also subsist between the northern and southern sides, conspicuous to Indians, being taught from their infancy to attend to them, which a common observer would, perhaps, never notice. Being accustomed from their infancy likewise to pay great attention to the position of the sun, they learn to make the most accurate allowance for its apparent motion from one part of the heavens to another: and in every part of the day they will point to the part of the heavens where it is, although the sky be obscured by clouds or mists.

An instance of their dexterity in finding their way through an unknown country came under my observation when I was at Staunton, situated behind the Blue Mountains, Virginia. A number of the Creek nation had arrived at that town on their way to Philadelphia, whither they were going upon some affairs of importance, and had stopped there for the night. In the

morning, some circumstance or other, which coula not
be learned, induced one half of the Indians to set off
withou their companions, who did not follow until some
hours erwards When these last were ready to pursue the . journey, several of the townspeople mounted
their horses to escort them part of the way. They proceeded along the high road for some miles, but, all at
once, hastily turning aside into the woods, though there
was no path, the Indians advanced confidently forward.
The people who accompanied them, surprised at this
movement, informed them that they were quitting the
road to Philadelphia, and expressed their fear lest they
should miss their companions who had gone on before.
They answered that they knew better, that the way
through the woods was the shortest to Philadelphia, and
that they knew very well that their companions had entered the wood at the very place where they did. Curiosity led some of the horsemen to go on ; and to their
astonishment, for there was apparently no track, they
overtook the other Indians in the thickest part of the
wood. But what appeared most singular was, that the
route which they took was found, on examining a map,
to be as direct for Philadelphia as if they had taken the
bearings by a mariner's compass. From others of their
nation, who had been at Philadelphia at a former period,
they had probably learned the exact direction of that
city from their villages, and had never lost sight of it,
although they had already travelled three hundred miles
through the woods, and had upwards of four hundred
miles more to go before they could reach the place of
their destination. Of the exactness with which they
can find out a strange place to which they have been
once directed by their own people, a striking example is
furnished, I think, by Mr. Jefferson, in his account of
the Indian graves in Virginia. These graves are nothing more than large mounds of earth in the woods,
which, on being opened, are found to contain skeletons
n au erect posture : the Indian mode of sepulture has

been too often described to remain unknown to you.
But to come to my story. A party of Indians that were
passing on to some of the seaports on the Atlantic, just
as the Creeks above mentioned were going to Philadelphia, were observed, all on a sudden, to quit the straight
road by which they were proceeding, and without asking any questions to strike through the woods, in a direct line, to one of these graves, which lay at the distance of some miles from the road. Now very near a
century must have passed over since the part of Virginia
in which this grave was situated had been inhabited by
Indians, and these Indian travellers, who were to visit it
by themselves, had unquestionably never been in that
part of the country before : they must have found their
way to it simply from the description of its situation,
that had been handed down to them by tradition.—
Weld's Travels in North America, vol. ii.

P. 106, l. 23.

Their fathers' dust,——

It is a custom of the Indian tribes to visit the tombs
of their ancestors in the cultivated parts of America,
who have been buried for upwards of a century.

P. 108, l. 26.

Or wild-cane arch high flung o'er gulf profound.

The bridges over narrow streams in many parts of
Spanish America are said to be built of cane, which,
however strong to support the passenger, are yet waved
in the agitation of the storm, and frequently add to the
effect of a mountainous and picturesque scenery.

P. 116, l. 22.

The Mammoth comes,——

That I am justified in making the Indian chief allude
to the mammoth as an emblem of terror and destruction, will be seen by the authority quoted below. Speaking of the mammoth or big buffalo, Mr. Jefferson states

that a tradition is preserved among the Indians of the animal still existing in the northern parts of America.

"A delegation of warriors from the Delaware tribe having visited the governor of Virginia during the revolution, on matters of business, the governor asked them some questions relative to their country, and, among others, what they knew or had heard of the animal whose bones were found at the Salt-licks, on the Ohio Their chief speaker immediately put himself into an attitude of oratory, and with a pomp suited to what he conceived the elevation of his subject, informed him that it was a tradition handed down from their fathers, that in ancient times a herd of these tremendous animals came to the Bick-bone-licks, and began an universal destruction of the bear, deer, elk, buffalo, and other animals which had been created for the use of the Indians. That the Great Man above looking down and seeing this, was so enraged, that he seized his lightning, descended on the earth, seated himself on a neighboring mountain on a rock, on which his seat and the prints of his feet are still to be seen, and hurled his bolts among them, till the whole were slaughtered, except the big bull, who, presenting his forehead to the shafts, shook them off as they fell, but missing one, at length it wounded him in the side, whereon, springing round, he bounded over the Ohio, over the Wabash, the Illinois, and finally over the great lakes, where he is living at this day."—*Jefferson's Notes on Virginia.*

P. 116, l. 28.

Scorning to wield the hatchet for his bribe,
'Gainst Brandt himself I went to battle forth.

I took the character of Brandt in the poem of Gertrude from the common Histories of England, all of which represented him as a bloody and bad man, (even among savages,) and chief agent in the horrible desolation of Wyoming. Some years after this poem appeared, the son of Brandt, a most interesting and intelligent youth, came over to England, and I formed an acquaintance with him on which I still look back with pleasure He appealed to my sense of honor and justice, on his own part and on that of his sister, to retract the unfair aspersions which, unconscious of their unfairness, I had cast on his father's memory.

He then referred me to documents, which completely satisfied me that the common accounts of Brandt's cruelties at Wyoming, which I had found in books ot Travels and in Adolphus's and similar Histories of England, were gross errors, and that in point of fact Brandt was not even present at that scene of desolation.

It is, unhappily, to Britons and Anglo-Americans that we must refer the chief blame in this horrible business. I published a letter expressing this belief in the *New Monthly Magazine*, in the year 1822, to which I must refer the reader—if he has any curiosity on the subject—for an antidote to my fanciful description of Brandt. Among other expressions to young Brandt, I made use of the following words:—" Had I learnt all this of your father when I was writing my poem, he should not have figured in it as the hero of mischief." It was but bare justice to say thus much of a Mohawk Indian, who spoke English eloquently, and was thought capable of having written a history of the Six Nations. I ascertained also that he often strove to mitigate the cruelty of Indian warfare. The name of Brandt, therefore, remains in my poem a pure and declared character of fiction.

P. 117, l. 4.

To whom nor relative nor blood remains,
No !—not a kindred drop that runs in human veins !

Every one who recollects the specimen of Indian eloquence given in the speech of Logan, a Mingo chief, to the governor of Virginia, will perceive that I have attempted to paraphrase its concluding and most striking expression :—" There runs not a drop of my blood in the

veins of any living creature." The similar salutation of
the fictitious personage in my story, and the real Indian
orator, makes it surely allowable to borrow such an expression ; and if it appears, as it cannot but appear, to
less advantage than in the original, I beg the reader to
reflect how d.fficult it is to transpose such exquisitely
simple words, without sacrificing a portion of their effec..

In the spring of 1774, a robbery and murder were
committed on an inhabitant of the frontiers of Virginia,
by two Indians of the Shawanee tribe. The neighboring whites, according to their custom, undertook to pun-
ish this outrage in a summary manner. Colonel Cresap,
a man infamous for the many murders he had committed on those much injured people, collected a party and
proceeded down the Kanaway in quest of vengeance ;
unfortunately, a canoe with women and children, with
one man only, was seen coming from the opposite shore
unarmed, and unsuspecting an attack from the whites.
Cresap and his party concealed themselves on the bank
of the river, and the moment the canoe reached the
shore, singled out their objects, and at one fire killed
every person in it. This happened to be the family of
Logan, who had long been distinguished as a friend to
the whites. This unworthy return provoked his vengeance ; he accordingly signalized himself in the war
which ensued. In the autumn of the same year a decisive battle was fought at the mouth of the great Kanaway, in which the collected forces of the Shawanees,
Mingoes, and Delawares, were defeated by a detach-
ment of the Virginian militia. The Indians sued for
peace. Logan, however, disdained to be seen among
the suppliants ; but lest the sincerity of a treaty should
be disturbed, from which so distinguished a chief ab-
stracted himself, he sent, by a messenger, the following
speech to be delivered to Lord Dunmore :—

" I appeal to any white man if ever he entered Logan's cabin hungry, and he gave him not to eat; if
ever he came cold and hungry, and he clothed him not.

During the course of the last long and bloody war Logan remained idle in his cabin, an advocate for peace. Such was my love for the whites, that my countrymen pointed as they passed, and said, Logan is the friend of the white men. I have even thought to have lived with you, but for the injuries of one man. Colonel Cresap, the last spring, in cold blood, murdered all the relations of Logan, even my women and children.

"There runs not a drop of my blood in the veins of any living creature :—this called on me for revenge. I have fought for it. I have killed many. I have fully glutted my vengeance.—For my country I rejoice at the beams of peace ;—but do not harbor a thought that mine is the joy of fear. Logan never felt fear. He will not turn on his heel to save his life.—Who is there to mourn for Logan? not one !"—*Jefferson's Notes on Virginia.*

P. 134, l. 4.

The dark-attired Culdee.

The Culdees were the primitive clergy of Scotland, and apparently her only clergy from the sixth to the eleventh century. They were of Irish origin, and their monastery on the island of Iona, or Icolmkill, was the seminary of Christianity in North Britain. Presbyterian writers have wished to prove them to have been a sort of Presbyters, strangers to the Roman Church and Episcopacy. It seems to be established that they were not enemies to Episcopacy ;—but that they were not slavishly subjected to Rome, like the clergy of later periods, appears by their resisting the Papal ordonnances respecting the celibacy of religious men, on which account they were ultimately displaced by the Scottish sovereigns to make way for more Popish canons.

P. 136, l. 28.

And the shield of alarm was dumb

Striking the shield was an ancient mode of convocation to war among the Gaël.

P. 141.

The tradition which forms the substance of these stanzas is still preserved in Germany. An ancient tower on a height, called the Rolandseck, a few miles above Bonn on the Rhine, is shown as the habitation which Roland built in sight of a nunnery, into which his mistress had retired, on having heard an unfounded account of his death. Whatever may be thought of the credibility of the legend, its scenery must be recollected with pleasure by every one who has visited the romantic landscape of the Drachenfels, the Rolandseck, and the beautiful adjacent islet of the Rhine, where a nunnery still stands.

P. 147, l. 14.

That erst the advent'rous Norman wore.

A Norman leader, in the service of the King of Scotland, married the heiress of Lochow in the twelfth century, and from him the Campbells are sprung.

P. 176, l. 11.

Whose lineage, in a raptured hour.

Alluding to the well-known tradition respecting the origin of painting, that it arose from a young Corinthian female tracing the shadow of her lover's profile on the wall, as he lay asleep.

P. 184, l. 24.

Where the Norman encamp'd him of old.

What is called the East Hill, at Hastings, is crowned with the works of an ancient camp; and it is more than probable it was the spot which William I. occupied between his landing and the battle which gave him England's crown. It is a strong position; the works are easily traced.

P. 188, l. 33.

France turns from her abandon'd friends afresh.

The fact ought to be universally known, that France

is at this moment indebted to Poland for not being in-
vaded by Russia. When the Duke Constantine fled
from Warsaw, he left papers behind him proving that
the Russians, after the Parisian events in July, meant
to have marched towards Paris, if the Polish insurrection had not prevented them

P. 197, l. 1.

Thee, Niemciewitz

This venerable man, the most popular and influential
of Polish poets, and president of the academy in Warsaw,
is now in London: he is seventy-four years old ; but his
noble spirit is rather mellowed than decayed by age.
He was the friend of Fox, Kosciusko, and Washington.
Rich in anecdote, like Franklin, he has also a striking
resemblance to him in countenance.

P. 197, l. 23.

Nor church-bell ———

In Catholic countries you often hear the church-bells
rung to propitiate Heaven during thunder-storms.

P. 208, l. 4.

Regret the lark that gladdens England's morn.

Mr. P. Cunningham, in his interesting work on New
South Wales, gives the following account of its song-
birds :—" We are not moved here with the deep mellow
note of the blackbird, poured out from beneath some
low stunted bush, nor thrilled with the wild warblings
of the thrush perched o_ the top of some tall sapling,
nor charmed with the blithe carol of the lark as we
proceed early a-field ; none of our birds rivalling those
divine songsters in realizing the poetical idea of ' *the
music of the grove :*' while ' *parrots' chattering*' must
supply the place of ' nightingales' singing' in the future
amorous lays of our sighing Celadons. We have our
lark, certainly, but both his appearance and note are a
most wretched parody upon the bird about which our

English Poets have made so many fine similes. He will mount from the ground and rise, fluttering upwards in the same manner, and with a few of the starting notes of the English lark; but on reaching the height of thirty feet or so, down he drops suddenly and mutely, diving into concealment among the long grass, as if ashamed of his pitiful attempt. For the pert, frisky robin, pecking and pattering against the windows in the dull days of winter, we have the lively 'superb warbler,' with his blue, shining plumage and his long tapering tail, picking up the crumbs at our doors; while the pretty red-bills, of the size and form of the goldfinch, constitute the sparrow of our clime, flying in flocks about our houses, and building their soft downy pigmy nests in the orange, peach, and lemon-trees surrounding them."—*Cunningham's Two Years in New South Wales*, vol. ii. p. 216.

P. 217, l. 24.

Oh, feeble statesmen—ignominious times.

There is not upon record a more disgusting scene of Russian hypocrisy, and (wo that it must be written!) of British humiliation, than that which passed on board the Talavera, when British sailors accepted money from the Emperor Nicholas, and gave him cheers. It will require the Talavera to fight well with the first Russian ship that she may have to encounter, to make us forget that day.

P. 227, l. 9.

A palsy-stroke of Nature shook Oran.

In the year 1790, Oran, the most western city in the Algerine Regency, which had been possessed by Spain for more than a hundred years, and fortified at an immense expense, was destroyed by an earthquake; six thousand of its inhabitants were buried under the ruins.

P. 232, l. 17.

The vale by eagle-haunted cliffs o'erhung.

The valley of Glencoe, unparalleled in its scenery for gloomy grandeur, is to this day frequented by eagles. When I visited the spot within a year ago, I saw several perch at a distance. Only one of them came so near me that I did not wish him any nearer. He favored me with a full and continued view of his noble person, and with the exception of the African eagle whom I saw wheeling and hovering over a corps of the French army that were marching from Oran, and who seemed to linger over them with delight at the sound of their trumpets, as if they were about to restore his image to the Gallic standard—I never saw a prouder bird than this black eagle of Glencoe.

I was unable, from a hurt in my foot, to leave the carriage ; but the guide informed me that, if I could go nearer the sides of the glen, I should see the traces of houses and gardens once belonging to the unfortunate inhabitants. As it was, I never saw a spot where I could less suppose human beings to have ever dwelt. I asked the guide how these eagles subsisted ; he replied, " on the lambs and the fawns of Lord Breadalbane." " Lambs and fawns !" I said ; " and how do *they* subsist, for I cannot see verdure enough to graze a rabbit ? I suspect," I added, " that these birds make the cliffs only their country-houses, and that they go down to the Lowlands to find their provender." " Ay, ay," replied the Highlander, " it is very possible, for the eagle can gang far for his breakfast."

P. 237, l. 28.

Witch legends Ronald scorn'd—ghost, kelpie, wraith.

The most dangerous and malignant creature of Highland superstition was the kelpie, or water-horse, which was supposed to allure women and children to his subaqueous haunts, and there devour them ; sometimes he would swell the lake or torrent beyond its usual limits,

and overwhelm the unguarded traveller in the flood.
The shepherd, as he sat on the brow of a rock on a
summer's evening, often fancied he saw this animal
dashing along the surface of the lake, or browsing on
the pasture-ground upon its verge.—*Brown's History
of the Highland Clans*, vol. i. 106.

In Scotland, according to Dr. John Brown, it is yet a
superstitious principle that the *wraith*, the omen or
messenger of death, appears in the resemblance of one
in danger, immediately preceding dissolution. This
ominous form, purely of a spiritual nature, seems to tes-
tify that the exaction (extinction) of life approaches. It
was wont to be exhibited, also, as "*a little rough
dog*," when it could be pacified by the death of any
other being "if crossed, and conjured in time."—
Brown's Superstitions of the Highlands, p. 182.

It happened to me, early in life, to meet with an
amusing instance of Highland 'superstition with regard
to myself. I lived in a family of the island of Mull,
and a mile or two from their house there was a burial-
ground without any church attached to it, on the lonely
moor. The cemetery was enclosed and guarded by an
iron railing so high, that it was 'thought to be unscalea-
ble. I was, however, commencing the study of botany
at the time, and thinking there might be some nice
flowers and curious epitaphs among the grave-stones, I
contrived, by help of my handkerchief, to scale the
railing, and was soon scampering over the tombs ; some
of the natives chanced to perceive me, not in the act of
climbing over to—but skipping over, the burial-ground.
In a day or two I observed the family looking on me
with unaccountable, though not angry seriousness: at
last the good old grandmother told me, with tears in her
eyes, "that I could not live long, for that my wraith
had been seen." "And, pray, where?" "Leaping
over the stones of the burial-ground." The old lady
was much relieved to hear that it was not my wraith,
but myself.

Akin to other Highland superstitions, but differing from them in many essential respects, is the belief—for superstition it cannot well be called (quoth the wise author I am quoting)—in the second-sight, by which, as Dr. Johnson observes, "seems to be meant a mode of seeing superadded to that which Nature generally bestows ; and consists of an impression made either by the mind upon the eye—or by the eye upon the mind, by which things distant or future are perceived and seen, as if they were present. This deceptive faculty is called Traioshe in the Gaelic, which signifies a spectre or vision, and is neither voluntary nor constant ; but consists in seeing an otherwise invisible object, without any previous means used by the person that sees it for that end. The vision makes such a lively impression upon the seers, that they neither see nor think of any thing else except the vision, as long as it continues ; and then they appear pensive or jovial, according to the object which was represented to them."

There are now few persons, if any, (continues Dr. Browne,) who pretend to this faculty, and the belief in it is almost generally exploded. Yet it cannot be denied that apparent proofs of its existence have been adduced, which have staggered minds not prone to superstition. When the connection between cause and effect can be recognised, things which would otherwise have appeared wonderful, and almost incredible, are viewed as ordinary occurrences. The impossibility of accounting for such an extraordinary phenomenon as the alleged faculty on philosophical principles, or from the laws of nature, must ever leave the matter suspended between rational doubt and confirmed skepticism. "Strong reasons for incredulity," says Dr. Johnson, "will readily occur." This faculty of seeing things out of sight is local, and commonly useless. It is a breach of the common order of things, without any visible reason or perceptible benefit. It is ascribed only to a people very little enlightened, and among them, for the most part, to the mean and ignorant.

In the whole history of Highland superstitions, there is not a more curious fact than that Dr. James Browne, a gentleman of the Edinburgh bar, in the nineteenth century, should show himself a more abject believer in the truth of second-sight, than Dr. Samuel Johnson, of London, in the eighteenth century.

P. 239, l. 1.

The pit or gallows would have cured my grief.

Until the year 1747, the Highland Lairds had the right of punishing serfs even capitally, in so far that they often hanged, or imprisoned them in a pit or dungeon, where they were starved to death. But the law of 1746, for disarming the Highlanders and restraining the use of the Highland garb, was followed up the following year by one of a more radical and permanent description. This was the act for abolishing the heritable jurisdictions, which, though necessary in a rude state of society, were wholly incompatible with an advanced stage of civilization. By depriving the Highland chiefs of their judicial powers, it was thought that the sway which, for centuries, they had held over their people, would be gradually impaired; and that by investing certain judges, who were amenable to the legislature for the proper discharge of their duties, with the civil and criminal jurisdiction enjoyed by the proprietors of the soil, the cause of good government would be promoted, and the facilities for repressing any attempts to disturb the public tranquillity increased.

By this act, (20 George II. c. 43,) which was made to the whole of Scotland, all heritable jurisdictions of justiciary, all regalities and heritable bailieries, and constabularies, (excepting the office of high constable,) and all stewartries and sheriffships of smaller districts, which were only parts of counties, were dissolved, and the powers formerly vested in them were ordained to be

exercised by such of the king's courts as these powers
would have belonged to, if the jurisdictions had never
been granted. All sheriffships and stewartries not dissolved by the statute, namely, those which compre-
hended whole counties, where they had been granted
either heritably or for life, were resumed and annexed
to the crown. With the exception of the hereditary
justiciaryship of Scotland, which was transferred from
the family of Argyle to the High Court of Justiciary,
the other jurisdictions were ordained to be vested in
sheriffs-depute or stewarts-depute, to be appointed by
the king in every shire or stewartry not dissolved by the
act. As by the twentieth of Union, all heritable offices
and jurisdictions were reserved to the grantees as rights
of property; compensation was ordained to be made to
the holders, the amount of which was afterwards fixed
by parliament, in terms of the act of Sederunt of the
Court of Session, at one hundred and fifty thousand
pounds.

P. 239, l. 3.

I march'd—when, feigning Royalty's command,
Against the clan Macdonald, Stairs's Lord
Sent forth exterminating fire and sword.

I cannot agree with Brown, the author of an able work,
" The History of the Highland Clans," that the affair of
Glencoe has stamped indelible infamy on the government
of King William III., if by this expression it be meant that
William's own memory is disgraced by that massacre. I
see no proof that William gave more than general orders to subdue the remaining malecontents of the Macdonald clan ; and these orders, the nearer we trace them
to the government, are the more express in enjoining,
that all those who would promise to swear allegiance
should be spared. As these orders came down from the
general government to individuals, they became more
and more severe, and at last merciless, so that they ultimately ceased to be the real orders of government

Among these false agents of government, who appears with most disgrace, is the "Master of Stair," who appears in the business more like a fiend than a man. When issuing his orders for the attack on the remainder of the Macdonalds in Glencoe, he expressed a hope in his letter "that the soldiers would trouble the government with no prisoners."

It cannot be supposed that I would for a moment palliate this atrocious event by quoting the provocations not very long before offered by the Macdonalds in massacres of the Campbells. But they may be alluded to as causes, though not excuses. It is a part of the melancholy instruction which history affords us, that in the moral as well as in the physical world, there is always a reaction equal to the action. The banishment of the Moors from Spain to Africa was the chief cause of African piracy and Christian slavery among the Moors for centuries; and since the reign of William III. the Irish Orangemen have been the Algerines of Ireland.

The affair of Glencoe was in fact only a lingering trait of horribly barbarous times, though it was the more shocking that it came from that side of the political world which professed to be the more liberal side, and it occurred at a late time of the day, when the minds of both parties had become comparatively civilized, the whigs by the triumph of free principles, and the tories by personal experience of the evils attending persecution. Yet that barbarism still subsisted in too many minds professing to act on liberal principles, is but too apparent from this disgusting tragedy.

I once flattered myself that the Argyle Campbells, from whom I am sprung, had no share in this massacre, and a direct share they certainly had not. But on inquiry I find that they consented to shutting up the passes of Glencoe through which the Macdonalds might escape; and perhaps relations of my great-grandfather— I am afraid to count their distance or proximity—might be indirectly concerned in the cruelty.

But children are not answerable for tl e crimes of their forefathers ; and I hope and trust that the descendants of Breadalbane and Glenlyon are as much and justly at their ease on this subject as I am

P. 245, l. 26.

Chance snatch'd them from proscription and despair.

Many Highland families, at the outbreak of the rebellion in 1745, were saved from utter desolation by the contrivances of some of their more sensible members, principally the women, who foresaw the consequences of the insurrection. When I was a youth in the Highlands, I remember an old gentleman being pointed out to me, who, finding all other arguments fail, had, in conjunction with his mother and sisters, bound the old laird hand and foot, and locked him up in his own cellar, until the news of the battle of Culloden arrived.

A device pleasanter to the reader of the anecdote, though not to the sufferer, was practised by a shrewd Highland dame, whose husband was Charles-Stuart-mad, and was determined to join the insurgents. He told his wife at night that he should start early to-morrow morning on horseback. " Well, but you will allow me to make your breakfast before you go ?" " Oh yes." She accordingly prepared it, and, bringing in a full boiling kettle, poured it, by intentional accident, on his legs !